D0291576

Prize Stories 2000

THE O. HENRY AWARDS

PAST JURORS

1997:   Louise Erdrich, Thom Jones, David Foster Wallace

1998:   Andrea Barrett, Mary Gaitskill, Rick Moody

1999:   Sherman Alexie, Stephen King, Lorrie Moore

PAST MAGAZINE AWARD WINNERS

1997:   *Epoch*

1998:   *The New Yorker*

1999:   *The New Yorker*

PRIZE STORIES

The O. Henry Awards

Edited and with an Introduction
by Larry Dark

ANCHOR BOOKS
A Division of Random House, Inc.
New York

AN ANCHOR ORIGINAL, SEPTEMBER 2000

Copyright © 2000 by Anchor Books, a division of Random House, Inc.

All rights reserved under International and Pan-American Copyright
Conventions. Published in the United States by Vintage Books,
a division of Random House, Inc., New York, and simultaneously
in Canada by Random House of Canada Limited, Toronto.

Anchor Books and colophon are registered trademarks of Random House, Inc.

Owing to limitations of space, permissions appear on pages 409–411.

Library of Congress Cataloging-in-Publication Data

Prize stories, 1947–

New York, N.Y., Doubleday.

v. 23 cm.

Annual.

The O. Henry awards.

None published 1952–53.

Continues: O. Henry memorial award prize stories.

1. Short stories, American—Collected works.

PZ1.011   813'.01'08—dc19   21-9372

ISBN: 0-385-49877-2

www.anchorbooks.com

Printed in the United States of America
10 9 8 7 6 5 4 3 2 1

Publisher's Note

WILLIAM SYDNEY PORTER, who wrote under the pen name O. Henry, was born in North Carolina in 1862. He started writing stories while in prison for embezzlement, a crime for which he was convicted in 1898 (it is uncertain if he actually committed the crime). His writing career was short and started late, but O. Henry proved himself a prolific and widely read short story writer in the twelve years he devoted to the craft, and his name has become synonymous with the American short story.

His years in Texas inspired many lively Westerns, but it was New York City that galvanized his creative powers, and his New York stories became his claim to frame. Loved for their ironic plot twists, which made for pleasing surprise endings, his highly entertaining tales appeared weekly in Joseph Pulitzer's *New York World*.

His best known story, "The Gift of the Magi," was written for the *World* in 1905 and has become an American treasure. Dashed off past deadline in a matter of hours, it is the story of a man who sells his watch to buy a set of hair combs as a Christmas present for his wife, who in the meantime has sold her luxurious locks to buy him a watch chain. "The Last Leaf" is another O. Henry favorite. It is the story of a woman who falls ill with pneumonia and pronounces that she will die when the last leaf of ivy she sees outside her Greenwich Village window falls away. She hangs on with the last stubborn leaf, which gives her the resolve to recover. She even-

Contents

Introduction

PRIZE STORIES 2000: The O. Henry Awards presents a significant mile-stone: the eightieth volume of this series. It is notable for two other reasons, as well. First, 1999 was a very good year for short fiction, and the twenty pieces in this book make for a particularly strong collection. Included are stories by well-known writers, such as Russell Banks, Andrea Barrett, Mary Gordon, Allan Gurganus, and John Edgar Wideman, along with a posthumously published story by Raymond Carver. In addition, you'll find work by writers whose names are less recognizable but are likely to become familiar in the years ahead—an important part of any O. Henry Awards volume. Although in previous years it would have been apt to describe the collection as a banquet, with individual stories akin to different courses, these twenty stories have a fullness and depth that make them each more like meals unto themselves. Strengthening the book further are the contributions of this year's prize jurors—Michael Cunningham, Pam Houston, and George Saunders—who deliberated thoughtfully and who have written insightful introductions to the stories selected for top honors: "Weight" by John Edgar Wideman, "The Man with the Lapdog" by Beth Lordan, and "The Deacon" by Mary Gordon.[1]

[1]Though this ground is covered in the Publisher's Note (page v), allow me to clarify: From among the thousands of eligible stories, the series editor chooses the twenty O. Henry Award winners in each volume. After reading just these twenty stories, the jurors select the first-, second-, and third-prize winners.

The second noteworthy aspect of *Prize Stories 2000* is that it closes the door on the stories of the twentieth century. Although the span of *Prize Stories: The O. Henry Awards* falls short of covering the entire period by twenty years, the 1,483 stories[2] published to date provide glimpses of and reflections on many of the important events of the 1900s, among these World War I, the Jazz Age, the Great Depression, World War II, the 1950s, the 1960s, the Vietnam war, and the incredible political and social changes that occurred in the last part of the century. Short stories, however, don't necessarily reflect the era during which they are written and published. Many of the great stories about the twentieth century, no doubt, have yet to be written, and this particular collection is no more limited in its focus to the past year than the first volume, in 1919,[3] was to the events of 1918. Most of these stories are set in a kind of timeless present, some refer to a more distant past. Computers make an appearance in only two of the stories,[4] and the current collective fixations on the Internet, popular culture, and consumerism barely register in these pages, nor in more than a handful of the three thousand or so stories that I read during the year.

By their nature, short stories aren't concerned with the here and now, nor with the newest technological development or the latest must-have infogadget. They are stubbornly timeless. What short stories have always done best is chart the smaller movements of individual experience, the changes that occur within a person, those rare opportunities for transcendence and grace that make the pressing concerns of the moment seem less than consequential in the long run. Certainly there's a place in our culture for mediums that aim to reflect what is happening this week, this day, or even this very moment. Newspapers, magazines, radio, television, and the Internet keep us informed, but their messages quickly pass out of our thoughts, rarely affecting us in a deep or lasting way. The best short stories, in contrast, communicate the essential aspects of human life that do not change at the speed of technological innovation. In a world grown

---

[2]That's roughly 18.5 stories per volume. In recent years, collections have had 20 stories per volume.

[3]Those of you doing the math yourselves may wonder why this is the eightieth rather than the eighty-second volume of the O. Henry Awards. Publication of the series was suspended in 1952 and 1953 following the death of series editor Herschell Brickell.

[4]Mary Gordon's "The Deacon" and John Biguenet's "Rose."

larger, they maintain the human scale. The stories in this year's volume are particularly strong in this way.

Although I don't consciously assemble a book along thematic lines, I invariably find common threads when I reread the stories I've chosen. There are few pursuits as solitary as writing, yet a story must connect with other people to be successful, and an author must draw upon something greater than him- or herself as part of the process. A set of stories published in the same year[5] is, therefore, likely to share some common concerns. Prominent among the larger issues tackled by the writers of these stories is death.[6] In half of the twenty stories someone dies—a mother, an ex-wife, a schoolgirl's best friend, various relatives over the course of many years, a young man's brothers, a father, parents, a child, a cousin, and a misunderstood but admired member of a community.[7] In other stories, we get a glimpse of those soon to die, the aged, the ill, and the walking dead.[8] The second, related element common to many of these stories is that of a striving for personal and spiritual development, whether through a life change, a newfound sobriety, religion, or a deeper understanding arrived at too late.[9]

Why is there so great an emphasis on death and other life changes in this collection? I can't say for sure. Perhaps the approach of a new millennium nudged these writers in the directions of self-examination and of

[5]Short stories usually take a while to be finished to an author's satisfaction, a while to be accepted for publication, and a while to see print. For this reason, I can't say that all of these stories were written in the same year. Some may have been started ten years ago or longer before they were published. Certainly, this is true of the posthumously published "Kindling," by Raymond Carver.

[6]For more on this, see George Saunders's introduction to Mary Gordon's "The Deacon," on page 38.

[7]Respectively: John Edgar Wideman's "Weight," Russell Banks's "Plains of Abraham," Melissa Pritchard's *"Salve Regina,"* Kiana Davenport's "Bones of the Inner Ear," J. Robert Lennon's "The Fool's Proxy," Allan Gurganus's "He's at the Office," Andrea Barrett's "Theories of Rain," John Biguenet's "Rose," Kate Walbert's "The Gardens of Kyoto," and Alice Elliott Dark's "Watch the Animals."

[8]Those soon to die: Beth Lordan's "The Man with the Lapdog." The aged: Tim Gautreaux's "Easy Pickings." The ill: Judy Budnitz's "Flush." The walking dead: Keith Banner's "The Smallest People Alive."

[9]Life change: Kevin Brockmeier's "These Hands" and Jeannette Bertles's "Whileaway." Life change and sobriety: Raymond Carver's "Kindling." Religion: Nathan Englander's "The Gilgul of Park Avenue," among others. Understanding: Michael Byers's "The Beautiful Days."

exploring their own mortality. In spite of the serious subjects of these stories, however, most are written with humor, irony, playfulness, or a lightness of touch that keeps them from becoming obvious or preachy. Good writing engages and entertains readers while still delivering deeper meaning. If there is any characteristic I look for in deciding whether or not to choose a story for the O. Henry Awards, it is this.

The skill, complexity, and richness of the works collected here are evidence that short fiction remains important. This volume presents just a small sample of the many accomplished stories written and published in 1999—far more, in fact, than could be collected in one volume or additionally cited among the fifty short-listed stories found in the back of this book. While I hope that being honored in *Prize Stories 2000: The O. Henry Awards* will serve as an affirmation to the writers and magazines included, I just as strongly hope that other writers will not feel slighted. Twenty out of more than three thousand, after all, represents rather long odds. In the end, for better or for worse, choices must be made and, regrettably, too few deserving stories can be honored.

It was, to say the least, a great century for the American short story. One need only recite the names of some of the writers who have graced the pages of the eighty previous O. Henry Awards volumes: Sherwood Anderson, F. Scott Fitzgerald, Ernest Hemingway, William Faulkner, Eudora Welty, Irwin Shaw, Jean Stafford, John Cheever, Richard Wright, Flannery O'Connor, J. D. Salinger, James Baldwin, Donald Barthelme, Grace Paley, John Updike, Joyce Carol Oates, Raymond Carver, and Alice Munro, to name but a few.[10] Who knows what changes the twenty-first century will bring to the way we read and write short fiction and to the mediums that deliver the written word? But from the vantage point of someone immersed in the steady flow of stories published in the 256 magazines consulted for this series, the prospects for the years immediately ahead look very promising. There are great reserves of talent and dedication to be found among the writers and editors currently devoted to this form. The American short story will likely prove to have been one of the twentieth century's most durable and significant creative endeavors, and I am certain it will continue to inform our lives just as richly in the century ahead.

LARRY DARK, 2000

[10]A complete list of O. Henry Award winners, from 1919 to 2000, is posted on the Internet at www.boldtype.com/ohenry or www.anchorbooks.com

Prize Stories 2000

THE O. HENRY AWARDS

F I R S T   P R I Z E

Weight

By John Edgar Wideman

INTRODUCED BY MICHAEL CUNNINGHAM

John Edgar Wideman's "Weight" does not directly resemble anything I've ever read before, and that is perhaps the highest praise I can offer any work of fiction. It is simultaneously a story in itself and a story about writing a story, though there is hardly a whiff of the formally experimental in it. Under its relatively straightforward surface lie subtler questions about storytelling as a complex assertion of love, rage, and consolation; and in this case it is an assertion that matters at least as much to the storyteller as it does to those for whom the story is intended. "Weight" is moving, in part, because the writer has not distanced himself in any way from his subject. Wideman lets autobiography and fiction spill over into each other because the story's messy, deeply personal emotions require it. We, as readers, are privy to the story itself and to the story's effects on the man who tells it.

If I say that I did not expect to like "Weight" when I started reading it, I mean it as a tribute to the story's, and Wideman's, power. The first few pages sounded an inner alarm of mine that is set to go off in the presence of the sentimental or the overly familiar. Oh-oh, I thought. Here's another story about a heroic mother who dies. The fact that it kept surging forward, without irony or apology, until it reached its marvelous, incantatory conclusion was stunning. I have read it several times and still can't quite tell how Wideman has built a story so alive out of such thoroughly used material. It has something to do with his passionate insistence on his mother's significance (yes, her weight), and it has considerably more to do with that central mystery, the writer's ability to do justice to the visible world in all its manifestations, from the innovative to the ancient.

A story like this, a story that risks embarrassing both writer and reader and ends up doing neither, suggests some sort of explanation as to why the icier, more cerebral and cynical fiction that was so plentiful thirty years ago—wonderful as some of it was—has not continued to be much written or read today. Although some readers at the start of the twenty-first century may go a bit glassy-eyed at the prospect of another ailing parent, another incurable disease, another lost child, our parents do continue to age and die, we continue to suffer diseases, our children continue to be lost. The fact that all these tragedies have occurred before, billions of times, does not in any way reduce their importance to us. It's hard to imagine a future in which we will no longer require the sense of companionship—simple companionship, without lessons or any other cheap attempts at uplift—that literature can offer us as we undergo our highly particular, unprecedented lives.

I hope it will in no way undercut Wideman's accomplishment if I say that choosing a set of "winners" from the twenty stories collected here was an extremely difficult business. Each of these stories is excellent in some way or other. The job of choosing the "best" felt counter to the whole purpose of stories, at least once the fraudulent, the inept, and the tiny had been eliminated. In trying to choose I was reminded of an obsession I developed as a child, when it seemed for some reason vitally important that I know the relative intelligence of different animals. I constantly asked whether a dog was smarter than a cat, or a pig smarter than a horse, and if I was unsatisfied at the time by my parents' repeated answer that a dog, cat, pig, or horse was a genius at being a dog, cat, pig, or horse, I consider the answer pure wisdom today. If a story creates life on its own terms, and gives the reader something the reader considers worth having, then it has worked, and deserves as much praise as we can give it.

"Weight" was, ultimately, the story among these twenty that affected me most, the one that resonated most potently after I'd read it. It is, however, very much in the generous, fearlessly emotional spirit of Wideman's story that I urge the reader to read every one of these selections, and to receive them all in the manner in which they are intended: as gifts.

—MICHAEL CUNNINGHAM

John Edgar Wideman

Weight

From *Callaloo*

MY MOTHER is a weightlifter. You know what I mean. She understands that the best laid plans, the sweetest beginnings have a way of turning to shit. Bad enough when life fattens you up just so it can turn around and gobble you down. Worse for the ones like my mother life keeps skinny, munching on her daily, one cruel, little, needle-toothed bite at a time so the meal lasts and lasts. Mom understands life don't play so spends beaucoup time and energy getting ready for the worst. She lifts weights to stay strong. Not barbells or dumbbells, though most of the folks she deals with, especially her sons, act just that way, like dumbbells. No. The weights she lifts are burdens, her children's, her neighbors, yours. Whatever awful calamities arrive on her doorstep or howl in the news, my mom squeezes her frail body beneath them. Grips, hoists, holds the weight. I swear sometimes I can hear her sinews squeaking and singing under a load of invisible tons.

I ought to know since I'm one of the burdens bowing her shoulders. She loves heavy, hopeless me unconditionally. Before I was born, Mom loved me, forever and ever till death do us part. I'll never be anyone else's darling, darling boy so it's her fault, her doing, isn't it, that neither of us can face the thought of losing the other. How could I resist reciprocating her love. Needing her. Draining her. Feeling her straining underneath me, the pop and cackle of her arthritic joints, her gray hair sizzling with static electricity, the hissing friction, tension and pressure as she lifts more than she can bear. Bears more than she can possibly lift. You have to see it to believe it. Like the Flying Wallendas or Houdini's spine-chilling escapes. One of the greatest shows on earth.

My mother believes in a god whose goodness would not permit him to inflict more troubles than a person can handle. A god of mercy and salvation. A sweaty, bleeding god presiding over a fitness class in which his chosen few punish their muscles. She should wear a T-shirt: *God's Gym*.

In spite of a son in prison for life, twin girls born dead, a mind blown son who roams the streets with everything he owns in a shopping cart, a strung out daughter with a crack baby, a good daughter who'd miscarried the only child her dry womb ever produced, in spite of me and the rest of my limp-along, near to normal siblings and their children—my nephews doping and gangbanging, nieces unwed, underage, dropping babies as regularly as the seasons—in spite of breast cancer, sugar diabetes, hypertension, failing kidneys, emphysema, gout, all resident in her body and epidemic in the community, knocking off one by one her girlhood friends, in spite of corrosive poverty and a neighborhood whose streets are no longer safe even for gray, crippled up folks like her, my mom loves her god, thanks him for the blessings he bestows, keeps her faith he would not pile on more troubles than she could bear. Praises his name and prays for strength, prays for more weight so it won't fall on those around her less able to bear up.

You've seen those iron pumping, musclebound brothers fresh out the slam who show up at the playground to hoop and don't get picked on a team cause they can't play a lick, not before they did their bit, and sure not now, back on the set, stiff and stone-handed as Frankenstein, but finally some old head goes on and chooses one on his squad because the brother's so huge and scary looking sitting there with his jaws tight, lip poked out you don't want him freaking out and kicking everybody's ass just because the poor baby's feelings is hurt, you know what I mean, the kind so buff looks like his coiled-up insides about to bust through his skin or his skin's stripped clean off his body so he's a walking anatomy lesson. Well, that's how my mom looks to me sometimes, her skin peeled away, no secrets, every taut nerve string on display.

I can identify the precise moment during a trip with her one afternoon to the supermarket on Walnut Street in Shadyside, a Pittsburgh,

Pennsylvania, white community with just a few families of us colored sprinkled at the bottom ends of a couple of streets, when I began to marvel at my mother's prodigious strength. I was very young, young enough not to believe I'd grow old, just bigger. A cashier lady who seemed to be acquainted with my mother asked very loudly, Is this your son, and Mom smiled in reply to the cashier's astonishment saying calmly, Yes, he is, and the doughy white lady in her yellow Krogers' smock with her name on the breast tried to match my mother's smile but only managed a fake grin like she'd just discovered shit stinks but didn't want anybody else to know she knew. Then she blurted, He's a tall one, isn't he.

Not a particularly unusual moment as we unloaded our shopping cart and waited for the bad news to ring up on the register. The three of us understood, in spite of the cashier's quick shuffle, what had seized her attention. In public situations the sight of my pale, caucasian featured mother and her variously colored kids disconcerted strangers. They gulped. Stared. Muttered insults. We were visible proof somebody was sneaking around after dark, breaking the apartheid rule, messy mulatto exceptions to the rule, trailing behind a woman who could be white.

Nothing special about the scene in Krogers. Just an ugly moment temporarily reprieved from turning uglier by the cashier's remark that attributed her surprise to a discrepancy in height not color. But the exchange alerted me to a startling fact—I was taller than my mother. The brown boy, me, could look down at the crown of his light-skinned mother's head. Obsessed by size, like most adolescent boys, size in general and the size of each and every particular part of my body and how mine compared to others, I was always busily measuring and keeping score, but somehow I'd lost track of my mother's size, and mine relative to hers. Maybe because she was beyond size. If someone had asked me my mother's height or weight I probably would have replied, *Huh*. Ubiquitous I might say now. A tiny, skin-and-bone woman way too huge for size to pin down.

The moment in Krogers is also when I began to marvel at my mother's strength. Unaccountably, unbeknownst to me, my body had grown larger than hers, yes, and the news was great in a way, but more striking and not so comforting was the fact, never mind my advantage in size, I felt hopelessly weak standing there beside my mom in Krogers. A wimpy shadow next to her solid flesh and bones. I couldn't support for one hot minute a fraction of the weight she bore on her shoulders twenty-four hours a day.

The weight of the cashier's big-mouthed disbelief. The weight of hating the pudgy white woman forever because she tried to steal my mother from me. The weight of cooking and cleaning and making do with no money, the weight of fighting and loving us iron-headed, ungrateful brats. Would I always feel puny and inadequate when I looked up at the giant fist hovering over our family, the fist of God or the Devil, ready to squash us like bugs if my mother wasn't always on duty, spreading herself thin as an umbrella over our heads, her bones its steel ribs keeping the sky from falling.

Reaching down for the brass handle of this box I must lift to my shoulder, I need the gripping strength of my mother's knobby-knuckled fingers, her superhero power to bear impossible weight.

Since I was reading her this story over the phone (I called it a story but Mom knew better), I stopped at the end of the paragraph above you just completed, if you read that far, stopped because the call was long distance, daytime rates, and also because the rest had yet to be written. I could tell by her silence she was not pleased. Her negative reaction didn't surprise me. Plenty in the piece I didn't like either. Raw, stuttering stuff I intended to improve in subsequent drafts, but before revising and trying to complete it, I needed her blessing.

Mom's always been my best critic. I depend on her honesty. She tells the truth yet never affects the holier-than-thou superiority of some people who believe they occupy the high ground and let you know in no uncertain terms that you nor nobody else like you ain't hardly coming close. Huh-uh. My mother smiles as often as she groans or scolds when she hears gossip about somebody behaving badly. *My, my, my* she'll say and nod and smile and gently broom you, the sinner, and herself into the same crowded heap, no one any better than they should be, could be, absolute equals in a mellow sputter of laughter she sometimes can't suppress, hiding it, muffling it with her fist over her mouth, nodding, remembering, how people's badness can be too good to be true, *my, my, my.*

Well, my story didn't tease out a hint of laugh, and forget the 550 miles separating us, I could tell she wasn't smiling either. Why was she holding back the sunshine that could forgive the worst foolishness. Absolve my sins. Retrieve me from the dead end corners into which I paint myself. Mama, please. Please, please, please, don't you weep. And tell ole Martha not to moan. Don't leave me drowning like Willie Boy in the deep blue sea. Smile, Mom. Laugh. Send that healing warmth through the wire and save poor me.

Was it the weightlifting joke, Mom. Maybe you didn't think it was funny.

Sorry. Tell the truth, I didn't see nothing humorous about any of it. God's t-shirt. You know better. Ought to be ashamed of yourself. Taking the Lord's name in vain.

Where do you get such ideas, boy. I think I know my children. God knows I should by now, shouldn't I. How am I not supposed to know youall after all you've put me through beating my brains out to get through to you. *Yes, yes, yes.* Then one youall goes and does something terrible I never would have guessed was in you. Won't say you break my heart. Heart's been broke too many times. In too many little itty-bitty pieces can't break down no more, but youall sure ain't finished with me, are you. Still got some new trick in you to lay on your weary mother before she leaves here.

Guess I ought to be grateful to God an old fool like me's still around to be tricked, Weightlifter. Well, it's different. Nobody ain't called me nothing like weightlifter before. It's different, sure enough.

Now here's where she should have laughed. She'd picked up the stone I'd bull's-eyed right into the middle of her wrinkled brow, between her tender, brown, all-seeing eyes, lifted it and turned it over in her hands like a jeweler with a tiny telescope strapped around his skull inspecting a jewel, testing its heft and brilliance, the marks of god's hands, god's will, the hidden truths sparkling in its depths, multiplied, splintered through mirroring facets. After such a brow scrunching examination, isn't it time to smile. Kiss and make up. Wasn't that Mom's way. Wasn't that how she handled the things that hurt us and hurt her. Didn't she ease the pain of our worst injuries with the balm of her everything's-going-to-be-alright-in-the-morning smile. The smile that takes the weight, every hurtful ounce and forgives, the smile licking our wounds so they scab over, and she can pick them off our skin, stuff their lead weight into the bulging sack of all sorrows slung across her back.

The possibility my wannabe story had actually hurt her dawned on me. Or should I say bopped me upside my head like the Br'er Bear club my middle brother loads in his cart to discourage bandits. I wished I was sitting at the kitchen table across from her so I could check for damage, her first, then check myself in the mirror of those soft, brown, incredibly loving mother's eyes. If I'd hurt her even a teeny-tiny bit, I'd be broken forever unless those eyes repaired me. Yet even as I regretted reading her the clumsy passage and prepared myself to surrender wholly, happily to the hounds of hell if I'd harmed one hair on her tender, gray head, I couldn't deny a sneaky, smarting tingle of satisfaction at the thought that maybe, maybe words I'd written had touched another human being, mama mia or not.

Smile, Mom. It's just a story. Just a start. I know it needs more work. You were supposed to smile at the weightlifting part.

God not something to joke about.

C'mon, mom. How many times have I heard Reverend Fitch cracking you up with his corny God jokes.

Time and a place.

Maybe stories are my time and place, Mom. You know. My time and place to say things I need to say.

No matter how bad it comes out sounding, right. No matter you make a joke of your poor mother . . .

Poor mother's suffering. You were going to say, *Poor mother's suffering,* weren't you.

You heard what I said.

And heard what you didn't say. I hear those words, too. The unsaid ones, Mom. Louder sometimes. Drowning out what gets said, Mom.

Whoa. We gon let it all hang out this morning, ain't we. Son. First that story. Now you accusing me of *your* favorite trick, that muttering under your breath. Testing me this morning, aren't you. What makes you think a sane person would ever pray for more weight. Ain't those the words you put in my mouth. More weight.

And the building shook. The earth rumbled. More weight descended like god's fist on his Hebrew children. Like in Lamentations. The Book in the Bible. The movie based on the Book based on what else, the legend of my mother's long suffering back.

Because she had a point.

People with no children can be cruel. Had I heard it first from Oprah, the diva of suffering my mother could have become if she'd pursued show-biz instead of weightlifting. Or was the damning phrase a line from one of Gwen Brooks's abortion blues. Whatever their source, the words fit and

I was ashamed. I do know better. A bachelor and nobody's daddy, but still my words have weight. Like sticks and stones, words can break bones. Metaphors can pull you apart and put you back together all wrong. I know what you mean, Mom. My entire life I've had to listen to people trying to tell me I'm just a white man in a dark skin.

Give me a metaphor long enough and I'll move the earth. Somebody famous said it. Or said something like that. And everybody, famous or not knows words sting. Words change things. Step on a crack, break your mother's back.

On the other hand, Mom, metaphor's just my way of trying to say two things, be in two places at once. Saying goodbye and hello and goodbye. Many things, many places at once. You know, like James Cleveland singing our favorite gospel tune, *Stood on the Bank of Jordan*. Metaphors are very short songs. Mini-mini stories. Rivers between like the Jordan where ships sail on, sail on and you stand and wave goodbye-hello, hello-goodbye.

Weightlifter just a word, just play. I was only teasing, Mom. I didn't mean to upset you. I certainly intended no harm. I'd swallow every stick of dynamite it takes to pay for a Nobel prize before I'd accept one if it cost just one of your soft, curly hairs.

Smile. Let's begin again.

It's snowing in Massachusetts / The ground's white in O-Hi-O. Yes, it's snowing in Massachusetts / And ground's white in O-Hi-O. Shut my eyes, Mr. Weatherman / Can't stand to see my baby go.

When I called you last Thursday evening and didn't get an answer I started worrying. I didn't know why. We'd talked Tuesday and you sounded fine. Better than fine. A lift and lilt in your voice. After I hung up the phone Tuesday said to myself, Mom's in good shape. Frail but her spirit's strong. Said those very words to myself more than once Tuesday. *Frail but her spirit's strong.* The perkiness I sensed in you helped make my Wednesday super. Early rise. Straight to my desk. Two pages before noon and you know me, Mom. Two pages can take a week, a month. I've had two page years. I've had decades dreaming the one perfect page I never got around to writing. Thursday morning reams of routine and no pages but not to worry I told myself. After Wednesday's productivity, wasn't I enti-

tled to some down time. Just sat at my desk, pleased as punch with myself till I got bored feeling so good and started a nice novel, *Call It Sleep*.
Dinner at KFC buffet. Must have balled up fifty napkins trying to keep
my chin decent. Then home to call you before I snuggled up again with
the little jewish boy, his mama and their troubles in old N.Y.C.

Let your phone ring and ring. Too late for you to be out unless you
had a special occasion. And you always let me know well ahead of time
when something special coming up. I tried calling a half hour later and
again twenty minutes after that. By then nearly nine, close to your bedtime. I was getting really worried now. Couldn't figure where you might
be. Nine-fifteen and still no answer, no clue what was going on.

Called Sis. Called Aunt Chloe. Nobody knew where you were. Chloe
said she'd talked with you earlier just like every other morning. Sis said
you called her at work after she got back from lunch. Both of them said
you sounded fine. Chloe said you'd probably fallen asleep in your recliner
and left the phone in the bedroom or bathroom and your hearing's to the
point you can be wide-awake but if the TV's on and the phone's not beside you or the ringer's not turned to high she said sometimes she has to
ring and hang up, ring and hang up two, three times before she catches
you.

Chloe promised to keep calling every few minutes till she reached you.
Said they have a prayer meeting Thursdays in your mother's building and
she's been saying she wants to go and I bet she's there, honey. She's alright,
honey. Don't worry yourself, O.K. We're old and fuddleheaded now, but
we're tough old birds. Your mother's fine. I'll tell her to call you soon's I
get through to her. Your mom's okay, baby. God keeps an eye on us.

You know Aunt Chloe. She's your sister. Five hundred miles away and
I could hear her squeezing her large self through the telephone line, see
her pillow arms reaching for the weight before it comes down on me.

Why would you want to hear any of this. You know what happened.
Where you were. You know how it all turned out.

You don't need to listen to my conversation with Sis. Dialing her back
after we'd been disconnected. The first time in life I think my sister ever
phoned me later than ten o'clock at night. First time a lightning bolt ever
disconnected us. Ever disconnected me from anybody ever.

Did you see Eva Wallace first, Mom, coming through your door, or
was it the busybody super you've never liked since you moved in.

Something about the way she speaks to her granddaughter you said. Little girl's around the building all day because her mother's either in the street or the slam and the father takes the child so rarely he might as well live in Timbuctoo so you know the super doesn't have it easy and on a couple of occasions you've offered to keep the granddaughter when the super needs both hands and her mind free for an hour. You don't hold the way she busies up in everybody's business or the fact the child has to look out for herself too many hours in the day against the super, and you're sure she loves her granddaughter you said but the short way she talks sometimes to a child that young just not right.

Who'd you see first pushing open your door. Eva said you didn't show up after you said you'd stop by for her. She waited awhile she said then phoned you and got no answer and then a friend called her and they got to running their mouths and Eva said she didn't think again about you not showing up when you were supposed to until she hung up the phone. And not right away then. Said as soon as she missed you, soon as she remembered youall had planned on attending the Thursday prayer meeting together she got scared. She knows how dependable you are. Even though it was late, close to your bedtime, she called you anyway and let the phone ring and ring. Way after nine by then. Pulled her coat on over her housedress, scooted down the hall and knocked on your door cause where else you going to be. No answer so she hustled back to her place and phoned downstairs for the super and they both pounded on your door till the super said we better have a look just in case and unlocked your apartment. Stood there staring after she turned the key, trying to see through the door, then slid it open a little and both of them Eva said tiptoeing in like a couple of fools after all that pounding and hollering in the hall. Said she never thought about it at the time but later, after everything over and she drops down on her couch to have that cigarette she knew she shouldn't have with her lungs rotten as they are and hadn't smoked one for more than a year but sneaks the Camel she'd been saving out its hiding place in a Baggie in the freezer and sinks back in the cushions and lights up, real tired, real shook up and teary she said but couldn't help smiling at herself when she remembered all that hollering and pounding and then tipping in like a thief.

It might have happened that way. Being right or wrong about what happened is less important sometimes than finding a good way to tell it.

What's anybody want to hear anyway. Not the truth people want. No-no-no. People want the best told story, the lie that entertains and turns them on. No question about it, is there. What people want. What gets people's attention. What sells soap. Why else do the biggest, most barefaced liars rule the world.

Hard to be a mother, isn't it Mom. I can't pretend to be yours, not even a couple minutes' worth before I go to pieces. I try to imagine a cradle with you lying inside, cute, miniature bedding tucked around the tiny doll of you. I can almost picture you asleep in it, snuggled up, your eyes shut, maybe your thumb in your mouth but then you cry out in the night, you need me to stop whatever I'm doing and rush in and scoop you up and press you to my bosom, lullabye you back to sleep. I couldn't manage it. Not the easy duty I'm imagining, let alone you bucking and wheezing and snot, piss, vomit, shit, blood, you hot and throbbing with fever, steaming in my hands like the heart ripped fresh from some poor soul's chest.

Too much weight. Too much discrepancy in size. As big a boy as I've grown to be, I can't lift you.

Will you forgive me if I cheat, Mom. Dark suited, strong men in somber ties and white shirts will lug you out of the church, down the stone steps, launch your gleaming barge into the black river of the Cadillac's bay. My brothers won't miss me not handling my share of the weight. How much weight could there be. Tiny, scooped out you. The tinny, fake wood shell. The entire affair's symbolic. Heavy with meaning not weight. You know. Like metaphors. Like words interchanged as if they have no weight or too much weight, as if words are never required to bear more than they can stand. As if words, when we're finished mucking with them, go back to just being words.

The word *trouble*. The word *sorrow*. The word *bye-and-bye*.

I was wrong and you were right, as usual, Mom. So smile. Certain situations, yours for instance, being a mother, suffering what mothers suffer, why would anyone want to laugh at that. Who could stand in your shoes a heartbeat—*shoes, shoes, everybody got to have shoes*—bear your burdens one instant and think it's funny. Who ever said it's O.K. to lie and kill as long as it makes a good story.

Smile. Admit you knew from the start it would come to this. Me trembling, needing your strength. It has, Mom, so please, please, a little, bitty grin of satisfaction. They say curiosity kills the cat and satisfaction brings it back. Smiling. Smile Mom. Come back. You know I've always hated spinach but please spoonfeed me a canful so those Popeye muscles pop in my arms. I meant shapeshifter not weightlifter. I meant the point of this round, spinningtop earth must rest somewhere, on something or someone. I meant you are my sunshine. My only sunshine.

The problem never was the word *weightlifter,* was it. If you'd been insulted by my choice of metaphor you would have let me know, not by silence, but nailing me with a quick, funny signifying dig, and then you would have smiled or laughed and we'd have gone on to the next thing. What must have bothered you, stunned you was what I said into the phone before I began reading. Said this is about a man scared he won't survive his mother's passing.

That's what upset you, wasn't it. Saying goodbye to you. Practicing for your death in a story. Trying on for size a world without you. Ignoring like I did when I was a boy, your size. Saying aloud terrible words with no power over us as long as we don't speak them.

So when you heard me let the cat out the bag, you were shocked, weren't you. Speechless. Smileless. What could you say. The damage had been done. I heard it in your first words after you got back your voice. And me knowing your lifelong, deathly fear of cats. Like the big, furry orange Tom you told me about, how it curled up on the porch just outside your door, trapping you a whole August afternoon inside the hotbox shanty in Washington, D.C., when I lived in your belly.

Why would I write a story that risks your life. Puts our business in the street. I'm the oldest child, supposed to be the man of the family now. No wonder you cried, Oh father. Oh son. Oh holy ghost. Why hath thou forsaken me. I know you didn't cry that. You aren't Miss Oprah. But I sure did mess up, didn't I. Didn't I, Mom. Up to my old tricks. Crawling up inside you. My weight twisting you all out of shape.

I asked you once about the red sailor cap hanging on the wall inside your front door. Knew it was my brother's cap on the nail, but why that particular hat I asked and not another of his countless, fly sombreros on display. Rob, Rob, man of many lids. For twenty years in the old house, now in your apartment, the hat a shrine no one allowed to touch. You never said it but everybody understood the red hat your good luck charm, your mojo for making sure Rob would get out the slam one day and come bopping through the door, pluck the hat from the wall and pull it down over his bean head. Do you remember me asking why the sailor cap. You probably guessed I was fishing. Really didn't matter which cap, did it. Point was you chose the red one and *why* must always be your secret. You could have made up a nice story to explain why the red sailor cap wound up on the nail and I would have listened as I always listened all ears but you knew part of me would be trying to peek through the words at your secret. Always a chance you might slip up and reveal too much. So the hat story and plenty others never told. The old folks had taught you that telling another person your secret wish strips it of its power, a wish's small, small chance, as long as it isn't spoken, to influence what might happen next in the world. You'd never tell anyone the words sheltered in the shadow of your heart. Still, I asked about the red sailor cap because I needed to understand your faith, your weightlifting power, how you can believe a hat, any fucking kind of hat, could bring my baby brother home safe and sound from prison. I needed to spy and pry. Wiretap the telephone in your bosom. Hear the words you would never say to another soul, not even on pain of death.

How would such unsaid words sound, what would they look like on a page. And if you had uttered them, surrendered your stake in them, forfeited their meager, silent claim to work miracles, would it have been worth the risk, even worth the loss, to finally hear the world around you cracking, collapsing, changing as you spoke your little secret tale.

Would you have risen an inch or two from this cold ground. Would you have breathed easier after releasing the heaviness of silent words hoarded so unbearably, unspeakably long. Let go, Mom. Shed the weight just once.

Not possible for you, I know. It would be cheating, I know. The man of unbending faith did not say to the hooded inquisitors piling a crushing load of stones on his chest, *More light. More light.* No. I'm getting my quotes mixed up again. Just at the point the monks thought they'd broken his will, just as spiraling fractures started splintering his bones, he cried, *More bricks. More bricks.*

I was scared, Mom. Scared every cotton picking day of my life I'd lose you. The fear a sing-song taunt like tinnitus ringing in my ear. No wonder I'm a little crazy. But don't get me wrong. Not your fault. I don't blame you for my morbid fears, my unhappiness. It's just that I should have confessed sooner, long, long ago, the size of my fear of losing you. I wish you'd heard me say the words. How fear made me keep my distance, hide how much I depended on your smile. The sunshine of your smiling laughter that could also send me silently screaming out the room in stories I never told you because you'd taught me as you'd been taught, not to say anything aloud I didn't want to come true. Nor say out loud the things I wished to come true. Doesn't leave a hell of a lot to say, does it. No wonder I'm tongue-tied, scared shitless.

But would it be worth the risk, worth failing, if I could find words to tell our story and also keep us covered inside it, work us invisibly into the fret, the warp and woof of the story's design, safe there, connected there as words in perfect poems, the silver apples of the moon, golden apples of the sun, blue guitars. The two of us like those rhyming pairs *never* and *forever, heart* and *part,* in the doo-wop songs I harmonized with the fellas in the alley around the corner from Henderson's barber shop up on Frankstown Avenue, first me then lost brother Sonny and his crew then baby brother Rob and his cut buddy hoodlums rapping and now somebody else black and young and wild and pretty so the song lasts forever and never ever ends even though the voices change back there in the alley where you can hear bones rattling in the men's fists, *fever in the funkhouse looking for a five* and hear wine bottles exploding and hear the rusty shopping cart squeak over the cobblestones of some boy ferrying an old lady's penny-ante groceries home for a nickel once, then a dime, a quarter, four quarters now.

Would it be worth the risk, worth failing.

Shouldn't I try even if I know the strength's not in me. No, you say. Yes. Hold on, let go. Do I hear you saying, Everything's gonna be alright. Saying, Do what you got to do, baby, smiling as I twist my fingers into the brass handle. As I lift.

SECOND PRIZE

The Man with the Lapdog

By Beth Lordan

INTRODUCED BY PAM HOUSTON

My boyfriend, Randy, read this story to me in the car, late one night between Santa Barbara and Berkeley. It was the fourth O. Henry story he had read in a row. We were somewhere near Gilroy, garlic capital of the world.

By the next time we would go to Santa Barbara, only three weeks later, we would have found out our beloved Irish wolfhound had terminal bone cancer. We'd begin our second road trip crying, spend most of it fighting, and arrive in Santa Barbara dazed by the enormity of what the dog meant to our relationship, the even more massive thing we meant to each other. But that first trip, until we read Beth Lordan's story, cancer was the farthest thing from our minds.

That's a lie. Cancer is never the farthest thing from my mind, especially when I get that feeling that my life is going just slightly better than I deserve, and I am appreciating it just slightly less than I should. In this way I am like Lyle, the protagonist in "The Man with the Lapdog."

Lyle is an American, retired to Ireland with his Irish wife, Mary, whom he appreciates somewhat less than his longhaired dachshund, "a pretty girlish little thing." It is on a walk with the lapdog that he meets Laura, a young American woman, and her terminally ill husband, Mark. Over the next several days Lyle watches Laura try to will Mark back to health, with Ireland— the land itself—complicit in the campaign. Lyle fantasizes about a reunion with Laura after Mark's death, and his disgust with Mary and her stout Irish temperament grows.

This story is clean and sure and delicate and deeply true. What is most beautiful about it is how quietly and completely it turns, leaving Lyle in a place that is absolutely believable, absolutely surprising, and absolutely satisfying to the reader all at once. The moment of grace this story allows its characters comes so softly it feels almost accidental, though it is both complete and profound. Like water coming to its level behind a dam.

In the car, near Gilroy, when Randy finished reading, we both made little noises of satisfaction, reached at the same moment for each other's hands, and then we were quiet for a long long time.

—PAM HOUSTON

Beth Lordan

The Man with the Lapdog

From *The Atlantic Monthly*

ALMOST EVERY morning, as Lyle was getting ready to take the dog for a walk along the bay, his wife would ask, "Are ye down the prom, then?" They had met and married thirty years before, in Vermont, when she was Mary Curtin and he'd thought her a happy combination of exotic and domestic. At sixty, after their life in the States, she still called herself a Galway girl; at sixty-seven, after two years of retirement in Galway, Lyle still considered a prom a high school dance, not two miles of sidewalk beside the water.

So he would say, "We're going to walk along the bay," and hope she'd leave it at that. When they had first come to Ireland, the exchange had had a bit of a joke to it, but he felt it now as unwelcome pressure. He had no intention of taking up Irish idioms—he'd have felt foolish saying "half-five" instead of five-thirty, "Tuesday week" instead of next Tuesday, "ye" for you. "Toilet" instead of bathroom was unthinkable. He called things by their real names—"pubs" bars, "shops" stores, "chips" French fries, and "gardai" police.

He didn't love the talk, and he didn't love the Irish people, who always stood too close and talked too fast, and he had trouble, still, understanding what they said. He had frightened and embarrassed himself trying to drive on the wrong side of the road with the steering wheel on the wrong side of the car, and had given it up. He disliked the weight of pound coins in his pocket, and he didn't care for Guinness.

And yet, somewhat to his surprise, he liked a lot about Ireland. He liked keeping the small garden in front of their house, the way things simply grew and thrived in the steady cool dampness. He liked the stone walls that surrounded every yard and separated one person's place from another's. He liked the little coal-burning fireplace in the sitting room. After forty years as an accountant for a hardware chain, he liked living in a place where people went for walks, and he liked going for walks. He liked the dog, a long-haired dachshund, a pretty, girlish little thing. He liked the opinionated newspapers, and he liked being a foreigner.

One day in early March, walking along the bay, he saw a couple he probably wouldn't have noticed among the other tourists if it had been summer. They stood arm in arm looking out over the water, the woman dark-haired and attractive in an unglamorous way, the man thin and frail, apparently very ill. Lyle heard her say, "Yes, County Clare—I'm sure of it," her American accent clear; he nodded as he passed, and they nodded in response. The next day their walks crossed at about the same place, and all three smiled in recognition. That evening something on television about pre-season tourists reminded him to say that he'd met an American couple.

"Have you?" his wife said. "Where are they from?"

"I don't know," he replied, sorry already that he'd said anything.

She tilted her head as if she was being playful and said, "So did ye talk about the weather, then?"

"Yes," he said. "We talked about the ugly weather."

On the third day, when they met again, Lyle gave the leash the small tug that told the dog to sit and said, "It's a beautiful day, isn't it?—good to see the sun again."

Something rippled between the man and the woman and came out as a quick laugh in her answer. "It's glorious," she agreed. "And you're American!" she said.

"I am," he said.

The man, too, seemed amused as he put out his hand in introduction. "I'm Mark; this is my wife, Laura. And we, too, are Americans."

"Lyle," he said. He shook Mark's thin hand. "Are you here on vacation?"

"For three weeks," Laura said, as if three weeks were a long, luxurious season. "And you?"

The dog was sitting patiently. "I'm retired, and my wife is Irish, so we came back here to live a couple of years ago."

They said where they were from, and how old their children were, and that this was their first trip to Ireland, long dreamed about, and then Laura reached out and put her hand lightly and briefly on the sleeve of Lyle's coat. "I have to tell you: we'd seen you walking here, and we made up a life for you—"

"We assumed you were Irish, of course," Mark said.

"I suppose it's because everything is so exactly as we expected it to be," Laura said. "The stone walls in the fields when we were coming over from Shannon, the pretty shops, the thatched roofs. We even saw a rainbow our first day here. So we just put you into the picture, the Galway gentleman, and when you turn out to be American, it's quite a joke on us." Her eyes sparkled.

Her eyes were very fine, her face strong, and Lyle admired even the simple way she held her dark hair in her fist to keep it from blowing across her face. She was coming into middle age with none of the artificiality of so many American women.

"So I've spoiled your postcard," he said, and all three of them laughed. When they parted, he kept the picture of himself her words had made: his overcoat and hat, his kindly aging face, the tidy small dog, obedient at the end of the leash. And he kept, too, the swift pleasure of her hand on his coat.

They met again the next day and the next, stopping to talk for a few minutes. Lyle would recognize them at some distance by Mark's brimmed hat and the bright shawl Laura wore over the shoulders of her coat. They walked in the mornings, she said, before the wind got too strong, because the wind tired Mark. He had lost his hair, and his face was swollen, but Lyle could see that in health he had been a handsome man. They always walked arm in arm, and she often seemed to be supporting him, more as a matter of balance than of strength, but something in the way they looked together led Lyle to believe that even before Mark's illness they had often walked this old-fashioned way, side by side, along streets or through parks. Lyle could almost remember the pleasure of that—the hand a warm pressure in the bend of his elbow, the wrist between his arm and his ribs eloquent and secret, the publicness of the linking.

. . .

The next evening his wife asked about his Americans, and he told her they were from Idaho, where Mark taught high school and Laura raised their four teenage children, who were with grandparents for these three weeks.

"A teacher," his wife said, wondering. "An expensive holiday for a teacher—and during the term."

"They have those deals," he said. "Two-for-ones. Off season." They were eating spaghetti, and he watched how she poked around among the strands, looking for something in particular.

"From the States to Ireland, do you think?" she said, doubtful.

"I don't know."

She chewed, and he could almost see her mind shifting. "If they did, Jimmy might be looking into it so."

Jimmy was their younger son, twenty-five years old without a dollar or a plan to his name. "He might," Lyle said cautiously.

She went on about fares and connections, and then safely into a story her sister Roisin had told her of a trip somebody had taken by bus from somewhere in Kerry to somewhere in Clare that sped along, if you counted all the time, at a rate of about six miles an hour. Lyle was relieved: they wouldn't have to talk about buying Jimmy a ticket, or how they weren't exactly rich themselves, or about his life-hating caution and how he'd always favored Kevin, and on and on. He finished his supper and waited for the end of the story, the ritual shake of her head, the "It's a terrible country." Back home she had told different stories about Ireland, ending them with "It's a grand country." Sometimes, now, he'd point this out to her, and ask why she had wanted to come back here if it was so damned terrible. But tonight, as he waited, in the noise of the long details of her telling, he thought of how simply Laura had spoken that morning.

She had asked about Saint Patrick's Day, how it would be celebrated, while Mark walked alone at a little distance, stooping unsteadily to pick up small shells. Lyle told her that the parade would be small compared with American parades, the day a quiet family holiday, more like Labor Day than Mardi Gras.

"Maybe we'll try the parade, then," she said, watching Mark's slow progress back. "If it's not likely to be a big crowd. He gets tired."

"Is his recovery expected to be long?" Lyle had wondered for days how to ask, and was pleased at how naturally the question came out.

"Oh, he won't recover," she said. "He's dying."

She put no drama into it at all, not into the words, not into the tone, not into the way she raised her hand against the sudden emergence of the sun. "I'm sorry," Lyle said.

She nodded. "So are we." And then they had stood there quiet, waiting for Mark to come back and for their walks in opposite directions to continue.

He hadn't told his wife any of that, and now she had passed the end of the bus story and had come to something else. "It's not the traveling, I told her, it's the staying that's so dear, and she was saying that that's where the money is, in B-and-Bs. Why, the people in Kerry, half of them, in the summer move into caravans in their own back gardens and let all their rooms to the tourists. I couldn't do that, I told her—you know how I am about motels, sleeping in other people's beds, and it'd be the same thing but worse, having strangers in your bed and then going back to it in October so, knowing they'd been there. I'd be thinking I could feel the heat of those bodies in the mattress." She stood and gathered up the plates and silverware.

There, in something that wasn't quite his mind and wasn't quite his body, he felt the sweet warmth a woman left in a bed, and knew that the shape and smell of the warmth were Laura's. So when his wife asked, "They're at a B-and-B, I'd think, your Americans?" he responded, "Why—are you going to go ask what their damned tickets cost?"

She stopped in her work and stared at him. "That was nasty," she said, but he saw that her eyes were only alert, not wounded.

"Oh, give it a rest," he said, and went into the sitting room and turned on the television and called the dog to his lap.

He discovered where they were staying by accident. The day before Saint Patrick's the rain was heavy, so he and the dog were trapped inside with the smell of damp coal ash and his wife's endless talk about the rain—lashing, she said, coming down in rods, she said, bucketing down, and how she hated rain in her face, she said, and, now, a soft day she didn't mind. But by midmorning the next day the rain had stopped, and he said he was going out. As he was putting on his overcoat, she came with a limp hank of shamrock and knelt on the kitchen floor to tie it to the dog's collar. "That looks pretty stupid," he said.

She patted the dog's head and stood up. "It looks lovely." She had two more bits, and he allowed her to pin one to the lapel of his coat. "Are you thinking of going to the parade, then?" she asked.

"It's not until noon." He hooked the leash onto the dog's collar. "Did you want to go?"

She made a wry face and pushed her hand in the air between them. "It's a poor excuse for a parade," she said. "Roisin's calling by for me to help her with her new curtains. I'll be back before tea."

Out of sight of the house, he stooped and adjusted the dog's greenery. The air was clean and cool. As he passed one of the schools, he could hear a few horns behind the building—kids preparing for the parade. Small family groups were slowly walking toward the parade route. Many people had small bunches of shamrock pinned to their coats. Children carried tricolors, and a few older boys had their faces painted green. He headed for the Salmon Weir Bridge, meaning to walk around the college and then circle back and maybe see the parade, maybe run into Mark and Laura. As he was waiting for the traffic to pass, he glanced down one of the side streets and saw Mark.

He was standing on the sidewalk, bareheaded, in jeans and a T-shirt, alone. Lyle had known he was thin, but there, coatless in the street, he was shockingly gaunt. As Lyle watched, Mark turned away, took two steps, and stopped. He put his arms up over his face and leaned against the building, like a child counting in a game of hide-and-seek. Farther up the street a door opened, and Laura came out. She hurried to Mark and put her hands on his shoulders. They spoke; Lyle could see that, and that Laura's hair was in a braid, and that her dark-green skirt rose and fell around her calves in the breeze, and that she was barefoot on the cold concrete. Then, slowly, she drew Mark from the wall and turned him to her. Still speaking, she took his hands and stepped backward, back toward the door she'd come out. He went with her a step, another step, and then she turned, pulling his arm around her waist. They walked together back inside, through the door of the Salmon Weir Hostel.

The rain began again.

Lyle was glad to find the house empty when he and the dog got home, empty and dim in the gray afternoon, with the glimmer of a coal fire in the sitting room. He threw away the shamrock, hung up his coat, and put the leash away. Mark would certainly die.

He jabbed at the fire with a small poker and put some more coal on, and then he sighed and sat down in his chair and watched the fire, listening to the coal whistling as it heated. He would die. She would stand as she had there on the sidewalk this morning and she would crumple, collapse in and down. Lyle rubbed his forehead with his fingertips.

The dog came and sat, alert, questioning, in front of him. "You're right," he said to her. "I forgot the treat. Come on." She followed him to the cupboard and gazed into his eyes as he gave her the little orange-colored biscuit.

Men would be lining up to take Mark's place, no doubt about it. The dog stayed in the kitchen to eat, as she always did, and Lyle went back to his chair. Poor bastard, knowing that. The idea of it was enough to send anybody out in shirtsleeves to grieve against the side of a building.

Then again. Maybe Laura would be one of those widows who didn't remarry. Maybe she'd dedicate herself to the children. Bring them back here in a year or two, show them where she and their father had spent these weeks. He would see her again, he thought, as the dog, her biscuit gone, trotted in; he lifted her into his lap, where she settled and fell immediately asleep. He'd see her, and she would be recovered from it.

He stroked the dog's smooth head. The wind was blowing across the chimney and making a low *hoo*ing sound; he had said before that sometimes he felt as if he were living in a jug, in this small room at the bottom of the chimney, but today he liked it. He relaxed into imagining Laura, in a few years, walking alone down by the Claddagh, and how he'd greet her, and how by then he'd have become, as he often did in dreams, younger and more attractive. Or he'd be in Idaho, somehow, and see her. At the edge of sleep, he imagined driving with her down the roads of his youth in rural Vermont, where small lanes branched off among the trees.

"Wrecked, are ye?" his wife said, chuckling, as his heart thudded two heavy strokes.

The next day Laura looked tired, but as they met, she smiled, her eyes bright, and she reached out and gripped his upper arm for an instant. He felt again that guilty lurch of his heart. "We're going adventuring," she said, releasing his arm.

"Adventuring?" He looked at Mark, whose smile seemed tight.

Laura said, "We're going to rent a car and drive the Ring of Kerry!"

"Drive it?" Lyle said, still to Mark. "Driving's a bit of a challenge here." Even to himself he sounded gruff, a spoilsport.

"She'll be doing it," Mark said, and Lyle heard the injury in his voice.

"I figure, if the other tourists can manage it, so can I," she said.

"Tourists are bad drivers," Lyle said, "especially on those narrow roads."

"You've been there, then," Mark said.

"Just once," Lyle said, and told hurriedly, gruffly, about the bus tour along the narrow roads, the number of tour buses, the hordes of rude Americans and Germans.

"But the car-rental man said that wouldn't be true now, this early in the year," Laura said, her eyes strained but her voice still gay. "And it would still be worth it—everybody says Kerry's beautiful."

You are beautiful, Lyle thought, before he could stop himself, and then his mouth went dry with the fear that he'd say it, make a fool of himself, and he lumbered on to say, "Oh, it is. It's very beautiful. The landscape."

Lyle's wife took her baths at bedtime, and sometimes talked to him through the half-closed door to their bedroom. Only watery sounds came from the bathroom tonight as he got into his pajamas, trying to think where that map of Kerry might have ended up. At one time, he was sure, the maps had all been in a drawer in the kitchen, but he had looked there earlier and found playing cards and string instead. So she'd reorganized at some point, and the maps could be anywhere. He opened the wardrobe door quietly and stared up at the stacks of shoe boxes on the top shelf. Where did you put the maps? he could say, and she'd say, Maps—and what'd you be wanting maps for and us with no car?

The bath water moved. "I've not seen that old dog outside Ward's shop all week," she said.

"No?" he said, to encourage her to go on, to cover the sound of the wardrobe door closing.

"John's had that dog for years on years, he has. A number of old dogs hereabout," she said. "Just past the school those two small dogs, the white one and the terrier, they're old. Judy down Canal Road, she's an old one, Maureen Ryder's dog. Oh—I dreamt of dogs," she said.

"Dogs?" he said, though encouragement wasn't really necessary now: she always told her dreams in endless detail.

"I'd the job of feeding them—big dogs on chains in a yard. I can still see two of them, these two bulldogs. The faces on them."

When he was a boy and something was lost, a shoe, say, or a hairbrush, his mother would stand in the kitchen and say, If I was a shoe, where would I be? So now Lyle stood beside the bed and closed his eyes and thought, If I was a road map, where would I be?

"I'd found this bright-blue plastic dish—half scoop, half dish, it was—and I'd filled it with dry dog food for the bulldogs." She gave a small laugh, and he heard the sound of dripping.

He bent and looked under the bed: four suitcases. If he were a road map, he might be in a suitcase, but he couldn't, certainly, get a suitcase out and open without her hearing, and he couldn't be sure the map was there, or if it was, that it would be in the first suitcase he opened.

"Pleased with myself, I was. And then your man comes up and he says, 'That's not enough,' he says, and then he says, 'Besides, they bite.' "

He stood up again, and knew that he was an aging man, with skinny legs inside the pajama pants that were snug around his bulging stomach, unfamiliar hair in his ears and nose. He stood still and heard his wife lifting herself from the bath water, and knew that the dream she was telling would go on in her rueful voice from behind the door until she'd finished it, and that when she came out, she'd get into bed behind him, damp in a way he'd once found so erotic that it nearly choked him. And maybe this would be one of the nights she'd put her moist hand on him.

"What the hell have you done with the damned road maps?" he said.

"Road maps?" she said. She pulled the bathroom door open and stood there in her worn nightgown, looking at him, the ends of her short gray hair dark and stringy with wet, dripping water down the sides of her neck. "And what'd you be wanting with road maps this time of night, cursing about it?"

"I wasn't cursing," he said.

"You were. You're cursing all the time now."

"I wouldn't be cursing if the damned maps had been where they belong."

"I'm not your housemaid," she said.

That was from an old, worn quarrel, almost a comfort, and he took up his part. "Just because I want to find things in my own God-damned house doesn't make me an ogre," he said.

"You should watch your language," she said. "And it wouldn't hurt to go to mass once in a while."

"Oh, mass! Sure—that's the answer to everything, isn't it? Maybe the priest could tell me where you've hidden the God-damned maps." He turned away, ready for her to say it was his fault that neither of the boys went to mass and that Kevin would probably marry that Jewish girl, and he'd say he hoped so, better a whining Jew than a whining Catholic. While they were saying those things, he would put on his slippers and his robe, she would get into bed, and he'd go downstairs and have a drink. And when he came back up in half an hour, she'd be asleep.

But she didn't say that, and she didn't move toward the bed. "For your Americans, is it?" she said, so mildly that he stopped and turned to look at her. She took her robe from the hook on the door, and nodded as she pulled it on and tied the belt. "I may have them in the hall press," she said. "Will I look for them so?"

He nodded, still confused and suspicious, and he knew he should say thank you, but she was gone down the stairs, the dog trotting behind her, and then he heard her in the hall closet, and then he heard her talking to the dog. He stood beside the bed and tried to imagine what he could say to her if he went downstairs; he could imagine nothing. When he heard the television come on, he got into bed. For many years, maybe always, she had gone to bed first or they had gone to bed together, and he found the freedom of being the only body on the mattress so comfortable and novel that he fell asleep quickly.

When he woke in the morning, the first thing he knew was that he was still alone, and a quick jolt of fear made him thrust his hand onto her side of the bed. It was warm, and at the same moment he smelled the coffee and rashers, and so he was irritated with her before he was even out of bed. It was irrational, and he knew that: for thirty years he'd waked alone in bed to the smell of the breakfast she was cooking. And yet this morning it seemed to him that she had pretended a larger absence, and the charade had forced from him a reaction that he found embarrassing.

But maybe she'd found the maps, he thought as he went down the stairs and into the kitchen. There lay the maps, beside his plate.

"You found them," he said.

"Was it Donegal they were wanting?" she said. "That one's gone missing."

"No—Kerry," he said.

"Grand, then—Kerry's there," she said, sounding relieved and pleased.

After breakfast, as he was putting on his coat, she said, "I thought I'd walk along with ye this morning. I'm to meet Roisin at ten at the Franciscans, and a walk will just fill the time." She was putting on her coat as she spoke, so there was nothing he could say. "Don't forget your map," she said, and he pushed it into his coat pocket and went out the door ahead of her.

"It's a grand morning," she said approvingly as they crossed the street onto the prom, and it was—nearly windless, a hint of sun. He didn't answer, and they walked on, she with her hands in her pockets, he with one hand in his pocket and the other holding the leash.

He had little hope that they wouldn't meet Mark and Laura, and when he saw them at a distance, Mark sitting on a bench and Laura standing beside him, looking out toward Mutton Island, he pulled the map from his pocket, half thinking to make a quick gift of it and be gone.

His wife took a sharp breath and murmured, "He's thin."

"He's sick," Lyle snapped, and then Laura turned and saw them, and they were too close to say more.

Mark stood, with obvious effort, and smiled, and Laura smiled, and as Mark took off his hat, Lyle realized that he couldn't look at either of them, so he smiled into the air between them and said, "Good morning. This is my wife, Mary—Mark, Laura," his voice too hearty for the words.

They shook hands and said the things people say—I've heard so much about you, a pleasure, how do you do, hello, Lyle smiling stupidly, helplessly, at the hotel across the road. Then his wife said, "How do ye find Galway?" and he could feel them hesitate and translate before Mark said, "It's a very friendly town. We'll be sorry to leave."

"But ye'll be back, then, after your trip to Kerry?"

Again a hesitation, in which Lyle heard the crying of the gulls, before Mark said, "Well—," and then Laura said, "Actually, we've been thinking about not going to Kerry after all. Given the roads."

Lyle looked down at the dog. Laura's voice was soft but strained. He wondered how obvious the map in his hand was, whether he could slide it back into his pocket without drawing attention.

"Ah, they're terrible, they are," his wife agreed, dismissing Kerry the Kingdom with a quick sigh as she sat on the bench. Mark sat beside her, his hat in his hand. "The thing ye might try is the Arans—have ye thought of that? There's a bus from town to Rossaveal, right to the ferry over, and then on the island there's the pony traps or the little buses, and back the same day." She laughed, comfortable, eager, sitting there with her purse on her lap as if this were a visit. "And, oh, the island's lovely, 'tis—it'll be gray here and the sun bright as Arizona over there."

"It sounds nice," Mark said.

"Ye might think of it," she went on. Lyle could see her thumbs on the purse, hidden from Mark and Laura, making rapid hard circles against the leather. "And Dublin, too—have ye been to Dublin?" She looked at Laura, who shook her head. "Oh, it's not to be missed, Dublin—just for a day, take the train over and back, the three museums and the Book of Kells. Of course, not all in a day, that'd be too much for anyone, it would, but just the National Museum, say, and they've a nice little tea shop there for your lunch." She stood up as if she'd settled something, but then she went on, hardly a breath between. "No, there's Ireland to see without Kerry, there is. Even right here in Galway. How much longer is your holiday?"

"Ten days?" Mark said, glancing at Laura.

"Or less," Laura said, "depending." She shrugged and drove her hands deep into her pockets. "The children," she said.

"I miss them," Mark said. His voice was quiet, but Lyle knew he was speaking to Laura. "I'd like to spend more time with them." His voice was like Mary's was when they fought about Jimmy—that soft tone, thinning with the threat of tears.

"Why, of course you would," Mary said. "Of course you would. But it takes a bit to change the tickets, doesn't it?" The sympathy in her voice seemed all for the difficulty of ticket changes.

"Yes," Laura said. She turned her face to the bay for a second and let the breeze push her hair back, and then she took a step closer to Mark and touched his cheek with the backs of her fingers. "It may take some doing." Mark closed his eyes for a second, and when Laura took her hand away, he put his hat back on.

So this was the end of what he'd seen on the street: Laura and Ireland had failed, and had surrendered. Mark would die, and Laura would not. They would not go together in joy to the edge of life.

"Well, then," Mary said, holding her purse over her stomach, smiling at Laura, "ye must come to tea, mustn't they, Lyle? Come to tea—let's see, could ye come today? No, wait—that won't work, will it? Maybe to-morrow?"

"That's very kind of you," Laura said.

Mark nodded to Lyle and said, "We'll meet again before then."

"Yes, of course—of course ye will, and you can tell Lyle, and we'll see about it, will we? It's grand by the fire on some of these days, it is, and ye should be in an Irish house before ye go back. It's lovely to have met ye so," she said, and shook Mark's hand again. Then she stepped in front of Lyle and put her arms around Laura and hugged her. Laura closed her eyes and for a second let her head touch Mary's.

Then they were apart, and the dog was up and ready to go, and Lyle found that he'd gotten the map back into his pocket somehow and had a hand free to shake Mark's. Then he and his wife were walking on, the dog trotting beside them, and after a few steps his wife slid her hand under his arm and his arm bent up to hold it, and so they walked on toward the Claddagh, the wind picking up at their backs.

"Coffee as well as tea, of course," she said, "since they're Americans, and tomorrow would be fine, it would, or Saturday."

"Let's make it Saturday," he said, because she was crying, and this was a decision they could make, although he didn't believe he'd ever see Mark or Laura again.

"Such lovely people," his wife said. "Such lovely people."

Lyle knew they were, and because his wife had said it, he wanted to say to her, So are we. He wanted to say that he wasn't a young man, but he wasn't dying, and that this hand on his arm was hers—that for them the end was still far off, with difficulties and complications still to come.

Instead he pressed her wrist against his side and said, "They are so. And it's a sad thing, it is."

The Deacon

By Mary Gordon

INTRODUCED BY GEORGE SAUNDERS

Fiction is an urgent business. It is the Dying Us telling stories to the Dying Us, trying to crack the nonsense in our heads open with a big hammer pronto, before Death arrives. What I love about this story is the way it briskly steps up to the Big Questions: Who was this Christ guy anyway? Did He really mean what He said? How are we supposed to love our neighbors when our neighbors tend to be such Gerards—not lovable, not really even likable, and, in fact, we sometimes even hate them? (Blessed are the poor, but not the extremely poor, especially not the unkempt extremely poor, and, boy oh boy, deliver us from the unkempt extremely poor who are sort of angry and inarticulate about it.)

This story works in a complex and beautiful way: our allegiance is with Joan throughout—we sense that, if we were nuns, we would be this kind of nun, if we were lucky. The Catholics among us have certainly known worse. (I remember one who routinely whacked us with a thick wooden dust broom; one who slapped my first-grade sister in the face for spilling her milk; one who asked for our ideas about Heaven and then ruthlessly corrected these, with a special venom reserved for anyone who doubted there were actual harps.) So we empathize with Joan, admire her even. And we can't help but viscerally share her disgust for Gerard. Gerard is beautifully done, delightfully hateable, passive, unaware, platitudinous, and his Mr. Potato Head ears are the perfect ears for him, metaphorically: not so great for actually hearing anything.

Then, in that magnificent scene at Gallagher's, the world is turned inside out. Retrospectively, in an instant, we see Joan's faults, which are glaring. She is a control freak, she likes almost no one, her Christianity is self-serving and strangely corporate. Every time I read this scene, I have a strong physical reaction, which includes tearage/chest flutters/hot face/euphoria/and an urge to deeply resolve to be kinder and more attentive forevermore. These reactions start at the line: "Gerard began to cry," and build throughout the rest of the story, as I see that Gerard, his bad ears and ploddingness and incompetence notwithstanding, has a deeper understanding of the true nature of compassion than Joan does (and than I did, until just that moment in the story)—compassion is not emotional, but dispassionate; not inspired, but solid; at its heart is attention. It has nothing to do with liking someone, and everything to do with easing suffering, with understanding one's self as essentially not separate from the sufferer. "The Deacon" itself, by that definition, is a profound act of compassion, by one of our very finest short story writers.

—GEORGE SAUNDERS

Mary Gordon

The Deacon

From *The Atlantic Monthly*

N O ROMANCE had been attached to Joan Fitzgerald's entering the convent. She wasn't that sort of person, and she hadn't expected it. A sense of rightness had filled her with well-being, allowed her lungs to work easily and her limbs to move quickly, removed her from the part of life that had no interest for her, and opened her to a way of being in the world that connected her to what she believed was essential. Her faith, too, was unromantic; the Jesus of the Gospels, who was with the poor and the sick, who dealt with their needs and urged people to leave father and mother to follow him—this was her inspiration. Yet when she thought of the word "inspiration," it seemed too airy, too silvery, for her experience. What she had felt was something more like a hand at her back, a light pressure between her shoulder blades. The images she had felt herself drawn toward had struck her in childhood and had not left the forefront of her mind: the black children integrating the school in Little Rock, the nuns in the Maryknoll magazine who inoculated Asian children against malaria. The source of their power was a God whose love she believed in as she believed in the love of her parents; she felt it as she had felt her parents' love; she believed that she was watched over, cared about, cared for as her parents had cared for her. She had never in her memory felt alone.

Her decision to become a nun, her image of herself as one, wasn't fed by fantasies of Ingrid Bergman or Audrey Hepburn. By the time she entered the Sisters of the Visitation, the number of candidates was dwindling and almost no one was wearing the habit except the very oldest sisters in the order; she'd been advised to get her college education first, and by the time she entered the order, in 1973, only two others were in her class. After twenty-five years she was a school principal in New York City and the only member of her class still in the order.

They joked about it, she and the other sisters, about how they'd missed the glamour days, and now they were just the workhorses, the unglamorous moms, without power and without the aura of silent sanctity that fed the faithful's dreams. "Thank God Philida's good-looking, or they'd think we were a hundred percent rejects," Rocky said, referring to the one sister living with them who was slender and graceful, with large turquoise eyes and white hands that people seemed to focus on—which she must have known, because she wore a large turquoise-and-silver ring she had gotten when she worked on an Indian reservation in New Mexico. Rocky and the fourth sister had grown roly-poly in middle age. They didn't color their hair, they had no interest in clothes, and they knew they looked like caricatures of nuns. "Try, as a penance, not to buy navy blue," Rocky had said. They seemed drawn to navy and neutral colors. They weren't very interested in how they looked. They had all passed through that phase of young womanhood, and sometimes, watching her Hispanic students, and the energy they put into their beauty (misplaced, she believed: it would bring them harm), Joan nevertheless understood their joy and their absorption, because she had been joyous and absorbed herself—though she had wanted to make things happen, to change the way the world worked.

All the sisters she lived with had the same sense of absorption. Rocky, who had been called Sister Rosanna, ran a halfway house for schizophrenics and was now involved in fighting the neighborhood in Queens where the house was located. "They want us out," she said, always referring to herself and the psychotics as "us"—believing, Joan understood, that they were virtually indistinguishable. Four days a week Rocky lived in the halfway house; the remaining three days she joined Joan and two other sisters—Marlene, who directed a homeless shelter, and Philida, who was the pastoral counselor at a nursing home. They shared a large apartment—owned by the order—on Fiftieth Street and Eighth Avenue. They had easy relations with the neighborhood prostitutes and drug dealers, who were thrilled to find that these people, whom they called "sister," seemed to have no interest in making them change their ways.

They could have been almost any group of middle-aged, unmarried women who made their living at idealistic but low-paying jobs and had to share lodgings if they wanted to live in Manhattan, housing costs being what they were. But at the center of each of their days was a half hour of prayer and meditation, led in turn by one of the four of them. They read the Gospel of the day and the Old Testament Scriptures; they spoke of their responses, although they didn't speak of either the texts or their thoughts about them once they had left the room they reserved for meditation. This time was for Joan a source of refreshment and a way of making sense of the world. If anyone had asked her (which they wouldn't have; she wasn't the type people came to for spiritual guidance), she would have said that this was why she loved that time and those words: they were the most satisfying consolation she could imagine for a world that was random and violent and endlessly inventive in its cruelty toward the weak.

Unlike the other sisters, including Philida, Joan had always been too thin. When she thought about it, she thought she had probably become stringy, and her skin, which had tanned easily, was probably leathery now. Perhaps her thinness and the coarse texture of her skin were traceable to her anomalous bad habit. Joan was a heavy smoker. She'd begun smoking in graduate school, the education program at the University of Rochester. Her study partners had all smoked, and she had drifted into the habit. She had wanted to persuade them—and herself, perhaps—that they didn't know everything about her just because she was a nun. Nuns didn't smoke; everyone knew that. But Joan did, though she had tried to quit. The women she lived with didn't allow her to smoke in the apartment; they had put a bumper sticker up on the refrigerator that said SMOKE-FREE ZONE. And of course she didn't smoke in school. She went over to the rectory to smoke.

She was the principal of Saint Timothy's School, at Forty-eighth Street and Tenth Avenue. Once all Irish, it was now filled with black and Hispanic children. Joan was proud of what Saint Timothy's provided. She knew that she suffered from what one of her spiritual advisers called "the vanity of accomplishment." She knew she had a tendency to believe that she could do anything if people would just go along with her programs, and she made jokes about it, jokes on herself, jokes she didn't really believe. When she made her last retreat, which was run by a Benedictine sister, the nun urged her to contemplate the areas of life that were unsusceptible to human action, the mysterious silences of God, the opportunities for holiness provided by failure. She tried, for a while, to center her meditations the way the Benedictine had suggested, but then concluded that this was a contemplative's self-indulgence; she was in the world, she was doing God's work in the world. There was work to be done, and (was this what she had grown up hearing described as "the sin of pride"?) she could do it. She had long ago given up heroic plans and dreams, but she could make her school run well, and she could give to children—who often didn't have it elsewhere—a place where they were made to feel important, where things were demanded of them, but where they were valued and praised.

Though Joan was frustrated and vexed by the poor quality of many of her teachers, she believed that the children got from her and her staff a quality of schooling they could never have gotten in the public schools. She came to understand that many of the teachers were at Saint Timothy's because they wouldn't have been tolerated anyplace else. She put up with most of them, because at least they created zones of energy and discipline. She drew the line, though, at Gerard Mahoney. Gerard had been teaching seventh grade at Saint Timothy's since he left his seminary studies, in 1956. Joan was sure he'd been thrown out, not for bad behavior or any spiritual failure but simply because he couldn't make the grade—not then, not in the years when the seminaries were full to overflowing. God knows, she said to herself, nowadays he would probably be ordained. But they'd sent him home, to his mother, who had been the housekeeper at Saint Timothy's since, Joan once speculated to Rocky, Barry Fitzgerald was a curate. Mrs. Mahoney had been there when Steve Costelloe arrived, fresh from the seminary, thirty years earlier. Steve had been the pastor at Saint Timothy's for the past fifteen years. Gerard's mother had died twelve years ago, after a long illness, when Gerard was fifty-two.

Joan and Steve got along, which was more, she thought, than a lot of women in her position could have said. Essentially, Steve was lazy; his saving grace was that he understood it. He was a pale redhead, with freckles under the gold hair that grew on his hands; he was going bald; he had broad shoulders, but then his body dwindled radically—he was hipless, and his legs (she'd seen them when he wore shorts) were hairless and broomstick-thin. He had a little pot—whimsical, like something he carried tucked in his belt, a crystal ball he tapped his fingers on occasionally, as if he were waiting for messages. He was incapable of saying no to people, which was one reason he was universally beloved. Saint Timothy's was a magnet for people who had nowhere else to go; Steve was constantly cooking up vats of chili (his recipe said: "feeds 50–65"), and some unfortunate was always in the kitchen.

Often someone who had no real business being there was found to have moved into one of the spare bedrooms; the rectory, built for the priests, was nearly empty. It housed only Steve and Father Adrian, from the Philippines, who giggled all the time; when faced with the desperate situations of junkies and abused wives, he would say "Pray and have hope," and giggle. Sometimes Joan and Steve said to each other—thinking of the hours they spent counseling people in trouble—that Adrian's approach might be approximately as successful as theirs, considering their rate of recidivism. In the Philippine parade he'd been on a float, playing a martyred Jesuit. His brother, who had contributed to the construction of the float, blamed Father Adrian for their failure to win the prize for best float. "You were laughing when they hanged you," he shouted at his brother. "That's why we didn't win." "I couldn't help it," Father Adrian said, giggling. "The children made me laugh." Steve was happy to have Father Adrian, because he was willing to take the seven o'clock mass, and Steve liked to sleep late. Joan suspected that Steve was often hung over. He was in good form by noon, for the larger mass that served the midtown workers, who came to him on their lunch hour and usually, she guessed, went back to work refreshed.

Problems arose when Steve felt that one of the people in the rectory rooms ought to be moving on; then he would come to Joan desperate for help. She would summon the person in question to the office (not in the rectory, of course, but in the school, next door) and speak firmly about getting a hold on life and going forward. Some of them just ignored her, and stayed on until some mysterious impulse sent them elsewhere. But a few of them listened, and that was bad: it encouraged Steve to ask for her help again, and she couldn't say no to his unhappiness; he was as hopeless as a hopeless child. She often said that the one temptation she could not resist was to try to fix something when it seemed broken and she believed she had the right tools. More often than not she felt she did.

Steve was dreadful with money, and a terrible administrator. He was saved by his connections; people he'd met when he played minor-league baseball, or when he sat in the Sky Box at the Meadowlands because someone had given him a Giants ticket, or people whose confessions he had heard on an ocean liner while he was a chaplain on a Caribbean cruise. Once a year Saint Timothy's would have a fund-raiser, and somehow he'd be bailed out. He left the administration of the school to Joan, allowing that she was much better at it than he, and saying, "Just don't get our name in the papers, unless it's for something good." He had no stake in proving himself the boss, and she was grateful for that; when her friends ran into trouble with their pastors, it was because those pastors resented a loss of power. Steve wasn't interested in power; but Joan believed he was genuinely interested in the welfare of his flock. When she was angry at him, because he had foiled her or screwed something up, she thought he was interested only in being universally liked, and that he'd become a priest because it gave him a good excuse for not being deeply engaged with human beings.

In the end he'd backed her up about Gerard, whose shortcomings were impossible to ignore. When she walked down the hall past his classroom, the sounds of chaos came over the frosted-glass pane above the door. She had taken to making random visits; the sight of her in the doorway quieted the kids. Pretending she was in full habit, pretending she was one of the nuns she'd been taught by, she could stand in a doorway and strike what her mother would have called the fear of God into any class. Even the rowdy seventh-graders—the boys who could have felled her with a punch, the girls who were contemptuous of her failure to get the knack of feminine allure—even they could be silenced and frozen in place by the sight of "Sister" staring down at them, as if from a great, sacral height. It couldn't go on.

She talked to Gerard first. Gerard smoked too, and she saw to it that their cigarette breaks in the rectory coincided. She asked him—gently, she hoped (though she'd been told that she wasn't tactful and lacked subtlety)—if things were going all right in his class. He said, "As well as can be expected." She had to hold her temper. Expected by whom? she wanted to say. She said that keeping order among adolescents was difficult, and if he wanted to brainstorm with her and some of the other teachers, she'd be glad to set something up. Then she looked into his dull black eyes, eyes that seemed to have been emptied of color and life and movement, and thought that if there was a brain behind them, it, too, would be inert and dull. No storming was possible in or from that particular brain.

She wasn't someone who thought much about people's looks (whether people were good-looking wasn't a judgment she made about them), but Gerard's looks annoyed her. It was as if he had sat passively by and allowed someone to push his face in; the area from his cheekbones to his lower teeth was a dent, a declivity, a ditch; his lower teeth jutted above his upper ones like a bulldog's. Something about the way his teeth fit made it difficult for him to breathe quietly; he often snorted, and he blew his nose with what Joan thought of as excessive, and therefore irritating, frequency. His ears were two-dimensional and flat, like the plastic ears that came with Mr. Potato Head kits. His clothes were so loose on him that she could not envision the shape of his body. He wore orthopedic shoes, and she imagined that he had a condition no one talked about anymore, something people didn't need to have, which he just held on to out of weakness or inertia. Gerard had flat feet.

He said he was doing just what he'd been doing for forty years, and it seemed to work out all right. He mentioned that one of his earliest pupils was already a grandfather.

She wanted to say to him, What the hell does that have to do with anything? But she was trying to keep in mind what would be best for the children. She suggested breaking up the class into focus groups; she suggested films and filmstrips; she offered him more time in the computer lab. They didn't actually have a computer lab; it was a room with one computer. But Joan thought that by calling it "the computer lab" she would encourage everyone to take it seriously. Gerard, remarkably, was more skilled with computers than most. She imagined him honing his skills alone in his apartment, the one he'd lived in with his mother, playing game after game of computer solitaire, or computer chess, or some other equally solipsistic and wasteful pastime. To whatever she suggested, he responded, "I guess I'll just go on doing what I've been doing. It seems to work out all right."

She was slightly ashamed of her glee when Sonia Martinez, the mother of Tiffany, one of the smartest girls in the seventh grade, came in to complain about Gerard. Sonia Martinez said that the children were learning nothing; that she wanted Tiffany to do well on her exams and get a scholarship to one of the good high schools, Sacred Heart or Marymount; and that Tiffany was going to be behind if she stayed in Gerard's class. She mentioned her tuition payments. You've got to be kidding, Joan wanted to say. Parents paid Saint Timothy's a tenth of what was charged at private schools—less if they were parishioners, which Tiffany's parents were. She didn't like Sonia Martinez, who was finishing a business degree at Hunter College and worked for the telephone company, whose children were immaculately turned out, who was obviously overworked and naturally impatient. But she admired her tenacity, and she knew that Mrs. Martinez was right. Sonia Martinez threatened a petition by the class parents.

"Just wait on that," Joan said. "Give me a little time."

Sonia Martinez trusted her; she said all right, but the semester was ticking on, and the placement exams came early in the fall of the eighth-grade year.

As Joan walked over to the rectory, she felt the liveliness in her bones. A salty, exciting taste was in her mouth, as if she'd eaten olives or a salad of arugula. She thought that if she tried to run now, she could run easily, and very, very fast. She felt no concern for Gerard; she told herself that his job was no good for him, either, the way things were, and anyway he was sixty-four; the time had come for him to retire. If Catholic schools were going to have credibility, they would have to have standards as high as those of other private schools. They had to get over the habit of thinking of themselves as refuges for people who couldn't make it elsewhere. Anyway, she told herself, I'm doing it for the students. They're my responsibility. My vocation is to serve them.

This is what she said to Steve, who, of course, said she was overreacting, that Sonia Martinez was overly ambitious, that they had, in charity, to think of their responsibility to Gerard, who had been with the parish all his life.

"So we have to forget our responsibility to the children we are pledged to serve?" she said.

"It's one year of their lives," Steve said. "This school is his whole life. It's all he has."

. . . .

When she talked it over with her friends, Rocky—who because she dealt
with schizophrenics was in an excellent position, she said, to deal with the
clergy—suggested that she tell Steve that Gerard probably wasn't happy:
dealing with chaotic, aggressive adolescents couldn't be pleasant. Joan
should think of something else for him to do.

"What, what can he do?" asked Joan, who was wishing more than ever
that their apartment wasn't a smoke-free zone. "He's a complete loser."

"He must be good at something."

"He can't even read the Gospel properly," Joan said. "Didn't you hear
him last week—'When Jesus rode on his donkey into Brittany'? You were
the one who had to dive under the seat and pretend you were looking for
a Kleenex."

"Everybody's good at something. What's he interested in?"

"Smoking."

"Didn't you say he did computers?"

She understood at that moment why people believed so literally in the
Holy Ghost, in the purges of fire. A heat came over her head; her own wisdom was visible to her. She would put him in charge of the computer lab.
That they had no computer lab was a minor problem. She had been reading about how obsolete computers sat around in offices. She would get
Steve to schmooze up his executive friends for donations: Steve would get
free lunches, the gift would probably be a tax deduction for them, and
they'd think they were buying a few years out of purgatory.

Steve, as she told her friends afterward, fell for the scheme like a ton
of bricks. Within a month they had six computers, none of them new but
all of them workable. Gerard was more adept at the technology than any
other teacher in the school, but so were most of the students. After he'd
given the teachers some minor instruction, he had little to do but sit in
the corner, watch the teachers and the students work, make sure the
switches were turned off at the end of the day, and occasionally dust the
keyboards. Everyone was happy—especially Sonia Martinez, who was
doing a paper on computer literacy and minority advancement. One of
Joan's friends, who taught education at the college run by their order in
Brooklyn, was able to pump up one of her students for a stint teaching
seventh grade. Joan knew this wouldn't last: the good young teachers left

because they could earn more elsewhere, or they got married and then pregnant. But for now things were much better. She hardly saw Gerard except when their cigarette breaks coincided. When she did, she congratulated him on his new job. He said, "We are all in the hands of the Lord."

She wanted to smack him.

Steve told her that the parish was going to celebrate Gerard's twenty-fifth anniversary as a deacon.

"What the hell does he do as a deacon anyway?" she said. "Besides mangle the Gospel?"

"He brings communion to the sick, though sometimes he gets lost and wanders around midtown with the Blessed Sacrament. To tell the truth, he doesn't do much. But it means a lot to him. His mother was heartbroken when he was sent down from the seminary. I think the old pastor really pushed for his deaconate. It's a good thing. Or, as my grandmother would have said, 'It does no harm.' And sometimes that's the best you can hope for."

She wanted to say to Steve, It's the best *you* can hope for, but she held her tongue.

"We're going to have a little party. We'll have mass, and then wine and beer and pretzels and chips in the basement. Can you organize the children?"

"To do what?"

"Have them sing something?"

"What do you think this is, *The Sound of Music?*"

"Come on, Joanie, give me a break. I'm stuck with this."

"So I provide the entertainment?"

"Entertainment—you? Do you think I'm crazy? Just the organization. That's more in your line."

Joan was surprised at how much what Steve said hurt her. But she determined to forget it. She asked him who was going to be in charge of the food and the decorations. "Marek," he said. Marek was from Poland; he had been an accountant there, but now he wanted to be an artist. He was living in one of the spare rooms at the rectory. He was supposed to be the sexton, and to do odd repairs, but he was as bad at that as Gerard was at reading the Gospel. She wasn't hopeful about the food and the decorations, but one of the things she had learned was that if she tried to do everything, nothing would get done well. It's not my problem, she said to herself; she would forget about the food, the decorations, what Steve had said to her, and concentrate on the children and their song.

She chose the littlest children, who still loved any excuse to perform. She herself had no musical talent; she had hired Josie Myerson, a niece of one of the sisters, who was getting a Ph.D. in music, to come to the school once a week to do music with the children. The girl was energetic and talented, and what she did, if inadequate in its extent, was at least first-rate in its quality. Josie, who was plain and misunderstood by her mother, looked at Joan with a hopefulness that made Joan uneasy. Soon, she expected, Josie would talk about wanting to enter the convent. Joan would discourage her; Josie was too neurotic, and the last thing the order needed was someone who joined because she couldn't make it in the larger world. But Joan knew how to use her power over Josie when she needed to, and she needed to now. Josie taught six of the girls and six of the boys the song "Memories," from *Cats,* which she thought would be appropriate for a twenty-fifth anniversary. Then they would break into a Latin medley, including dancing, which would make them all happy and lighten the tone.

Steve announced at the beginning of the mass that it was to be said in thanksgiving for Gerard's ministry. Most people, he said, didn't understand the role of the deacon. He could do all the things a priest did except consecrate the Host. His ministry was in the community, and he was of the community; Gerard certainly was, having lived here, on the same block, all his life. Joan was sure that almost none of the parishioners had any idea who Gerard was, other than that he was funny-looking and often made mistakes in the reading. Nevertheless, they applauded him when Steve called for applause, and because it was a Sunday, enough people were there to make the applause sound genuine and ample.

Just after communion Joan went downstairs to determine where the children should stand; she didn't know where Marek would have put the tables, and how she would accommodate the arrangement. When she turned on the light, her heart sank. Marek had done nothing to make the place festive. On one long table were two boxes of Ritz crackers; a slab of cheddar cheese on a plate; some unseparated slices of Swiss, the paper still between the slices; a plate of dill-pickle spears; a bowl of green olives;

two bags of potato chips; and a bag of Chee-tos. There were two half-gallon jugs of red wine, a bottle of club soda, and a bottle of ginger ale. Two dozen paper cups, still in their plastic. A packet of napkins, also wrapped. On the four pillars that supported the ceiling were taped white paper plates with the number 25 written on them in blue ballpoint.

Desperate, Joan ran upstairs to the rectory kitchen for bowls to put the crackers and the chips in. Frantically she unwrapped the paper cups and unwrapped and spread out the napkins. She ran upstairs again for some ice and looked for an ice bucket; unable to find one, she emptied the ice trays into a large yellow bowl. When the children came downstairs, she told them to stand in front of the food table; somehow, she thought, they made the whole thing less dispiriting.

She'd been worried that there wasn't enough food, but only three adults came downstairs from the church: Father Adrian; Lucinda, the Peruvian housekeeper; and Mrs. Frantzen, who had taught in the school until her retirement, fifteen years earlier. Then Steve came downstairs— he was always surrounded after mass, and had a hard time getting away—but said he could stay only a minute. He had a baptism in Westchester—one of the assistant coaches of the Knicks had had a baby, and no one but Steve could baptize her. He told Gerard he'd take him to Gallagher's for dinner—that he'd be back at five. "You, too, Joan," he said, running out the doorway. "You'll join us too." He didn't wait for a reply.

She told the children they could eat what they wanted, and they dived for the potato chips. Their activity was a welcome spot of color, because no one had anything to say. They kept congratulating Gerard, and saying what a wonderful thing the deaconate was, and how wonderful it was that he had served the parish all these years, in all these ways. No one said what the ways were exactly. Mrs. Frantzen said how proud his dear mother would be. Father Adrian offered a prayer for the repose of Gerard's mother's soul. The children sang their song but skipped the Latin medley. Father Adrian and Lucinda drifted upstairs. Mrs. Frantzen said she'd have to be going.

Gerard lingered while Joan collected the food to take upstairs. She supposed that eventually Marek would get around to it, but she much preferred being busy over trying to think of something to say to Gerard.

"Well, Gerard, it's quite a day for you," she said, with a false brightness that turned her stomach.

"I count my blessings," he said. She could think of nothing else to say. He helped her carry the leftovers up the stairs. She thought of the up-coming dinner at Gallagher's. She thought that Steve had selected the restaurant because the management knew them, and because they could smoke there. She rarely thought about drinking, but she planned that as soon as she sat down, she'd order a Scotch and soda.

When she got to the apartment, the other sisters were watching a video of W. C. Fields's *My Little Chickadee*. She was glad to take her shoes off, set-tle on the couch, and join the laughter—much too raucous, they said happily, for a bunch of nuns. It was three o'clock. At four she'd have to get ready for dinner, and at four-thirty she'd leave. But she had time to watch the movie. Marlene had made chocolate-chip cookies, and Philida was putting coffee Häagen-Dazs into their blue-and-white ice-cream bowls.

"Now, this is heaven," Rocky said. "Forget eternal light and visions of unending bliss. This is it."

"Ten years in purgatory for blasphemy," Marlene said.

"If only this weren't a smoke-free zone," Joan said.

"If only you weren't trying to kill yourself," Rocky said.

"All right, all right, I'm sorry I brought it up," Joan said. She thought about how Fields's cruelty was delightful, and wondered what it had to do with Gospel generosity, and decided that it had everything and nothing to do with it and she should just relax. She wondered what W. C. Fields would do with Gerard. He certainly wouldn't be going to Gallagher's with him. Or maybe he would. For the steak and the Scotch.

At four-thirty the phone rang. It was Steve, from his car, or from the highway beside his car. He was waiting for a tow truck. He wasn't going to be able to get to the city by five. They'd have to go on without him; he'd be there as soon as he could.

"Don't do this to me, Steve," Joan said.

"I'm not doing it. It's in the hands of God, Sister."

"God has nothing to do with it. Just get here. Can't one of your rich friends lend you a car?"

"I'm in the middle of the highway. I have to deal with this first."

"Just hurry. Just go as fast as you can."

"Aye, aye, sir," he said, and clicked off.

When she told the other nuns what had happened, Philida was suspicious. "I'll bet he's sitting in someone's rumpus room and just said his car broke down."

"Steve wouldn't lie."

"Steve takes care of Steve."

"And a lot of other people, too. You can't say he's not generous, Philida."

"When it's easy for him."

"I'm just not going to think about it," Joan said, angry at Philida for making things more difficult. "It's impossible enough as it is. Will one of you come with me? Steve'll pay for it. Or probably no one will pay. The people who run Gallagher's are in the parish; Steve probably baptized all their kids."

"Joan, if you had a choice between dinner with Gerard and watching *The African Queen* and ordering in Thai food, which would you choose?" Marlene asked.

"In solidarity with a sister, I'd go to Gallagher's."

"Solidarity is one thing; being out of your mind is another. Offer it up, for the poor souls," Rocky said.

"This is community life? This is my support network?"

"We'll keep the movie out for an extra day, so you can see it tomorrow. The community will pay the late fee."

"That's Christian charity at its most heroic."

"We gave up the virgin-martyr thing years ago, Joan. Hadn't you heard?"

She had what she thought was a brilliant idea. She phoned Gerard and explained what had happened to Steve, and asked if he'd like to put off the dinner until another day, when Steve could join them.

"But then it wouldn't be my anniversary," he said.

"Well, it could still be a celebration."

"This is the day of my anniversary," he said. "No other day will be that."

She gave up. People's wanting something so much often wore her down. She very rarely wanted anything for herself enough to try to force someone into giving it to her. Gerard wanted this, and like a lot of people who had very little else in or on their minds, he had plenty of room for a stubborn will to grow in.

"Great, then I'll meet you at Gallagher's," she said. She couldn't remember when the prospect of anything had made her so sick at heart.

Slabs of beef hung from hooks in the restaurant window. On the pine-paneled walls, behind the red-leather booths, were pictures of New York sporting, political, religious, and show-business figures from the 1890s to the 1950s. Diamond Jim Brady, Fiorello La Guardia, Jack Dempsey, Yogi Berra. Stiff-looking monsignors beside men in fedoras and coats with collars made of beaver or perhaps mink. An age of easy, thoughtless prosperity, a slightly outlaw age, of patronage and conquest and last-minute saves from on high. She thought how odd it was that she liked this place so much, since it had nothing to do with the way she had always lived her life—was the opposite of the way she had lived her life. Yet she didn't feel out of place here; she felt welcomed, as if they had made an exception for her, and she liked the feeling, as she liked the large hunks of bloody meat and the home-fried potatoes and the creamed spinach, more than the Thai food the sisters would be eating, more than the cookies they would devour while they watched the film.

"So, Gerard, it's a great day for you," she said with what she hoped he wouldn't notice was a desperate overbrightness, masking her terror at the fact that after she said this, she would have nothing to say.

"I thank God every day of my life. I count my blessings. Except I have to say I was a little disappointed. None of the old students came. I thought they'd come. The celebration was mentioned in the parish bulletin."

"Oh, Gerard, most of the old students don't live in the parish anymore. And besides, you know how busy people are."

"Still, you'd think at least one of them."

"I'm sure they were at the mass. You know how shy people are to come to anything after mass. Catholics simply weren't brought up to do it."

"I was surprised, though."

He wouldn't let it go. She felt, at the same time, hideously sorry for him and angry that he wouldn't accept the ways out she offered him. Did he have any idea how horribly he had failed as a teacher? Was today the first news of it for him? If it was, her mixture of pity and dislike was even stronger, though equal in its blend.

"I'm surprised Father Steve went off to the baptism. You'd think he could have found a substitute."

"I think it was a very good friend."

"He's known me for years."

"Well, you know Steve, he always thinks he can do everything. I'm sure he'll show up. You know his way of pulling things off in the end."

"It's a very important day to me."

"Of course it is, Gerard, of course."

"It was a great blessing, my being called to the deaconate."

Yes, she wanted to say, a job with so little to it that you couldn't screw it up.

"My mother was very upset when I was sent home from the sem. I just couldn't cut it. The pressure was very tough. I think these days they'd say I had a nervous breakdown."

Suddenly she wondered if she had to think of him in a new way, as someone with an illness rather than with a series of bad habits. She didn't know which she preferred, which was more hopeless, which less difficult to bear.

"My mother wanted a son as a priest more than anything. All those years being a housekeeper in the rectory. I really disappointed her. I just couldn't cut it."

"I'm sure you were a great comfort to her in her last days."

His dull eyes brightened. "Do you think that's it? Do you think it's the will of God? That I couldn't cut it at the sem because if I had been a priest, she would have been alone in her last illness?"

"I've heard you were very devoted to her."

"I took care of her for fifteen years. It was a privilege. It was a very special grace."

"Well, then, you see," Joan said, not knowing what she meant at all.

"Still, I was a big disappointment to her. There was no getting around that. And I was disappointed today, that so few people came. Next to my investiture, it was the most important day of my life."

Gerard began to cry. The waiter hovered behind them and then disappeared. Joan wondered what on earth people in the restaurant imagined was going on between them, who people thought they might be to each other—this unfortunate-looking old man and the underdressed old maid across from him.

She tried to give her attention to him, not to think of the waiter or the other diners, not to be mortified at the sight of this man—he was an old man, really—crying, trying to light a cigarette.

"Sometimes I just don't know what it all means."

A wave of anger rose up in her. Anger toward Gerard and toward the institution of the Catholic Church. What was it all worth, the piety, the devotion, if it left him crying, struggling helplessly over an ashtray? Seeing life as meaningless. At least it should have provided him with sustenance. He had missed the whole point; he had taken only the stale, unnourishing broken crusts and missed the banquet. She was angry at him for having missed the whole point of Jesus and the Gospels, when he had been surrounded by them every day of his life, and angry at the Church for having done nothing to move him.

"Surely, Gerard, you know that you are greatly beloved."

He stopped crying and shook his head like a dog who had been fighting and had had a bucket of cold water thrown on him.

"I appreciate that, Sister. I appreciate that very much. That's why even Father's not showing up is the will of God, I think. I always thought that of all of them, you were the one who really cared about me."

She felt sick and helpless. How could she say to him, I wasn't talking about me, I was talking about God. He was looking down at the tablecloth; his shoulders were relaxed, not hunched and knotted as usual. He lifted his head and gave her a truly happy smile.

"You see, you were the only one who cared enough to notice what I was going through. Everybody just let me go on teaching, doing a terrible job, giving me class after class to screw up. Do you think I liked it in there? I was just afraid of losing my job. It's all I have, coming to the school."

"There's the deaconate—you could make something of that."

"I'm not very good with people," he said. "But you figured out what I was good at. You looked at what I was really like. You saw that I had a talent for computers. You paid attention. That's what caring really means. You were the only one since my mother who cared enough to tell me I had to improve. Everybody else thought I was hopeless. They didn't want to look at me, just kept me around so I wouldn't be on their conscience. You really looked, and you found my gift."

Turning computer switches on and off? she wanted to say. Dusting keyboards? Turning out the lights and locking the door.

"Now I know I have a real place, a place where I'm needed, and it's all thanks to you. That's the kind of thing Jesus was talking about."

Oh, no, Gerard, she wanted to say, oh, no, you're as wrong as you can be. Jesus was talking about love, an active love that fills the soul and lightens it, that draws people to each other with the warmth of the spirit, that makes them able to be with each other as a brother is with a sister or a mother with her child. Oh, no, Gerard, I do not love you. You are a person I could never love. Never, never, will I feel anything for you when I see you but a wish to flee from your presence. She prayed: Let me stay at the table. Let me feel happy that I made Gerard happy. Let me not hate him for his foolishness, his misunderstanding, his grotesque misinterpretation of me and the whole world. She prayed to be able to master the impulse to flee.

But she could not.

"Excuse me," she said, and ran into the ladies' room. In the mirror her eyes looked dead and cold to her. She believed what she had said to Gerard, that all human beings were, by virtue of their being human, greatly beloved. But the face she saw in the mirror did not look as if it had ever been beloved, or could ever love.

She looked in the mirror and prayed for strength—not to make herself love Gerard but to sit at the table with him. Only that.

He believed that she loved him. He believed that she had his interest at heart, when all she cared about was keeping him from doing damage to her children, whom she did, truly, love. Only Steve had prevented her from throwing him out on the street. Steve, who, she was more sure than ever now, was relaxing in Westchester.

The poor you always have with you. She heard the words of Jesus in her head. And she knew that she would always have Gerard. He was poorer than Estrelita Dominguez, thirteen years old and three months' pregnant, or LaTrobe Sandford, who might be in jail this time next year.

The poor you always have with you. She thought of Magdalene and her tears, of the richness of the jar's surface and the overwhelming scent of the ointment—*nard* she remembered its being called—and the ripples of the flowing hair. She saw her own dry countenance in the greenish bathroom mirror. She combed her hair and smoothed her skirt down over her narrow hips. She returned to Gerard, who had been brought a Scotch and soda by the waiter.

"On the house," Gerard said. "I told him we were celebrating my anniversary."

"And you, Sister," the waiter said. "What can we give you? A ginger ale?"

"Just water, please," she said. "A lot of ice."

The waiter was an Irishman; he'd be scandalized by a nun's ordering Scotch. She didn't want to disappoint him.

Russell Banks

Plains of Abraham

From *Esquire*

Had he known everything then that he'd know later, Vann still would have called it a coincidence, nothing more. His was a compact, layered mind with only a few compartments connected. He had been married three times and was unmarried now, and this morning he couldn't shake Irene, his second wife, from his mind. He shaved and dressed for work, tightened the covers and slid the bed back under the sofa, all the while swatting at thoughts of Irene, the force of his swipes banging doors and walls, making him feel clumsy and off-balance. *Thinking about problems only aggravates problems,* but the way these random scraps of memory, emotion, and reflection flew at him—even now, four years after the divorce from Irene, with the lump of a whole third marriage and divorce in between—was strange. Vann and Irene had not seen each other or spoken in person once in those years.

It was a coincidence, that's all, and would have been one even if Vann had known that on this particular morning, a Wednesday in November, Irene, who was forty-eight years old and close to a hundred pounds overweight and suffering from severe coronary disease, who normally would herself be getting ready for work, was instead being prepared at Saranac Lake General Hospital for open-heart surgery. The procedure, to be performed by the highly regarded vascular surgeon Dr. Carl Ransome, was to be a multiple bypass. It was a dangerous although not an uncommon operation, even up here in the north country, and had Irene not collapsed in pain two days earlier while grocery shopping at the Grand Union in Lake Placid with her daughter, Frances, the procedure would have been put off until she had lost a considerable part of her excess weight. Too late for that now.

"Jesus," Dr. Ransome had said to the night nurse after visiting Irene in her room for the first time, "this'll be like flaying a goddamned whale." The nurse winced and looked away, and the young surgeon strode whistling down the corridor.

Vann stirred a cup of instant coffee and wondered if he ever crowded Irene's mornings the way she was crowding his. Probably not. Irene was tougher than he, a big-bellied joker who had seemed nothing but relieved when he left her, although he himself had been almost surprised by his departure, as if she had tricked him into it.

"Good riddance," she liked saying to Frances. "Never marry a construction man, doll baby. They're hound dogs with hard hats."

Vann wasn't quite that bad. He was one of those men who protect themselves by dividing themselves. He regarded love and work as opposites—he loved to work but had to work at love. Yet, with Irene, what Vann thought of as love had come easy, at least at first. When they married, Irene and Vann were in their mid-thirties, lonely, and still shaky from the aftershocks of belligerent first divorces, and for a few years they managed to meet each other's needs almost without trying. Vann was a small man, wiry, with muscles like doorknobs, and back then he had liked Irene's size, her soft amplitude. He had regarded her as a large woman, not fat. And she had liked and admired his crisp, intense precision, his pale crew-cut hair, his tight smile.

To please her, and to suit himself, too, he had come in off the road and for a while kept his tools in the trunk of his car and worked locally. He started his own one-man plumbing-and-heating business, limited mostly to small repairs and renovations, operating out of a shop that he built into the basement of Irene's house in Lake Placid. Frances, who was barely a teenager then, had resented Vann's sudden, hard presence in her mother's life and home and stayed away at boarding school, except for holidays, which was fine by Vann, especially since Irene's first husband was paying the tuition.

Irene quit her job at the real estate office and kept Vann's books. But after four barely break-even and two losing years in a row, his credit at the bank ran out, and the business collapsed, and Vann went on the road again. Soon he saw his needs differently. He guessed Irene saw her needs differently then, too. He knew he had disappointed her. He allowed himself a couple of short-term dalliances, and she found out about one. He told her about one other. He drank a lot, maybe too much, and there were some dalliances he barely remembered. Those he kept to himself. A year later, they were divorced.

Vann had known from the moment he and Irene first spoke of marriage that if he failed at this, his second shot at domestic bliss, he would have to revise his whole view of life with women. This was going to be his second and probably last chance to get love and marriage right. Vann knew that much. You can't make a fresh start on anything in life three times. By then, if a man gets divorced and still goes on marrying, he's chasing something other than romance and domestic life; he's after something strictly private. Vann had gone on anyhow. And now, in spite of the third divorce, or perhaps because of it, whenever he told himself the story of his life, the significance of his second marriage remained a mystery to him and a persistent irritant. Vann remembered his ten years with Irene the way men remember their war years: the chapter in the story of his life so far that was both luminous and threatening and loomed way too large to ignore.

He picked up his coffee cup and went outside and stood on the rickety, tilted porch of the cottage, where he deliberately studied the smear of pink in the eastern sky and the rippling ribbons of light on the small, man-made lake in front of him. *Lake Flower. Weird name for a lake.* He decided that it was going to be a fine day. Which pleased him. He'd scheduled the ductwork test for today and did not want to run it in a nasty, bone-chilling autumn rain. Vann was field superintendent for Sam Guy, the mechanical contractor out of Lake Placid, on the addition to Saranac Lake General Hospital. Tomorrow, if today's test went smoothly—he had no reason to think it wouldn't—he'd have the heat turned on in the new wing. After that, they'd be working comfortably inside.

It was still dark—dark and cold, a few degrees below freezing—when he got into his truck and drove from the Harbor Hill Cottages on Lake Flower out to the hospital, and despite his studied attempts to block her out, here came Irene again. He remembered how they used to sit around the supper table and laugh together. She had a loose, large face and no restrictions on distorting it to imitate fools and stupid people. Her tongue was as rough as a wood rasp, and she had a particular dislike of Sam Guy, who, the day after Vann's business folded, had hired him and sent him back on the road. "That man needs you because without you he can't pour pee from a boot," she'd declare, and she'd yank one of her own boots off and hold it over her head and peer up into it quizzically.

Vann had never known a woman that funny. Toward the end, however, she had started turning her humor on him, and from then on, there was no more laughing at Irene's comical faces and surprising words. His only recourse had been to slam the door behind him while she shouted, "G'wan, go! Good riddance to bad rubbish!"

He switchbacked along tree-lined streets, crossing the ridge west of the narrow lakeside strip of hotels, motels, stores, and restaurants, and entered a neighborhood of small wood-frame houses and duplexes. The pale light from his headlights bounced off frost that clung like a skin to yellowed lawns, glassed-in porches, and steeply pitched rooftops. Strings of smoke floated from chimneys, and kitchen lights shone from windows. *Jesus, family life.* Which, despite all, Vann still thought of as normal life. *And a proper breakfast.* Vann could almost smell eggs and bacon frying. Moms, dads, and kids cranking up their day together: He could hear their cheerful, sleepy voices.

Vann had lived that sort of morning, but not for nearly fifteen years now, and he missed it. Who wouldn't? Way back in the beginning, up in Plattsburgh, with his own mom and dad, he'd been one of the kids at the table; then later, for a few years, with his first wife, Evelyn, and the boys, he had been the dad. But family life had slipped from his grasp without his having noticed, as if, closing his eyes to drink from a spring, he'd lost a handful of clear water and was unable afterward to imagine a way to regain it. The spring must have dried up. A man can't blame his hands, can he?

Instead, he'd learned to focus his thoughts on how, when he was in his twenties and married to Evelyn and the boys were young, he simply had not appreciated his good luck. That was all. Evelyn had remarried happily and wisely right after the divorce, and the boys, Neil and Charlie, raised more by their stepfather than by Vann, had turned into young men themselves—gone from him forever, or so it seemed. A postcard now and then was all, and the occasional embarrassed holiday phone call. Nothing, of course, from Evelyn—his child bride, as he referred to her—but that, especially as the years passed, was only as it should be.

The way Vann viewed it, his main sin in life had been not to have appreciated his good luck back when he had had it. If he had, he probably would have behaved differently. His was a sin of omission, then. To reason that way seemed more practical to him and more dignified than to wallow in regret. It helped him look forward to the future. It had helped him marry Irene. And it had eased his divorce from Inger, his third wife. The Norwegian, was how he thought of her now.

At the variety store where Broadway turned onto Route 86, he picked up a *Daily Enterprise* and coffee to go and a fresh pack of Marlboros. He was driving one of Sam Guy's company pickups, a spruce-green three-quarter-ton Jimmy, brand-new. It had been assigned to him directly from the dealer, and though he liked to pretend, at least to himself, that the vehicle belonged to him and not his boss, Vann would not have said aloud that it was his. That wasn't his style. He was forty-nine, too old to say he owned what he didn't. And too honest.

Besides, he didn't need to lie: He was making payments to the Buick dealer in Plattsburgh on a low-mileage, two-year-old black Riviera that he'd bought last spring to celebrate his divorce from the Norwegian. She'd gotten sole ownership of the house he'd built for them in Keene Valley, but she was also stuck with the mortgage, which gave him some satisfaction. His monthly payments for the car had worked out to six dollars less than his monthly alimony checks, a coincidence Vann found oddly pleasant and slightly humorous, although, when he told people about it, no one else thought it funny or even interesting, which puzzled him.

The Riviera was loaded. A prestige car. It cheered Vann to be seen driving it, and he hoped that over the summer the Norwegian, who was a legal aide for the Adirondack Park Agency in Ray Brook, had accidentally spotted him in it once or twice. He didn't particularly want to see her, but he sure hoped that she had seen him and had noted that Vann Moore, yes indeedy, was doing just fine, thanks.

Out on Route 86 a few miles west of town, he turned right at Lake Colby and pulled into the hospital parking lot, drove to the rear of the three-story brick building, and passed along the edge of the rutted field to the company trailer, where he parked next to a stack of steel pipe. From the outside, the new wing, a large cube designed to merge discreetly with the existing hospital building, appeared finished—walls, roof, and windows cemented solidly into place. Despite appearances, however, the structure was little more than a shell. The masons hadn't started the interior walls yet, the plumbers hadn't set any of the fixtures or run the aboveground water, vacuum, and air lines, and the electricians were still hanging overhead conduit. The painters hadn't even hauled their trailer to the site.

The ductwork for the air-conditioning and heat was finished, though. Three days ahead of schedule. Vann was a good super. He'd risen in the ranks from journeyman pipe fitter to foreman to super. He'd run his own business and could read drawings and engineering specs, could do estimates for new work in Sam Guy's shop in Lake Placid when the weather turned bad and everyone else got laid off. And he was a good boss, respected and liked by his men. Sam Guy regarded Vann as his right hand and had no compunctions about saying so, and he paid him appropriately. To people who wondered about Vann's way of life, and there were a few, Sam said that if Vann hadn't been tagged over the years with alimony payments and hadn't lost three houses, one to each wife, he'd be living well on what he earned as a super. He wouldn't be renting furnished rooms and shabby, unused vacation cottages, following the work from town to town across the north country. To Vann, however, the opposite was true: If he hadn't followed the work, he'd not have been divorced three times.

Inside the hospital, in the physicians' scrub room, Dr. Ransome and his assistant this morning, Dr. Clark Rabideau, the resident cardiologist who was Irene's regular physician, and Dr. Alan Wheelwright, the anesthesiologist, were discussing the incoming governor's environmental policies while they slowly, methodically washed their hands and arms.

Their patient, Irene Moore, dozy with sedatives, her belly shaved from chin to crotch, was being wheeled on a gurney down the long, windowless second-floor hallway from her room to the main operating room at the end. Her twenty-year-old daughter, Frances, sat alone by the window in Irene's room, flipping through a copy of *Cosmopolitan*. Frances was a tall, big-hipped girl, a second-year student at St. Lawrence University planning to major in psychology. Her straight, slate-colored hair fell limply to her shoulders, and her square face was tight with anxiety.

With her mother unconscious, or nearly so, Frances felt suddenly, helplessly alone. *I'm over my head in this,* she said to herself, *way over,* and quickly turned the pages, one after the other. *What the hell am I supposed to be thinking about? What?*

It was nearly daylight. In the northeast, the flattened sky over Whiteface Mountain was pale gray. In the southeast, over Mount Marcy and Algonquin Peak, a bank of clouds tinted pink was breaking apart, promising a clear day. The other workers were rumbling onto the job site—electricians, masons, plumbers, steamfitters—driving their own cars and pickups while the foremen and supers arrived in company vehicles. It was light enough for Vann, smoking in his truck, sipping his coffee, to read the front page of the paper and check the NFL scores. It got his mind finally off Irene.

He folded his paper and left the warm truck, but as he crossed to the trailer, key in hand, he glanced out across Lake Colby at the pink morning sky and the dark line of pines below, and the scenery sent him drifting again. He remembered an afternoon four years ago, shortly after the divorce. He was running the public high school job over in Elizabethtown and living in the Arsenal Motel on Route 9 at the edge of town, and one Friday when he drove in from work, a large, flat package was waiting for him at the front desk.

Vann knew at once that it was from Irene—he recognized her handwriting and the return address, their old Lake Placid address. He lugged the crate back to his room and lay it flat on the bed and studied it for a while. What the hell kind of joke was she playing on him this time?

Finally, he pried open the crate and removed several layers of brown paper and plastic bubble-wrap from the object inside. It was a large, framed picture. He recognized it instantly and felt a rush of fear that made his heart pound as if he had unwrapped a bomb. It was a signed color photograph of Adirondack scenery by a well-known local photographer. Very expensive, he knew. A few years back, when they were still happily married, he and Irene had strolled into a Lake Placid crafts shop, and Vann had glanced up at a picture on the wall and had felt himself leap straight up and into it, as if into someone's dream. It was called *Plains of Abraham* and the scene was of a late-summer day, looking across a field of tall grasses and wildflowers toward Algonquin Peak. The golden field, wide and flat, lay in sunshine in the foreground at eye level. A dark, jagged line of trees cut across the middle, and the craggy, plum-colored mountain towered in the distance, a pure and endless blue sky behind and above it.

This was the first and the only picture that Vann had ever wanted to own. He asked the saleswoman how much, figuring he could maybe spring for a hundred bucks.

"Twenty-two hundred dollars," she said.

He felt his ears and face flush. "Pretty pricey," he said and moved quickly on to the maple cutting boards and ceramic bowls.

For months afterward, Irene had teased him about it, imitating his high, thin voice and pursed lips. "Pretty pricey," she chirped, checking out a restaurant menu. Or speculating about local real estate: "Pretty pricey." But she had seen the strange, distant, pained look on her husband's face as he gazed at the picture on the wall of the crafts shop. And now here it was before him, as if staring at him from his bed, while he stood over it, confused, frightened, stubbornly resisting awe. He no more wanted to live with that picture than he wanted to live with the woman who had sent it to him. It made him feel invaded, trapped, guilty. Just as she did. If he kept it, what was he supposed to do, write her a thank-you note? What he *should* do, he thought, is return the picture to the crafts shop and pocket the money himself. Serve Irene right.

He took down the large print of an antlered deer that hung above his bed in the motel room and replaced it with *Plains of Abraham* and stepped back to examine it. It was like a window that opened onto a world larger and more inviting than any he had ever seen. No, the picture was too personal between him and Irene and too mysterious to return for cash, he decided. He would wrap it up and recrate the thing and mail it back to her tomorrow. She's so damned smart, let *her* figure out why she sent it to him.

He washed and changed out of his work clothes and went for supper and a few drinks at the Ausable Inn in Keene Valley, where he'd arranged to meet Inger, the Norwegian, whom at that time he'd not quite decided to marry, although he was sleeping with her three and four nights a week. He didn't return to the motel until halfway through the next day, Saturday, and by then, hungover, fuddled with sex and sleeplessness, he had all but forgotten the picture. But when he entered the small room and saw the photograph hanging above his bed, he remembered everything.

He sat down on the chair facing it, and his eyes filled with tears. He could not believe that he was actually crying. Crying over what? An overpriced picture of some *scenery*? A damned *divorce*? An *ex-wife*?

He took down the photograph and rehung the deer print. Carefully, he wrapped the picture, returned it to its crate, and stuck the crate into his closet, where it remained more or less forgotten for the entire summer. When the school job was finished and Vann moved fifty miles south to Glens Falls, where a shopping mall was going in, he lugged the picture along and stashed it in the back of his motel-room closet down there. He still owned the thing, although it remained in its crate, and the crate stayed in his closet, hidden, barely acknowledged by Vann, except when one job was over and he packed to move to the next. He'd pull it out and sit on the bed and study Irene's original mailing label as if it could somehow tell him why he couldn't seem to get rid of the damned thing.

To Irene, her mind and body muffled by sedatives, the washed-out blue tile walls of the operating room looked almost soft, as if covered with terry cloth. The operating table, shaped like a cruciform, was in the middle of the room under a bank of white lights. Irene felt her body being eased off the cart by a female nurse and the two male attendants who had brought her here. They arranged themselves alongside her in a line and slid her smoothly onto the table. Her body felt like cold butter. She could see what was happening, but it seemed to be going on elsewhere, in a room beyond glass, and to someone else. Her arms were extended and strapped down, and a long, dark-blue curtain was drawn around her upper and lower parts, leaving only her enormous trunk exposed.

"We're outta here, Dale," one of the attendants said, and Irene heard the squeaky wheels of the cart and the swish of the closing door.

Hidden behind her, Alan Wheelwright, the anesthesiologist, in a blue cotton gown and cap and white surgical mask, stood at the head of the table preparing bags of blood for transfusion, while the nurse, her flecked green eyes expressionless above her mask, swabbed Irene's belly with orange antiseptic, covering her mounded body from hip to throat, back to front, humming as she worked, as if she were home alone painting her toenails. Then, into each of Irene's thick, chalk-white arms, the nurse inserted an intravenous catheter.

Irene saw a man's face, which she recognized, despite the mask, as Dr.

Rabideau's, and next to him another man, taller, with bushy white eyebrows, whom she did not recognize but felt she should. There were more nurses now, and the room suddenly seemed crowded and small. A man laughed, genuinely pleased. Someone sang, *I'm forever blowing bubbles*.

She wondered where in the room Vann was standing. Maybe he was one of the people in the masks. She looked at the eyes; she knew Vann's eyes. Her own eyelids seemed to be semitransparent sheets, shutting over and over, in layers. She blinked and left a film; then another. She wondered if her eyes had been shut for a long time already.

What we have here, folks, is hard labor.

Vann's eyes were sapphire-blue and crinkly at the corners, even when he wasn't smiling, like now.

Break out the retractors, Dale. We have liftoff.

Vann was down in the dim basement of the new wing, a huge, cold, open space cluttered with cinder blocks, unused rolls of pink insulation, and stacks of conduit. It took him several tries, but he finally got the gas-powered Briggs & Stratton compressor chugging smoothly. The pump was tied to the overhead ductwork through a three-quarter-inch gate valve with a pressure gauge that Vann had installed strictly for the purposes of the test. He had a kid, Tommy Farr, to help him, but Vann made the connections himself, using Tommy to hand him the tools as he needed them—hose clamps, screwdriver, pipe-joint compound, Stillson wrench. His bare hands were red and stiff from the cold; Vann didn't like working with gloves.

The rest of his crew was scattered over the first and second floors of the wing, installing plumbing fixtures in the lavatories and running the vacuum and oxygen lines. The sheet-metal guys had been released for a new job, a supermarket in a mini-mall over in Tupper Lake. He figured if any blowouts or blocks in the ductwork showed up, he and Tommy could locate and fix them themselves. He wasn't worried. It was a routine test under fairly low pressure, twenty-five pounds per square inch. It wasn't as if the ducts were going to carry water. Just heated air from the large, dark furnace that sat ready to be fired in a shadowed corner of the basement and cooled air from the crated air-conditioning units that had been lifted to the rooftop by crane a week ago.

"All right, Tommy," Vann said, and he stood away from the valve and handed the skinny kid the wrench. "You wanna do the honors?" Vann lit a cigarette, clenched it between his lips, inhaled deeply, and stuck his chilled hands into his jacket pockets.

"Just turn the sucker on?"

"Let 'er rip. When you hit twenty-five psi's on the gate-valve gauge, close 'er up."

The kid knelt down and with one large hand slowly opened the valve and released a jet of compressed air into the pipeline that led to the threaded gate valve soldered to the side of the sheet-metal duct directly overhead. That duct in turn led from the cold furnace behind them to elaborate crosses and intersections at several places in the basement, where it split into smaller ducts that passed through the reinforced concrete ceiling on to the floors above. At each floor the ducts split again and snaked between and above the yet-to-be-installed walls and ceilings of the new rooms and corridors. These ducts, carefully blocked and baffled at the openings, turns, T's, and Y's, eventually crossed out of the new wing into the old hospital and tied into its system, which carried heated air from the outdated but still adequate furnace in the basement of the main wing of the hospital to the 150 private and semiprivate rooms and wards, the scrub rooms and surgeons' dressing rooms, the physical-therapy center, the operating rooms, the emergency room, the maternity ward and nursery, and all the large and small, public and private lavatories, the janitors' closets, kitchens, dining rooms, nurses' lounges, computer center, labs, billing offices, administrative offices, and the gift shop and florist shop, which was closed this early in the day, and the nearly empty waiting rooms, and even into the large, glass-fronted lobby, where Frances, the daughter of Irene Moore, was at this moment strolling from the hospital, down the steps to the parking lot. Frances was on a run into town for some small present to greet her mom when she woke, something sentimental and silly, like a teddy bear, that her mom would pretend to hate, the way she always did, but Frances knew that her mom would store the gift in a secret drawer so that she could take it out and look at it whenever she wanted to realize anew how much her daughter loved her.

Something was going wrong. The first sign was a cool puff of air that carried a gray plume of ash—probably cigarette ash—from a wall register into the cafeteria on the first floor of the old wing. A janitor leaned against his mop and with some annoyance watched the gray powder float onto his clean floor.

In a laboratory on the second floor, bits of dirt fell from the ceiling vent onto the head and shoulders of a puzzled technician, causing her to jump from her seat and stare at the vent for a moment. When no further debris fell, she sat back down and resumed cataloging urine samples.

Then along one corridor after another and in the maternity ward and in several of the private rooms, on all three floors of the hospital, nurses, doctors, maintenance people, and even some patients began to see tiny scraps of paper, ashes, shreds of pink insulation, metal filings, sawdust, and unidentifiable bits of dirt fly from the registers and ceiling vents, float through the air, and land on sheets and pillows, sterilization cabinets, stainless-steel counters, computers, desks, spotless equipment, and tools of all kinds, dusting hairdos, nurses' caps, starched white uniforms, and even the breakfast trays. Nurses, doctors, administrators, and staff people strode up and down hallways and made phone calls, trying to locate the cause of this invasion of flying debris. Attendants grabbed sheets and blankets and covered the newborn infants in the nursery and patients in the wards, shouting orders and firing angry questions at one another, while patients pressed their buzzers and hollered for help and brushed the floating bits of dirt and trash away from their faces, bandages, casts, and bedding. Those patients who were mobile ran, limped, and rolled in wheelchairs from their rooms and wards to the hallways and nurses' stations, demanding to know what was happening. Had there been an explosion? Was there a fire?

In the operating room, Dr. Rabideau shouted, *Close her up! For Christ's sake, close her up and get her the hell out of here!*

In the cold basement of the new wing, Vann stood in the light of a single bulb and puzzled over the gauge on his compressor. He rubbed his cigarette out on the cement floor.

"She's not holding any pressure at all now. Not a damn bit," he said to Tommy Farr. "Something's open that shouldn't be. Or else we've got one hell of a blowout someplace," he said and reached up and shut off the air to the main duct. He switched off the compressor motor, and the basement was suddenly silent.

"How we gonna find out what's open?" Tommy asked.

"We got to check everything that's supposed to be closed. One of you guys must've left a cap off one of the register openings."

"Hey, not me! I ain't no sheet-metal guy. I was in the trailer counting fittings all day Friday."

"I know, I know. I just need somebody to blame," Vann said, smiling. He clapped the kid on the shoulder. "C'mon, let's get the drawings from the trailer. We'll go room to room and check every vent until we find the missing cap. Then we'll cap 'er and try again."

Vann had done his job the way he was supposed to, and his men had done theirs. He could not have known what had occurred beyond the thick fire wall that separated the new wing from the old, could not have known that over there, when he finally shut his compressor down, the debris had instantly ceased to fall. And he could not have known that seconds after Drs. Ransome, Rabideau, and Wheelwright in a panic had closed their incisions and rushed her from the operating room, his ex-wife Irene had gone into cardiac arrest in the recovery room. They had managed to get her heart pumping again and her blood pressure back, but an embolism had formed in her left carotid artery and had started working its way toward her neck. Shortly after noon, a blood vessel between the left temporal and parietal lobes of her brain burst, and Irene Moore suffered a massive stroke and immediately lapsed into a coma.

The only surgeon in the area capable of removing the clot from her brain was driving over from Plattsburgh. They hoped to have the operating room cleaned up and ready for him by early evening. With her heart condition, however, and the trauma inflicted on her by the interrupted surgery this morning, the likelihood of still more embolisms, the anticoagulants, and now the stroke, "I'm sorry, but it truly does not look good," Dr. Rabideau told Frances.

She did not know where to turn for consolation or advice. She was the only one left in the world who loved her mother, and her mother was the only one left who loved her. Frances's father, Irene's long-gone first husband, had his new life, a new wife and new kids out in California. Irene's second husband, Vann, had his new life, too, Frances supposed. He and Frances had never liked each other much, anyhow.

A little after lunch, the supervisor of maintenance in the hospital found Vann on the second floor of the new wing, still tracing the overhead ducts with Tommy Farr. The supervisor, Fred Noelle, was a man in his mid-sixties who had worked for the hospital since high school. He knew every inch of the old building, every valve, switch, pump, and fitting, and had been an especially useful consultant when they were designing the addition. Cautiously, Fred asked Vann if earlier this morning he might have done something in the way of connecting the heat and ventilation ducts of the new wing to the ducts of the old. Tied them together, say, and then opened them up, maybe.

"No," Vann said. "Why? You got problems over there?"

"Have we got problems? Yes, we've got problems. We'll be cleaning the place up for the rest of the year." He was a balding, heavyset man with a face like a bull terrier, and he looked very worried. He knew there were lawsuits coming. A lot of finger-pointing and denials.

"What the hell happened?" Vann asked him.

Fred told him. "They got crap on patients, in the labs, all over. Even in the operating rooms."

Vann was silent. Then he spoke slowly and clearly, directing his words to the kid but speaking mainly for Fred Noelle's benefit. "It couldn't have been us. There are baffles between the two systems, blocks, and they don't come out till after we get everything installed and blown out and balanced and the whole wing is nice and clean and ready for use. Then we open it to the old system. And that won't be till next summer," he said, his voice rising. He knew he was telling the truth. He also knew that he was dead wrong.

Somewhere, somehow, one of the baffles between the two networks had not been installed by his men or else had been left off the drawing by the mechanical engineer who had designed the system for the architect. Either way, Vann knew the fault was his. This morning, before cranking up the compressor, on the off chance that one of his sheet-metal guys had screwed up, he should have checked the baffles, every damned one of them. No one ever did that, but he should've.

He placed the drawing on the floor and got down on his hands and knees to examine it. "See," he said to Fred. "Take a look right here. Baffle. And here. Baffle. And here," he said, pointing to each of the places where the ducts crossed through the thick wall between the two wings of the hospital.

But then he saw it. No baffle. The mechanical engineer had made a terrible mistake, and Vann, back when they'd installed the ducts, hadn't caught it.

Fred got down beside him, and he saw it, too. "Uh-oh," he said, and he placed his fingertip where a barrier should have been indicated and where, instead, the drawing showed a main duct flowing through the old exterior wall and connecting directly to the heat and ventilation system of the hospital. A straight shot.

Tommy squatted down on the other side of Vann and furrowed his brow and studied the drawing. He didn't see anything wrong. "Bad, huh, Vann?"

Vann followed Fred Noelle out of the structure and across the parking lot and through the main entrance of the hospital. They went straight to the large carpeted office of Dr. Christian Snyder, the hospital director. Fred made the introductions, and Dr. Snyder got up and shook Vann's hand firmly.

"We think we got this thing figured out," Fred said. Dr. Snyder was a crisply efficient fellow in his early forties with blond, blow-dried hair. He wore a dark pinstripe suit and to Vann looked more like a downstate lawyer than a physician. Fred unrolled the drawing on Dr. Snyder's large mahogany desk, and the three men stood side by side and examined the plan together, while Fred described Vann's test and how it was supposed to work and how it had failed.

"You're the subcontractor for the sheet-metal work?" Dr. Snyder said to Vann.

"No. No, I'm just the field super for him. Sam Guy, he's the subcontractor."

"I see. But you're responsible for the installation."

"Well, yes. But I just follow the drawings, the blueprints."

"Right. And this morning you were testing the new ductwork, blowing compressed air through it, right?"

"Yes, but I didn't realize—"

Dr. Snyder cut him off. "I understand." He went around his desk, sat down heavily, and picked up a pencil and tapped his teeth with it. "Fred, will you be able to attend a meeting here this evening? Seven-thirty, say?"

Fred said sure, and Dr. Snyder reached for his phone. Vann picked up the drawing and started to roll it up. "Please, leave that here," Dr. Snyder said, and then he was speaking to his secretary. "Celia, for that meeting with Baumbach, Beech, and Warren? Fred Noelle, who's in charge of maintenance, he'll be joining us."

He glanced up at Vann as if surprised to see him still standing there. "You can go, if you want. Thanks for your help. We'll be in touch," he said and went back to his telephone.

Outside in the lobby, alone, Vann pulled out a cigarette and stuck it between his lips.

"Sir! No smoking!" the receptionist barked at him, and he shoved the cigarette back into the pack and made for the door.

On the steps he stopped and lit up and looked across the road at Lake Colby and the pine trees and hills beyond. There was a stiff, cold breeze off the lake, and it was starting to get dark. Vann checked his watch. Three-thirty-five. Off to his left he saw a woman with her back to him, also smoking and regarding the scenery. Vann couldn't remember when he had done anything this bad. Not at work, anyhow. In life, sure— he'd messed up his life, messed it up lots of ways, most people do. But, Jesus, never at work.

The woman tossed her cigarette onto the parking lot below and turned to go back inside, and Vann recognized her—Frances, his ex-wife's daughter. For a second, he was afraid of her, but then he realized that he was glad to see her and blurted, "Hey, Frances! What're you doing here?" Startled, she looked up at him, and he saw that she was crying. He took a step toward her. She was taller than he remembered, a few inches taller than he, and heavier. Her face was swollen and red and wet with tears. "Is it your mom?"

She nodded yes, like a child, and he reached out to her. She kept her arms tight to her sides but let him hold her close. He was all she had; he would have to be enough.

"Come on inside and sit down, honey, and tell me what's happened," Vann said, and with one arm around her, he walked her back into the lobby, where they sat down on one of the blond sofas by the window. "Jeez," he said, "I don't have a handkerchief."

"That's okay, I got a tissue." She pulled a wrinkled tissue from her purse and wiped her cheeks.

"So tell me what happened, Frances. What's wrong with your mom?"

She hesitated a second. Then she inhaled deeply and said, "I don't understand it. She's in a coma. She went in for open-heart surgery this morning and something happened, something went wrong, and they had to bring her out in the middle of it."

"Oh," Vann said. "Oh, Jesus." He lowered his head. He put his hands over his face and closed his eyes behind them.

"There were complications. She had a stroke. The doctors don't think she'll come out of it," she said, and started to cry again.

Vann took his hands away from his face and sat there staring at the floor. The beige carpet was decorated with the outlines of orange and dark-green rectangles. Vann let his gaze follow the interlocking colored lines from his feet out to the middle of the room and then back again. Out and back, out and back. There were six or eight other people seated in the sofas and chairs scattered around the lobby, reading magazines or talking quietly with one another, waiting for news of their mothers and fathers, their husbands and wives and children in the rooms above.

"Do you think maybe could I go and see her?" he said in a low voice.

"I don't think so. She's in intensive care, Vann. She won't even know you're there. I saw her a little while ago, but she didn't know it was me in the room."

Slowly Vann got to his feet and moved toward the receptionist by the elevator. He wanted to see Irene. He could say it to himself. It didn't matter if she knew he was there or not; he had to see her. He needed to fill his mind with her actual, physical presence. No fading memories of her, no tangled feelings of guilt for things done and undone, no dimly remembered hurts and resentments. Too late for all that. He needed to look at her literal existence, see her in the here and now, and take full-faced whatever terrible thoughts and feelings came to him there.

"I need to see my wife," he said to the receptionist. "She's in intensive care."

The woman peered at him over her horn-rimmed glasses. "Who's your wife?"

"Irene. Irene Moore."

He signed the book that the woman pushed at him and stepped quickly toward the elevator. "Third floor," she said. He got into the elevator, turned back, and saw Frances seated across the lobby, looking mournfully at him. Then the door slid closed.

At the nurses' station outside the intensive-care unit, an elderly nurse pointed him down a hallway to a closed door. "Second bed on the right. You can't miss her; she's the only one there."

The room was dark, windowless, lit only by the wall lamp above the bedstead. Irene's body was very large; it filled the bed. Vann didn't remember her as that big. She made him feel suddenly small, shrunken, fragile. There were IV stands and oxygen tanks and tubes that snaked in and out of her body and several thick black wires attached to cabinet-sized machines that blinked and whirred, monitoring her blood pressure, heart, and breathing.

For a long time he stood at the foot of the bed peering through the network of tubes and wires at his ex-wife's body. She was covered to her neck by a sheet. Her arms lay limp and white outside the sheet. A tube dripped clear liquid into a vein at one wrist. On the other wrist she wore a plastic identification band.

No wedding ring, he noticed. He looked down at his own left hand. No wedding ring there, either. *Irene, you're the one I loved.* He said the words silently to himself, straight out. *And I'm only loving you now. And, Jesus, look at what I've done to you, before I could love you.*

What's that love worth now, I wonder, to you or me or anybody?

He felt a strong wind blow over him, and he had to grab hold of the metal bed frame to keep from staggering backward. The wind was warm, like a huge breath, an exhalation, and though it pummeled him, he wasn't afraid of it. He turned sideways and made his way along the bed. The wind abated, and he found himself looking down at Irene's face. There was a tube in her slightly open mouth and another in one of her nostrils. Her eyes were closed. Somewhere behind her face, Irene was curled in on herself like a child, naked, huddled in the darkness, alone, waiting.

Vann slipped his hands into his jacket pockets and stood with his feet apart and looked down on the woman he had been able to love for only a moment. He stood there for a long time, long after he had ceased to love her and had only the memory of it left. Then he turned away from her.

When he emerged from the elevator to the lobby, he quickly looked around for Frances and found her seated in a far corner of the room, slumped in a chair with her head on one arm and her eyes closed as if she was asleep. He sat down next to her, and her eyes fluttered open.

"Did you see her?" Frances asked.

"Yeah. I did. I saw her."

"She didn't know you were there, did she?"

"No. No, she didn't," he said. "But that didn't matter."

"Where're you going now, Vann? From here."

"Well, I don't know. I thought maybe I'd wait here, Frances. Keep you company. If you don't mind, I mean."

The girl didn't answer him. They both knew that Irene was going to die, probably before morning. Like a father, Vann would wait here with her and help the girl endure her mother's death.

People coming into the lobby were brushing snow off their shoulders and hats. Vann looked out the window at the parking lot and the lake. It had been snowing for a while, and the cars in the lot were covered with powdery white sheets. Sam Guy would fire him, no doubt about it, and both Vann and Sam would be lucky if no one sued them. Vann would go back to working locally out of his car, like he'd done when he first married Irene. He was coming in off the road too late, maybe, to make anyone happy, but here he was anyhow, trying.

Judy Budnitz

Flush

From *McSweeney's*

I CALLED my sister and said: What does a miscarriage look like?

What? she said. Oh. It looks like when you're having your period, I guess. You have cramps, and then there's blood.

What do people do with it? I asked.

With what?

The blood and stuff.

I don't know, she said impatiently. I don't know these things, I'm not a doctor. All I can tell you about anything is who you should sue.

Sorry, I said.

Why are you asking me this? she said.

I'm just having an argument with someone, that's all. Just thought you could help settle it.

Well, I hope you win, she said.

I went home because my sister told me to.

She called and said: It's your turn.

No, it can't be, I feel like I was just there, I said.

No, I went the last time. I've been keeping track, I have incontestable proof, she said. She was in law school.

But Mich, I said. Her name was Michelle but everyone called her Mich, as in Mitch, except our mother, who thought it sounded obscene.

Lisa, said Mich, don't whine.

I could hear her chewing on something, a ball-point pen probably. I pictured her with blue marks on her lips, another pen stuck in her hair.

It's close to Thanksgiving, I said, why don't we wait and both go home then?

You forget—they're going down to Florida to be with Nana.

I don't have time to go right now. I have a job, you know. I do have a life.

I don't have time to argue about it, I'm studying, Mich said. I knew she was sitting on the floor with her papers scattered around her, the stacks of casebooks sprouting yellow Post-its from all sides, like lichen, Mich in the middle with her legs spread, doing ballet stretches.

I heard a background cough.

You're not studying, I said. Neil's there.

Neil isn't doing anything, she said. He's sitting quietly in the corner waiting for me to finish. Aren't you, sweetheart?

Meek noises from Neil.

You call him sweetheart? I said.

Are you going home or not?

Do I have to?

I can't come over there and make you go, Mich said.

The thing was, we had both decided, some time ago, to take turns going home every now and then to check up on them. Our parents did not need checking up, but Mich thought we should get in the habit of doing it anyway. To get in practice for the future.

After a minute Mich said: They'll think we don't care.

Sometimes I think they'd rather we left them alone.

Fine. Fine. Do what you want.

Oh all right, I'll go.

I flew home on a Thursday night and though I'd told them not to meet me at the airport, there they were, both of them, when I stepped off the ramp. They were the only still figures in the terminal; around them people dashed with garment bags, stewardesses hustled in pairs wheeling tiny suitcases.

My mother wore a brown coat the color of her hair. She looked anxious. My father stood tall, swaying slightly. The lights bounced off the lenses of his glasses; he wore jeans that were probably twenty years old. I would have liked to be the one to see them first, to compose my face and walk up to them unsuspected like a stranger. But that never happened— they always spotted me before I saw them, and had their faces ready and their hands out.

Is that all you brought? Just the one bag?

Here, I'll take it.

Lisa honey, you don't look so good. How are you?

Yes, how are you? You look terrible.

Thanks, Dad.

How are you, they said over and over, as they wrestled the suitcase from my hand.

Back at the house, my mother stirred something on the stove and my father leaned in the doorway to the dining room and looked out the window at the backyard. He's always leaned in that door-frame to talk to my mother.

I made that soup for you, my mother said. The one where I have to peel the tomatoes and pick all the seeds out by hand.

Mother. I wish you wouldn't do that.

You mean you don't like it? I thought you liked it.

I like it, I like it. But I wish you wouldn't bother.

It's no bother. I wanted to.

She was up until two in the morning pulling skin off tomatoes, my father said, I could hear them screaming in agony.

How would you know, you were asleep, my mother said.

I get up at five thirty every morning to do work in the yard before I go in to the office, he said.

I looked out at the brown yard.

I've been pruning the rose bushes. They're going to be beautiful next summer.

Yes, they will.

Lisa, he said, I want you to do something for me tomorrow, since you're here.

Sure. Anything.

I want you to go with your mother to her doctor's appointment. Make sure she goes.

O.K.

She doesn't have to come, my mother said. That's silly, she'll just be bored.

She's supposed to get a mammogram every six months, my father said, but she's been putting it off and putting it off.

I've been busy, you know that's all it is.

She's afraid to go. She's been avoiding it for a year now.

Oh stop it, that's not it at all.

She always finds a way to get out of it. Your mother, the escape artist.

She crossed her arms over her chest. There was a history. Both her mother and an aunt had had to have things removed.

It's the same with all her doctors, my father said. Remember the contact lenses?

That was different. I didn't need new contacts.

She stopped going to her eye doctor for fifteen years. For fifteen years she was wearing the same contacts. When she finally went in, the doctor was amazed, he said he'd never seen anything like it, they don't even make contact lenses like that anymore. He thought she was wearing dessert dishes in her eyes.

You're exaggerating, my mother said.

Mich I mean Lise, my father said. He's always gotten our names confused; sometimes, to be safe, he just says all three.

She's afraid to go because of the last time, he said.

What happened last time? I said.

I had the mammogram pictures done, she said, and then a few days later they called and said the pictures were inconclusive and they needed to take a second set. So they did that and then they kept me waiting for the results, for weeks, without telling me anything, weeks where I couldn't sleep at night and I kept your father up too, trying to imagine what it looked like, the growth. Like the streaks in bleu cheese, I thought. I kept feeling these little pains, and kept checking my pulse all night. And then finally they called and said everything was fine after all, that there was just some kind of blur on the first pictures, like I must have moved right when they took it or something.

You were probably talking the whole time, my father said. Telling them how to do their job.

I was probably *shivering*. They keep that office at about forty degrees and leave you sitting around in the cold in a paper robe. The people there don't talk to you or smile; and when they do the pictures they mash your breast between these two cold glass plates like a pancake.

My father looked away. He had a kind of modesty about some things.

My mother said to me: All those nights I kept thinking about my mother having her surgery; I kept feeling for lumps, waking up your father and asking him to feel for lumps.

Leah, my father said.

He didn't mind that. I think he might have enjoyed it a little.

Please.

Didn't you?

Promise me you'll go, he said.

She's not coming, she said.

The next day we drove to the clinic an hour early. My mother had the seat drawn as close to the steering wheel as she could get it; she gripped the wheel with her hands close together at twelve o'clock. She looked over at me as often as she looked out at the road.

There were squirrels and possums sprawled in the road, their heads red smears.

It's something about the weather, my mother said, makes them come out at night.

Oh.

We're so early, my mother said, and we're right near Randy's salon. Why don't we stop in and see if he can give you a haircut and a blowout?

Not now.

He wouldn't mind, I don't think. I talk about you whenever I go see him to have my hair done. He'd like to meet you.

No.

If you just got it angled on the sides, here, and got a few bangs in the front—

Just like yours, you mean.

You know, I feel so bad for Randy, he looks terrible, circles under his eyes all the time, he says his boyfriend is back in the hospital. Now whenever I go to get my hair cut, I bake something to bring him, banana bread or something. But I think the shampoo girls usually eat it all before he can get it home.

That's nice of you.

I worry about him. He doesn't take care of himself.

Yes.

Why are you still getting pimples? You're twenty-seven years old, why are you still getting pimples like a teenager?

Not everyone has perfect skin like you, I said. Green light. Go.

I do not have perfect skin, she said, bringing her hands to her face.

Both hands on the wheel please. Do you want me to drive?

No, I don't. You must be tired.

I touched my forehead. Small hard bumps like Braille.

She drove. I looked at the side of her face, the smooth taut skin. I wondered when she would start to get wrinkles. I already had wrinkles. On my neck, I could see them.

So, how is it going with this Piotr?

He's all right.

Still playing the—what was it? Guitar?

Bass guitar.

She turned on the radio and started flipping through stations. Maybe we'll hear one of his songs, she said brightly.

I said: I told you he was in a band. I didn't say they were good enough to be on the radio.

Oh. I see. So the band's just for fun. What else does he do?

Nothing. Yet.

So. What kind of name is Piotr? Am I saying it right?

Polish, I said.

I did not feel like telling her that only his grandmother lived in Poland; his parents were both born in Milwaukee, and he had grown up in Chicago and had never been to Poland; Piotr was a name he had given himself; he was not really a Piotr at all, he was a Peter with pretensions and long hair. I did not tell her this.

A black car cut into the lane in front of us. My mother braked suddenly and flung her right arm out across my chest.

Mother! Keep your hands on the wheel!

I'm sorry, she said, it's automatic. Ever since you kids were little . . .

I'm wearing a seatbelt.

I know honey, I can't help it. Did I hurt you?

No, of course not, I said.

When we reached the parking garage my mother rolled down her window but couldn't reach; she had to unfasten her seatbelt and open the car door in order to punch the button and get her parking ticket. I looked at her narrow back as she leaned out of the car, its delicate curve, the shoulder blades like folded wings under her sweater, a strand of dark hair caught in the clasp of her gold necklace. I had the urge to slide across the seat and curl around her. It only lasted for a second.

She turned around and settled back into her seat and the yellow-and-black-striped mechanical bar swung up in front of the car, and I tapped my feet impatiently while she slammed the door shut and rolled up the window. Now she was fiddling with her rearview mirror and straightening her skirt.

Come on, I said, watching the bar, which was still raised but vibrating a little.

Relax honey, that thing isn't going to come crashing down on us the minute we're under it. I promise you.

I know that, I said, and then closed my eyes until we were through the gate and weaving around the dark oil-stained aisles of the parking lot. I would have liked to tell her about some of the legal cases Mich had described to me: freak accidents, threshing machines gone awry, people caught in giant gears or conveyor belts and torn limb from limb, hands in bread slicers, flimsy walkways over vats of acid. Elevator cases, diving board cases, subway train cases, drowning-in-the-bathtub cases, electrocution-by-blender cases. And then there were the ones that were just called Act of God.

I didn't tell her.

Remember where we parked, she said.

O.K.

But she did not get out of the car right away. She sat, gripping the wheel.

I don't see why we have to do this, she said. Your father worries . . .

He'll be more worried if you don't go, I said, and anyway there's nothing to worry about because everything's going to be fine. Right? Right.

If there's something wrong I'd just rather not know, she said to her hands.

We got out; the car shook as we slammed the doors.

She was right about the clinic. It was cold, and it was ugly. She signed in with the receptionist and we sat in the waiting room. The room was gray and bare, the chairs were old vinyl that stuck to your thighs. The lights buzzed and seemed to flicker unless you were looking directly at them.

We sat side by side and stared straight ahead as if we were watching something, a movie.

There was one other woman waiting. She had enormous breasts. I could not help noticing.

I took my mother's hand. It was very cold, but then her hands were always cold, even in summer, cool and smooth with the blue veins arching elegantly over their backs. Her hand lay limply in mine. I had made the gesture thinking it was the right thing to do, but now that I had her hand I didn't know what to do with it. I patted it, turned it over.

My mother looked at me strangely. My hand began to sweat.

There was noise, activity, somewhere, we could hear voices and footsteps, the crash and skid of metal, the brisk tones of people telling each other what to do. But we could see nothing but the receptionist in her window and the one woman who looked asleep, sagging in her chair with her breasts cupped in her arms like babies.

I need to use the restroom, my mother said and pulled her hand away.

The receptionist directed us down the hall and around the corner. We went in, our footsteps echoing on the tiles. It was empty, and reeked of ammonia. The tiles glistened damply.

Here, do something with yourself, my mother said and handed me her comb. She walked down to the big handicapped stall on the end and latched the door.

I combed my hair and washed my hands and waited.

I looked at myself in the mirror. The lights were that harsh relentless kind that reveal every detail of your face, so that you can see all sorts of flaws and pores you didn't even know you had. They made you feel you could see your own thoughts floating darkly just under your skin, like bruises.

Mother, I said. I watched her feet tapping around.

Lisa, she said, there's a fish in the toilet.

Oh, please.

No, I mean it. It's swimming around.

You're making it up.

No I'm not. Come see for yourself.

Well, it's probably just some pet goldfish someone tried to flush.

It's too big to be a goldfish. More like a carp. It's bright orange. Almost red.

You're seeing things—maybe it's blood or something, I said; then I wished I hadn't. The clinic was attached to the county hospital; all sorts of things were liable to pop up in the toilets—hypodermic needles, appendixes, tonsils.

No, no, it's a fish, it's beautiful really. It's got these gauzy fins, like veils. I wonder how it got in here. It looks too large to have come through the pipes. It's swimming in circles. Poor thing.

Well then come out and use a different one, I said. I suddenly started to worry that she was going to miss her appointment. You're just stalling, I said.

Come in and see. We have to save it somehow.

I heard her pulling up her pantyhose, fixing her skirt. Then she unlatched the door to the stall and opened it. She was smiling. Look, she said.

I followed her into the stall.

Come see, she said. Together we leaned over the bowl.

I saw only the toilet's bland white hollow, and our two identical silhouettes reflected in the water.

Now where did he go? my mother said. Isn't that the strangest thing?

We looked at the empty water.

How do you think he got out? she said. Look, you can see, the water's still moving from where he was. Look, look—little fish droppings. I swear. Lisa honey, look.

My mother is going crazy, I thought. Let's go back to the waiting room, I said.

But I still have to use the bathroom, she said.

I stood by the sink and waited. You're going to miss your appointment, I said. I watched her feet. Silence.

I was making her nervous. I'll wait for you in the hall, I said.

So I left, leaned against the wall, and waited. And waited. She was taking a long time. I started to wonder if she had been hallucinating. I wondered if something really was wrong with her, if she was bleeding internally or having a weird allergic reaction. I didn't think she was making it all up; she couldn't lie, she was a terrible, obvious liar.

Mother, I called.

Mom, I said.

I went back into the bathroom.

She was gone.

The stall doors swung loose, creaking. I checked each cubicle, thinking she might be standing on the toilet seat, with her head ducked down the way we used to avoid detection in high school. In the handicapped stall the toilet water was quivering, as if it had just been flushed. I even checked in the cabinets under the sink and stuck my hand down in the garbage pail.

I stood there, thinking. She must have somehow left and darted past me without my noticing. Maybe I had closed my eyes for a minute. She could move fast when she wanted to.

Had she climbed out the window? It was a small one, closed, high up on the wall.

She had escaped.

I walked slowly down the halls, listening, scanning the floor tiles.

I thought of her narrow back, the gaping mouth of the toilet, pictured her slipping down, whirling around and vanishing in the pipes.

I tried to formulate a reasonable question: Have you seen my mother? A woman, about my height, brown hair, green eyes? Nervous-looking? Have you seen her?

Or were her eyes hazel?

I came back to the waiting room with the question on my lips, I was mouthing the words she's disappeared, but when I got there the receptionist was leaning through the window calling out in an irritated voice: Ms. Salant? Ms. Salant? They're ready for you, *Ms. Salant.*

The receptionist was opening the door to the examining rooms; the nurses and technicians were holding out paper gowns and paper forms and urine sample cups, Ms. Salant, Ms. Salant, we're waiting, they called; people were everywhere suddenly, gesturing impatiently and calling out my name.

So I went in.

Later I wandered up and down the rows of painted white lines in the lot. I had forgotten where she parked the car. When I finally came upon it I saw her there, leaning against the bumper. For a moment I thought she was smoking a cigarette. She didn't smoke.

When I drew closer I saw that she was nibbling on a pen.

We got in the car and drove home.

All of a sudden I thought of something I wanted to pick up for dinner, she said at one point.

Some fish? I said.

We drove the rest of the way without speaking.

So how did it go today, ladies? my father said that evening.

My mother didn't say anything.

Did you go with her? he asked me. Yeah, I said.

So, you'll hear results in a few days, right? he said with his hand on my mother's back.

She looked away.

Right, I said.

She looked at me strangely, but said nothing.

I told them not to but they both came to the airport Sunday night when I left.

Call me when you get the news, all right? I said.

All right, she said.

I wanted to ask her about the fish in the toilet, whether it had really been there. Whether she had followed the same route it had. But I couldn't work myself up to it. And the topic never came up by itself.

We said good-bye at the terminal. My hugs were awkward. I patted their backs as if I were burping babies.

I told them to go home but I knew they would wait in the airport until the plane took off safely. They always did. I think my mother liked to be there in case the plane crashed during take-off so she could dash onto the runway through the flames and explosions to drag her children from the rubble.

Or maybe they just liked airports. That airport smell.

I had a window seat; I pushed my suitcase under the seat in front of me. A man in a business suit with a fat red face sat down next to me.

I wondered if my mother even knew what I had done for her. I had helped her escape. Although at the time I hadn't thought of it that way; I hadn't really thought at all; I had gone in when I heard my name, automatic school-girl obedience, gone in to the bright lights and paper gowns and people who kneaded your breasts like clay. I began to feel beautiful and noble. I felt like I had gone to the guillotine in her place, like Sydney Carton in *A Tale of Two Cities*.

I called Piotr when I got home. I'm back, I said.

Let me come over, he said, I'll make you breakfast.

It's seven thirty at night.

I just got up, he said.

My apartment felt too small and smelled musty. I'd been gone three days but it seemed longer. Piotr came and brought eggs and milk and his own spatula—he knew my kitchen was ill-equipped for anything but sandwiches.

He seemed to have grown since I last saw him, and gotten more hairy; I looked at the hair on the backs of his hands, the chest hair tufting out of the collar of his T-shirt.

He took up too much space. As he talked his nose and hands popped out at me huge and distorted, as if I were seeing him through a fish-eye lens. He came close to kiss me and I watched his eyes loom larger and larger and blur out of focus and merge into one big eye over the bridge of his nose.

I was embarrassed. My mouth tasted terrible from the plane.

What kind of pancakes do you want? he asked.

The pancake kind, I said.

He broke two eggs with one hand and the yolks slid out between his fingers.

I can do them shaped like snowmen, he said, or rabbits or flowers.

He was mixing stuff up in a bowl; flour slopped over the edges and sprinkled on the counter and the floor. I'll have to clean that up, I thought.

Round ones please, I said.

There was butter bubbling and crackling in the frying pan. Was that pan mine? No, he must have brought it with him—it was a big heavy skillet, the kind you could kill someone with.

He poured in the batter, it was thick and pale yellow; and the hissing butter shut up for a while. I looked in the pan. There were two large lumpy mounds there, side by side, bubbling inside as if they were alive, turning brown on the edges.

He turned them over and I saw the crispy undersides with patterns on them like the moon; and then he pressed them down with the spatula, pressed them flat and the butter sputtered and hissed.

There was a burning smell.

I'm not feeling very hungry right now, I said.

But I brought maple syrup, he said. It's from Vermont, I think.

The pan was starting to smoke. Pushing him aside, I took it off the flame and put it in the sink. It was heavy; the two round shapes were now charred and crusted to the bottom.

Well, we don't have to eat them, he said. He held out the bottle of syrup. Aunt Jemima smiled at me. She looked different, though. They must have updated her image; new hairstyle, outfit. But that same smile.

There's lots of stuff we can do with syrup, he said, it's a very romantic condiment.

He stepped closer and reached out and turned the knob on the halogen lamp. His face looked even more distorted in the dimness.

What? I said. Where did you get such a stupid idea?

Read it somewhere.

I'm sorry, I'm just not feeling very social tonight, I said. Peter, I said.

Oh come on.

I missed my parents very much suddenly. You're so insensitive, I said. Get out.

Hey, I *am* sensitive. I'm *Mr.* Sensitive. I give change to bums. Pachelbel's Canon makes me cry like a baby.

Like a what? I said.

Why are you screaming at me? he said.

Don't let the door hit you in the ass on the way out, I said. I thought I was being smart and cutting. But he took it literally; he went out and closed the door behind him with great care.

My sister called later that night.

So how were they? she asked.

Fine, I said. Same as always.

Your voice sounds funny; what happened? she said.

Nothing.

Something's wrong. Why don't you ever tell me when something's wrong?

There's nothing, Mich.

You never tell me what's going on; when you think I'll worry about something you keep it to yourself.

I tell you everything.

Well then, tell me what was wrong with you earlier this fall.

Nothing . . . I don't know . . . there's nothing to tell.

That was the truth. All that happened was I got tired of people for a while. I didn't like to go out, didn't shower, and didn't pick up the phone except to call my office with elaborate excuses. The smell of my body became comforting, a ripe presence, nasty but familiar. I lay in bed telling myself that it was just a phase, it would pass. Eventually the bulb on my halogen lamp burned out and after two days of darkness I ventured out to buy a new one. The sunlight out on the street did something to my brain, or maybe it was the kind bald man who sold me the bulb. I went back to work.

So how are you? How's Neil?

Oh we broke up, she said. We had a big fight, and he couldn't see that I was right and he was wrong. It was high drama, in a restaurant with people watching, us screaming and stuff, and this fat waitress pushing between us using her tray as a shield and telling us to leave. So we finished it outside on the street, I made my points, one two three, and did my closing arguments. If we were in court I would have won.

I'm sorry, I said. Why didn't you tell me right away?

Oh, I didn't want you feeling bad for me. I'm glad, really. Small-minded jerk. Did I ever tell you he had all this hair on his back? Gray hair, like a silverback gorilla.

Yes, well. I don't know that I'll be seeing Piotr any more either.

That's too bad.

No, it's not.

That night as I lay in bed I thought of my mother and I felt my body for lumps the way she said she felt hers, and I put two fingers to the side of my throat. And I began to think of her and think of an undetected cancer, spreading through her body unnoticed. It began to dawn on me that I had done a very stupid thing.

I thought of her lying in bed beside my father at that moment, oblivious to the black thing that might be growing and thickening inside her, maybe in tough strands, maybe in little grainy bits, like oatmeal. She would avoid thinking about it for another six months or a year or two years; she'd deny it until her skin turned gray and she had tentacles growing out of her mouth and her breasts slid from her body and plopped on the floor like lumps of wet clay. Only when all that happened would she give in and say, Hmmm, maybe something is wrong, maybe I should see a doctor after all.

I lay awake for most of the night.

At one point I got up to use the bathroom, and as I sat on the toilet in the dark I suddenly became convinced that there was something horrible floating in the water below me. I was sure of it. A live rat. Or a length of my own intestines lying coiled bloody in the bowl. I sat there afraid to turn on the light and look, yet couldn't leave the bathroom without looking.

I sat there for half an hour, wracked with indecision. I think I fell asleep for a bit.

And when I finally forced myself to turn on the light, turn around and look—I was so convinced there would be something floating there that I was horribly shocked, my stomach lurched to see only the empty toilet.

I went back to work on Tuesday.

Did I miss anything? I asked one of the men.

You were gone? he said.

I didn't know his name; all the men who worked there looked alike. They were all too loud, and had too much spit in their mouths.

I had a cubicle all my own, but I dreamed of an office with a door I could close.

A few days later my father called. Your mother heard the results from the clinic, he said, the mammogram was fine.

That's great, I said.

She doesn't seem happy about it, he said, she's acting very strange.

Oh, I said.

What's going on, Lisa? he said. There's something fishy going on here.

Nothing, I said. Ask your wife, I said. Can I talk to her?

She just dashed out for an appointment, told me to call you. She said you'd be relieved.

Yes.

I'm going to call your sister now, she was waiting to hear. Or do you want to call her?

I'll do it, I said.

It seemed strange to me then that I would need to call Mich; a phone call implied distance, but our family seemed so close and entwined and entangled that we could hardly tell each other apart. Why should you need a phone to talk to someone who seems like she's living inside your skin?

We both went home for Christmas.

Later Mich visited them.

Then I visited.

Then it was Mich's turn again.

When I called home during Mich's visit my father said: Your mother was due for another mammogram, so I sent Lisa with her to make sure she goes.

You mean you sent Mich, I said. I'm Lisa.

Yes, right, you know who I mean.

A few days later my father called, his voice sounding strained. Your mother talked to the mammography clinic today, he said, but she won't tell me anything. She's been in her room, crying. She's been talking on the phone to your sister for an hour. I guess the doctors found something, but I'll let you know when we know for sure.

O.K.

I hung up and called Mich.

Hello, she said. She sounded like she was choking on one of her pens.

Mich, I said, it's yours, isn't it?

She sighed and said: It's ridiculous, but I thought I was doing her a favor, I thought I was sparing her some worry.

You went in for her, didn't you?

You know, Mich said, she's more worried about this than if she was the one with a lump in her breast. She feels like it's her lump, like it was meant for her, like she gave it to me somehow.

That's ridiculous, I said. I felt like I was talking to myself.

Although, you know, if it were possible, I would, Mich said. I mean, if there was somehow a way to magically take a lump out of her breast and put it in mine, I'd do it in a second.

I wish I could do that for you, I said.

Yeah, we could all share it.

One dessert and three forks, I said.

And later as I sat alone on the floor in the apartment I started to lose track of where I stopped and other people began, and I remembered standing in a white room with my breast clamped in the jaws of a humming machine, and I felt for the lump that I thought was mine, and sometimes I thought it was my mother's, and I imagined the mammogram pictures like lunar landscapes. Then I could not remember who had the lump anymore, it seemed we all did, it was my mother's my sister's and mine, and then the phone rang again and I picked it up and heard my father call out as he sometimes did: Leah-Lise-Mich.

Kevin Brockmeier

These Hands

From *The Georgia Review*

THE PROTAGONIST of this story is named Lewis Winters. He is also its narrator, and he is also me. Lewis is thirty-four years old. His house is small and tidy and sparsely furnished, and the mirrors there return the image of a man inside of whom he is nowhere visible, a face within which he doesn't seem to belong: there is the turn of his lip, the knit of his brow, and his own familiar gaze; there is the promise of him, but where is he? Lewis longs for something not ugly, false, or confused. He chases the yellow-green bulbs of fireflies and cups them between his palms. He watches copter-seeds whirl from the limbs of great trees. He believes in the bare possibility of grace, in kindness and the memory of kindness, and in the fierce and sudden beauty of color. He sometimes believes that this is enough. On quiet evenings, Lewis drives past houses and tall buildings into the flat yellow grasslands that embrace the city. The black road tapers to a point, and the fields sway in the wind, and the sight of the sun dropping red past the hood of his car fills him with sadness and wonder. Lewis lives alone. He sleeps poorly. He writes fairy tales. This is not one of them.

The lover of the protagonist of this story, now absent, is named Caroline Mitchell. In the picture framed on his desk, she stands gazing into the arms of a small tree, a mittened hand at her eyes, lit by the afternoon sun as if through a screen of water. She looks puzzled and eager, as if the wind had rustled her name through the branches; in a moment, a leaf will tumble onto her forehead. Caroline is watchful and sincere, shy yet earnest. She seldom speaks, and when she does her lips scarcely part, so that sometimes Lewis must listen closely to distinguish her voice from the cycling of her breath. Her eyes are a miracle—a startled blue with frail green spokes bound by a ring of black—and he is certain that if he could draw his reflection from them, he would discover there a face neither foreign nor lost. Caroline sleeps facedown, her knees curled to her chest: she sleeps often and with no sheets or blankets. Her hair is brown, her skin pale. Her smile is vibrant but brief, like a bubble that lasts only as long as the air is still. She is eighteen months old.

A few questions deserve answer, perhaps, before I continue. So then: The walls behind which I'm writing are the walls of my home—the only thing padded is the furniture, the only thing barred the wallpaper. Caroline is both alive and (I imagine—I haven't seen her now in many days) well. And I haven't read Nabokov—not ever, not once.

All this said, it's time we met, my love and I.

It was a hopeful day of early summer, and a slight, fresh breeze tangled through the air. The morning sun shone from telephone wires and the windshields of resting cars, and high clouds unfolded like the tails of galloping horses. Lewis stood before a handsome dark-brick house, flattening his shirt into his pants. The house seemed to conceal its true dimensions behind the planes and angles of its front wall. An apron of hedges stretched beneath its broad lower windows, and a flagstone walk, edged with black soil, elbowed from the driveway to the entrance. He stepped to the front porch and pressed the doorbell.

"Just a minute," called a faint voice.

Lewis turned to look along the street, resting his hand against a wooden pillar. A chain of lawns glittered with dew beneath the blue sky—those nearby green and bristling, those in the distance merely panes of white light. A blackbird lighted on the stiff red flag of a mailbox. From inside the house came the sound of a door wheeling on faulty hinges, a series of quick muffled footsteps, and then an abrupt reedy squeak. *Hello,* thought Lewis: *Hello, I spoke to you on the telephone.* The front door drew inward, stopped short on its chain, and shut. He heard the low mutter of a voice, like residual water draining through a straw. Then the door opened to reveal a woman in a billowy cotton bathrobe, the corner of its hem dark with water. A lock of black hair swept across her cheek from under the dome of a towel. In her hand she carried a yellow toy duck. "Yes?" she said.

"Hello," said Lewis. "I spoke to you on the telephone." The woman gave him a quizzical stare. "The nanny position? You asked me to stop by this morning for an interview." When she cocked an eyebrow, he withdrew a step, motioning toward his car. "If I'm early, I can—"

"Oh!" realized the woman. "Oh, yes." She smiled, tucking a few damp hairs behind the rim of her ear. "The interview. I'm sorry. Come in." Lewis followed her past a small brown table and a rising chain of wooden banisters into the living room. A rainbow of fat plastic rings littered the silver-gray carpet, and a grandfather clock ticked against the far wall. She sank onto the sofa, crossing her legs. "Now," she said, beckoning him to sit beside her. "I'm Lisa. Lisa Mitchell. And you are . . . ?"

"Lewis Winters." He took a seat. "We spoke earlier."

"Lewis . . . ?" Lisa Mitchell gazed into the whir of the ceiling fan, then gave a swift decisive nod. "Aaah!" she lilted, a smile softening her face. "You'll have to excuse me. It's been a hectic morning. When we talked on the phone, I assumed you were a woman. Lois, I thought you said. *Lois* Winters. We haven't had too many male applicants." Her hand fluttered about dismissively as she spoke, and the orange bill of the rubber duck bobbed past her cheek. "This *would* seem to explain the deep voice, though, wouldn't it?" She smoothed the sash of her bathrobe down her thigh. "So, tell me about your last job. What did you do?"

"I'm a storyteller," said Lewis.

"Pardon?"

"I wrote—write—fairy tales."

"Oh!" said Lisa. "That's good. Thomas—that's my husband, Thomas—" She patted a yawn from her lips. "Excuse me. Thomas will like that. And have you looked after children before?"

"No," Lewis answered. "No, not professionally. But I've worked with *groups* of children. I've read stories in nursery schools and libraries." His hands, which had been clasped, drew apart. "I'm comfortable with children, and I think I understand them."

"When would you be free to start?" asked Lisa.

"Tomorrow," said Lewis. "Today."

"Do you live nearby?"

"Not far. Fifteen minutes."

"Would evenings be a problem?"

"Not at all."

"Do you have a list of references?" At this Lisa closed her grip on the yellow duck, and it emitted a querulous little peep. She gave a start, then laughed, touching her free hand to her chest. She held the duck to her face as it bloomed with air. "Have I had him all this time?" she asked, thumbing its bill.

Somewhere in the heart of the house, a child began to wail. The air seemed to grow thick with discomfort as they listened. "*Some*one's cranky," said Lisa. She handed Lewis the duck as she stood. "Excuse me," she said. She hurried past a floor lamp and the broad green face of a television, then slipped away around the corner.

The grandfather clock chimed the hour as Lewis waited, its brass tail pendulating behind a tall glass door. He scratched a ring of grit from the dimple of the sofa cushion. He inspected the toy duck—its popeyes and the upsweep of its tail, the pock in the center of its flat yellow belly—then waddled it along the seam of a throw pillow. *Quack,* he thought. *Quack quack.* Lewis pressed its navel to the back of his hand, squeezing, and it constricted with a squeak; when he released it, it puckered and gripped him. He heard Lisa's voice in an adjacent room, all but indistinct above a siren roll of weeping. "Now, now," she was saying. "Now, now." Lewis removed the duck.

When Lisa returned, a small child was gathered to her shoulder. She was wrapped in fluffy red pajamas with vinyl pads at the feet, and her slender neck rose from the wreath of a wilted collar. "Shhh," Lisa whispered, gently patting her daughter's back. "Shhh."

Lisa's hair fell unbound past her forehead, its long wet strands twisted like roads on a map. Her daughter clutched the damp towel in her hands, nuzzling it as if it were a comfort blanket. "Little Miss Grump," chirped Lisa, standing at the sofa. "Aren't you, sweetie?" Caroline fidgeted and whimpered, then began to wail again.

Lisa frowned, joggling her in the crook of her arm.

"Well," she said, "let's see how the two of you get along. Caroline—" With a thrust and a sigh, she presented her daughter, straightening her arms as if engaged in a push-up. "This is Lewis. Lewis . . ." And she was thrashing in my hands, muscling away from me, the weight of her like something lost and suddenly remembered: a comfort and a promise, a slack sail bellying with wind.

Her voice split the air as she twitched from side to side. Padding rustled at her waist.

"Oh, dear," said Lisa. "Maybe we'd better . . ."

But Lewis wasn't listening; instead, he drew a long heavy breath. If he could pretend himself into tears, he thought, perhaps he could calm her. For a moment as sharp as a little notched hook, he held her gaze. Then, shuddering, he burst into tears. His eyes sealed fast and his lips flared wide. With a sound like the snap and rush of a struck match, his ears opened and filled with air. Barbs of flickering blue light hovered behind his eyes. He could hear the world outside growing silent and still as he wept.

When he looked out at her, Caroline was no longer crying. She blinked out at him from wide bewildered eyes, her bottom lip folding in hesitation. Then she handed him the damp towel.

It was a gesture of sympathy—meant, Lewis knew, to reassure him—and as he draped the towel over his shoulder, a broad grin creased his face.

Lisa shook her head, laughing. "Look," she said, "Thomas and I have plans for this evening, and we still haven't found a baby sitter. So if you could come by around six—?"

Caroline heard the sound of laughter and immediately brightened, smiling and tucking her chin to her chest. Lewis brushed a finger across her cheek. "Of course," he said.

"Good." Lisa lifted her daughter from his arms. "We'll see how you do, and if all goes well . . ."

All did. When Lisa and Thomas Mitchell returned late that night—his keys and loose change jingling in his pocket, her perfume winging past him as she walked into the living room—Caroline was asleep in his lap. A pacifier dangled from her mouth. The television mumbled in the corner. Lewis started work the next morning.

As a matter of simple aesthetics, the ideal human form is that of the small child. We lose all sense of grace as we mature—all sense of balance and all sense of restraint. Tufts of wiry hair sprout like moss in our hollows; our cheekbones edge to an angle and our noses stiffen with cartilage; we buckle and curve, widen and purse, like a vinyl record left too long in the sun. The journey into our fewscore years is a journey beyond that which saw us complete. Many is the time I have wished that Caroline and I might have made this journey together. If I could, I would work my way backward, paring away the years. I would reel my life around the wheel of this longing like so much loose wire. I would heave myself past adolescence and boyhood, past infancy and birth—into the first thin parcel of my flesh and the frail white trellis of my bones. I would be a massing of tissue, a clutch of cells, and I'd meet with her on the other side. If I could, I would begin again—but nothing I've found will allow it. We survive into another and more awkward age than our own.

Caroline was sitting in a saddle-chair, its blue plastic tray freckled with oatmeal. She lifted a bright wedge of peach to her lips, and its syrup wept in loose strings from her fist to her bib. Lewis held the back of a polished silver spoon before her like a mirror. "Who's that?" he said. "Who's inside that spoon? Who's that in there?" Caroline gazed into its dome as she chewed her peach. "Cah-line," she said.

Lewis reversed the spoon, and her reflection toppled over into its bowl. "Oh my goodness!" he said. His voice went weak with astonishment. "Caroline is standing on her head!" Caroline prodded the spoon, then taking it by the handle, her hand on his, steered it into her mouth. When she released it, Lewis peered inside. "Hey!" he said. His face grew stern. "Where did you put Caroline?"

She patted her stomach, smiling, and Lewis gasped. "You *ate* Caroline!"

Caroline nodded. Her eyes, as she laughed, were as sharp and rich as light edging under a door.

The upstairs shower disengaged with a discrete shudder, and Lewis heard water suddenly gurgling through the throat of the kitchen sink. Mr. Mitchell dashed into the kitchen swinging a brown leather briefcase. He straightened his hat and drank a glass of orange juice. He skinned an apple with a paring knife. Its cortex spiraled cleanly away from the flesh and, when he left for work, it remained on the counter like a little green basket. "Six o'clock," said Mrs. Mitchell, plucking an umbrella from around a doorknob. "Seven at the outside. Think you can make it till then?" She kissed her daughter on the cheek, then waggled her earlobe with a fingertip. "Now you be a good girl, okay?" she said. She tucked a sheaf of papers into her purse and nodded goodbye, extending her umbrella as she stepped into the morning.

That day, as a gentle rain dotted the windows, Lewis swept the kitchen and vacuumed the carpets. He dusted the roofs of dormant appliances—the oven and the toaster, the pale, serene computer. He polished the bathroom faucets to a cool silver. When Caroline knocked a pair of ladybug magnets from the refrigerator, he showed her how to nudge them across a tabletop, one with the force of the other, by pressing them pole to common pole. "You see," he said, "there's something there. It looks like nothing, but you can feel it." In the living room, they watched a sequence of animated cartoons—nimble, symphonic, awash with color. Caroline sat at the base of the television, smoothing fields of static from its screen with her palm. They read a flap-book with an inset bunny. They assembled puzzles onto sheets of corkboard. They constructed a fortress with the cushions of the sofa; when bombed with an unabridged dictionary, it collapsed like the huskwood of an old fire.

That afternoon, the sky cleared to a proud, empty blue, and Lewis walked with Caroline to the park. The children there were pitching stones into a seething brown creek, fat with new rain, and the birds that wheeled above them looked like tiny parabolic *M*'s and *W*'s. The wind smelled of pine and wet asphalt.

Lewis strapped Caroline into the bucket of a high swing. He discovered a derelict kickball between two rocking horses and, standing before her, tossed it into the tip of her swing, striking her knee, her toe, her shin. "Do it 'gain," she said as the force of her momentum shot the ball past his shoulder, or sent it soaring like a loose balloon into the sky. It disappeared, finally, into a nest of brambles. Pushing Caroline from behind, Lewis watched her arc away from him and back, pausing before her return like a roller toy he'd once concocted from a coffee can and a rubber band. She weighed so little, and he knew that—if he chose—he could propel her around the axle of the swingset, that with a single robust shove she would spin like a second hand from twelve to twelve to twelve. Instead, he let her swing to a stop, her arms falling limp from the chains as she slowed. A foam sandal dangled uncertainly from her big toe. Her head lolled onto her chest. She was, suddenly, asleep. As Lewis lifted her from the harness, she relaxed into a broad yawn, the tip of her tongue settling gently between her teeth. He carried her home.

After he had put her to bed, Lewis drew the curtains against the afternoon sun and pulled a small yellow table to her side. He sat watching her for a moment. Her breath sighed over her pillowcase, the turn of fabric nearest her lips flitting slightly with each exhalation. She reached for a stuffed bear, cradling it to her heart, and her eyes began to jog behind their lids. Gingerly, Lewis pressed a finger to one of them—he could feel it twitching at his touch like a chick rolling over in its egg. What could she be dreaming, he wondered, and would she remember when she woke? How could something so close be so hidden? And how was it that in the light of such a question we could each of us hold out hope—search eyes as dark as winter for the flicker of intimacy, dream of seizing one another in a fit of recognition? As he walked silently from her bedroom, Lewis lifted from the toyshelf a red plastic See 'n Say, its face wreathed with calling animals. In the hallway, he trained its index on the picture of a lion, depressing the lever cocked at its frame. *This,* said the machine, *is a robin,* and it whittered a little aria. When he turned the dial to a picture of a lamb on a tussock of grass, it said the same thing. Dog and pony, monkey and elephant: *robin—twit twit whistle.* Lewis set the toy against a wall, listening to the cough of a receding car. He passed through the dining room and climbed the back stairway, wandered the deep and inviolate landscape of the house—solemn with the thought of faulty lessons, and of how often we are shaped in this way.

An old story tells of a man who grew so fond of the sky—of the clouds like hills and the shadows of hills, of the birds like notes of music and the stars like distant blessings—that he made of his heart a kite and sailed it into the firmament. There he felt the high mechanical tug of the air. The sunlight rushed through him, and the sharp blue wind, and the world seemed a far and a learnable thing. His gaze (the story continues) he tethered like a long string to his heart—and never looking down, lest he pull himself to earth, he wandered the world ever after in search of his feet.

Talking about love, I suspect, is much like this story. What is it, then, that insists that we make the attempt? The hope of some new vision? The drive for words and order? We've been handed a map whose roads lead to a place we understand: *Now,* says a voice, *disentangle them.* And though we fear that we will lose our way, still, there is this wish to try. Perhaps, though, if we allow our perceptions of love to brighten and fade as they will, allow it even if they glow no longer than a spark launched from a fire, perhaps we will not pull our heart from its course: surely this is possible.

My love for Caroline, then, is what slows me into sleep at night. It is a system of faith inhabiting some part of me that's deeper than I've traveled. The thought of her fills me with comfort and balance, like heat spilling from the floor register of an old building. Her existence at this moment, alongside me in time—unhesitating and sure—all of this, the *now* of her, is what stirs through me when I fail. My love for Caroline is the lens through which I see the world, and the world through that lens is a place whose existence addresses the fact of my own.

Caroline chews crayons—red like a firetruck, green like a river, silver like the light from passing airplanes—and there's something in my love for her that speaks this same urge: I want to receive the world inside me. My love for Caroline is the wish that we might spend our lives together: marry in a hail of rice, watch the childhood of our children disappear, and think to ourselves someday: when this person is gone, no one in all the world will remember the things I remember.

Salient point is an early and sadly obsolete term for the heart as it first appears in the embryo: I fell upon it in a book of classical obstetrics with a sense of celebration. The heart, I believe, is that point where we merge with the universe. It is salient as a jet of water is salient—leaping continually upward—and salient as an angle is salient—its vertex projecting into this world, its limbs fanning out behind the frame of another. What I love of Caroline is that space of her at rest behind the heart—true and immanent, hidden and vast, the arc that this angle subtends.

I would like to cobble such few sentences into a tower, placing them in the world, so that I might absorb what I can of these things in a glance. But when we say *I love you,* we say it not to shape the world. We say it because there's a wind singing through us that knows it to be true—and because even when we speak them without shrewdness or understanding, it is good, we know, to say these things.

The dishwasher thrummed in the kitchen, and the thermostat ticked in the hallway, and the dryer called from the basement like a tittuping horse. Caroline lay on the silver-gray carpet, winking each eye in turn as she scrutinized her thumb. Her hair was drawn through the teeth of a barrette, and the chest of her shirt was pulled taut beneath one arm. Lewis could see her heartbeat welling through the gate of her ribs. It called up in him the memory of a time when, as a schoolboy, his teacher had allowed him to hold the battery lamp during a power failure. He had lain on the floor, balancing the lamp atop his chest, and everywhere in the slate-black schoolroom the light had pulsed with his heart. Like a shaken belief or a damaged affection, the life within such a moment could seem all but irreclaimable.

The seconds swayed past in the bob-weight of the grandfather clock.

"Come here," said Lewis, beckoning to Caroline, and when she'd settled into his lap, he told her this story: In a town between a forest and the sea there lived a clever and gracious little girl. She liked to play with spoons and old buttons, to swat lump-bugs and jump over things, and her name was Caroline.

("I don' like *spoons,*" said Caroline. *Spoons?* said Lewis. *Did I say spoons? I meant goons.* Caroline giggled and shook her head. "No-*o.*" *Prunes?* "Nuh-uh." *Baboons?* Caroline paused to consider this, her finger paddling lazily against her shirt collar. "Okay.")

So then: Caroline, who played with buttons and baboons, had all the hours from sun to moon to wander the city as she wished, scratching burrs from her socks or thumping dandelion heads. The grownups offered her but one caution: if ever the sky should threaten rain, the clouds begin to grumble, or the wind blow suddenly colder, she must hurry indoors. The grownups had good reason to extend such a warning, for the town in which they lived was made entirely of soap. It had been whittled and sliced from the Great Soap Mountains. There were soaphouses and soapscrapers, chains of soap lampposts above wide soap roadways, and in the town center, on a pedestal of marbled soap, a rendering of a soapminer, his long proud shovel at his side. Sometimes, when the dark sky ruptured and the rains came daggering across the land, those of the town who had not taken shelter—the tired and the lost, the poky and the dreamy—would vanish, never to return. "Washed clean away," old-timers would declare, nodding sagely.

One day, Caroline was gathering soapberries from a glade at the lip of the forest. Great somber clouds, their bellies black with rain, had been weltering in from the ocean for hours, but she paid them no mind: she had raced the rain before, and she could do it again. When a cloud discharged a hollow growl, she thought it was her stomach, hungry for soapberries—and so ate a few. When the wind began to swell and chill, she simply zippered her jacket. She bent to place a berry in her small blue hat and felt her skin pimpling at the nape of the neck, and when she stood again, the rain was upon her.

Caroline fled from the forest. She arrowed past haystacks and canting trees, past empty pavilions and blinking red stoplights. A porchgate wheeled on its hinges and slammed against a ventilation tank. A lamplight burst in a spray of orange sparks. *Almost,* thought Caroline, as her house, then her door, then the glowspeck of her doorbell came into view. And at just that moment, as she blasted past the bakery to her own front walk, a tremendous drift of soapsuds took hold of her from behind, whipping her up and toward the ocean.

When Caroline awoke, the sunlight was lamping over her weary body. Her skin was sticky with old soap. Thin whorls of air iridesced all around her. She shook her head, unfolded in a yawn, and watched a bluebird flap through a small round cloud beneath her left elbow. That was when she realized: she was bobbing through the sky inside a bubble! She tried to climb the inside membrane of the vessel, but it rolled her onto her nose. She prodded its septum with her finger and it stretched and recoiled, releasing a few airy driblets of soap that popped when she blew on them. *Bubble, indeed,* she thought—indignant, arms akimbo. Caroline (though a clever and a gracious little girl) could not think of a single solution to her dilemma—for if her craft were to erupt she would surely fall to earth, and if she fell to earth she would shatter like a snowball—so she settled into the bay of her bubble, watching the sky and munching the soapberries from her small blue hat.

There is little to see from so high in the air: clouds and stars and errant birds; the fields and the hills, the rivers and highways, as small and distinct as the creases in your palm. There is a time as the morning brightens when the lakes and rivers, catching the first light, will go silvering through the quiet black land. And in the evening, when the sun drops, a flawless horizon will prism its last flare into a haze of seven colors. Once, Caroline watched a man's heart sail by like a kite, once a golden satellite swerving past the moon. Preoccupied birds sometimes flew straight toward her—their wings stiff and open, their beaks like drawn swords—yawing away before they struck her bubble. On a chilly afternoon, an airplane passed so close that she counted nineteen passengers gaping at her through its windows, their colorless faces like a series of stills on a filmstrip. And on a delicate, breezy morning, as she stared through a veining of clouds at the land, Caroline noticed that the twists of color had faded from the walls of her bubble. Then, abruptly, it burst.

Caroline found herself plummeting like a buzz bomb from the sky, the squares of far houses growing larger and larger. Her hair strained upward against the fall, tugging at her scalp. Her cheeks beat like pennants in the wind. She shut her eyes. As for what became of her, no one is certain—or rather there are many tales, and many tellers, each as certain as the last. Some say she spun into the arms of a startled baboon, who raised her in the forest on coconuts and turnip roots. Some say she dropped onto the Caroline Islands, striking the beach in a spasm of sand, and so impressed the islanders with the enthusiasm of her arrival that with a mighty shout they proclaimed her Minister of Commerce. And some say she landed in this very house—on this very couch, in this very room—where I told her this story and put her to bed.

The human voice is an extraordinary thing: an alliance of will and breath that, without even the fastening of hands, can forge for us a home in other people. Air is sent trembling through the frame of the mouth, and we find ourselves admitted to some far, unlikely country: this must, I think, be regarded as nothing short of wondrous. The first voice I remember hearing belonged, perhaps, to a stranger or a lost relation, for I cannot place it within my family: it sounded like a wooden spool rolling on a wooden floor. My father had a voice like cement revolving in a drum, my mother like the whirring of many small wings. My own, I've been told, resembles the rustling of snow against a windowpane. What must the mother's voice—beneath the whisper of her lungs, beneath the little detonations of her heartbeat—sound like to the child in the womb? A noise without design or implication—as heedless as growth, as mechanical as thunder? Or the echo of some nascent word come quaking through the body? Is it the first intimation of another life cradling our own, a sign that suggests that this place is a someone? Or do children—arriving from some other, more insistent landscape—need such testimony? If the human voice itself does not evince a living soul, then that voice raised in song surely must.

Things go right, things go wrong/hearts may break but not for long/you will grow up proud and strong/sleepy little baby.

Of all the forms of voice and communion, a song is perhaps the least mediated by the intellect. It ropes its way through the tangle of our cautions, joining singer to listener like a vine between two trees. I once knew a man whose heart percussed in step with the music that he heard; he would not listen to drums played in hurried or irregular cadence; he left concerts and dances and parties, winced at passing cars, and telephoned his neighbors when they played their stereos too loudly—in the fear that with each unsteady beat he might malfunction. Song is an exchange exactly that immediate and physiological. It attests to the life of the singer through our skin and through our muscles, through the wind in our lungs and the fact of our own beating heart. The evidence of other spirits becomes that of our own body. Speech is sound shaped into meaning through words, inflection, and modulation. Music is sound shaped into meaning through melody, rhythm, and pitch. A song arises at the point where these two forces collide. But such an encounter can occur in more than one place. Where, then, is song most actual and rich—in the singer or in the audience?

Dream pretty dreams/touch beautiful things/let all the skies surround you/swim with the swans/and believe that upon/some glorious dawn love will find you.

A successful song comes to sing itself inside the listener. It is cellular and seismic, a wave coalescing in the mind and in the flesh. There is a message outside, and a message inside, and those messages are the same, like the pat and thud of two heartbeats, one within you, one surrounding. The message of the lullaby is that it's okay to dim the eyes for a time, to lose sight of yourself as you sleep and as you grow: if you drift—it says—you'll drift ashore: if you fall, you will fall into place.

And if you see some old fool/who looks like a friend/tell him good night old man/my friend.

Lewis stood with a washcloth before Caroline's highchair, its tray white with milk from a capsized tumbler. A streetlamp switched on outside the kitchen window, and as he turned to look, another did the same. The sun had left channels of pink and violet across the sky in which a few wavering stars were emerging. He could hear the rush of commuter traffic behind the dry autumn clicking of leaves—motor horns calling forlornly, a siren howling in the distance. The highchair stood like a harvest crab on its thin silver stilts. Lewis sopped the milk up from its tray and brushed the crumbs from its seat, rinsing his washcloth at the gurgling sink. All around the city—he thought, staring into the twilight—streetlamps were brightening one by one, generating warm electric purrs and rings of white light. From far above, as they blinked slowly on and off, they would look like rainwater striking the lid of a puddle.

In the living room, Caroline sat at the foot of the television, several inches from the screen, watching a small cartoon Martian chuckle perniciously as he fashioned an enormous ray gun. Lewis knelt beside her and, just for a moment, saw the black egg of the Martian's face shift beneath his gleaming helmet—but then his eyes began to tingle, and his perception flattened, and it was only a red-green-blueness of phosphorescent specks and the blade of his own nose. He flurried his hand through Caroline's hair, then pinched a dot of cookie from her cheek. "Sweetie," he said to her, standing. When his knees cracked, she started.

A set of cardboard blocks—red and blue and thick as bread loaves—were clustered before a reclining chair. They looked like something utterly defeated, a grove of pollard trees or the frame of a collapsed temple. Earlier in the day, Lewis had played a game with Caroline in which he stacked them two on two to the ceiling and she charged them, arms swinging, until they toppled to the carpet. Each time she rushed them, she would rumble like a speeding truck. Each time they fell she would laugh with excitement, bobbing up and down in a stiff little dance. She rarely tired of this game. As often as not, actually, she descended upon the structure in a sort of ambush before it was complete: Lewis would stoop to collect another block, hear the drum of running feet, and down they would go. Now, as she peered at the television, he stacked the blocks into two narrow columns, each its own color, and bridged them carefully at the peak; satisfied, he lapsed onto the sofa.

Propping his glasses against his forehead, he yawned and pressed his palms to his eyes. Grains of light sailed through the darkness, like snow surprised by a headlamp, and when he looked out at the world again, Caroline had made her way to his side. She flickered her hands and burbled a few quick syllables, her arms swaying above her like the runners of a sea plant: in her language of blurt and gesture, this meant *carry me,* or *hold me,* or *pick me up*—and swinging into her, Lewis did just that. She stood in his lap, balancing with one smooth-socked foot on either thigh, and reached for his forehead. " 'Lasses," she said. Lewis removed his glasses, handing them to her, and answered, "That's right." An ice-white bloom of television flashed from each lens as Caroline turned them around in her palms. When she pressed them to her face, the stems floated inches from her ears; then they slipped past her nose and hitched around her shoulders, hanging there like a necklace or a bow tie. Lewis felt himself smiling as he retrieved them. He polished them on the tail of his shirt and returned them to their rightful perch.

He looked up to find Caroline losing her balance, foundering toward him. Her foot slid off his leg onto the sofa and her arms lurched up from her side. "Whoa," he said, catching her. "You okay?" She tottered back onto his lap, her head pressing against his cheek. He could feel the dry warmth of her skin, the arching of her eyebrows, the whiffet of her breath across his face. Then, straightening, she kissed him. The flat of her tongue passed up his chin and over his lips, and, stopping at the ledge of his nose, inverted and traveled back down. Lewis could feel it tensed against him like a spring, and when it swept across the crest of his lips, he lightly kissed its tip. Caroline closed her mouth with a tiny pecking sound. She sniffled, brushed her nose, and settled into him. " 'Lasses," she said, and her warm brown hair fell against his collarbone. Lewis blinked and touched a finger to his dampened chin. His ears were tingling as if from a breeze. His head was humming like a long flat roadway.

From the front porch came the rattle of house keys. As the bolt-lock retracted with a ready chink, Caroline dropped to his lap. She turned to watch the television and pillowed her head on his stomach.

"Home!" called Mr. Mitchell, and the door clapped shut behind him.

My brother is three years my senior. When I was first learning to speak, he was the only person to whom my tongue taps and labial stops seemed a language. I would dispense a little train of stochastic syllables—*pa ba mi da,* for instance—and he would translate, for the benefit of my parents: *he wants some more applesauce.* My brother understood me, chiefly, from basic sympathy and the will to understand: the world, I am certain, responds to such forces. It was in this fashion that I knew what Caroline told me—though when she said it she was mumbling up from sleep, and though it sounded to the ear as much like *igloo* or *allegory*—when with a quiet and perfect affection she said, "I love you."

With fingers spidery weak from the cold, Lewis worked the tag of Caroline's zipper into its slide, fastening her jacket with a tidy *zzzt*. He tightened her laces, straightened her mittens, and wiped her nose with a tissue. He adjusted her socks and trousers, and the buttonless blue puff of her hood. "All right," he said, patting her back. "Off you go." Caroline scampered for the sandbox, her hood flipping from her head to bob along behind her. When she crossed its ledge, she stood for a moment in silence. Then she growled like a bear and gave an angry stamp, felling a hillock of abandoned sand. Lewis watched her from a concrete bench. She found a small pink shovel and arranged a mound of sand into four piles, one at each rail, as if ladling out soup at a dinner table. She buried her left foot and kicked a flurry of grit onto the grass.

Brown leaves shot with threads of red and yellow skittered across the park. They swept past merry-go-rounds and picnic tables, past heavy gray stones and rotunda bars. A man and his daughter tottered on a seesaw, a knot of sunlight shuttling along the rod between them like a bubble in a tube of water. Two boys were bouncing tennis balls in the parking lot—hurling them against the asphalt and watching them leap into the sky—and another was descending a decrepit wire fence, its mesh of tendons loose and wobbling. Caroline sat on her knees in the sandbox, burrowing: she unearthed leaves and acorns and pebbles, a shiny screw-top bottlecap and her small pink shovel. A boy with freckles and cowboy boots joined her with a grimace, a ring of white diaper peering from above his pants. His mother handed him a plastic bucket, tousling his plume of tall red hair. "Now you play nice," she told him, and sat next to Lewis on the bench. She withdrew a soda can from her purse, popping its tab and sipping round the edge of its lid. Caroline placed her bottlecap in her shovel, then scolded it—*no, no, no*—and tipped it to the side. The woman on the bench turned to Lewis—gesturing cheerily, nonchalantly. "Your daughter is a*dor*able," she said.

For a moment Lewis didn't know how to respond. He felt a strange coldness shivering up from inside him: it was as if his body were a window, suddenly unlatched, and beyond it was the hard aspen wind of December. Then the sensation dwindled, and his voice took hold of him. "Thanks," he said. "She's not mine, but thank you."

The woman crossed her legs, tapping her soda can with a lacquered red fingernail. "So," she asked, "you're an uncle, then?"

"Sitter."

From the back of her throat came a high little interrogatory *mm*. In the sandbox, her son slid his plastic bucket over his head. *Echo,* he hollered, his face concealed in its trough: *echo, echo, echo.* He was the sort of boy one might expect to find marching loudly into weddings and libraries, chanting the theme songs from television comedies and striking a metal pan with a wooden spoon. "I'm Brooke," said the woman, bending to set her soda can at her feet. "And you are . . . ?"

"Lewis."

She nodded then rummaged in her purse, a sack of brown woven straw as large as a bed pillow. "Would you like some gum, Lewis? I know it's in here somewhere." Her son lumbered over to Caroline and clapped his bucket over her head. It hit with a loud thumping sound. Lewis, watching, stepped to her side and removed it, then hoisted her to his shoulder as she began to cry.

The woman on the bench glanced up from her purse. "Alex*ander,*" she exclaimed. She stomped to the sandbox in counterfeit anger. "*What* did you do?" The boy glowered, his mouth pinching shut like the spiracle of a balloon. He threw the small pink shovel at a litter bin and began punching his left arm. "*That* settles it," said his mother, pointing. "No more fits today from *you,* Mister. To the car."

"Your bucket," said Lewis—it was dangling from his right hand, fingers splayed against Caroline's back.

"Thanks," said the woman, hooking it into her purse. She waved as she left with her son.

Caroline was nuzzling against his neck, her arm folded onto her stomach. Her chest rose and fell against his own, and Lewis relaxed his breathing until they were moving in concert. He walked to a wooden picnic table and sat on its roof, brushing a few pine needles to the ground. The wind sighed through the trees, and the creek rippled past beneath a ridge of grass. Silver minnows paused and darted through its shallows, kinks of sunlight agitating atop the water like a sort of camouflage for their movements. Lewis tossed a pine cone into the current and watched it sail— scales flared and glistening—through a tiny cataract. An older couple, arms intertwined, passed by with their adolescent daughter. "I'm not sure I even be*lieve* in peace of mind," the girl was saying, her hands fluttering at her face as if to fend off a fly. He could hear Caroline slurping on her thumb. "You awake?" he asked, and she mumbled in affirmation. "Do you want to go home or do you want to stay here and play for a while?"

"Play," said Caroline.

Lewis planted her on her feet and, taking her by the hand, walked with her to the playground. A framework of chutes and tiered platforms sat in a bed of sand and gravel, and they climbed a net of ropes into its gallery. A steering wheel was bolted to a crossbeam at the forward deck, and when Caroline spun it, they beeped like horns and *whoa*ed from side to side. They snapped clots of sand from a handrail. They ran across a step-bridge swaying on its chains. A broad gleaming slide descended from a wooden shelf, its ramp speckled with dents and abrasions, and ascending a ladder to its peak, they swooped to the earth. They jumped from a bench onto an old brown stump and climbed a hill of painted rubber tires. They wheeled in slow circles on a merry-go-round, watched the world drift away and return—slide tree parking lot, slide tree parking lot—until their heads felt dizzy and buoyant, like the hollow metal globes that quiver atop radio antennas. Beside a bike rack and a fire hydrant, they discovered the calm blue mirror of a puddle; when Lewis breached it with a stone, they watched themselves pulse across the surface, wavering into pure geome-try. A spray of white clouds hovered against the sky, and an airplane drifted through them with a respiratory hush. "Look," said Lewis, and Caroline followed the line of his finger. Behind the airplane were two sharp white condensation trails, cloven with blue sky, that flared and dwindled like the afterlight of a sparkler. Watching, Lewis was seized with a sudden and inexplicable sense of presence, as if weeks and miles of sur-rounding time and space had contracted around this place, this moment. "My God," he said, and filled his lungs with the rusty autumn air. "Look what we can do."

A man with a stout black camera was taking pictures of the playground equipment. He drew carefully toward the slide and the seesaw, the mon-key bars and tire-swings, altering his focus and releasing the shutter. Each print emerged from a vent at the base of the camera, humming into sight on a square of white paper. Lewis approached the man and, nodding to Caroline, asked if he might borrow the device for a moment. "Just one picture?" he asked, his head cocked eagerly. "Well," said the man—and he shrugged, giving a little flutter with his index finger. "Okay. One."

Caroline had wandered in pursuit of a whirling leaf to the foot of a small green cypress tree. Its bough was pierced with the afternoon sunlight, and she gazed into the crook of its lowest branches. A flickertail squirrel lay there batting a cone. She raised a mittened hand to her eyes, squinting, and when Lewis snapped her picture, a leaf tumbled onto her forehead.

"Your daughter," said the man, collecting his camera, "is very pretty."

Lewis stared into the empty white photograph. "Thank you," he said. He blew across its face until the dim gray ghost of a tree appeared. "She is."

Though it often arises in my memories and dreams, I have not returned to the playground in many days. It is certain to have changed, however minutely, and this is what keeps me away. Were I to visit, I might find the rocking horse rusted on its heavy iron spring, the sidewalk marked with the black prints of leaves, the swings wrapped higher around their cross-bars—and though they seem such small things, I'd rather not see them. The sand may have spilled past the lip of the sandbox, and the creek may have eaten away at its banks. The cypress tree might have been taken by a saw or risen a few inches closer to the sun. Perhaps a pair of lovers have carved their signet into its bark—a heart and a cross, or a square of initials. My fear, though, is that the park has simply paled with all its contents into an embryonic white—that, flattening like a photograph too long exposed, it has curled at its edges and blown away. In my thoughts, though, it grows brighter each day, fresher and finer and more distinct, away from my remembering eyes.

Caroline was nestled in bubbles. Sissing white hills of them gathered and rose, rolling from the faucet to each bank of the tub. They streamed like clouds across the water, rarefying as they accumulated—as those bubbles in the center, collapsing, coalesced into other, slightly larger bubbles, which themselves collapsed into still larger bubbles, and those into still larger (as if a cluster of grapes were to become, suddenly, one large grape), which, bursting, opened tiny chutes and flumes to the exterior—and there sat Caroline, hidden in the thick of them, the tips of her hair afloat on the surface. When she scissored her feet, the great mass of the bubbles swayed atop the water. When she twitched her arm, a little boat of froth released itself from the drift, sailing through the air into a box of tissues. She looked as if she had been planted to her shoulders in snow.

Lewis shut the water off, and the foam that had been rippling away from the head of the tub spread flat, like folds of loose skin drawing suddenly taut. The silence of the faucet left the bathroom loud with hums and whispers—intimate noises were made vibrant and bold: effervescing bubbles, gentle whiffs of breath, metal pipes ticking in the walls. Caroline leaned forward and blew a cove the size of her thumb into a mound of bubbles. The bathwater, swaying with her motion, rocked the mound back upon her, and when she blinked up from inside it, her face was wreathed in white. Lewis pinched the soap from her eyelashes. He cleaned her with a hand towel—brushed the swell of her cheeks and the bead of her nose—and dropped her rubber duck into the bubbles. It struck the water with a *ploop,* then emerged from the glittering suds. "Wack, wack," said Caroline, as it floated into her collarbone. She pulled it to the floor of the tub and watched it hop to the surface.

Lewis squirted a dollop of pink shampoo into his palm and worked it through the flurry of her hair. Its chestnut brown, darkened with water, hung in easy curves along her neck and her cheek and in the dip of skin behind each ear. His fingers, lacing through it, looked as white as slants of moonlight. He flared and collapsed them, rubbing the shampoo into a rich lather, and touched the odd runnel of soap from her forehead. One day, as he was bathing her, a bleb of shampoo had streamed into her eye, and she had kept a hand pressed to it for the rest of the day, quailing away from him whenever he walked past. Ever since then, he had been careful to roll the soap back from her face as it thickened, snapping it into the tub. When it came time to rinse, Caroline tilted her head back and shut her eyes so tightly that they shivered. Lewis braced her in the water, his palm against the smooth of her back.

With a green cotton washcloth and a bar of flecked soap, he washed her chin and her jaw, her round dimpled elbows, the small of her back and the spine of her foot. His sleeves were drawn to his upper arms, his fingertips slowly crimping. His hands passed from station to station with careful diligent presses and strokes. Caroline paddled her duck through the water, then squeezed it and watched the air bubble from under its belly. He washed her arms and her legs and the soft small bowl of her stomach. He washed the hollows of her knees, soaped her neck and soaped her chest, and felt her heart, the size of a robin's egg, pounding beneath him. Her heart, he thought, was driving her blood, and her blood was sustaining her cells, and her cells were investing her body with time. He washed her shoulder blades and the walls of her torso and imagined them expanding as she grew: her muscles would band and bundle, her bones flare open like the frame of an umbrella. He washed the shallow white shoulders that would take on curve and breadth, the waist that would taper, the hips that would round. The vents and breaches, valleys and slopes, that would become as rare and significant to some new husband as they now were to him. The face that, through the measure of its creases, would someday reveal by accident what it now revealed by intent: the feelings that were traveling through her life. He washed her fragile, dissilient, pink-fingered hands. The hands that would unfold and color with age. The hands that would learn how to catch a ball and knot a shoelace, how to hold a pencil and unlock a door—how to drive a car, how to wave farewell, how to shake hello. The hands that would learn how to touch another person, how to carry a child, and on some far day how to die.

The water was lapping against the wall of the tub. Lewis found himself gazing into the twitch of his reflection: his lips and eyes were tense with thought beside a reef of dissipating bubbles. Caroline watched for a moment, then splashed him with a palm of cupped water. When Lewis looked at her through the tiny wet globes that dotted his glasses, she laughed, and he felt some weary thing inside of him ascend and disperse, like fog lifting from a bay. He polished his glasses and his mouth curled into a smile.

When he pulled the bath plug, Caroline started—surprised, as she often was, by the sudden deep gurgle and surge. He welcomed her into the wings of a towel as the water serpent-whirled into the drain.

SUMS

Number of days we spent together: 144. Number of days we spent apart (supposing that Archbiship James Usher of Meath, who calculated the date of the Creation at 23 October 4004 BC, was correct): 2,195,195. Number of days since I last saw her: 43. Number of days since I began writing this story: 3. Number of days in her life thus far: 613. Number of days in mine thus far: 12,418; projected: 12,419. Number of times we walked to the park: 102. Number of swings on the swingset there: 3; strap swings: 2; bucket swings: 1. Number of times she rode the bucket swing: 77; the strap swing: 1. Number of times she rode the strap swing and fell: 1. Number of times I pushed her on the bucket swing, average per session: 22; total: 1,694. Number of puzzles we constructed: 194. Number of towers we assembled from large cardboard blocks: 112; demolished: 111. Number of stories I told: 58. Number of diapers I changed: 517. Number of lullabies I sang: 64. Number of days I watched while Caroline napped, Caroline: 74; the television: 23; the sky: 7. Number of times, since we met, that I've laundered my clothing: 93; that I've finished a book: 19; that I've heard songs on the radio with her name in them: 17 (*good times never felt so good:* 9; *where did your long hair go?:* 2; a song I don't know whose chorus chants *Caroline Caroline Caroline* in a voice like the clittering of dice in a cup: 6). Number of footlong sandwiches I've eaten since we met: 12. Number of Lewises it would take to equal in height the number of footlong sandwiches I've eaten since we met: 2.1; number of Carolines: 4.9. Number of times I've thought today about the color of my walls: 2; about the shape of my chin: 1; about airplanes: 4; about mirrors: 3; about the inset mirror in one of Caroline's flap-books: 1; about Caroline and the turn of her lips: 6; about Caroline and macaroni and cheese: 1; about how difficult it can be to separate one thought from another: 1; about Caroline and moths and childhood fears: 4; about my childhood fear of being drawn through the grate of an escalator: 1; about my childhood fear of being slurped down the drain of a bathtub: 2; about eyes: 9; about hands: 6; about hands, mine: 3. Number of lies I've told you: 2. Number of lies I've told you about my behavior toward Caroline: 0; about fairy tales: 0; about Nabokov: 1. Number of times I've dreamt about her: 14; pleasant: 12. Number of times I've dreamt about her mother: 3; nightmares: 3. Number of nightmares I recall having had in my life: 17. Number of hours I've spent this month: 163; in vain: 163.

Lewis tidied the house while Caroline napped, gathering her toys from the kitchen and the bathroom, the stairway and the den. He collected them in the fold of his arms and quietly assembled them on her toyshelves. Warm air breathed from the ceiling vents and sunlight ribboned in through the living-room windows, striking in its path a thousand little whirling constellations of dust. Lewis pulled a xylophone trolley from under the couch. He stacked rainbow quoits onto a white peg.

He carried a pinwheel and a rag doll from the hallway and slipped a set of multiform plastic blocks into the multiform sockets of a block-box. He walked from the oven to the coatrack, from the coatrack to the grandfather clock, fossicking about for the last of a set of three tennis balls, and, finding it behind the laundry hamper, he pressed it into its canister. Then he held the canister to his face, breathing in its flat clean scent before he shelved it in the closet of the master bedroom. Lewis often felt, upon entering this room, as if he had discovered a place that was not an aspect of the house that he knew—someplace dark and still and barren: a cavern or a sepulcher, a tremendous empty seashell. The venetian blinds were always sealed, the curtains drawn shut around them, and both were overshadowed by a fat gray oak tree. The ceiling lamp cast a dim orange light, nebular and sparse, over the bed and the dressers and the carpet. Lewis fell back on the bedspread. The cable of an electric blanket bore into his shoulder, and his head lay in a shallow channel in the center of the mattress—formed, he presumed, by the weight of a sleeping body. He yawned, drumming his hand on his chest, and listened to the sigh of a passing car. He gazed into the tiny red eye of a smoke alarm.

When he left to look in on Caroline, he found her sleeping contentedly, her thumb in her mouth. A stuffed piglet curled from beneath her, its pink snout and the tabs of its ears brushing past her stomach. Her back rose and fell like a parachute tent. He softly shut her door. Returning to the living room, he bent to place a stray red checker in his shirt pocket, then straightened and gave a start: her mother was there, sitting on the sofa and blinking into space. Lisa Mitchell rarely arrived home before the moon was as sharp as a blade in the night sky, never once before evening. Now she sat clutching a small leather purse in her lap, and a stream of sunlight delineated each thread of her hair. It was midafternoon.

"Early day?" asked Lewis. He removed a jack-in-the-box from the arm of a chair, sealing the lid on its unsprung clown. Lisa Mitchell neither moved nor spoke; she simply held her purse and stared. "Hello . . . ?" he tested. She sat motionless, queerly mute, like a table lamp or a podium. Then her shoulders gave a single tight spasm, as if an insect had buzzed onto the nape of her neck, and her eyes glassed with tears. Lewis felt, suddenly, understanding and small and human. "Do you need anything?" he asked. "Some water?" Lisa drew a quick high breath and nodded.

Lewis rinsed a glass in the kitchen sink, then filled it from a bay on the door of the refrigerator, watching the crushed ice and a finger of water issue from a narrow spout. When he handed it to Lisa, she sipped until her mouth pooled full, swallowed, and placed it on a side table. Her fingertips left transparent annulets across the moist bank of the glass, her lips a wine-red crescent at its rim. Lewis sat next to her on the sofa. "Do you want to talk about it?" he asked. His voice had become as gentle as the aspiration of the ceiling vents.

"I . . . ," said Lisa, and the corner of her mouth twitched. "He said I . . ." Her throat gave out a little clicking noise. She trifled with the apron of her purse—snapping it open and shut, open and shut. "I lost my job," she said. And at this she sagged in on herself, shaking, and began to weep. Her head swayed, and her back lurched, and she pressed her hands to her eyes. When Lewis touched a finger to her arm, she fell against him, quaking.

"It's okay," he said. "It will all be okay." Resting against his shoulder, Lisa cried and shivered and slowly grew still. Her purse dropped to the floor as she relaxed into a sequence of calm, heavy breaths. Then, abruptly, she was crying once again. She wavered in this way—between moments of peace and trepidation—for what seemed an hour, as the white midday light slowly windowed across the carpet. After she had fallen quiet, Lewis held her and listened to her breathing. (She sighed placidly, flurrying puffs of air through her nose; she freed a little string of hiccups that seemed both deeply organic and strangely mechanical.) The sleeve of his shirt, steeped with her tears, was clinging to his upper arm, and his hand was pinpricking awake on her back. He could feel the warm pressure of her head against his collarbone. When she shifted on the cushions, he swallowed, listening to the drumbeat of his heart. He slid his fingers over the rungs of her spine, smoothing the ripples from her blouse, and she seemed to subside into the bedding of the sofa. It was as if she were suddenly just a weight within her clothing, suspended by a hanger from his shoulder, and he thought for a moment that she had fallen asleep—but, when she blinked, he felt the soft flicker of her eyelashes against his neck. Her stockings, sleek and coffee brown, were beginning to ladder at the knee, and Lewis reached to touch a ravel of loose nylon. He found himself instead curling a hand through her hair.

Lisa lifted her head, looking him in the eye, as his fingers swept across a rise in her scalp. He felt her breath mingling with his own. Her eyes, drawing near, were azure blue, and walled in black, and staring into his own. They seemed to hover before him like splashes of reflected light, and Lewis wondered what they saw. The tip of her nose met with his, and when she licked her lips, he felt her tongue glance across his chin. His lips were dry and tingling, his stomach as tight as a seedpod. When his hand gave a reflexive flutter on her back, Lisa stiffened.

She tilted away from him, blinking, the stones of her teeth pressing into her lip. The grandfather clock voiced three vibrant chimes, and she stood and planed her blouse into the waist of her skirt.

When she looked down upon him, her eyes were like jigsawed glass. "I think you'd better go now," she said.

Certain places are penetrated with elements of the human spirit. They act as concrete demonstrations of our hungers and capacities. A sudden field in the thick of a forest is a place like reverence, a stand of corn a place like knowledge, a clock tower a place like fury. I have witnessed this and know it to be true. Caroline's house was a place like memory—a place, in fact, like my memory of her: charged with hope and loss and fascination. As I stepped each morning through her front door, I saw the wall peg hung with a weathered felt hat, the ceiling dotted with stucco, the staircase folding from floor to floor, and it was as if these things were quickened with both her presence and her ultimate departure. The stationary bicycle with its whirring front fan wheel and the dining room table with its white lace spread, the desk cup bristling with pencils and pens and the books shelved neatly between ornamental bookends: these were the hills and trees and markers of a landscape that harbored and kept her. The windows were the windows whose panes she would print with her fingers. The doorstop was the doorstop whose spring she would flitter by its crown. The lamps were the lamps in whose light she would study for school. The sofa was the sofa in whose lap she would grow toward adulthood. The mirrors: the mirrors there were backed in silver and framed us in the thick of her house. Yet when we viewed the world inside of them, we did not think *here is this place made silver,* but simply *here is this place:* what does this suggest, we wondered, about the nature of material existence? When I was a small boy, I feared my attic. A ladder depended from a hatch in the hallway, and when my father scaled it into the darkness, I believed, despite the firm white evidence of the ceiling, that he was entering a chamber without a floor. A narrow wooden platform extended into open space, and beneath it lay the deep hidden well of my house: I could see this when I closed my eyes. Though Caroline's house suggested no such fear, it was informed by a similar logic of space: the floors and partitions, the shadows and doorways, were each of them rich with latent dimensions.

It is exactly this sense of latitude and secret depth that my own house is missing. The objects here are only what they are, with nothing to mediate the fact of their existence with the fact of their existence in my life. The walls may be the same hollow blue as a glacier, the carpet as dark as the gravid black sea, and I may be as slight as a boat that skirts the pass—but the walls are only walls, the carpet only carpet, and I am only and ever myself. In the evening, as the sun dwindles to a final red wire at the horizon, I switch on every light and lamp but still my house mushrooms with shadow. I walk from room to room, and everything that belongs to me drifts by like a mist—the wooden shelves banded with book spines, the shoes aligned in the closet, the rounded gray stone that I've carried for years . . . they are my life's little accidents, a sediment trickled through from my past: they are nothing to do with me. I look, for instance, at the photograph framed on my desk: it sports a slender green tree, and a piercing blue sky, and a light that is striking the face that I love—and how, I wonder, did I acquire such a thing? It is a gesture of hope simply to open the curtains each morning.

In truth, I don't know why it ended as it did. When Lewis arrives the next morning, the sun has not yet risen. The sidewalks are starred with mica, and the lawns are sheeted with frost, and the streetlamps glow with a clean white light. He steps to the front porch and presses the doorbell. When the door swings open, it is with such sudden violence that he briefly imagines it has been swallowed, pulled down the gullet of the wide front hall. Thomas Mitchell stands before him wearing striped red night clothes, his jaw rough with stubble. He has jostled the coatrack on his way to the door, and behind him it sways into the wall, then shudders upright on its wooden paws. He places his hand on the lock plate, thick blue veins roping down his forearm.

"We won't be requiring your services any longer," he says, and his eyebrows shelve together toward his nose, as in a child's drawing of an angry man.

"Pardon?" asks Lewis.

"We don't need you here anymore." He announces each syllable of each word, dispassionate and meticulous, as if reciting an oath before a silent courtroom. His body has not moved, only his mouth and eyes.

Lewis would like to ask why, but Thomas Mitchell, taut with bridled anger, stands before him like a dam—exactly that solemn, exactly that impassable—and he decides against it. *(You know why,* the man would say: Lewis can see the words pooled in writing across his features. And yet, though Lewis is coming to understand certain things—that his time here ran to a halt the day before, that his actions then were a form of betrayal—he does not, in fact, know anything.) Instead he asks, "Can I tell her goodbye?" and feels in his stomach a flutter of nervous grief.

"She's not here," says Thomas.

Lisa Mitchell's voice comes questioning from the depths of the house: "What's keeping you?"

Thomas clears his throat. He raises his hand from the lock plate, and his breath comes huffing through his nostrils like a plug of steam. "You can go now," he says, tightening his lips. "I don't expect to see you here again." Then, sliding back into the house, he shuts the door. The bolt lock engages with a heavy thunk.

Lewis does not know where to go or what to do. He feels like a man who, dashing into the post office to mail a letter, discovers his face on a wanted flyer. He stands staring at the doorbell—its orange glow like an ember in a settling fire—until he realizes that he is probably being watched. Glancing at the peephole, he feels the keen electric charge of a hidden gaze. Then he walks across the frost-silvered lawn to his car, his staggered footprints a dark rift in the grass. Lewis drives to the end of the block and parks. He looks into the crux of his steering wheel, his hands tented over his temples, and wonders whether Caroline has been told that he won't be returning.

On the sidewalk, he passes a paperboy who is tossing his folded white missiles from a bicycle; they sail in neat arcs through the air, striking porches and driveways with a leathery slap. Lewis walks around the house to the window of Caroline's bedroom, his heart librating in his chest like a seesaw. The sun will soon rise from behind the curved belly of the fields. The frost will dissipate in the slow heat of morning, and his footprints will dwindle into the green of the lawn.

Caroline is awake in her bed, a sharp light streaming across her face from the open bedroom door. Her pacifier falls from her mouth as she yawns. She wiggles in a pair of fuzzy blue pajamas. Lewis presses himself to the brick of the house and watches her for a few moments. Her body casts a wide shadow over her rumpled yellow bedspread, and it looks as if there is an additional head—his—on the pillow next to hers. He touches his fingers to the window. When he curves and sways them, they look like the spindled legs of an insect. He wants to rap against the glass, to pry it from its frame, to reach across Caroline's blankets and pull her into his arms, but he doesn't.

Instead, he lowers his hand to his side, where it hangs like a plummet on a string, and as a hazy form moves into the glare of the doorway, he turns and retreats to his car. Driving away, he spots a filament of dawn sunlight in the basin of the side-view mirror. He will realize as he slows into his driveway that he has just performed one of the most truly contemptible acts of his life. If he were a good man, he would have found a way, no matter the resistance, to tell her goodbye; to hand her like an offering some statement of his love; to leave her with at least this much. He could certainly have tried.

He did not, though. He simply left.

Memories and dreams are the two most potent methods by which the mind investigates itself. Both of them are held by what is not now happening in the world, both of them alert to their own internal motion. I have begun to imagine that they are the same transaction tilted along two separate paths—one into prior possibility, the other into projected. In one of my earliest memories, I am walking through a wooded park with a teacher and my classmates. I carry in my hands a swollen rubber balloon, cherry red and inflated with helium. I don't know where it was purchased, whether it was mine or how long I'd held it, but it was almost as large as the trunk of my body—I remember that. Something jostles me, or my arm grows tired, and I lose my grip. I do not think to reach for the balloon until it has risen into the trees. It floats through a network of leaf-green branches and shrinks in the light of the midday sun. Soon it is only a grain of distant red, and then it vanishes altogether, leaving the blue sky blue and undisturbed.

Remembering this moment, I often dream of Caroline. I dream her resting in my lap and dream her swaying on the swingset. I dream that she is beside me, or I dream that she is approaching. One day, perhaps, we will flee together in my car. We will pass from this town into the rest of our lives, driving through the focus of the narrow black road. On bird-loud summer mornings, as a warm breeze rolls through our windows, we'll watch yellow-green grasshoppers pinging along the verge of the highway. In autumn, the leaves will fall red from the trees as our windshield blades fan away pepperings of rain. The heat will billow from our dashboard vents in winter, and the houses will chimney into the low gray sky. And on the easy, tonic nights of spring, we'll pull to the side of a quiet street and spread ourselves across our ticking hood: we'll watch the far white stars and the soaring red airplanes, ask *Which is the more beautiful, which the more true?*—and in finding our answers, we will find what we believe in.

Melissa Pritchard

Salve Regina

Every angel is terrifying.
—Rainer Maria Rilke

From *The Gettysburg Review*

NORAH LOFT tightened the scarlet strip with its notchings of white numbers around her naked hips. After two weeks of traversing the bedroom floor on her rear end—one hip thrusting out then the other, "walking" back and forth, back and forth—tonight's measurement mocked all her efforts. Stuffing the measuring tape into her ballerina jewelry box, Norah doused a cotton square with Bonnie Bell 1006 and drove it up and down her face as if she were cleaning a rug. She performed the eye widening exercises Lacey had shown her, convinced she was doing them backwards. Lacey liked to describe her own eyes as hopeless, small and too gray, like wet, dead guppies. Dropping on a rosebud-sprigged nightie, Norah skewered empty beer cans on her head, two on top, one on each side, three down the back, so her hair, by tomorrow morning, might almost resemble Lacey's.

Norah snapped off all the lights except the yellow bean-pot lamp on her nightstand. She's hated this room ever since her mother redecorated it in marigold yellows and orange, with the baffling and pointless theme of Spain. Directly over Norah's bed hung a framed travel poster showing a matador in pink balletic shoes, poised to gore a bull, ESPAÑA written in red letters down one side. Her only option was to ignore her surroundings, as if she were stranded in some foreign, second-rate motel. Now, removing her glasses and dropping to her knees, Norah began a fervent series of prayers to the Blessed Virgin Mary as set forth by Reverend Mother Stewart in one of her pocket-size booklets distributed by Holy Rood Press in Long Island. If Norah's dispute with her flesh had ended in yet another rout, then her will to acquire saintliness seemed, if only by mulish reaction, to be accelerating.

Mo and Mitzi Loft, Norah's parents, went on being pleased with last year's decision to send their only child, in her sophomore year, to a private school. Without appearing prejudiced, they had neatly sidestepped the issue of public school integration. Removing their daughter from a politically volatile climate insured Norah a superior education at the hands of nuns said to be the female equivalent of Jesuits. The Convent of the Sacred Heart was academically rigorous, the architecture impressive, the grounds parklike and secluded. And though she had never been to Europe, Mitzi exclaimed that the convent looked like something you would surely drive past in France, certainly Paris, where the mother school, Sacre Coeur, was said to still exist. This local convent was attended mainly by the daughters of wealthy capitalists, Catholics naturally, many of whom were boarders. Norah, neither a Catholic nor a boarder, rode her Sears bicycle to and from school each day.

Although there had been the possibility of a second private school in San Francisco, the Lofts deemed it less costly, wiser, to keep Norah home. Mo particularly wanted to supervise his daughter's orthodontia. As a dentist, the alignment of her teeth was of professional and even competitive concern to him. Mitzi felt this a little silly, overinvolved, but didn't think it politic to complain. After all, hadn't she met Morris when he had appeared with a group of dental students at the tooth factory in Scranton? Few people, the tour guide had said, stopping to ogle Mitzi, could appreciate the skill involved, sorting and matching teeth. As if on cue, Mitzi had glanced up from her task of pairing three hundred adult male incisors and paralyzed Mo, or so he would forever claim, by smiling directly, blazingly, at him. People didn't realize, the guide continued, how many thousands of teeth, made here in Scranton, were shipped overseas—even as the demand for false teeth dropped in the United States, other parts of the world, and England especially, where people lost as many teeth as ever. In the midst of this, Mo and Mitzi exchanged phone numbers. Eventually they married and moved to California, where Mitzi embarked upon the long and occasionally gratifying process of reinventing herself. The Lofts were Goldwater Republicans, members of the Menlo Country Club, and Mitzi herself kept up with several vaguely prestigious volunteer activities as well as her monthly bridge group, referred to affectionately by its eight members as "Sherry & Therapy."

Mitzi Loft had done well; at the moment, fifteen-year-old Norah was her single vexation. The child was stiff-limbed, morose, socially regressive. Stepping into Norah's room yesterday afternoon to put up the Costa Brava travel poster she'd had reframed in yellow, Mitzi literally stumbled over an untidy heap of religious paraphernalia sticking out from under the orange chenille bedspread. A gloomy-looking black and silver rosary, half a dozen dogeared prayer booklets written in zealous purple prose, three holy cards—one with the image of a crown of thorns wrapped around a heart spurting blood—and of all dreary things, a cheap black face veil. She didn't dare tell Morris.

In the best of times, Mo referred to himself as an agnostic; in the worst, a hard-boiled cynic. His moods hinged entirely upon the state of his practice. What no one had warned her about was that dentists, after psychiatrists, had the highest rate of suicide. This terrified Mitzi, so she worked to keep her husband at a constant temperature, like a coddled egg. She had overcome his loudest objection to sending Norah to a convent, saying she would see to it that Norah did not convert, turn into a nun or a missionary in Calcutta; nothing religiously untoward would happen. Now this. Face veils. Rosaries. Thorns poking into hearts.

On a lesser note, Mitzi held out optimism that in a school of girls all wearing the same dull, triangular blue skirts and god-awful cropped boleros (uniforms imported from Cairo, Egypt, for pity's sake), Norah's homeliness would hardly distinguish itself. Behind convent walls, she might outgrow her ugly-ducklingness.

Riding her bicycle to school that first morning after Christmas vacation, Norah wore her new black knit cap and mittens. The brilliant winter air left her cheeks flushed and her eyes watering as she cycled past the gold-lettered sign, Sacre Coeur, past the spiked ironwork gates of the convent, as if she were departing one way of life, even one century, for another. The serpentine road she cycled along, bordered by semicircular beds of sky blue agapanthus and half-wild rose hedges splashed with scarlet, was irregularly shaded by thick stands of oak and feathery palms with regal, supple-seeming gray trunks. Norah rode up to the three-story building made of rose-colored granite with its great columned porte cochere, its crenellated towers and cupolas, feeling, spiritually at least, by way of sanctuary and relief, home. The Sacred Heart religious presided over their domain with the same century-old discipline established by the mother school in Paris. Theirs was a serene, fastidious government, the school and its vast estate sealed as if under a bell jar in an atmosphere rich and seductive, faintly erotic, where school rituals were called by their French names, *prime, gouter, congé*. By contrast, the Lofts' house was a show of modern, one-dimensional conformity. Neighbors commented on how well-kept it was, but to Norah, her home seemed an arid card house imbued with anxiety; indeed, she could scarcely distinguish its square rooms from her father's bland dental suites.

Leaving her bicycle in the small rack by the kitchen, Norah ascended a set of side stairs and went into the building. Passing the library, she went up yet another set of wide, red-carpeted stairs to the second floor, where she slipped into an alcove, knelt on a plain, wooden prie-dieu, and gazed up at the seated life-size figure of the Virgin. On an altar banked by green glass vases of thickly fleshed white lilies, Mary's indigo mantle fell in solemn, anchored folds over her pale rose gown. The twelve stars of the apocalypse encircled her humbly inclined head, and her canted gaze— Norah always felt it personally—was tender, brimming, enigmatic. The Virgin saw nothing, saw without judgment into the heart of everything.

Remember, O Most Gracious Virgin Mary, that never was it known, that anyone who fled to thy protection, implored thy help or sought thy intercession was left unaided. Inspired by this confidence, I fly to thee O Virgin of virgins, my mother; to thee I come, before thee I stand, sinful and sorrowful. O Mother of the word incarnate, despise not my petitions, but in thy mercy hear and answer me. Amen.

Norah left the alcove and stealthily went downstairs to the chapel. One of her most frequent prayers was to please not be seen in either place. The nuns would surely press for conversion, and the other girls, even Lacey, most of all Lacey, jaded from years of Catholic schooling, might tease her, or worse. The way the two queer girls were shunned was instruction enough. Rose and Deirdre. Norah had never spoken to them. Marooned on an ugly spar of talk, they clung tightly to the wreckage of one another, incurring further derision. No one actually knew if they were queer or not—rumor itself condemned them. On occasion Norah prayed for their souls, but like everyone else she was repulsed by their cowed, doughy faces, their moist, nail-bitten hands, their downcast expressions of shame. Norah had a secret terror of being like them. Not that she was queer, surely not— half the girls in the school had a crush on Mother Fitzgerald, she wasn't alone in that. It was this other, increasing devotion to Mary, to the Virgin (whose image Norah generally mixed up with Mother Fitzgerald's) that caused her to feel generally outcast and mildly disgraced. In the middle of her third academic year, Norah could not help being what she was, a diligent girl. Respected but plain. Never left out, never first to be included. Nun's pet. A model girl, intelligent, obedient, dull as dust.

Shortsighted even with her glasses, Norah, as she walked into the darkened chapel, made out a large, vague object—a table or so she thought— set before the altar. She walked straight up to it. The nun's freckled hands were modestly crossed, a plain black rosary wrapped around them, her black habit and white wimple stiff and pleated, a pair of gold pince-nez placed (as if she would need them!) over her closed eyes. She looked like a small human made of paper or a large doll made of powdered, papery flesh. With her heart flaring, Norah raced from the chapel, bolted up two flights of stairs to the study hall, and entered, breathless, from the back door just as Mother Fitzgerald, mistress of studies for the third and fourth academics, swept in from the front, her black skirts and long, sheer veil pulsing with sensual vitality behind her.

The third floor study hall was a high-ceilinged room, its cream-colored walls trimmed with varnished oak wainscoting. A row of tall, deeply recessed windows along the room's north side overlooked Palm Court, a circular patio area shaded by palm trees, where, during the more clement months of April and May, the girls ate their lunch, and in June, each year's graduating class held a small but elegant commencement ceremony.

Inside the pocket of her habit—designed after a nineteenth-century French mourning costume—Mother Fitzgerald carried a palm-size mahogany clapper, an instrument brought out and clicked in the manner of castanets, not with any rhythm of course, but to command silence, attention, obedience. She now used her clapper, as briskly and confidently as she did everything. As she mounted the platform and stood to one side of her wooden lectern, flanked by the American flag and large color photographs of John F. Kennedy, Jr. and Pope John XXIII, Mother Fitzgerald surveyed the sixty or so blue-uniformed girls seated before her. She was aware that some of them were infatuated with her, though none more so, or more obviously, than Norah Loft. She had been receiving small, delicately folded notes from Norah for weeks now, usually discussing points of theology. Mother Fitzgerald interpreted these as camouflaged love notes. Accustomed to receiving such notes from girls, along with sly, hot glances and small gifts, tokens of affection, she prayed regularly to be forgiven the deep sense of pleasure these aroused in her. She reminded herself that her main task was to take a misguided love and direct it to its true source, God. Still, and she felt some thrilling shame over this, she had saved each letter, each note, sweet evidence of her students' affection for her, in a small pine box with a key.

The girls, she announced, were to proceed down to chapel where they were to attend a funeral mass for Mother Logan, who had been living these past nine years in the nuns' retirement home. The convent's property was quite immense; beyond the main building, the girls were restricted to the tennis courts, hockey field, swimming pool and, on special occasions, the school's religious gardens, a damp, disorienting maze of grottoes where stained marble statues of St. Agnes, St. Joseph, Mater, Our Lady of Lourdes, all with voluptuous yet stern expressions, were enshrined then forgotten. None of the girls had ever been inside the retirement home; none of them knew Mother Logan. They were, said Mother Fitzgerald, her cheeks turning their irresistible rose color, to retrieve their missals and veils from their desks and form ranks. The ordinary school day, she added with a small, reassuring smile, would resume after Mass.

They filed past the closed coffin and, with black veils covering their young faces, knelt to receive communion. Norah sat alone, listening to the elderly nuns in the front two pews sing "*Salve Regina*" in rehearsed, silvery unison. Mantled in black, diminutive and round-shouldered, most wore the same gold pince-nez as Mother Logan and they seemed to have the same parsnip pallor. Except that they were upright, open-eyed, and harmonizing, Norah thought they were no different from their now dead companion. She could never imagine Mother Fitzgerald becoming this, turning into this, could not imagine everything distinctive and vitally exquisite about her stripped away. Perhaps that was the point. Perhaps it was a fact of becoming old. One's personality fell away.

Carrying a batch of essays on martyrdom to Reverend Mother's office as a favor for Mother Fitzgerald, Norah was surprised to see the crèche still in place weeks after Christmas. At the beginning of Advent, each girl's name was typed and glued, a paper girth, around the midsection of a small woolen lamb. The lambs, sixty or so, stood in a solid, snowy bank on the long bottom step of a series of shallow, green-felted stairs leading up to the manger. By Christmas Eve, they were all to have reached the top step, to assemble meekly before the holy family. But throughout the season, infractions of rules, the most minor lapses in conduct, were taken note of by the nuns until the flock was broken into punished, straggling ranks. A wild, refractory few lagged four or more steps behind. Norah's lamb, as it had the year before, ascended without incident or interruption to Jesus. Lacey Jenks's was detained five steps down, gazing sideways toward the lavatory, where she had twice been caught smoking. Far from being chastened, Lacey had laughed. She had been obedient for too many years, and where in the world, she asked Norah, had it gotten her?

Norah met Lacey Jenks at the fall tea her first year at Sacred Heart. Lacey had been appointed Norah's "Angel," to watch over and guide her. Despite Norah's resolution never to laugh at the expense of others, she took immediate guilty pleasure in her new friend's humor, a sly, sometimes sniping wit fed by unerring perception. It was Lacey who first pointed out that the backs of Madame Sesiche's legs were unshaven—you could see them when she turned to conjugate active and passive verbs on the blackboard—and that the music appreciation teacher, Miss Trammel, was going bald on the top of her head, a plight she failed to disguise with tortoise barrettes and artful shiftings of her part. And it was Lacey who told her about Mother Fitzgerald, who, it was rumored, the night before her wedding to the son of a Greek prince, took refuge in the convent, where she has been ever since.

Though it was never spoken of, another factor bound these two. Both Norah and Lacey rode bicycles to school, both were reminded in constant, subtle ways by their parents that private school was a privilege, that sacrifices were being made. The boarders, on the other hand, accustomed to an unvarying climate of wealth, were oblivious, even careless of its intimidating effect on girls like Norah and Lacey. No one spoke of money, yet friendships fell plainly along economic lines. The wealthier girls kept to themselves, while girls like Lacey and Norah found themselves unexpectedly and sometimes fiercely compatible.

From the very beginning, Mitzi had been unhappy with Norah's Angel. Lacey Jenks was a day student, her mother a city librarian, her father a retired army colonel. They lived in an older, slightly run-down section of Menlo Park. Why couldn't Norah have gotten one of the other girls, one of the Dial soap heiresses, for instance? While she tolerated the friendship between her daughter and this Lacey, she did little to encourage it. Several of the other girls Norah invited home at different times seemed pleasant enough, but these, too, Mitzi ascertained from a few calculated inquiries, were less than sterling liaisons. The task fell to Mitzi to chip out an acceptable social niche for her daughter. Currently, through her connections at the Menlo Country Club, she was lobbying for Norah's invitation to the upcoming cotillion. Were she to attend, her name might well appear in the society column of the *San Francisco Chronicle,* linked with those of local debutantes. She was horrified to see, however, that Norah's complexion was worsening. The crescent-shaped rash of pimples around her chin was migrating up toward her temples. Mo would have to agree to getting her into weekly acne treatments again. Though it gave Norah's skin something of the suggestion of a bad sunburn, the ultraviolet light worked wonders. Besides, Mitzi enjoyed flirting with the dermatologist, Dr. Ferraye. Flirting stabilized a marriage, and Mitzi had long been aware when she "dolled up"—Mo's phrase—to do her errands, men eagerly attended and things got done. She wished Norah could understand the efficiency, the pragmatism of beauty.

DEAR BOOBS,

Merci for your letter. I'm in a poopy mood but you're not ugly. You'd blush if you knew how cute you are. For lunch I had two pieces of white bread, one lamb and gravy, on other peanut butter and jelly. Thing of jello, five round teeny crackers, 500 cal. or more, ergo: no dinner. Ughy Ughy. Helen just asked me if I was writing an encyclopedia. What does life mean—what is love—I want to find out this weekend—Does

*Mother F. really hate me?—Miss Trammel forgot to put on D. O.—I
am a boob—I think I shall take down my girdle and go to pot. I hate
you cause you're everything I wish I could and should be—I have a hate
complex. Am I a boob? Do I look like a boob? Helen is upset cause I
won't let her read this and she thinks I am writing nasties about her. Je
ne sais quoi.*

I love you with all my toe. Respectful au revoirs, One Little Boob

Such notes to Norah had begun to change. Since the onset of her guitar lessons, Lacey's notes were dominated by someone named Arthur
Webb. Even her handwriting grew crimped and stupidly curlicued. For
Christmas, her parents had succumbed and given Lacey a Sears guitar
along with six months of paid lessons. Classical lessons, not what she'd
wanted, but as she told Norah, how else would she ever have met Arthur?
Her first lesson was at Kepler's, a small, popular music store in downtown
Menlo Park. Arthur, she wrote Norah, had taken her into a tiny, white
soundproof cubicle and, sitting inches away, demanded she open her legs
wide, no much wider, like so, the guitar had to lie properly across her lap.
He made her sing "On Top of Old Smokey" without any accompaniment,
in order to get, he said, some idea of her pitch. The whole time she was
singing he'd stared at her, his eyes narrowed. Arthur was a graduate student at San Francisco State College, and Lacey thought he was twenty-
three or -four, though she'd never asked. She'd brought a news clipping to
show Norah, a minuscule announcement of a recital, with his picture. But
Norah couldn't tell much; his face was blurred. The impression she got
was of two mournful eyes and a great mop of dark shaggy hair. Twice
Lacey asked Norah to come to the music shop, but Norah, reticent, embarrassed, said no. Much later, she would wish she had gone, had seen
them together, but some part of her dug in, was mad. She missed the old
notes, the sly, catty ones, the ones that made her laugh so hard she could
only hope to be forgiven.

A second tiresome consequence of Lacey's "romance" was her constant
absorption in her appearance. From one day to the next her hair changed,
her diet altered, her mood swung. By contrast, Norah's acne had worsened, she'd stopped bottom walking, and her hair, minus Mo's empty beer
cans, hipped out on the sides and dwindled like a dying plant on top.
Though one day, after flipping through an issue of *Seventeen* (for

Christmas—a stocking stuffer—Mitzi had given her a year's subscription) she rubbed her lips with talcum powder, then smeared Vaseline over them, an inexpensive trick, the article promised, to get that ethereal English look. Over dinner, Mo har-harred that his daughter looked next in line for Rasputin's Funeral Home. Mitzi tried shushing him, but Norah fled to her room and whammed the door. Alone with Mitzi's wrath, Mo waggled his eyebrows and made an O with his mouth, a ridiculous expression intended to absolve him.

So while Lacey practiced guitar scales, her fingertips turning white with callus and slightly bloodied—for Arthur, she'd sigh—Mitzi got Norah a volunteer job at Stanford Hospital. Now she wore a second uniform, a bibbed, red and white seersucker jumper with white sneakers. She assisted new mothers, helped them into wheelchairs, handed over their newborn infants, rolled them into an elevator, then out to the curb where husbands waited beside the family car like soldiers, like doormen or butlers, like nervous new fathers. Norah held each infant as the mother was helped by her husband into the car, then leaned down to hand over the small bundle. What made these people trust her with an infant? What if she dropped it, what if it rolled under the car? She told Lacey the husbands almost always insisted on a picture of her holding the baby, standing beside the new mother in her wheelchair. Why would they want a picture like that? Norah imagined herself appearing in photo albums of strangers all over the state of California. As a candy striper, she liked the sanitized cheerfulness of the hospital, she liked helping people who invariably expressed curious gratitude for what she found so intolerably awkward, her own youth. Eventually, Norah would receive a red and white enameled pin for working one hundred hours; this would be noted in a small column of the hospital newsletter. Goody Two-shoes, Lacey teased. Norah Brownnoser. Wait until Reverend Mother plops one of her ribbons on you. Lacey was referring to honor ribbons awarded at the school ceremony known as Prime, satin sashes crossing the chest and shoulders, fastened at the hip with a small, bronze medal. Norah did want a pale blue sash across her chest, placed there, in front of the whole school, by Reverend Mother McGwynn, as a sign of her exemplary behavior.

How, the Lofts agreed, could you fault a child for taking life seriously? Mo was mainly relieved she had not picked up what he called the God bug. Mitzi tried to be proud of her daughter—she understood she should be. Still, she didn't care for studiousness, for this sort of earnestness in a young girl. Ambition wasn't feminine, it frightened people. And, privately, Mitzi equated religion with moral insurance for the old or dying. Regularly, she checked Norah's room. The gloomy articles were still there. Some nights, unable to sleep, she pictured Norah announcing a vocation. She and Mo would have to drive out to some godforsaken cloister somewhere to visit their former daughter, now Mother Loft, sitting behind bars, prim, humorless, bespectacled. No wedding. No grandchildren. Mitzi would instead bring boxes of unscented soap, rough washcloths, sets of plain homespun underwear. It was her worst nightmare. She had read enough about teenagers to understand you couldn't confront them directly. You couldn't even agree with them. The best strategy was to feign indifference to whatever wrong direction they were headed in, then plop in little facts, like Alka-Seltzers, round innocuous comments, let those sink in, take slow, antidotal effect . . . on average, nuns die a full fifteen years before normal women . . . nuns cannot take vacations . . . have you ever seen a nun on a roller coaster or riding a horse . . . nuns can't dance or marry or swim in the sea . . . imagine, up at three every morning, grinding away at the same silly prayers, rain or shine, year in, year out. Casually, Mitzi tapped out such little notions of monotony, usually when they were driving somewhere. And though Norah never said a word, never responded, Mitzi never gave up hope.

Norah was responding. She saw what her mother was up to—persecution. Each night, on her knees beneath the picture of the pink-slippered matador, Norah asked for a vision. Sometimes she felt translucent, as though light were pouring through her, as though the air around her were heavy as syrup and she herself were light, porous, all her weight vanishing into her soul and flying upward. She counted these among the happiest sensations she had known.

With the latest note crumpled in her hand (Noser: Music Room, 12:30, News!), she found Lacey sitting on the piano bench, her face ignited by the as yet undisclosed "news." Stealthily, Norah shut the door behind her. No doubt this had to do with what's-his-face, Arthur Webb.

"Come over to me, Nose. Close your eyes. Are they closed? Ok."

Norah stood blind in the center of the small practice room, her hands loosely clasped behind her back. First she felt Lacey's hands on her shoulders, smelled her gingery breath, then came the kiss—brief, warm, lovely.

The piano bench dragged on the floor a little. Lacey plinked a bit of "Heart and Soul," softly, on the piano.

"Norah. Open your eyes. Do they look different? My lips? God, I needed to call you, but I didn't want the Colonel eavesdropping, which he would, the big boob. And I didn't dare write anything in case someone else read it. Oh my God. Yesterday, after my lesson, Arthur kissed me. He's been wanting to since the first time he saw me. That's what he said."

Norah thought Lacey's lips looked unchanged, maybe drier. She'd assumed Arthur didn't know what Lacey felt about him, or if he did know, wouldn't care. After all, he was twenty-three or -four and went to college. She and Lacey weren't even sixteen. Now Lacey was pursing her lips and rolling her eyes in the most asinine way.

"You shouldn't do that."

"Why, Norah? He loves me. He's practically said so."

"The man is older than you. Not to mention he's your teacher."

"So? I'm sixteen in two months. We've already decided to wait."

"Wait for what?"

"Honest to God, Norah. Don't be dense. To have sex. Arthur is mature, and he's got this friend who's got a place at the beach we. . . ."

"Lacey will you stop? I can't hear this anymore."

"Why? I've been talking to you for months."

Norah was sure their absence from study hall had been noticed, that they were about to be caught, that because of Lacey, she would lose her chance for a ribbon.

"I'm sorry if I'm boring you. There's just no one else I can trust with this. I trust you with my life, Norah. I promise to talk about Arthur less. Not one word. I won't use any word that starts with A. I'll . . ."

"Lacey. We've got to get back to study hall."

"Ok, ok. We're gone. We're there. What about this? If I promise not to say another word about A (she silently mouthed his name) can I still give you a signal that says we've done it? Had sex?"

Norah found herself agreeing just to get out of the music room. And for the next three weeks, Norah did get a respite from his name, did get some part of their old, Arthur-less relationship back, at least until the signal came, a silly double thumbs-up, after which nothing was the same.

• • •

On the same night Lacey Jenks was to lose her virginity in, of all places, Kepler's music shop (there was no friend's beach house, only a ratty old maroon sofa in the back, where Arthur had already seduced two other girls—he was beginning to think he had a knack for this), on that same evening, Mitzi Loft was putting the finishing touches on Norah. Considering the obstacles she'd climbed over, one damned thing after another, she had a right to feel pleased. The biggest obstacle had turned out to be Mo, who was in one of his funks. His practice was down—he had lost three clients in one month—though Mitzi reminded him two of the three had died which could hardly be taken personally, and the third was Sam Widdle, so a high, holy good riddance. But Mo took anything to do with his dentistry to heart, and what Mitzi didn't know was he had also made investments without consulting her and was steadily losing money on them. (In fact, if Mitzi lifted the lid on what a kettle of fish he was in, she would throw a fit, exactly why he hadn't told her. They would have to shag his broken keester down some long, lonesome road, creditors braying all the way, before he'd unload his troubles to her. All he could bring himself to suggest was that Mitzi keep the expenses down to a dull roar.) And Mitzi, ever nervous about his statistical weakness for suicide, accepted a friend's loan of her daughter Helen Marie's cotillion dress from last year. Both girls, it turned out, wore the same size, and the dress, while nondescript, was at least a Lanz original. So she had only to pay for Norah's hair and a pair of white brocade pumps she found at Payless and had dyed emerald green.

So now her daughter—fifteen!—stood before her, wearing a midcalf, white chiffon dirndl skirt with a sleeveless gold lamé top, in emerald heels with a dyed-to-match purse, a wide, emerald velveteen bow perched slightly past the crown of her head, her hair professionally done—to match Mitzi's—in a lacquered, bouffant flip.

"Morris!" This came gaily from Norah's bedroom. "Picture time!"

Helmet head. Freakdoody. With strangely reticent bitterness, Norah regarded her reflection. Her own mother could not see how tacitly ugly she had become, how ready she was to die.

Mo shambled in with the camera, picked his unlit cigar out of his mouth, told his daughter that, orthodontia aside, she was an eyeful. Indeed she did look almost dazzling, reminding him of Mitzi when he'd first seen her—you have got to be the tooth fairy, he'd teased, partly to hide how defenseless he'd suddenly felt. Now he noticed even Norah's acne had been cleverly camouflaged.

"Gorgeous, honey. Let me get some pictures, record this moment for future generations, huh?" A comment which, as soon as he made it, depressed him. A future generation implied his own absence. In the living room, he took the obligatory pictures in front of the fireplace and the picture window. He snapped several of Mitzi and Norah together, pictures that Mitzi would crunch into a ball and plunge into the trash when she saw how, next to her daughter, she looked at least a decade older than she felt.

"Ready for the ball, Cindyfella?" Mo joked, and with that chauffeured Norah to her first and last cotillion, a cramp in her left toe and her mouth aching from having had her braces tightened that morning.

At the expansively lit entrance to the Menlo Country Club, Norah got out of her father's new red Mustang, stood there a moment, leaned down and asked, "Can I come home now?"

Poor kid, Mo thought. I should take her out for a hamburger and a movie, let her mother think she went to this monkey-ass thing. But Mitzi was waiting. She had a surprise, she'd winked almost lewdly from the garage as he backed the Mustang out, and he knew, or hoped he knew, what that meant. The sight of his daughter maturing into a woman made him remember his own and Mitzi's youth, what was it called, splendor in the grass, and he found himself excited about the how and when and where of her surprise. Would she be hiding stark naked in the laundry room, or wearing some flimsy negligee, waving a bottle of champagne and two glasses—things she had done before—the memories, the possibilities distracted him, and he started to answer his daughter by saying oh, ten, eleven, twelve, when he saw Norah's pleading, myopic expression. He really ought to find a way to finance contact lenses for her.

"Nine-thirty should make your mother happy. You just give your old popster a jingle."

"Ok," her voice sounded small.

He watched his daughter wobble away from him in her cheap, green, obviously painful shoes, so young, the world sweeping her up, the world ahead of her. What if she turned around? Would he be able to resist saving her? Mo forced himself to look away, to drive on home to what was waiting for him, the tooth fairy from Scranton, light of his life.

• • •

Norah pinched her glasses off and crammed them in the small green "clutch," as her mother called it, exactly what she was doing, clutching it in her icy hands. Inside its black satin interior were things her mother had tucked in: a monogrammed, lace-edged hankie, a tube of Hot Polka Dot lipstick, a small plastic comb, and change for a phone call. Norah had added her rosary beads, one of Mother Stewart's prayer booklets, and the most recent note Mother Fitzgerald had written to her, on the back of a holy card: *My dearest Norah, Though our paths be different, our goal is still the same.*

Seven o'clock. Two and a half hours. Norah hid behind a feathery broom of potted palms before forcing herself to walk, her feet killing her, into the dimly lit ballroom. Without her glasses, she felt as if she were underwater, a stolid obelisk that whole schools of exotic fish darted around, shot past. She was the only one standing, unasked. And what if she was? Asked? What was she to do with her purse? Her feet were already numb, used to their thick sport socks and old saddle shoes. Norah stood there, grateful for the semidarkness, when she heard or rather felt someone ask her to dance. A tall, gangling, extra-lanky boy, he reminded her of a pinkish, faintly wet looking daddy longlegs, wearing glasses, as she should have been. She hadn't heard him over the noise of the band, so he had poked her in the shoulder to get her attention. Now he clamped her into a wooden-legged box step, and they labored together, he blinking across her shoulder, she staring into his armpit for one whole Frank Sinatra song, then another. Clearly, they were victims of the same ballroom dance lessons. During a break in the music, her partner towered beside her, his arm soldered to her waist, happy to have zeroed in on his matching half. Norah freed herself, waving in what she hoped was the direction of the powder room.

"I'll be back," she shouted. Not waiting for his reaction, she limped away.

The ladies' lounge was a suite of two huge, expensively furnished rooms, the toilets and sinks like unpleasant, functional afterthoughts. Both lemon-scented rooms glittered feverishly with pale, nervous girls, bobbing and primping in front of long, gold-flecked wall mirrors. Upon coming in, Norah had felt their cold, collectively dismissive glance. The velvet bow on her head condemned her. No one else wore one, and her dress, she saw instantly, was last year's. For some reason, she'd imagined the bathroom would be empty, that she would be able to sit down on one of the dark green club chairs and read. Instead, she walked down to a stall at the far end marked Out of Order, went in, latched the door, nudged her shoes off, and sat sideways on the toilet, her stockinged feet propped on the silver toilet paper dispenser. She planned to say her rosary and read and reread Mother Fitzgerald's notes until, say, nine o'clock.

At six minutes to nine, Norah emerged holding her shoes and purse clipped together and limping since her left leg and buttock had gone completely to sleep. There was a white telephone in the lobby. Her father answered on the fifth ring.

"Sentence served, babydoll?" That made her smile. The dance wouldn't be over until twelve-thirty, yet there he would be, within ten minutes, the door to his Mustang opened for her. Mo took Norah out for a milkshake while Mitzi waited at home in her red silk kimono, pleased at having so easily restored her husband's spirits. Men were simple creatures with primitive needs. She could not yet guess, waiting for Mo and Norah to return—where were they?—how crestfallen she would be by Norah's laconic answers to her inquiries . . . who was there, what were the other girls wearing, whom did she dance with? One would think she hadn't gone at all. The next morning she would search for her daughter's name in the society column (Norah Loft, daughter of Dr. and Mrs. Morris Loft, wearing an all-season gold lamé and white chiffon gown . . .), but there were just the same names that appeared week after week: Leslie Malone, Cindy Rambeault, Betsy Farasyn. . . . She refused to dwell on the hypocrisy of the rich, how doors looked as if they might open but rarely did, how smiles might seem genuine but rarely were. With her usual energy, she launched into her next plan, to have Norah volunteer as a docent at the local art museum. She had heard that a number of girls from the wealthier families over in Atherton had begun doing that.

Lacey Jenks raised the black veil from her face to accept communion from the handsome young seminary priest who had proclaimed in his homily that a girl's sins could be seen in her eyes, that God had so designed it. Coming back down the aisle of the chapel, she paused beside Norah to flash the double thumbs-up—old news, since she and Arthur had already had sex nine times. Still, she had waited so as not to shock Norah, who, if possible, was becoming ever more shockable. Now, Lacey prayed—

though it was more like begging—not to be pregnant. Nine times, Arthur had talked her into letting him "pull out." Foolproof, he had whispered. But desperate, with her period three weeks late, Lacey had read in her mom's medical book that it wasn't foolproof at all. Yesterday, Arthur had taken her to a doctor he knew for a test. Today, he would take her back for the results. All morning, during the first day of the school's annual three-day spiritual retreat, instead of contemplating God or reading from the exhausted heap of religious books the nuns trotted out every year, Lacey had written and rewritten her married name, Mrs. Arthur Webb, inked a chain of marguerite daisies, her favorite, around the edges of the letters. She'd designed bride and bridesmaid dresses, imagined a wedding along the lines of the one she had seen in *The Sound of Music*. But unshared happiness was lonely. Arthur didn't talk. He was a musician, he said, not a conversationalist. It still amazed her how easily she'd fooled her parents. At seventy-nine the Colonel could be declared legally senile, and her mother was always at the library, working overtime, or else in the house somewhere, lying down with one of her migraines. Lacey had discovered if she did her chores and her homework without complaint, her parents were so paralyzed by gratitude that they believed whatever she told them. And what she'd been telling them was she had theater rehearsals after school. Arthur waited for her on his motorcycle, took her to his apartment, afterward dropping her off by her bicycle, stashed under some pomegranate bushes near the school grounds. Handsome Father O'Malley was barking out his ass, as the Colonel liked to say. Her eyes, for she had gazed boldly up at him as he placed the dry, white host on her tongue, revealed nothing at all.

CHER HOLY NOSER,
I know, I know. I'm not sixteen (seize) yet, so DBM (don't be mad) at me, will explain ALL later. . . .
    If I'm not at school tomorrow, pray for me. I know how much you like to do that (pray) . . . and right now people like me could use that (prayer).

Toot mon amour,
Mrs. Arthur Webb
(hee)

• • •

As she knelt by her bed that night, praying for Lacey, the Virgin Mary appeared like a bit of floating gauze in a corner of the room by Norah's
closet, looking somewhat like the pink and blue statue in the alcove, only
without any solidity. The apparition, which she later realized also resembled Mother Fitzgerald, lasted perhaps a second, during which Norah received the distant impression she had been asked—or commanded—to
befriend the two queer girls, Rose and Deirdre. Feeling foolish yet rar-
efied, she bowed her head before the hovering, mothlike figure and said,
yes, she would obey. When she lifted her head, it was gone.

The next morning, Norah felt as if a thick, satiny light swam around her.
She felt calm, slowed with holy purpose. At lunchtime, in the dining hall,
she took her tray of food and sat directly across from the two girls, Rose and
Deirdre. Because of the retreat's rule of silence, Norah smiled, as beatifically
as she could. Suspicious, the girls glowered back, but Norah, undeterred, remained confident in the mission she had been given. And lying across her
bed that night, Norah wrote to Mother Fitzgerald (a letter she would later
tear up), telling her about the vision. After brushing her teeth—since the
cotillion, she had given up any other form of self-improvement—she turned
out all the lights except the small yellow lamp beside her bed and waited. She
didn't want to appear greedy, but she desperately needed a second vision to
prove the validity of the first, which she had begun, ever so slightly, to doubt.
She identified with those children who had seen Our Lady of Fatima, with
young Bernadette of Lourdes. That led to Norah picturing herself on top of
a small hill, her eyes turned heavenward, her arms uplifted, thousands of
people gathered below, waiting. Was she crazy? What if this was like *The
Screwtape Letters,* that C. S. Lewis book where Wormwood, or whatever the
devil's name was, knew your every vanity, his job to corrupt you through di-
abolical temptations, semblances of virtue? Was spiritual pride tempting her
to see herself as famous, chosen, special? As she knelt by her bed, squinting
at the corner where she had seen Mary / Mother Fitzgerald the night before,
there was a timid rap at her window, then another, then a third, more insistent. Norah got up and went over to see Lacey staring at her, her beautiful
long hair flattened with rain, dripping about her face.

"Nose."

Norah could barely hear. She raised the window. "What are you doing here?" The rain became audible, wind blew coolly in. She thought she heard a motorcycle. Arthur's? It was raining hard.

"Norah. This is *très* serious. I have to go away. But I'll be back in three, maybe four days, by Monday for sure."

"Where are you going?"

"I got in a righteous argument with my parents and left a note on my bed saying I'd walked over to your house. So here's the thing. If they call, can you say I'm here and that I'll be home after school tomorrow. . . ."

"If you were here, wouldn't they want to talk to you, not me?"

"Say I'm in the shower or something. Say I'm asleep. Throwing up. The point is, I need to keep them from looking for me right away."

"Why?" Norah felt frightened. "Are you going somewhere with him?"

"We're going to Mexico. Just for a few days."

"Mexico?"

"Arthur knows this clinic in Tijuana where girls from his college go. It's really safe, and he's paying for the whole thing. Jesus, Norah. Now you'll hate me. I wish I was like you, as good as you, but I probably won't ever be. Please. Will you do that? Just tell my parents, if they call, that I'm here, staying with you?" Lacey was crying, her long hair like two shining blades down her shoulders.

"You said his motorcycle was a joke—how will you get all the way to Mexico?"

"He's been working on it all week."

When she heard that, Norah decided to really hate Arthur Webb. His dumb motorcycle. Dumb everything.

"Ok, I'll tell them. Wait." Norah put her hand out the window, felt cold rain sting her wrist. "Take this?"

Lacey wiped her nose on the hem of her big sweater. "Jesus, Mary, and Joseph. You've gone Catholic on me, Norris. That's ok. I already knew. I was watching you before I knocked, you looked holier than hell. Hey, my mom always says converts make the best saints." Lacey pocketed the rosary in a solemn motion. "I'll hang onto it the entire time."

She looked for Lacey's bicycle on the last day of the retreat, knowing it wouldn't be there, how could it be? Still. After morning Mass, Norah wandered the rain-drenched school grounds until she happened upon the nuns' plain, two-story retirement home. Behind it was a neatly kept orchard of apple trees. She sat on a patch of damp, long, yellow grass, struggling to pray, imagining instead what might be happening to her friend. Norah ended up going back to the empty study hall, sitting at Lacey's desk and impulsively writing a letter. In it, she recklessly declared how beautiful and perfect she believed Mother Fitzgerald to be. She did not set this letter in the usual place, upon the lectern used by the mistress of studies, but carried it down to the west wing of the second floor, a cloistered area where the nuns lived. The long, low-lit hall looked deserted. She ran down its length before finding the door marked M. Fitzgerald. Amazed by her own audacity, she bent down and slid the letter underneath.

At lunch, with somewhat less conviction, she sat across from Rose and Deirdre, who, this time, smiled with a combined, breathtaking trust in her. Norah moved her food around, worrying about the letter, thinking she should write another, retracting what she'd said in the first, when there was a disturbance in the hallway just outside the dining room, a breach of the retreat's heavy silence, the sound of voices conferring. Then Mother Fitzgerald, accompanied by Reverend Mother McGwynn, the mistress general, and the school's Latin teacher, Mother Flaherty, walked in. Mother Fitzgerald looked distraught. At the familiar command of the wooden clapper, the roomful of girls rose, curtsied in the direction of their reverend mother, and received news that during last night's storm, there had been an accident, resulting in the premature death of one of their third academic students. They were to proceed immediately to chapel, to pray for the soul of Lacey Ann Jenks.

Hail Mary, full of grace, the Lord is with thee, blessed art thou amongst women and blessed is the fruit of thy womb, Jesus. Holy Mary, Mother of God, pray for us sinners now and at the hours of our death, amen. Hail Mary . . .

To Mitzi's credit, she did not pry. She calmly held her daughter, then went with her to the funeral at Our Lady of Angels. Mo stayed home. All funerals, he said, especially those of children, depressed him.

At the service, Mitzi thought the parents looked terrible, as though they couldn't live through this, and indeed, Colonel Jenks would die in less than a year's time, in a car accident less than a mile from his home, due, it was said, to his failing eyesight. There was an older brother, who, with other male relatives, bore the casket, which was white and draped in a blanket of pink baby roses. Newspaper details would be scarce, though there would be the most recent yearbook photograph of Lacey. What

Mitzi would later hear through friends was that Lacey had been sneaking out of the house to see her guitar instructor. Mo, hearing this from his wife, felt newly protective of Norah, restrictive of her whereabouts. On several heated occasions, Mitzi argued with him, heedless, for once, of his mood. If he didn't want his daughter becoming a nun why in god's name did he suddenly insist on treating her like one, what was the matter with him, couldn't he see the child scarcely left her room anymore? But that would be weeks later, weeks after the death of Lacey Jenks.

At the end of her third year at the Convent of the Sacred Heart, during Prime, an awards ceremony held in the Little Theater, Norah Loft's name was called. Again and again she was made to leave her seat and go up on the stage to be congratulated by Reverend Mother and the other nuns. She accepted medals of merit, academic certificates, even what she had once so dearly wished for, a pale blue honor ribbon. For her scholarship, in particular, for her essay on the benefits of martyrdom, which had won third place in a national Catholic youth essay contest, for her leadership potential and community service, Norah Loft received special commendation. The following year she would be elected valedictorian, and her speech, poetic and slightly scathing—not what anyone expected—would be dedicated to Lacey Jenks. But now, kneeling to receive her ribbon from Reverend Mother, applause rising respectfully behind her, Norah felt nothing she could identify, nothing at all.

Then, at the point when Prime usually ended, Mrs. Jenks, wearing a kelly green suit and matching hat, came forward to announce a small scholarship in her daughter's name, funded by the city's library. She wept as she spoke of the lifelong values instilled in Sacred Heart girls. Then Mrs. Jenks sat down, and the best singer in the school, Kathy Murphy, played her guitar and sang "Today, While the Blossom Still Clings to the Vine," followed by another girl Norah didn't know well, who had composed a villanelle about death, comparing it, in a tedious chain of verses, to a dance whose steps were ever the same. Afterward, all four classes stood to recite a mimeographed prayer in honor of Lacey Jenks, in memory of her innocent, untried soul.

That summer, Mo recouped his losses and was able to pay for Norah's first pair of contact lenses. Her braces had been removed as well, so with straight ivory teeth and wide, impassive eyes, Norah Loft seemed, over that summer, to have traded her ugly-ducklingness for some new, abject radiance. Mitzi noted, with no small relief, the disappearance of her daughter's religious articles. Though Norah now burned purple cones of Bombay incense in her room and wrote poetry, verse after gloomy verse wherein lovers suffered sudden, unjust deaths on the moors, or gypsies rode on horseback down white roads to the sea, disconsolate scenes all set apparently in England. Not a problem, Mo said, when Mitzi waved the poems around, having located them in her daughter's desk while Norah was away at an exclusive girls camp in Lake Tahoe and Mitzi'd begun re-decorating her room in a French provincial theme. A phase, he said. No doubt she was copying the stuff out of some book somewhere, it seemed pretty sophisticated, he couldn't make head nor tail of it. Though he did remember writing some pretty sour material when he was trying to get over his first girlfriend's leaving him. Death and heartbreak, he reminded Mitzi, throw you the hardest.

Cecilia Mornay, the daughter of a high government official in Haiti, sat in a yellow damask chair, a cup of tea balanced on her lap, gazing up at the senior girl introduced by Mother Fitzgerald as her Angel. The fall tea, as always, was held in the immaculately appointed front parlor, and up to this point, Norah had successfully avoided looking at Mother Fitzgerald. Her letter, shot under the nun's door, with its reckless avowal of passion, had never been acknowledged. There had been no reply, the long summer had ensued and now, Norah thought to herself, hearing Mother Fitzgerald prattle on about the school's soccer and tennis teams, gesturing with fa-miliar, ruddy, athletic movements, how pathetically jolly, how ignorant. How could she have thought this nun graceful or sensitive, attached hope or perfection to her? The spell was broken, a spell much like that cast by the Blessed Virgin over innocence. What she could not know was how hungrily her letter had been received, how Mother Fitzgerald had, after many written and discarded replies, expressions of love returned in kind, added Norah's cri de coeur to all the others she had saved from various girls, and taken them downstairs to the basement incinerator. With a prayer that she be forever spared wanting to be loved in such deplorable ways, Mother Fitzgerald pitched the letters, bound together, cries of love identical and shallow in each girl's heart, the same in her own, into the in-cinerator's constant, dirty fire.

· · ·

After some weeks, Cecilia Mornay found herself content, adjusting to this newest school. She was popular with the other girls and felt some guilt that she no longer relied upon Norah Loft, avoided her anyway, always so serious and, worse, openly critical of the one person she liked best, Mother Fitzgerald. As her soccer team's captain, Cecilia excelled in part to see the nun's face flush with pleasure, to hear her ringing shouts of triumph. Only recently they had begun exchanging small notes handwritten in French, Cecilia's first language. Norah showed no interest in athletics; her attitudes were those of a nihilist, a nonparticipant, an unsmiling intellectual, all of which Cecilia found abhorrent and unappealing. Norah commanded respect, certain cold attributes of leadership and realms of knowledge were hers, but Cecilia felt unsettled in her presence. Back home in Haiti, her mother would explain such a sensation by saying a ghost walked with that one, you can be sure.

> Queen of Angels
> Of Martyrs
> Of Virgins
> Of Peace
> Of Sinners and Saints
> Singular Vessel,
> Save us.

Three days after the motorcycle accident, Norah knelt before the Virgin. When at last she stood up, she saw Lacey Jenks sitting beside the statue. Neatly dressed in her school uniform, her hair was darkened, glittering with rain. On her lap was a white index card with blurred red lettering Norah could not decipher. That night, waking up in her bed, Norah thought she saw Lacey, haloed in silver mist, moving toward the window. And for what would prove to be the last time, during Mass the following morning, Norah would see her dead friend, floating and naked, as if on her stomach, above the handsome but obstinate Father O'Malley, her fingers splayed in a V above his head. She smiled, tenderly and without judgment, before her features were washed over by a fierce, impenetrable gaze, a look Norah Loft began, without awareness, to reflect, drawing to herself all who desired to see what it was that overturned human love, what mystery it was that so crowned the heart with cold braided thorns, one strand glory, the other a blind, perdurable grace.

Keith Banner

The Smallest People Alive

From *The Kenyon Review*

I

PHYLLIS MADE liver and onions the first night I was there, with peas and microwaved hash browns. Ben, her son and my used-to-be best friend, ate Cinnamon Toast Crunch cereal as an act of defiance.

"Yummy yummy," Phyllis whispered loudly, chewing and smiling, as if it were a commercial for the Liver and Onions Council.

Chuck, Ben's dad, just laughed at his end of the table. He had on his greasy Armco cap, his face pale and in need of a shave. Phyllis, by the way, was barefoot, in a pair of red sweats pulled up to her knees with one of Chuck's old flannel shirts on, her dyed-black hair ponytailed with a rubber band.

Ben sat above his bowl of cereal, not furious, just resolute. He was skinny, his face drawn in, the tracheotomy scar glowing pink above the neckline of a faded Hootie and the Blowfish T. With that, he wore acid-washed jeans and hiking boots with sweat socks. Resting his left arm on the dinette table, the arm that didn't work that well, he spooned cereal in with the right. His walker, silver aluminum with dirty white tape on the tops for handles, little wheels on its front legs, sat beside the brown refrigerator behind the table like a robot sidekick.

Chuck said, "Good God Phyllis, this is just the best liver, I mean *ever*.

You outdid yourself." He looked around the table, then wheezed out his sweet-toned, red-neck laugh.

It was obvious this whole dinner-thing they were doing was a great big put-on, a way of taunting Ben into eating what they were, and also a way to get rid of some other feelings without really going into anything serious. After Chuck laughed, though, it just went quiet again.

Me? I was sitting next to Phyllis, eating what Chuck and Phyllis were, and I guess I could describe myself as a twenty-two-year-old, not very tan male, on the verge of obesity, with short, professionally cut hair, done by Adam, the guy I live with. I was wearing a button-down shirt, jeans a little too tight because I refuse to go above a forty-two waist size. This, tonight, believe it or not, was the start of my vacation here in McCordsville, Ohio, with Ben and Phyllis and Chuck. I had come all the way from Dayton, sixty miles from the north.

Intermittently I looked at Ben as he ate his cereal, as I cut up my liver. He looked up and got the feeling that he knew I was pitying him, so he was playing his part, spooning cereal slowly into his twenty-two-year-old baby mouth, the milk dripping from the spoon onto the vinyl tablecloth. Defiant, situated in his chair as if to be spotlighted.

To break the silence again, Phyllis said, "These hash browns . . ." but then she stopped chewing so elaborately, stopped smiling. "These hash browns are not done," she said to herself, pissed. She got up as if she were putting out a fire, went to the counter and grabbed a spatula and platter, scooped the hash browns from Chuck's and my plates. Silent, Phyllis put the platter into her huge, ancient microwave, turned it on with the dial.

Ben started laughing.

"Shut up," said his mom.

Ben laughed sluggishly, as his speech had been affected, his voice, his face, his eyes, his everything. It happened two years ago. *It*, like the book by Stephen King. It was pretty simple, though, not enough maybe for a whole novel of unrelenting terror, but tragic, the way things out in the country can get. Two years ago, October 10, 1995, Ben had tried to off himself in the garage, the one right outside the kitchen window over there. Ben parked his piece-of-shit, sky-blue bucket-of-bolts Plymouth Volare in that garage, clogged what gaps existed in windows and doors with cheap caulking, attached a hose to the exhaust pipe with silver duct tape, then slipped the hose into the front seat and sat back to die. Even though he had taken as many precautions as humanly possible, obviously Ben still survived. The roof was full of holes. His dad came home to get lunch, found him, and called 911.

Ben looked up when Phyllis told him to shut up, laughing like that. Then he stopped. He slammed his spoon into his bowl, milk going everywhere.

"What . . . What. Did you. Say?" he yelled in his brain-damaged speak, sentences chopped up into stalled segments. His face got completely red. It was as if he were going to wish them into the cornfield, like that little kid on the "Twilight Zone" episode.

"I told you to shut up that awful laughing," Phyllis said, turning around, this time grinning. The microwave dinged.

Chuck went, "Hey, Ben. Mike's here. Mikey."

I smiled, as if my presence meant anything. Ben did not look at me, milk dripping onto the beige linoleum. He continued to sit in his chair, his face puppet-like when a puppet is in a suitcase waiting to be used, the left eye bigger than the right, blinkless and bigger.

Suddenly, he let out a blood-curdling scream. Phyllis brought the hash browns back. Ben kept howling. It was like that *Scream* painting that's been turned into blow-up dolls at Spencer's Gifts.

"We just ignore," Phyllis says, her face disgusted, and yet too full of the kind of hopelessness only people with dyed-black ponytails and greasy white foreheads can manufacture.

Chuck ate the hash browns, keeping his head down.

Ben stopped finally. Panting, he stared at me. He looked exhausted, but also you could see in his eyes that he wanted to scream more, scream louder, knowing it would not do anything anyway. Still the desire was there.

I smiled again. My own stupid smile. Christ. Milk kept dripping.

"Yes," Phyllis said. "He will clean that up." She was talking to herself.

Of course, Phyllis cleaned it. Ben just got up and got his walker and went into the living room. The walker had been a matter of contention for most of the time I'd been here, since two that afternoon, arriving in my own piece-of-shit bucket-of-bolts Dodge Colt, me the Vacation Boy having gotten a week off from Winn Packaging, where I took hot plastic bottles from molding machines 6 P.M.–6 A.M. four nights a week.

That walker was there greeting me on the front porch of their blond-brick ranch-style. Phyllis had put it out there like a bad dog. I knocked on the screen door upon arriving. There was Ben inside the house, inside the screen, wobbling. He looked at me with sour curiosity.

"Get. That," he ordered.

I had my duffel bag, so I put that down and scooted the walker toward me, opened the door, gave the walker to him.

"Thanks," he said, gripping and fondling the top handles.

I joked, "Nice to see you too."

He raised his eyes slowly and smiled. "Hey," he said.

His mom came in then, same outfit as she would be wearing at dinner: "The physical therapist said he should try going without that." Tense, she walked up, drying her hands on a dishtowel. Then her expression changed to formal, all-out happiness. "Welcome, Mikey," she said, looking at the walker with disgust. "We are glad to have you come back out here to the country and see us."

Ben's walker rattled and squeaked all the way down the long, ranch-style hall to his bedroom.

"He still acts up a little," Phyllis said. "Brain damage," she whispered, walking back into the kitchen.

Once upon a time, in a galaxy far, far away, Ben and I were close, if that's the right word, not just kids who grew up together, but closer even than that, as close as Ben would allow. Especially a couple summers before *It*, when I was kind of lost right after high school and so was he. We hung out, his coming up weekends to Dayton, the two of us, almost as a joke, going to that one gay bar they put into the used-to-be Target strip mall by the interstate. We would get drunk as shit, me commenting whore-like on the men, Ben pretending to be "bi" and macho—wincing when I got too faggy. He was trying to act as if this was all just a phase and that soon he would find a lady and "lay lady lay" down with her and get married and move into a farmhouse all their own.

Right now, though, it's me sitting in the living room with Ben and Chuck, Phyllis in the kitchen, cleaning off the table, bitching that she has to do everything, but not wanting any help. Ben is staring at a plaster-of-paris statue of a fuzzy-faced bunny on the coffee table. Chuck is watching "Entertainment Tonight." I am wanting suddenly and desperately to call Adam, who wouldn't be home anyway on a goddamn Friday night. Adam lives with me, but shares his room with his boy-toy now, who shall from now on be called Nameless. The other day, Adam told me, "Me and Nameless are gonna have to get a place of our own," looking all hurt and damaged in the living room of the apartment *I* was paying for. Adam said that just because I threw a little tantrum. I had gotten off work and come home and they were in the shower together, and I went into the kitchen and as a joke got a big knife, the biggest goddamn knife, and reenacted the famous *Psycho* shower scene. I did not kill anyone, however.

You see, I wanted to tell Ben, I am not all there either.

"We are out of water!" Phyllis yells from the kitchen.

To add to the glamour of my visit, the McCordsville Water Treatment Plant had issued a water advisory around four o'clock, having problems with bacteria in the supply, and people in the surrounding area were told to boil all tap water for drinking and oral hygiene. "Happens all the time," Chuck told me, arriving home from work. But Phyllis, being Phyllis, has taken it one step further to include using store-bought water for everything.

She comes into the completely sedate country-decorated living room. "You hear me?" She's talking to Chuck.

"Yeah." He just stays in his lounger, kind of laughing under his breath.

Phyllis laughs, "Well?"

"Well, just boil regular tap water like everybody else," he says.

Phyllis laughs louder. Then stops, like an old-time comedian trying to get more yuks, bugging her eyes out. "No, buddy. You get up off your big ass. And you go out and get us some store water. I am not—repeat *not*—touching that bacteria. You know that. No."

Chuck stays seated, his under-the-breath laughing growing into a grunt.

This is when I step in. "Ben and I can go get you some." I had to say something. It was like their arguing was my fault, like I had brought the plague of dirty water with me.

Phyllis looked at me, not smiling this time. "You sure?"

"We. Are going," Ben said right off.

I took this as recognition, that even though his life was totally screwed, we still had a relationship.

Chuck sat back in his La-Z-Boy, knocking the back of the chair into the wall. "Let 'em go," he said, angry, following that up with his laugh. "Let 'em fucking go."

Phyllis marched back into the kitchen and came out with her purse, a white, scuffed one, got out her wallet, gave me a ten-dollar bill. "Buy as much as you can with that," she instructed me. It felt as if this was her admitting defeat, this was her handing her responsibilities over to me, like the smallest thing had just killed her. "Go on," she said.

Ben had already gotten up, using his walker. He stood by the couch, holding onto it, not grinning, his left eye glowing big and dumb in the bright light from the TV. Chuck took off his socks. I crumpled up the ten-dollar bill. Rose. Walked toward the kitchen, hearing the rattling walker behind me, hearing Ben's huffing breath.

Outside, a big orange October moon and the flat-topped earth, cornstalks shaved to stubble, the smell of burning leaves. At least now, Ben and I had something to do. I looked at Ben beside my car. He was staring out behind the garage, at a little path that snaked to the other side, beside a stack of firewood covered in a blue plastic tarp, lit by an old pole light.

The walker sinking slightly into the mud, Ben started walking toward the path. "Come. On. Come," he said.

I followed, watching his back, his legs, as he hobbled across gravel. I flashed to when he was not who he is now, but just a plain old geek, cute, at least to me. Back when we were best friends, he allowed me to suck him off, in his bedroom on this very property. I mean what are the odds? Two queers (except yeah he was "bi") in rural Ohio, one slightly obese, the other skinny, tight-lipped, wanting to escape but not knowing how. Ben truly, in a way, loved Phyllis and Chuck. Loved the silence of the green, green grass and the anonymity of radio towers in the middle of nowhere and going fishing and hunting and mowing long, hot acres without his shirt on. Loved the simplicity and exactness of where he was. And just like escaping to Dayton with me, at times, to the bar, to drink but never really do anything, pick up anybody, or even dance. Never talk to me seriously about any of it. His gayness was this private, burning *thing* he kept away from himself, from them in there in the house right now. Sure he went to the rest stop on I-75N a few times, he told me, in stalls jerking off with truck-driving angels. But with me, it was like he was allowing me to go down on him as a gift, silent as a gifted actor playing a guilty homo on a prestigious "Hallmark Hall of Fame."

Now we are back behind the garage, the Death Garage, his gripping the walker. Three pie pans nailed to little wood planks are jutting out of the weeds back here. I look at Ben's face. He is staring at the pie pans. After a short while, I get nervous.

"Larry," he says. "Moe," he says. "Curly." Each time pointing at a separate pie pan. I try to figure out what he means. I can't.

He starts laughing. "Dead, man," he says. "Dead." He laughs, like I should laugh too. So I do, the way a hostage laughs during a bank heist when ordered. I smile after I stop. There's the wind-blown silence. There's the pie pans rattling softly.

"Mine," he says. But he is not crying. He is grinning. It's like he gets the joke that is now his life, and when he turns around to go back I can hear him humming something almost intelligible. Maybe a top-ten hit. Maybe Boyz II Men.

The Kroger's is at the bottom of a hill. It's small and old, like most everything in McCordsville. He is using the walker, of course, going through ancient automatic doors, walker-wheels squeaking on worn linoleum. A wicked-witch dummy stands before a display of Dr Pepper. The musty smell of an old building mixes in with the smell of new groceries, fruity and papery. The fat, young woman behind the service desk has dyed-blond hair and a tanning-booth tan. Her name is Candy. Ben and I both know her from school.

"Look who's here." Candy waves and smiles. Ben goes up, but I stay back, having never really *known*-known her. Ben talks. Her face gets the strained kind of expression people have when they listen to people who can't talk fast. He is talking about the Three Stooges.

"Oh, they get me too," she says. "Every time." She looks over at me, "Hey, Mike. How's it going?"

"Just fine."

She smiles. "You still in Dayton?"

"Yeah."

She doesn't know what else to ask, so I nod and walk on to the water, not wanting to get into it because I think of the times she and her friends called me a faggot in the lunch line. Too much bullshit to get into at the McCordsville Kroger's, six years after the fact. I grab a cart along the way. Then pull ten plastic jugs of water off the shelves, hearing his goddamn walker crashing down the aisle. He stops by the cart and motions over to the liquor bottles, which are catty-corner.

"What?" I say, lugging the last water.

"Schnapps," he says.

"What kind?"

"Peach."

"You are gonna drink peach schnapps?"

He just blows his lips out in frustration, almost like he is trying to be cute. "Fuck. Yes."

I laugh. "OK." I get a bottle of peach schnapps.

It's Candy who checks us out, as the other two old-lady cashiers are busy. She's all extra-crispy and big-chested in the express lane. I have this feeling that she thinks her super tan might buy her a ticket out of here. She looks me directly in the eye, and she knows and I know what she and her fucking friends thought of me, not really Ben as Ben stayed in the ag department for most of his high-school career, focusing on cows. She runs the jugs of water over the radar pricer, looking back down. Then, like she is apologizing, Candy says, "He is the bravest person I think I know. Coming back from that."

I nod. Ben is right next to me, but he is letting her talk about him.

"You want your water in a sack?" Candy goes.

"No thanks," I say. I look at Candy's face. This smile she has is something she learned after high school, like she took an adult-ed class on how to act once everything is over and you still have to go on.

I load it all up and go, Ben behind me clanging his walker.

"Bye, Ben! Bye, Mike!" Candy says. I don't look back. "Stay in touch!"

At the ranch, Phyllis helps us get all the water in and starts boiling two gallons of it to make it hot enough to do the stacked pans and dishes. It is 8:30 P.M. Chuck already is asleep with "Sabrina the Teenaged Witch" on. Ben and I sit on the couch again, leaving the schnapps out in the car. I get up almost as soon as I sit down, though, antsy as hell.

Phyllis is wiping down the sink as if it is her version of martyrdom. I feel like I have come across her doing something very private, so I smile out of shock and politeness.

"He really is glad you're here," she says.

"Maybe we'll go to the movies tonight," I say.

"Yeah. Get out and blow the stink off," she says, trying to be friendly. "How's your mom doing?"

"Fine," I say. "She's still at Dayton General Hospital." Mom got her LPN license right after the divorce. That's why we moved to Dayton too.

I stop there, of course, thinking of when Mom comes over to see me now, how I try to hide the fact that I am living with Adam and Nameless, as it would be too perverse to explain, or too embarrassing. So I play it up in front of Mom when she comes, like Adam is my lover, and I am completely, completely happy. I always schedule her visits for when Adam and Nameless are not home. I see her sitting on my couch, looking worried, but smiling. Her dark hair is cut Peter-Pan short for convenience, her eyes glass from pulling third trick. She says, "Well, looks like you are very happy, Mike."

"Yeah, Mom's fine, doing good," I say, standing there.

"Good." Phyllis keeps wiping.

"Hey," I go. "Who are Larry, Moe, and Curly anyway?" Smiling. "Ben took me out behind the garage and showed me these pie-pan tombstones and—"

Phyllis's face went pale. She stopped wiping. "Don't you remember?"

"What?" My smile drops then, as Phyllis turns toward the living room.

"The three kittens," she says, fading it into a whisper.

"What?" I get closer and can see through the kitchen doorway that Chuck must have snored himself awake. Now he is sitting up.

"The cats were in the garage when he did it," Phyllis whispers loudly. "Remember? Remember? The momma put them inside a big tire in there and nobody knew."

That same stupid smile I have worn all day reignites. I can see in the door-shape Ben's feet on the floor, the walker, Ben's fingers digging into the sofa cushion. I pull back, Phyllis now going over and pouring another gallon jug of store water into another pot on the stove to heat, possibly to wash her hands.

"Oh yeah," she whispers, screwing the lid back on the empty jug. "Oh yeah. Larry, Moe, and Curly. He didn't know. I mean it wasn't on purpose. His dad buried them, and it was only like two weeks back when Ben made the markers. His memorial, he said, except he couldn't get the whole word out. *Morial,* that's what came out. His language skills are all screwed up."

Phyllis walks out to the utility room where they put recyclables. Yes, I think. Language skills. Phyllis tries to make some order out of the pile of water bottles.

Then Chuck starts yelling. "Did you cut up the goddamn newspaper again for coupons before I get to read it?"

Phyllis yells back from the utility room: "No, I certainly did not!"

In the doorway, Chuck is holding the paper, which has been cut into with scissors. He is super hyper-pissed. Not laughing at all.

"Fucking ruins the paper!" he says, looking at me but talking to himself. "Can't even have a newspaper around this house."

2

The night after his "accident," Ben was driven by ambulance to the hospital where my mom works. The one in McCordsville could not handle brain injuries like his. This was close to the same time Adam was about to move in with me, as well as close to the time I landed my Winn Packaging job. It's like all Ben's tragedy was counterbalanced by my good fortune, right?

I figured Adam's moving in with me meant he loved me (he was without Nameless at the time), not that he wanted free rent. Plus I would be the breadwinner, as Adam made diddley at Helene's as a hairdresser. I would have that power over him, and even though his being a hairstylist sounds stereotypical, Adam is not a fairy, as much as elegant and pouty, with a kind of snotty distance from the real world. Like he is just too good, which makes me only want to somehow conquer his ass, but lovingly, being diligent and loving till the day he caves in.

Or at least that is how the fantasy goes.

At that time, then, I was feeling like Ben's suicide attempt was just this hideous, pathetic predicament. I remember thinking what a loser he was, like he can't even kill himself right. Fucking scaredy-cat faggot. I think I might have even said those exact words to Adam, later that same night, as we had drinks at TGI Friday's in the mall where his hair salon was. I was being all melodramatic and upset about my now ex–best friend doing something so stupid. Seeking Adam's sympathy. Adam nodded, sipping his cocktail. Tan and tall, he had on a stylish ensemble, a white button-down shirt and black jeans, his hair slicked back, his face smooth and sleek.

"Oh, I just hate homosexuals who hate themselves," he said and then he sipped again luxuriantly. I watched his lips on the glass.

Anyway, before that, Mom and I met Phyllis and Chuck in the cafeteria at the hospital, where we had coffee and big chocolate-chip cookies prior to Ben's arrival, Phyllis then sporting a hideous perm, Chuck the same in his Armco uniform. Mom was in her white uniform, obese yet pristine, and I—I was her slightly obese son who just got a really good factory job. Both Mom and I, I think back now, were acting superior. After all, it was Dayton Memorial Hospital Ben had to come to after their homophobic hatred fucked him up.

"This is a great rehab hospital," Mom said. "Best in the state."

Phyllis and Chuck nodded. They were truly defeated, but it was like in their defeat they were relieved. Mom was all proper and shit. She was delicately wording her sentences, sipping her coffee like a teacher. She looked at me with her superior, loving gaze.

Mom said, "He's going to need all our help."

Phyllis said, "Yes."

Chuck said, "You just got to love your kid. That's all." It was like he'd been talking in another imaginary discussion inside his head and that last part slipped out.

"He tried to kill himself," Mom whispered, glaring at her own plump hands on the tabletop. "So he is gonna need a reason to live when he recovers. He is going to need parents who don't judge him."

Phyllis took that without saying anything. Chuck got up and got more coffee from the self-serve machine. I pictured Ben one time when I sucked him off. I think it was Christmas Eve when we were both fifteen, right when Mom and Dad were first getting divorced. Ben stood against his bedroom wall like he was about to be executed, smiling, though, in the light of the aquarium he once kept.

Phyllis got pissed, not from anything Mom said in the cafeteria. It was upstairs in the rehab unit, after Ben had arrived. We were all in the waiting room, CNN on the wall TV, waiting till they got all the machinery hooked up in his room.

Mom was preaching about me: "He has a boyfriend, Phyllis. A good job. He is not hating himself."

I was nodding like a back-up singer.

Phyllis turned red. "Stop it." She got up and walked over to Chuck, who was watching soldiers marching on CNN. They walked toward Ben's room.

Mom laughed. "Come on. Come on. I have to start my shift." Mother and son walked to the elevator. "We can check on Ben later," Mom said. "Come on up with me. We'll talk."

We went up to the preemies unit, where she was working at the time. She let me come with her to this glass-surrounded warehouse of incubators, Mom and I walking in front of it toward the nurse's station. Looking in at the incubators, I thought, Jesus fucking Christ, these are the smallest people alive. But I kept my mouth shut. Soon I would be starting my own dead-end job, after quitting my first semester of community college. Soon I would hurl myself full-fledged into my obsession with Adam, my only reason left on earth to live, only heartache and heartburn and reenactments of *Psycho* awaiting me.

But for now I was my mom's special, queer son in the nursery of premature infants, some blue, some red, some pink, some brown, all so tiny they were like little dreams floating in Plexiglass cubes in their own recording studio inside the hospital. The machines keeping them breathing and their kidneys going and their hearts beating sounded like experimental music no one really wants to hear.

Mom and I walked past them all to the back, where there was a low-lit nurse's station. Two or three other nurses were doing paperwork.

"This is Mike, my son," Mom said, putting her purse down on a counter. They did not seem to care. Mom looked at me, "I have a whole shift ahead."

"I know," I said, scanning the eleven incubators, eleven kids. Out there, a skinny red-headed nurse with gloves on opened one, turned over a child the size of a knick-knack.

"I just want you to know, Mike, that I am proud of you," Mom said.

"Thanks." I could not look at her. Right then it hit me. The reason Ben tried to do what he did was he was lonely, and I felt kind of triumphant that I was not, or at least I had the ability to pretend I was not, because I *was* lonely, pathetically so.

"I know you're worried about Ben," Mom had tears in her eyes. "But I love you."

I loved her too. I still felt this thrilling dullness inside when she hugged me, though. This was a show she had put on in front of Chuck and Phyllis, and even now in front of the other nurses, this hugging bullshit was a show, was it not?

But too I melted. And I told Mom how much I loved her.

I left the nursery of incubators to go see Ben a little while later. He was still hooked up to his ventilator. His skin was silvery, his eyelids like tiny gray clouds. Ben's parents sat off to the side by the window, just silhouettes. In silence, they were allowing me this glimpse at the wet blackness of Ben's hair, and his preemie-like face, fetal from carbon monoxide, fetal from trying to push himself out, fetal from having nowhere else left to go.

3

Ben is in his bedroom now, sitting on the bed in the bright light from an old-fashioned, cut-glass light fixture in the ceiling, the kind moths like. Sitting there in jeans and a black cowboy kind of dress shirt, his face calm, cowboy boots on his feet, the ever-present walker there too. I wonder if he sleeps with the thing.

I smell like Safari by Ralph Lauren, the stuff Mom got me for my birthday. (We went out to Olive Garden, the waiters and waitresses sang to me. Mom goes, "It's a shame Adam had to work.") I have on brown corduroys and an extra-extra-extra-large shirt and loafers, my hair moussed a little, my face fat and totally plain.

"Ready?" I try to sound encouraging, poking my head into his room. Posters on the walls have not changed, the same mix of *Garth Brooks Live!* and Counting Crows and Hootie, the same twin bed with plaid spread, the same desk with an ancient computer. I step in.

"Yeah. Ready," he says.

I sit down beside him, moving the walker. "I thought we might go to the 4120—you know, the Fort, the bar we used to go to?"

He does not say anything.

"OK?" Smiling. It seems like that is all I've been doing here. "OK?"

Ben looks at me. His eyes are sleepy. "Fine."

I want to kiss him then. Kiss him for making those pie-pan tombstones, kiss him for still being alive. It is a sudden rush, a twitch inside that can't get out, and it's not about love as much as about fear. I'm afraid that I won't ever be kissed, and afraid too that Ben won't ever be kissed either.

Ben and The Walker and I walk down the hall, out to the kitchen. Phyllis escorts us out in her housecoat.

"What you gonna see?" Phyllis asks. We are on the back porch. She

clutches her upper arms, her ponytail unrubberbanded, her hair unrav-
eled threads.

"Don't know yet," I say.

Ben just keeps walking with his trusty sidekick. Phyllis nods. Terrified
that I will take her damaged boy to an evil place, worried that I won't
bring him back. She walks backwards then into the house, talking, "Ben,
don't walk fast. You'll trip over that walker. You took your seizure pills,
right? Good. Be careful."

Her love is about walking backwards into her house. Her love is on the
phone with me, "Sure you can come for a visit, Mike. Ben misses having
people around," as if she and Chuck are not people: her love is about forgetting she and Chuck and Ben are people.

Peach schnapps and Dilantin. Sure I worry. Ben drinks the schnapps
though, downs it, his face stiff from the wonderful flavor. I figure it is all
I can give him.

Night-driving is like a dream out here, flat, grim little roads folding
back, out and around, barbed-wire fences like thousands of stitches after
a serious operation, anonymous houses you remember without ever having committed them to memory. I sip too. It is sixty or so miles, and we
get on the interstate around 10:30. Ben falls to sleep, the walker sleeping
on its side in the backseat in the rearview mirror. Tossing and turning a
little with each bump.

I pull into the place finally, the old, closed Target strip mall. Lots of
cars. I pull up, always uncomfortable coming here, but then where else do
I go? To a fucking country bar with my fellow employees at Winn? That's
where I belong, right? Not with the Sexy and the Fashion-Conscious and
the CK-One-Wearing of Dayton, but with the Lowdown and the
Haggard listening to Alan Jackson and Shania Twain, drinking Bud Light,
ordering wings. And of course Ben does not belong here either. He belongs at home, saying prayers to the dead kittens, throwing fits, sobbing.

I wake him up, though. He starts, the schnapps bottle dropping.

"Fuck," he says.

"Dreaming?"

"Yes," he snaps.

This is when I get out. I get out and stretch, look around, and then I
see Adam and Nameless getting out of Nameless's Tercel. I just stand
there, and it hits me that I must have done this on purpose. He and

Nameless start walking toward the throbbing techno temple. Meanwhile, groggy and awkward, Ben has gotten out of the passenger side on his own. Adam and Nameless do not wave. Nameless in leather pants! Nice hair. Reminds one of George Michael. And Adam. Once, one time only, he let me kiss him right after the Gloria Estefan concert I won tickets to from the radio. Kissed, once, and then me allowing myself to be fucked over again and again and again until I learned to love it.

"Adam!" I yell.

They stop and point.

I guess this is when I realize Ben has fallen down drunk, or with a seizure. My fault, my fault. Adam and Nameless run over. I go and I see Ben on the concrete, one little bloody place on his forehead from hitting the door maybe on his way down (goddamn he fell so silently), and I get the panic, the electrical fear plugged into the socket in my brain, and I start to cry but then again it's not crying. It's like a miscarriage.

Ben's face is peaceful on the ground, in seizure bliss, a dumb, half-shaky tranquility. I bend down and take his head in my hands, and maybe you are not supposed to lift people during a seizure or whatever, I don't know, but I am freaked, and Adam goes, I hear Adam go: "Mike, you want me to call 911?"

"No!" I scream.

Ben's eyes slide open. I think of Jesus in a movie, having been taken off the cross, Jesus's eyes opening, beautiful symphonic music playing.

"Just get the hell away," I say, not looking at Adam or at Nameless, just seeing their shoes on the pavement. Other shoes too.

Adam goes, "Mike, come on."

Nameless: "I am calling 911."

"No!" That one is a howl.

I look up and there they are, others gathering. Ben sits up on his own then, like a toddler learning about gravity.

"Home," he says. "Home." Like E.T.

I help Ben up. He slides into the seat. I walk toward Adam. "You can shove 911 up your ass," I say, or maybe just think it.

Adam tells me to stop, Nameless right beside him still. I stop.

"What is wrong with you?" Adam says. "That guy passed out!" His face is full of fear and disbelief. "You need to call an ambulance, Mike. Come on."

I stare at him for a few seconds, into his face, without saying anything. "Have you lost it?" Nameless says.

I walk backwards to the car, then get in.

The crowd all stand in my headlights, like the end of some serious movie, one nominated for several Oscars, but then it ends up winning zilch.

Phyllis and Chuck are fast asleep. I assist Ben to the bathroom by his bedroom. He slept most of the hour back, and he puked only a little. I was way too afraid to go to a hospital.

I am wiping his forehead as he sits on the toilet. Ben mumbles he is sorry. As I put a Band-Aid on the little cut, I picture him making the three pie-pan grave markers, picture him walking with them awkwardly outside, planting them into the ground, like finally he has sense enough to do this. Then it is a flash forward, but then backward too, from here in the bathroom making him better, to the day he did it, the time right before. I see him uninjured, just sitting in his room, plain but not ugly, alone. Then he gets it, like a bird landing on his windowsill, he gets it: *hey, it's time.*

Maybe he has a sore throat, or a long-lost love I don't know about, boy or girl, or a hatefulness so deep it requires immediate action, or maybe Phyllis left a note on the fridge for him to *start pulling his weight around here!,* or maybe he thought about being a little boy forever in a tree house, his face the size of a dime in a sweet, sunny world of after-life tree houses and butterflies singing Carpenters' songs and no reminder of what the world once fucking was.

In his room, now bandaged, Ben is fine. I realize I left his walker out in my car. I offer to go get it, but he does not hear me. He slides to the floor. I wonder if I should have woke Phyllis, told her about the seizure or whatever, but it would have gotten ugly I'm sure, and I did not need ugly right then in my life.

Ben pulls out a cardboard box from under his bed, and he says, looking up from it, on his knees: "Shut. The. Door. Lock. It."

I do. Nervous, crazy, knowing something is happening, knowing it. Maybe I should call Mom, tell her he drank schnapps with his Dilantin, she would not judge, she would—

The lid is off. Inside the box are three photo albums. You know the kind: floral-patterned vinyl covers with FAMILY ALBUM in curlicue gold leaf. He tells me to take one. I open the cover. Inside are crudely cut-out pictures of men. Just men, preserved under acetate. Men not naked or pornographic, but from Sears catalogs in work clothes, neckties, under-wear, men from Wal-Mart mail supplements in plaid shirts, hands in pockets, staring off into space with masculine skin and crystalline eyes. Men in B.V.D.s cut out from Christmas underwear gift packs. Black and white pictures of men from the newspaper: John F. Kennedy, Jr., riding a bike in Central Park; Al Gore smiling from a porch; an anonymous coun-cilman with a cute mustache. Men—hallelujah—it's raining men. Nameless, foreign, healthy, not gay not straight, men in regular everyday clothes and in tuxedos. Pierce Brosnan, Tom Cruise, Harrison Ford, the Diet Coke guy. A baseball player spitting out tobacco on the mound, a Marlboro man lighting up at sunrise.

All three are like that. Filled up. He is going to need to buy another album. "This is wonderful," I tell him. "You did this?"

Ben rolls his eyes, sarcastic and sleepy, understanding his own foolish pride. It hits me then that his life now is about his own nursery of men who do not speak or see or feel or hear or smell or taste, frozen by him, cut out with hands that have gross motor problems. He waits all day for magazines and supplements and the newspaper to arrive in the U.S. Mail so that he can search, find, preserve.

After a while I stop looking, help him put them back up. I don't know what to say. But he says, "So?"

"Nice," I say. His room is too bright from the ceiling fixture. I feel dim inside, though. Beautifully dim. I feel like we have been forgotten by the rest of the world, and this is just fine. I don't experience my usual late-night panic, my Adam-induced insomnia. I don't. Ben looks almost like he used to: backwards, kind, and a little confused.

Then I am tucking Ben into bed, kissing him good night, deeply kiss-ing him good night, feeling his hard-on under the plaid spread. My fat ass and I climb into his twin bed, after I turn out the lights. We do it.

It's not lovely, God knows, but it means everything. I feel like as we do it we are going back to a time when we were almost the same people, two kids, two stupid boys. I won't go into it anymore, though. There's noth-ing left to say, except to tell you that we don't say a single word, knowing we have a week. A whole week.

Kiana Davenport

Bones of the Inner Ear

From *Story*

LIGHTNING, AND a woman breaks in two. Zigzag of ions, her bone-snap of scream. I remember skies crackling. A roasted peacock falling from a tree. I remember a man's hair turning fright-wig blue. Is what one remembers what really occurred? Uncle Noah said every moment has two truths.

We came from the rough tribes of Wai'anae, wild west coast of the island. Here, native clans spawned outcasts and felons, yet our towns had names like lullabies. Makaha, Ma'ili, Nanakuli, Lualualei. In Nanakuli, a valley slung like a hammock between mountain and sea, I was born in a house known for its damaged men.

Long before my birth time, Grandpa came home from World War I with his nose shot off. Doctors built him a metal nose, which he removed at night before he slept. Folks said that's why Grandma went insane, lying under his empty face. Uncle Ben came back from World War II without an arm. His younger brother, Noah, returned from combat in Korea, silent as a grub. In time, my cousin Kimo would come home from Vietnam carrying eighteen ounces of shrapnel that they took from his leg before they amputated it.

When Grandma finally died in the crazy asylum, folks came from everywhere, bringing baskets of food, then sat watching our men like people at a zoo. Grandpa and his boys drank too much, stripped off their clothes, raved and danced with savage grace while light hung in the space of their missing limbs. Their mutilations glowed. They wrestled their boar hounds to the ground, played pitch and catch with Grandpa's nose till everyone went home.

After his war, Grandpa worked as a coffin repairman at DeMarkles Mortuary, so we grew up on his corpse tales—the terminally infected, the futilely stitched. Women outrunning their stillborns. Bullets outrunning young men. Sometimes while he told his eerie tales, things flew out of the windows of our house. A kitchen knife when our uncles were at it. Bottles aimed at garbage-tipping dogs. Once Kiki flew through a window, thrown by her mother, Aunty Ava, one of Grandpa's daughters.

Five headstrong Hawai'ian beauties, they were famous up and down the coast. Pua, Ginger, and Jade. My mother, Lily. And Ava. She was the one I kept my eye on. Ava and Mama were taxi dancers. Slow-hipped, honey-colored, each night they dressed for the dance halls, Ava rice-powdering her cheeks and arms, trying to make them paler, Mama puckering and rouging her perfect lips. Sometimes in sleep I climb behind my mother's eyes. I slip into her skin. I glide with handsome mix-bloods at the dance halls, legs wrapped around thighs that rudder me round the floor.

Some nights Kiki's father came, a handsome Filipino drummer. He'd close the door to Ava's room. Their singing bedsprings, call-and-response of human moans. Then, the sound of him slapping her, a series of screams. Grandpa aiming his pig-hunting rifle, the drummer running down the road. One night Ava roared up the lane, arms slung around a new man, a surfer on a Harley. Grandpa threw her suitcase in the yard and locked the door. Weeks later, she came begging, and he took her back. She stood in the doorway, flicking ashes, throwing off perfumes. For a while I worshipped her.

One day for no reason, she hit Kiki so hard, the girl flipped sideways, landing on her head. Her eyes rolled backward, showing white, a trick that took my breath. That night it was quiet; I was careful where I looked. Then Grandpa walked up to the chair Ava sat in, lifted her and the chair over his head, and threw them both across the room. She just lay there, her cheekbone's shadow on the floor.

My father was a saxophonist on inter-island cruise ships. When he was in port, he liked to surprise Mama by climbing through her window. After he left, she would sleep for days. I would sit outside her door, listening as she snored softly, cousin Kiki beside me. We girls grew so close, we could just look at each other and feel safe.

Life went on in Nanakuli. Shootings. Whirl-kick karate death gangs. Marijuana farmers were hauled off to Halawa prison, while girls gave birth in high-school johns. But there was Nanakuli magic, too. Wild-pig hunting with our uncles, their boar hounds singing up jade mountains. Or, torch-fishing nights, elders chanting, bronze muscles flashing, strained by dripping haunches of full nets. In tin-roofed shacks, women swayed, stirring meals at rusty stoves, their shadows epic on the walls.

When all five daughters brought their men home, our house bulged and rocked with human drama. In the mornings while they slept, my cousins and I slicked mulberry juice on our lips, turning them a ghoulish blue, scraped green mold from the walls and smeared it on our eyelids, then pinned plumeria in our hair and slow-danced in couples like the grown-ups.

Then Ava's husband reappeared. The clang of his belt buckle as he draped his pants over the end of their bed. Sounds of passion, then, predictably, her screams. For years, I blamed her temper on that man. Now, I know she was swollen with Grandma's genes. She was blister-tight. She slammed Kiki's head with an iron skillet. Shaved her bald for telling a lie. One day she held Kiki's hand over open flames until Uncle Noah pinned her to the wall.

Year after year, I watched him retreat, observing the world from his window, the windowsill growing shiny through the years of his forearms. He did not remember Korea. When we mentioned that war, Noah frowned, asked if we had made it up. Having dismissed the past, he grew acutely aware of the present, focusing more and more on Ava.

She had grown up wanting to be an Olympic swimmer but then she turned beautiful and the dance halls found her. Folks said she looked like Lena Horne. Ava had a second child. The father, a graceful Chinese famous for his tango, was only five years older than Kiki and me. Grandpa threw Ava out again. She never made it to the clinic. Her baby slid out in the backseat of Nanakuli's only taxi while the driver knelt in the bushes vomiting.

Much later Ava told us how she bit the umbilical cord, swung the baby upside down, slapped it till it screamed, and wrapped it in her skirt. Then she climbed up to the driver's seat, stuffed the man's jacket between her legs, and stole his taxi. For years I pictured her speeding off in a rusty Ford, her newborn yelling itself purple while she shifted gears and struggled with her afterbirth.

She and the tango-man hid out in Chinatown, living off the sale of the stripped-down cab. When they were finally arrested, Grandpa posted bail, Ava was put on probation, and he brought her home. The baby, Taxi, was beautiful. But when Kiki bent to lift her little brother, Ava lunged at her.

"Touch him, I break your arm!"

Kiki stood straight, so she and her mother were eye to eye. "Guarantee. I never again come near your little bastard."

It was the first time I saw Kiki's edge. I saw something else that day. Her walk was becoming obvious. For several years now, she had listed slightly, as if her right foot were deprived of a natural heel. Each year the lopsided walk was more pronounced. Grandpa took her to a foot doctor who found nothing, but an ear specialist said her equilibrium was off. Tiny bones of her inner ear were permanently damaged. I thought of Kiki flying headfirst through a window, her mother swinging an iron skillet like a baseball bat. Kiki's flame-scarred hand that took away her lifeline. I crawled into her bed and held her.

That summer was so dry, barking deer stumbled down from the mountains, licking windows of air-conditioned stores. The piss of boar hounds sizzled on tar. Mongooses crawled under our house, coughing and sucking at the pipes. And in the midst of it, my father. A word that always silenced me. He came with his somber eyes and closed the door to my mother's room. I know he loved her at one time. I don't believe he lied. I think that time moved on.

I lifted the window shade, watching moonlight on my feet, imagining my father pacing Mama's room, saying he would not be back. I thought how folks appeared and vanished in our lives, and wondered what controlled them. I pictured a big celestial genie, rubbing whatever makes humans come and go. He left and she played dead as usual. I thought she was playing. Grandpa cried for nights on end, and then we buried her. Shortly after, I slept through a hurricane that lasted three days.

At sixteen Kiki discovered dancing, that when she danced she did not limp. She began to smell of aftershave. Someone was teaching her to tango.

One night she knelt beside my bed. "Ana! I'm in love with Gum. Father of little Taxi."

I sat up, stunned. "You crazy? What about your mama."

"She never loved him. Or anyone."

Gum tried to explain it to Ava; we knew because we heard her screams. We started running up the road, on into the valley, into deep jungle throats that swallowed us. For hours, we shinnied up lava boulders, clinging to roots and knotted vines. Up to our refuge behind a waterfall. Years back when we first braved the falls, we discovered, behind them, an eerie grotto draped in moss, full of scattered bones.

Now, crawling behind those thundering drapes, we fell exhausted into the cave, into man-shaped hollows centuries old. In the dimness, bones glowed green and blue. We lay side by side, feeling warmth from the sun the earth had swallowed. We were children again, cradled in stone.

"Sometimes I see things," Kiki whispered. "I hope they don't see me . . . I hope they don't come after me."

I knew she was afraid she would inherit her mother's temper. "Do you think Grandma did the same thing to your mama?"

"Maybe. Maybe if Mama shaved her head, we'd see the scars."

We stayed behind the falls all night, and in those hours Kiki tried to change her life. Take it off like a coat, leave it behind.

"I'm a woman now. She strike again, I strike back."

Next day we shot out of those falls like bullets, plunging feet-first into thundering foam, down into a swirling river. Grandpa, out searching in his grass rain-cape, found us exhausted on the shore. We marched home like woman warriors, full of resolution.

Ava must have sensed it. She never mentioned Gum, but at night she stood in Kiki's room, staring at the empty bed. One day I heard Taxi scream, then muffled silence. Blue moons appeared on his arms and legs, little bruises the size of a pinch. Grandpa saw them too and started throwing chairs again, telling Ava to get out for good, he would raise her kids. She fell to her knees, screaming and pleading.

Grandpa gave in, of course, and Ava stayed. Then our family began to rinse away. One sister stepped into a chauffeured car, was never seen again. Another joined the Catholic order. Third sister married a Samoan who swallowed fire for a living and smelled of gasoline. One-legged Cousin Kimo shocked us all by enrolling at the island's big university.

Soon there was just Ava, Noah, and Ben, assorted cousins left with Grandpa.

He began complaining about his nose, and doctors gave him a new one, an ugly prosthetic that looked eerily real. It had a bitter plastic smell and gave him pain. Then he felt nothing. His nasal passages had gangrened. Grandpa's face was so damaged when he died, we buried him wearing a mask, laid out in his mildewed white linen suit, a ti leaf across his chest for safe journey. Clans came from up and down the coast, leaning into his coffin, trying to see the horror beneath the mask. They twisted in their pews, staring at us like the old days.

I kept my eyes on Ava, still beautiful in a menacing way. Taxi, beside her, five years old, a timid, jumpy little thing, but slender and graceful like his father. Mama had been Grandpa's favorite, but I think Ava loved him best of all. Now she moved to his coffin, her voice growing ugly and amplified.

"Papa! How come all these years you never give me credit? Always yelling how I raise my kids? How come all these years you never *love* me!"

She rocked the coffin back and forth, trying to heave it over. When Father Riley ran down from the altar and tried to pull her back, Ava picked him up and threw him to his knees so hard he skidded. Uncle Ben shouted, reached out with his arm, and knocked her down. In that moment, Kiki moved to little Taxi, took his hand, and quickly led him up the aisle, her walk still lopsided, listing to the right. We buried Grandpa and brought Ava home. She sat in her room, whispering and rocking.

One night she stood in my doorway, then crept close and, with dreamy precision, tapped my hand.

"Your father was real mischief. He once put a lizard in my handbag. Oh, *he* was a dancer!"

I couldn't move. I felt like something with its mouth stitched shut.

She leaned so close, I saw her fillings, blue-black as lava. Strands of saliva clung to the roof of her mouth.

"I had him first, you know. But he was nothing. He just lived. I gave him to your mama."

I looked straight into her eyes. "She killed herself, didn't she?"

"Yes! She was pregnant." She threw back her head and laughed. "Men. They just lay there."

"Maybe they're afraid of you," I said. "Even Kiki's afraid of you. She should hate you . . . all those scars."

Ava laughed again. "Scars make her *interesting.*"

Then her skin grew tight, her cheekbones looked whittled down to knuckles. "Where's my boy, Taxi?"

"I won't tell you."

She grabbed my wrist, shook it like a club. "You get him back. Else I burn this house down."

For days, cars dragged up and down our road. One of the boar hounds had dropped a litter and twelve puppies were for sale. Two were bought by a drag queen out shopping for accessories. She had seen Taxi with Kiki and Gum, practicing at Castro Dance Hall. "Such a little Fred Astaire!"

Hearing that, Ava climbed out of her window and stole the drag queen's truck. She found Taxi asleep in Gum's car beside the dance hall. Nowhere else to run, she drove home and locked the boy in her room with her. At first he screamed, then she calmed him down, holding him, rocking him like a mother. I watched her through the keyhole.

A day and a night we pleaded, banging on the door. Then Ben lowered a bottle of milk on a rope from the second floor down to her window. Ava opened it just enough to grab the bottle. For three days we passed her baskets of food dangled from the rope. She and the child messed in a bucket which she emptied out the window every night. We heard them laughing. Singing kid songs. When we called Taxi's name, he answered. He and his mama were playing games.

Ben grew impatient. At night while Ava and the boy slept, he tried to wedge her door loose near the hinges. One day, as she reached out the window for their food, Ben tried to break the door in.

Ava went berserk. "You not going take my boy! I warned! I warned!"

Her screams were so awful Kiki dropped to her knees, praying out loud. We called their names for hours, then finished breaking in the door. She lay in the corner with her smothered child. She had slashed her neck to pieces trying to cut her artery. Noah picked up the blood-red boy, carried him outside, and sat in sunlight, hugging him. He opened and closed his mouth like a fish, rocking the body to and fro.

We buried Taxi next to Grandpa, and Ava followed Grandma to Kanehoe State Hospital. Folks drove past our house, taking pictures. I ran out with Grandpa's camera and shot back. But images came after me, tracking me by body heat like morays. I started running in my dreams. One night I boarded a bus, following the ruby-strung arrow of taillights bound for Honolulu.

I learned fast, woman-fast, and in time became a nurse, finding a whole new lineup of humans among the injured and diseased. People who asked nothing of me but comfort. I learned detachment, how to cure, or turn away. I learned you can save a life by lying. And that some folks *need* to die. I hugged the dead even when they'd rigored, in case a soul was hanging back. I held a man's heart outside his chest and found the pulse consoling.

A bifurcated woman. Half of me nursing strangers, the other half nursing drinks at 2 A.M. Stroking slips the color of old peach skin, smelling perfume still clinging to her hairpins. Somewhere, my father had been measured for a hat. Mama had kept that piece of paper with the figures. That's all I was sure of, my mother's slip size, my father's head measurements. Some nights I listened to saxophones. Sometimes at dusk I wept.

Why they released Ava was never clear. Crowded wards. Her age, her edges turning soft and blurred. Uncle Ben signed the release and brought her home, then called me. I stood in that road, beloved slum of potholes, chicken coops, animal fat frying. The house ran out to meet me. Uncle Noah waved, still polishing the windowsill with his forearms. Swimming in the bright aquarium of his thoughts. For years now, he had watched an empty chair rock to and fro, remembering the boy who sat there. That's when I understood how much he had loved little Taxi.

Ava was wearing an ink-colored wig, her forehead pressed to her bedroom wall, telling her confession. Her teeth were gone, eyes empty craters, neck a pearly grid of scars. She turned and ran at me headfirst, then jerked back, like something leaping the length of its chain. She didn't know me. But she had started again on Kiki, whispering outside her door at night. Lurid, obscene things no daughter should have heard. I packed Kiki's bags, planning to take her to Honolulu. But she retreated, up to her elbows in pastries. She had stopped dancing, stopped everything. All she did was eat. Ava kept stalking her, even tried to climb in bed with her.

Uncle Ben shook his head, stroking the shoulder where his arm had been. "Bad thing, I brought her home. She drive dat girl to suicide."

Lightning season came. Air so electric, the fillings in our teeth hummed. Everything we touched just sparked. There were flash floods;

the seas gave off a yellow glow. For days lightning zigzagged up the valley. It hit a wild pig that rolled into our yard, completely roasted. Voltaged peacocks fell from trees. One night herringbones of ions, lightning striking everywhere. No one saw Ava leave the house. But then, sky crackling, her awful scream. We found Ben standing over her, his hair electrified a gaseous blue.

She lay facedown, spread out like a pelt. Paramedics said lightning. But her body seemed untouched. Then they said she must have tripped and fallen. The medical examiner found a big crack in the back of her skull from a powerful blow. He thought lightning had hit a branch which struck her. Folks said Ben struck the blow. Or, Kiki. The skies calmed down. We buried Ava, then sat back, tipping long-necked beers, letting the wounded world become green glass. Those moments were as kind as life would get.

Several years passed before I walked that road again. I stood before the house, completely shocked. Kiki was sitting on the porch, so absolutely huge, she looked like a sofa. She now weighed almost four hundred pounds. She had a heart condition and was deaf in one ear. She was peeling something in a bowl when she looked up. Slowly, almost impossibly, she rose to her feet, which were so swollen, they looked like loaves of bread. She tried to struggle down the steps; I ran forward, flung my arms around her legs, and wept. Kiki bent and stroked my hair.

That night, Ben took me aside, explaining how a year after Gum moved to Seattle, Kiki had tried to hang herself. She thought no one was home. A burglar roaming the house stepped into her room just as she started to kick the chair from under her feet. The man shouted, climbed up beside her on the chair, held her round the waist, and talked to her for hours. Kiki fell in love with the burglar who saved her life.

He moved into the house, and he and Kiki had a child. He sounded like a good man, good to her, but one night he took off down the road forever. Ben said it was Kiki's "fits" that drove him off. They came out of nowhere, like her mother's. Her baby girl was almost two now, a chubby little thing named Lily, for my mother. I found her tethered to a clothesline like a dog. I knelt, looking for bruises, then held her for a while.

I came home again for Uncle Noah. Most of his years had been lived in silence and now, nearing seventy, he was ready to come to a stop. I knelt beside his bed.

"You were always my hero, did you know? I loved how you had all the answers, and kept them to yourself."

He smiled, drifted for a while, then half sat up, pointing to his closet. Inside was something big and round wrapped in moldy cloth. He said two words. "Bury it." That night I unwrapped it in my room. Rusty now, the way iron gets. The weight of the skillet still profound. The back still matted with blood, gray strands of hair, bits of her skull like ice chips. I wiped it clean, buried it with Noah, and went back to Honolulu.

Some nights I sit with patients, placing my hand on their chests to make sure they're still breathing, adjusting my breathing to theirs. Sharing the rhythmic rise and fall. Sometimes the moon-metal blade of a scalpel is like a candle in my face by which I see my life reflected. A careful life, no shocks, no faulty perceptions. A life completely watered-down. Once, I proposed to a man while I emptied his bedpan. I said I liked the way he snored; snores let you know where people are. He thought I was joking. I checked a mirror to see if my face was behaving, then went home and slept for days.

Sometimes I visit cousin Kimo, a lawyer now, pride of Nanakuli. I watch how gently his son unstraps his father's artificial leg. I stir the ashes of our childhood, wondering why some of us managed to escape that house while others didn't. Kimo says it's in the egg. He says I look like my mother. He says I sleep too much.

Kiki's still living there with Ben's widow and come-and-go cousins. Her heart is worse; medications leave her drowsy. She has forgotten the metaphysics of walking. Her seizures take her unaware. Some days I sit beside her while she naps, her body a breathing mountain. Her features have almost disappeared, but somewhere in that mask of flesh is the girl behind the waterfall: edgy, tough, full of resolution.

One day she wakes and smiles at me. "Even in my sleep, Mama's trying to catch up with me. But, ho! I still outrun her."

I love this woman more and more. Our genes are warped together. Her morphology is mine. And I love her because she's still fighting the hole that wants to suck her in.

Young Lily is eight now. Brown skinned, lovely. Very bright. Books and toys, a star chart on her ceiling. But something fractured in her eyes. She stands in the kitchen, playing with knobs, watching the slow transformation of electric stove rings turn from gray to orange. She broods in her room full of secrets. One day, I hear her voice, eerie and old. I hear dull thuds and open her door. She's holding a doll I've never seen, an ugly, twisted, broken thing.

"I warned you and warned you," she whispers. "You selfish little bitch." She slaps its face repeatedly. She bangs its head against the floor.

I turn away, keeping myself blind to signals, avoiding the Morse of Lily's steps. That is, I look down when she walks toward me, and when she walks away. I don't want to see that her walk is funny, that she seems to tilt.

But then she comes dragging that ugly, battered doll, its head wrapped in bandages, makeshift Band-Aids on its legs. Lily thrusts herself between my arms, half sitting in my lap, demanding, not asking for, my attention. A quirky and aggressive child. I hug her, pointing to the doll.

"What's all this? I thought you hated her."

She pats its head. "Yeah. But, she needed medical attention."

I laugh. "Well, Lily. Maybe one day you'll be a nurse."

She steps back and studies me. Then adamantly she shakes her head. "No, Aunty! I going be one *doctor*. I going tell folks what to do."

I hug her again, because she is the best of her mother—edgy, full of resolution. She hugs me back with young-girl arms, yet I feel her toughness and her tremor, as if her blood is already marshaling tiny armies that will reinstruct her genes. As if she is already breaking the mold, honoring the daughters born with no clues or codes, and the mothers of those daughters—golden, slow-hipped women who should have been running, not dancing.

J. Robert Lennon

The Fool's Proxy

From *Harper's Magazine*

WHEN THE war was over, Grant clipped his hair close to the scalp and rode to Eleven, where he found a man to drive him out to the station. The man's name was Harper. He was a textile dealer who wore good clothes often stained with the juice from exotic fruit he'd had sent special from California, which he could be found casually eating at any time. He wasn't eating now, but Grant could smell it on his sweet breath. The car he drove was sleek and new but beaten around the runners and tire wells by rocks and bits of hardened mud. He asked Grant if he was taking a trip and Grant said he was, and the two said nothing more to each other until they reached the station. By Grant's reckoning, it was not yet six A.M.

There had been a town here called Grissom, but nobody lived in it now. When Grant was a boy two Mexicans had been hanged here for stealing somebody's horses. This was long after such things were decreed by courts, but the men had no local family and not much English, and no one who knew of their crimes objected to the punishment. That they were guilty was beyond doubt. They were found on the range asleep by the stolen horses, with their Winchesters stupidly lashed to the riggings. Grant was not sure where they'd been hanged, possibly the lowest rung of the water tower, but he did remember that for some time nobody bothered to cut down their bodies. Not long afterward the last inhabitants of Grissom quit the area for good.

Take care of yourself, Harper told Grant, and extended his soft hand. Grant took it and nodded his thanks and got out of the car.

There was some doubt that the train would stop at all. He had sent a letter saying he would be here to meet it, but he had not requested a reply. If the train came he planned to get on it and ride it as far as it took him, and if it didn't he would go back to the ranch and resume work as if nothing had happened. His parents and brother would know what he had tried to do but would not be inclined to say anything about it.

As it happened an old man was waiting here, wearing a crisp new suit and clutching a shabby carpetbag. His jaw worked with an involuntary motion, but he regarded Grant with clear eyes that followed him as he walked to the only other bench on the tiny platform. The bench shifted under him, then steadied. Above him hung a sign with GRISSOM painted clearly on it. The windows of the station house behind him were covered by bare boards. Across the tracks stood a silo with its elevator in ruins at its foot, and behind it rose a solitary table of earth in the indeterminate distance, disfigured by a weird rocky outcrop the wind appeared to have ignored and that could have served as a stage on which giants performed for travelers of the past.

Grant took off his hat and looked over at the old man. The old man had been watching and now looked away.

Since the victory over Japan, Grant had given this journey a great deal of thought, and he had pictured himself much as he was right now, seated and calmly awaiting his train. He had imagined the rocking motion the train would make and the swaying of his fellow passengers with it and the soundless slosh of his breakfast coffee in the dining car. Less clear in his mind was his destination or what he might do when he got there. He supposed there would be a railroad hotel with whores and a bar and a soft-spoken bartender who would tell him where to go to find work. He intended to reach the Atlantic Ocean and walk barefoot into it, his shoes and socks behind him on the beach. Beyond that, imagination failed him.

Something moved in his peripheral vision, and he looked up to find the old man coming toward him, holding his bag close as if someone might take it from him.

Time? the man said.

Grant had no watch. He said he didn't know. This didn't seem to satisfy the old man, but he asked nothing further and remained standing between the benches, as if to return was more effort than he could bear to expend. A strong wind passed like a ghost train through the station, and both men touched their hands to their hats. Light began to gather as if pulled by the wind. Grant offered the man a seat on his bench.

'Bliged, said the man.

He was on his way to Chicago, he said, to visit with a son and his wife and children. The journey filled him with dread, because he could not remember the name of his son's wife or the names of his grandchildren or even how many of them there were. He feared that he wouldn't recognize them at the station and that they would turn him away. Additionally, he feared the ride in his son's car to their home outside the city. He had seen pictures of the thousands of cars that raced along the highways and worried about an accident. Grant didn't know what to tell him. These seemed like valid fears. He asked the man where he lived.

Oh, right 'round here.

Grissom?

The old man frowned without meeting Grant's eyes. Not no more, he said.

Sometime later the train came into view in the distance. It came slowly and didn't seem to get any larger as it approached, so that when it stopped before them it appeared a small thing to Grant, powerless to take them any significant distance. Its doors fell open, but no one came to usher them inside. Grant stood up and asked the old man if he'd like a hand with his bag, but the man ignored the question and made his own way onto the train and disappeared.

Grant followed with neither reluctance nor eagerness, mounting the three steps because it was what he had anticipated doing. Although the day was now bright, the car was dark. A few passengers sat in grimy pools of light cast through soiled windows, while unoccupied seats remained shadowed by heavy opaque curtains. The passengers were asleep. Grant walked to the center of the car, raised his bag to the overhead rack, then thought better and set it down on a nearby seat. He slid in after it. No pull was visible for the curtain, so he grabbed two handfuls of the fabric and pushed it aside. Already the train had begun to move. He watched the strange butte roll out of view, then brought his bag onto his lap as if he might open it. But there was nothing inside that he needed and he put it back.

He fell asleep. He sensed the braking of the train and the passage of others in the aisle. Around him more curtains were opening and whispered conversations grew louder. He felt a hand on his shoulder and opened his eyes to find the conductor standing over him, one hand holding his tickets and punch and the other plunged into his change pocket. He asked how far Grant was going.

Where's it headed to?

Chicago.

Okay, Grant told him, and paid. Then he fell back to sleep.

When he next woke the sun was high outside over a miniature range of hills with cattle walking on them, and a heavy man of about sixty sat beside him. The man had one hand in Grant's bag, which Grant had left open when he paid the conductor. Now the man removed his hand.

Where're you headed, soldier?

Grant met the man's eyes, which were small and hard, like plum stones. Chicago, he said.

Son, you ought to know this ain't Company B. You leave your belongings unguarded beside you like that and you will find them made off with.

Grant zipped the bag shut and pushed it underneath the seat with his calves resting against it. When he had settled himself, the stranger stretched his body out, shoving both feet under the seat in front, and slipped off each shoe using the toe of the opposite foot. With his creased wool trousers and starched shirt mussed by travel, he carried the air of a modest businessman and an odor of monotonous work reluctantly done. An occasional tic wrinkled his nose and mouth. He was ewe-necked, with a large head that swayed like a daisy when he talked. He had not taken his eyes off Grant.

Been out on the Pacific coast, have you? Back from where?

Grant glanced out the window. A motte of tall leaning cottonwoods passed, cupping a cluster of what could have been broken tombstones. He felt played out, though he'd just woken up. He would have been out riding line right now, seeking fence to fix. Instead, it was likely to be his brother Max doing it. About now they would all be acting like Grant had never been.

Okinawa, he said, as the graveyard hove out of sight. Peleliu.

The man nodded. Not Iwo, huh?

No.

Ever eat dog?

No, Grant said.

The man was laughing. Damn good thing, he said. These boys come back saying they ate dog as if it's an admirable thing. God damn. He stuck out a bent hand, the knuckles tough and enlarged like knots in a branch. Sam Kroch, he said, high at the end like a question, so that Grant did not immediately know it was his name the man was speaking.

Grant Person, Grant said presently and shook the hand.

You a farm boy, son? You have got a sun-pecked look to you.

Yessir.

You going home? Indiana? Illinois?

Indiana.

So you're a hero back home, are you? Look at you, all in one piece. Some of these boys come back all tied up together like a pot roast. You get yourself shot?

The wound grew hot at the question, the one thing Grant had as evidence if he needed it. Scarred white and without hair, it had resulted when a horse dragged a rope hard around his calf, cutting a channel through his trousers and into the flesh. This was four years before. It could pass as a bullet wound if it had to.

I took a bullet in the leg at Peleliu, he said. Healed up good. He cleared his throat. I still favor it some, he said.

Kroch laughed as if at a clever joke. I don't doubt that, he said, not a bit. And he tipped his head back, still smiling, and went to sleep.

For a short time there were six of them, all boys. The oldest was called Edwin. He was eight the winter Grant was seven, naturally broader in the shoulders and face and taller due to his age. This was at the onset of the Depression, and of all the children only Edwin seemed to understand the gravity of the situation and under it grew serious and sure, like a person expected to take control of the outfit at any moment if necessary, which in fact he was. At seven Grant was still thought of as a child, his horsemanship a form of play not work, his assigned tasks around the place chores as opposed to duties. The others truly were children: Thornton, who was slow, even for a four-year-old; Robert, who at two and a half was Thornton's playmate and protector; Max, who was barely walking; and Wesley, the sickly newborn. In which way he was sick was unclear initially. He was declared colicky and cried evenings for many hours before sleep. He refused milk. When Grant thought about this time, which was not often, he remembered Max sucking greedily at the breast, his shod feed dangling off the chair, while Wesley lay silent and watchful nearby in the bassinet. Wesley was born tiny and did not grow significantly.

Their mother's name was Asta and their father called her Ann. His name was John. He was raised in the north of England and collected her from her home in Iceland during the first war. She had kept house with her mother there while her father raised sheep, and now in America she kept house and bore sons while her husband raised sheep. Growing up, Grant never heard a single word of Icelandic from her, and few of anything else. Nevertheless her English was perfect. Although she would not have been called beautiful, she stood apart from other women in the clarity and fullness of her features and by her great height, nearly six feet. She was feared and respected by the ranch men, most of whom she stood taller than. Among those who feared her was John, who was small and talkative and boastful, and whose strange skills, such as carving toys from pinewood and playing the fiddle, distracted him from ranch work, at which he was mediocre at best. Away from Asta he seemed to blame her for his ineptitude. He could often be heard wondering what good she had done him, with all of her supposed sheep smarts. In earshot of her he would blame the shiftlessness and disobedience of the boys, once they were old enough to blame. For her part Asta ignored his complaints and continued to provide him with sons. She knew as well as he did the worth, on a ranch, of six boys.

On Christmas night 1929 they ate dinner together alone, without the hands. This uncharacteristic family privacy made them all uncomfortable, and they struggled for things to say. Wesley nursed weakly for a short time, then once laid down began to cry, and the sound seemed to unhinge Asta, who held her knife and fork tightly but didn't touch them to her food. When John told her to go quiet him, Edwin got up from the table, went to the bassinet, and whispered in the baby's ear. In minutes he was asleep.

The following morning Wesley woke congested in the nose and throat and spent the day facedown on their mother's lap, expelling mucus. Two days later he began to turn gray, then dull purple in large blotches, and his fingers went cold and stiff. The following afternoon his head began to bulge at the fontanel. He stopped crying. That night he fell into a coma, and he died under the doctor's care in the late morning of January 1.

Grant had dreamed that a gentle horse, a blood bay, had entered the house and knelt before the bassinet, and tiny Wesley had climbed onto its red back and ridden away into the night. That afternoon he went to his mother where she lay next to the baby's still body and told her what he had dreamed, and without turning over to face him she reached back and slapped him hard enough to knock him down. In the morning they buried the baby in a wind-scraped corner of the pasture starveout where even the horses never bothered going. John enclosed the grave with fence, leaving ample room around it as if he knew what was to come.

While Kroch slept Grant tried to imagine what life in Indiana might have been like had he actually lived there. He expected it was gentler in Indiana, with more time for sleep and less sickness among the animals. Or perhaps there wouldn't have been animals. They might have grown corn, just that one thing, and the world would have bought it from them. The train was nearly to Minnesota now, and night was falling. Passengers filled the compartment. The look of them made Grant glad Kroch had chosen him. It was not uncommon during the war to see women alone or alone with children, but the women in this car were accompanied, and all the solitary travelers were men. They varied in age and appearance, but all had the eyes of outlaws, or so it seemed to Grant. They carried bought bags with few signs of use, as if they were only props stuffed with balled-up newspapers. This train rocked much as he had imagined, but he had no sense of nearness to anyone on it. Activity in towns they passed looked staged, and of course with his first lie he had turned into an actor. This was not a simple matter of making up a story and telling it to whomever he encountered; it was himself he was inventing, a version of him who had spent years in the company of other young men and had known the drudge and racket of war.

But he hadn't. He had spent his youth in ever-increasing solitude, without reference to others. He had gone among the men back home and made no impression, and had never paid his own looks or talk any mind. He could vanish in the creases of land and not be thought of by anyone. Now suddenly he was traveling in a landscape of eyes.

He was able to sleep with his heels clinched tight against his bag for safekeeping. When he woke it was to a scene of straight, flat paved roads and cars that waited at intersections for the train to go by. Towns flashed past until they ran together, and this was the city. Passengers woke as if by a sixth sense. Kroch was among them, his clear eyes on Grant.

There she is, son, he said.

Grant looked out to make sure he meant Chicago and not some specific structure. I reckon my daddy's here to meet me, he said.

Maybe I ought to wait around and see that. A hero's welcome.

Grant reached out and steadied himself against the seat in front, quelling nausea. The train was slowing. I ain't any kind of hero, he said.

Kroch was laughing. The way you tell that story, I believe it.

I don't follow, he said without looking.

Kroch was close now, right up at his ear. You have got to convince yourself before you can convince other people, boy. You don't even say your name like you mean it.

Grant felt him retreat, felt his body rise from the seat. He turned fast and found Kroch in the aisle peering down at him.

It's my name, Grant said, and saw people turn.

A smile found Kroch's face. Okay, Grant Person. Now you sound like a honest man. The train moaned and stopped, and Kroch kept his balance like a steel beam. People got up all at once, but Kroch was ahead of them, down the stairs and across the filthy platform.

Grant followed the other passengers through heavy glass doors into a room of stupendous size crammed tight with the sounds of footsteps and their echoes. It was like a cathedral where you worshiped by walking. He stood with his eyes shut while people arced around him from behind as if herded. He wondered if they would crush one another to death if obstructed, as sheep were known to do. His bag, bumped by passersby, was tugging at his hand like a leashed dog, so he found a place on a long high-backed pew and caught his breath. In time a man and woman and child sat down nearby, and he looked toward the woman and said, I want to get a train to New York City.

She wore a pink dress with frills and a hat with fake flowers on it, and her hand went to her child's shoulder and then her husband's.

What? the man said turning. You said what?

I want to get the train to New York.

The man was holding a cigar, turning it in his hand. Well, you go to New York, soldier. It isn't any of my business. He brought out a silver guillotine from his coat and sliced the cigar end clean off. The cut end dropped to the floor.

Where? Grant asked him.

What! now with the cigar between his teeth. The child, a boy, was staring.

Where do I get the train?

The man snorted and pointed, then shook his head as if flinging Grant free of it. Then the woman stood, pulled her son from his seat, walked to her husband's opposite side, and sat down.

The man lit his cigar. Well? he said.

There was a train leaving on the hour. He bought a ticket and was shown where to go to get on. While waiting he came across a machine that dispensed sandwiches, and he put his coins into it. The carousel turned and he opened a door, then thought better of his choice and quickly shut it. But the next door he tried wouldn't give, and neither would the first one when he tried it again.

Nearby two doors yawned into light, and he could see cars moving on a street. He went out. The city looked like it did in pictures, except lived in, with buildings faded or crumbling from use and the cars nudging around one another with the scattershot instinct of insects. The order of city streets now seemed an illusion, like the smooth contours of rough land viewed from a distance. In each direction traffic lights changed in slow succession, a wave of red and then green sweeping across the city. A taxi stopped before him, and a man dashed toward it and climbed in. Grant watched the taxi pull away. He was hungry.

The train stopped frequently at stations and sometimes stood still in lush countryside for no apparent reason. When it moved it moved slowly. Grant's compartment was full. He washed himself in a rural station bathroom and changed his clothes. When he learned the price of food in the dining car he tried to abstain in part from regular meals, but at times hunger overtook him and he ate without concern for money or manners. The men and women who shared his table didn't speak to him, and he offered nothing to their conversation. He listened while they talked about Atlantic City. Men spent entire days making sand castles there. One could witness a seven-foot shark in a glass tank and a horse that jumped from a great height into the ocean. This last seemed hard to believe. His fellow diners asked their waiter if he knew the city, and when he said he did asked him if there really was a beach for coloreds and special entertainment for them as well. The waiter said that indeed there was, it was the hottest spot on the coast. One woman in the group occasionally met Grant's eyes with a kind look, and he thought of her soft features and long neck at great length as he went to sleep that night.

By the time the train reached the station Grant understood that he didn't want to be in New York after all. He considered the cars and lights he'd seen in Chicago, and the thought made him very tired. For a while he sat on a bench much like the one he'd sat on there, and he closed his eyes and daydreamed about home. The routine in which his days were milled was absent utterly, like a cycle of weather going on halfway around the world. He wished he had a horse to ride. He would find the beach, and the horse would test itself on the shifting sand. It would shy at first from the advancing water, then master itself and crash through the tide, leaving prints that washed away behind it. When he opened his eyes he watched his dining companions pass without noticing his presence there. When they had disappeared he made his way to a ticket window and asked how to get to Atlantic City.

He was told he could get a bus at Grand Central.

Which way? he said.

But when he went outside and saw the whole of New York, the directions he'd been given eluded him. He watched travelers motion to taxis and tuck themselves inside and the taxis fold into the flow of cars. He took his money from his bag and counted it.

How much? he asked when he got in. The driver told him and Grant considered getting back out, but the driver was shrewd enough to have already started driving, and anyway he'd made his decision and ought to stick to it.

At Grand Central Terminal he paid all but three of his dollars for a ticket. The bus took him out of the city and along a busy road where identical house fronts crowded together like men lined up at a bar. They were traveling south, so he looked left in the hope of seeing the ocean, but he could not. Soon they turned away from the evening sun, and sand began to appear along the road. The bus turned golden inside like the heart of a minor star. Where it stopped he saw the backs of tall buildings and between them a mass of people walking. He got off and heard the odd cacophony of a big band and smelled fried food. On the other side of a packed parking lot rose a flight of wooden steps, and he climbed them and found himself on a wide wooden thoroughfare, where people laughed and clutched one another falling down drunk in fine clothes, and publicly embraced in the backs of carts towed by running men, and pushed in and out of penny arcades and theaters and bars. Beyond all this was a cloudless purple sky that grew darker as it descended to the horizon. The horizon was flat and absolute, the authentic edge of the world. This at last was the ocean.

He sat shoeless mere inches out of reach of the ocean's tongue, eating from a paper plate of hot potato pastries. He had wanted meat but ended up buying the first thing he laid eyes on. Beside him his lemonade was already empty. He had two dollars and ten cents, and all his clothes were foul and wrinkled. Night came sooner here, so back home his mother was cooking supper for the men. By now they had stopped wondering about him. Less than a week ago the house had been emptier at night than Grant could bear, and now, without him, it was emptier still.

He would not have thought it possible for an entire family to go wrong. They had been strong and numerous and lived in a small valley that was theirs alone, or seemed that way: when anyone entered, the dust they raised was visible from miles away, and visitors, even if unexpected, could be met on the road. Home was a domain. It was permanent and unbreachable. In retrospect this was a childish way of thinking. Families die out, even the hardiest lines. No blood could resist bad luck.

The second to die was Robert. He turned six on the same June day in 1933 that Edwin turned twelve. That same month a man just hired fell drunk off his horse and walked for several weeks afterward with a crutch. The boys were poking fun out in front of the house, with Grant dramatizing the fall and Thornton looking on from under a shade tree, laughing appreciatively in his weird, hoarse adult's voice. Robert impersonated the remorseful hired man stuttering apologies and jerking his crutch about, using as a prop the shotgun he'd been chasing pheasants with earlier in the day. He had forgotten to engage the safety, and when the stock struck his boot top something caught the trigger and a barrel discharged under his arm and nearly took it off his body. Robert remained standing. No one appeared at the noise; there were a lot of people on the ranch and a lot of reasons to fire a shotgun. Robert's shirt swallowed up blood like a patch of dry ground and quickly turned black. He held the shot arm with the opposite hand and dropped to his knees. Thornton had continued to laugh after the shot but now perceived something amiss and fell silent. Grant ran to his brother, who had pitched onto his side now, and took the boy's gray face in his hands, telling him stay still, don't move. He ran to the barn screaming to his father to come hurry, grabbed a rotted wool sack, and balled it up as he ran back to Robert's side. The boy had his eyes shut and his dry lips together. Grant shoved the sack under the bleeding arm and pressed it there to stop the flow. If this hurt Robert he made no sign. Bits of grease wool were poking from the sack and lapping up the blood and shrinking to slick strands with it. The shotgun lay in the dirt nearby, and Grant snaked out a foot and kicked it away. Thornton sat blubbering in the shade. Their father arrived cursing and Edwin behind him with a face that seemed already to have considered the possibility of such an incident and fully accepted its inevitability. Unlike their father, Edwin was not surprised.

And neither was their mother, when John returned in the truck with Robert's body to bury it. They had aimed for the hospital in Ashton but Robert died on the way. John didn't stop at the house, only drove across the bare dirt of the starveout to the corner where Wesley lay, and waited for Asta and the boys to follow. Edwin brought the shovel.

She was not seen to cry then or ever again that Grant could recall, not even when Edwin shot himself in the stand of lodgepole they harvested from the hillside, or when the telegram came informing her that Thornton had perished at sea. The years those incidents spanned were compressed in Grant's memory like frayed patches on a coiled rope. Certainly there were other things in between, his childhood adventures and schooling and the reckless driving of gravel roads, but these recollections faded quickly in the intense tragic light and made his short life seem worthless and futile. As for his mother, he could not recall any expression on her face save for the stoic glare she had adopted, a figurehead's face of the sort a person contrived for staring into a wild wind as if it were possible to find the source.

Night fell and the noises behind him died. The ocean crept up toward where he sat, and he moved himself back. When it approached a second time he stood and turned toward the city. The sand was treacherous, with broken bits of shell and rotting crabs that he could see in the light from the moon and from the buildings ahead. A sign was posted at the base of the steps that read: SHOES MUST BE WORN ON BOARDWALK. He sat on the steps and put them on. A group of young men passed behind him singing. On a bench a man was kissing a woman. After a moment he took his shoes off and climbed back down into the sand. The boardwalk was built on wooden pilings that created a sheltered space, and he ducked his head and situated himself under there, with a mound of sand as a pillow and his bag close beside him. He fell asleep to the sound of footsteps overhead.

It had to be noon, or nearly so. The traffic on the boardwalk was a relentless rumble and the air hot, even here in the shade. He came out into the daylight. People in various states of undress sunned themselves and leaped in the surf. Women's arms and legs were bare, and men held them close walking along the water's edge. A tall Negro was building a sand castle and had already finished one just beside it. Grant recognized the completed castle, from pictures he'd seen, as the Roman Colosseum. As he watched, two men approached the Negro and dropped money into a nearby paper cup, and he responded with a nod, not taking his eyes from the work. It seemed to Grant that the war's end had driven people to forget who they were and where their lives were leading, and to relinquish their money and secrets as if now there would be an unlimited supply. He wondered what the day of the week was—he had forgotten—and if it mattered to anyone.

On the boardwalk he bought a breakfast of sausage and eggs and toast for one dollar and ate it standing up, under a colorful umbrella. He walked as far as the boardwalk would take him, peering down each extravagant pier through its gaudy archway, to the massive halls, and costumed people passing handbills, and food stands and games of chance. Graceful birds of a sort he hadn't seen before swooped in loose formation around small children, who tossed bread in the air for them to catch.

Walking back, he stopped before a small crowd of people playing ball and ring-tossing games. One game involved throwing a baseball over the wooden counter and into a shallow basket. The basket had a convex bottom and was angled sharply toward the player. In another game players tried to throw a wooden ring onto a milk bottle. Both games were cheats. The ball reliably bounced out of the basket every time, and the rings were too small. What interested Grant was a parrot, gripping a perch to which it was tied by the foot with string. The parrot tottered back and forth on the perch, two steps one way and two the other, as far as it could go in either direction. It did this compulsively, silently.

Give him a coin, the proprietor said. He was ropy looking, with a crooked nose and a frayed straw hat, and his black eyes, which he blinked rapidly, were like the parrot's.

Go ahead, he said. Give him a coin, see what he does.

Grant had a penny, which he placed on the counter in front of the parrot.

It'll take at least a nickel, the parrot man said. As if in agreement, the parrot made a strangled sound, like a squawk.

Grant replaced the penny with a nickel. The parrot grabbed the nickel in its beak, flapped its wings, and flew to the rim of a tall glass container standing behind the perch. The string went nearly taut. Having steadied itself, the parrot dropped the coin, which landed with a dull sound on a pile of nickels, dimes, and quarters at the bottom of the container. Then the parrot returned to the perch. Behind Grant someone applauded.

Hey, is that something else? the parrot man said.

Ain't it supposed to talk? Grant asked him.

The parrot man glared. He's supposed to do exactly what he just did. Parrots are supposed to talk.

Well, this one does exactly what I tell him to, mister. He's supposed to fly over there and drop that nickel, and that's exactly what he did.

Grant gave this some thought. All right then, he said, and, deciding he'd been duped like everybody else, moved on.

He bought dinner. This left him with thirty cents. The afternoon passed, and he considered that he might skip supper and sleep again on the sand, but what then in the morning? He went back to the parrot man and asked him if he had any work. Nobody else was at the stand. The parrot man blinked. Do I look like I got any work for you, mister?

I just got here. I don't have any money.

What do I care? the parrot man said, but then, Where do you come from anyway?

As if to balance against future lies, Grant told him about Eleven.

You fought the war?

Yes.

The parrot man nodded. I was a cook over in France. Boy, I don't ever want to pick up a fry pan again, you know?

What about the bird? Grant said. The parrot paced, occasionally opening and closing its beak.

What about him?

You probably got better things to do than clean up after it, Grant said. I could look after that bird. I could feed it and clean up after it.

The parrot man shook his head. I told you I ain't got no work. But something about the idea appealed to him, Grant could tell. For the briefest moment the skin of his face, which heretofore had not seemed sufficient to cover his skull, slackened, and he took on the look of a normal man, free of the burden of the parrot.

I'll take whatever you can give me, Grant told him. I don't want for much. Just enough to eat with.

You're staying someplace respectable, right? This bird needs a roof over his head. And as if recognizing that he had committed himself to Grant's offer, his face snapped back into its original configuration.

I got a room, Grant lied. They agreed on an amount and it was done. Grant went off to get a room, with instructions to return later for the parrot.

There was not much in the way of rooms. As he walked west the rates dropped. When they got low enough he walked north until he found a woman who would let him wait until the next day to start paying. She was heavy and old, with a pale expressionless face like a reflection in a china plate, and she sat in a wooden folding chair behind a grimy linoleum counter. A scratched glass bowl was sitting on the counter with a handlettered sign: DO NOT HAND ME YOUR MONEY PUT IT IN THE CUP. From an open door behind her issued the sound of a radio. She dropped a key into the glass bowl and he took it out. She said that he had better pay two nights tomorrow night or she would send her husband up to kick him out. Grant said he understood.

She leaned forward ever so slightly and said in a low voice, This place is full of niggers. They will steal the fillings out of your teeth.

Yes, ma'am, said Grant.

The lobby was painted with what might once have been a cheerful yellow but had been corrupted by water stains and the husks of dead insects. A low table had old magazines on it, and there was a dry astringent smell as if hundreds of newspapers were stored nearby.

He went to his room. It was about six feet by ten, with a high ceiling and a narrow mattress bowed in the middle as if a ghost were sleeping on it. There was a chair and a small table and a tiny closet with three wire hangers inside. A shallow sink had a sliver of soap on it and a square mirror above. The walls were stained but not too badly. His window overlooked an alley and a smaller building, and if he leaned to one side and pressed his head to the glass he could see a strip of beach far off to the north. For a while he watched the strip of beach until the shadows of the fancy hotels threw themselves over the sand, obscuring its bathers. He lay down on the sunken mattress. It was not uncomfortable, but he doubted its strength. He lay gingerly as he might ride a very old horse.

This room was all right, though it had too much in it for its size. He looked up and considered the ceiling's great height. All that empty space up there with no way to use it. He closed his eyes and reviewed his war story. Japan. He pictured palm trees and little flat thatch houses, and the Emperor's men peering out of them with their rifles.

That story ought to have been true. The local board had considered their deferment applications and told John to send one of the boys, one only. Max was too young to go, though he begged. Thornton did not understand what he was getting into. It ought to have been Grant who went and who was sunk in the South Pacific. But their father kept him, because he did not trust Max to work reliably and because Thornton was the kind of help he could easily hire. With Edwin dead he needed to teach someone to run the ranch. Max argued that he could take Thornton's place, that he could go and call himself Thornton Person and pass for eighteen, but John would have none of it. I won't have my sons lying, he said, there's no honor in a lie.

No honor in staying home, Max said.

Grant might have said anything at all, but he kept his mouth shut. It is awful quiet around here, Max said to him, and their father did not speak up in Grant's defense.

I got work to do, Grant said and got up from his chair. They were all in the kitchen, the three boys and their mother, her back to them, washing a sink-load of dishes.

Hey Grant! Thornton was saying, Hey, where you going? We're just talking. It was intolerable to Thornton that they quarreled and intolerable that their father's will be questioned. The boys towered above John Person like miraculous crops.

It was never clear to Grant why their father mistrusted Max, who was fifteen in 1943 when Thornton was sent away, and who had never once appeared late to do his work or skipped school or engaged in any foolish thing more than once. But John disliked him. He made no effort to conceal it. And every time he opened his mouth in criticism of Max, he would praise Grant before he closed it, and while Grant had no use for this misplaced attention he was powerless to refuse it, the way a thirsty man can't help drinking bad water. John acknowledged the rivalry that sprang up between them but did nothing to set it right, believing the boys ought to be able to work out their problems themselves.

He often said with apparent disgust that Max took after his mother, and this was true. Like her, Max was competent and self-reliant. She was the braver of their parents, Grant saw now, because she never hesitated to love them and did not stop when they began to die. She once surmised to Grant that she was chosen to lose her children because she was strong enough to withstand it, which gave Grant to wonder if he then was chosen to be lost.

He returned to the stand a few hours past dark and waited on a nearby bench for the parrot man to close down. When he did he gave Grant a wooden box with a handle and a cage with a thick cloth draped over it. He explained that the box had the parrot's food in it and told Grant how much to give the parrot and when.

It's in here? Grant said, lifting the cage.

He goes to sleep, said the parrot man. Okay, you all set?

I need some money.

You ain't done anything yet.

You'll pay me tomorrow? My landlady needs her money.

The parrot man backed up a step as if he thought he was being tricked. If you bring him here and take care of him all day you'll get your money. I can't give you any more or less than that.

Grant nodded, satisfied, and left. But he went back. Hey, he said, this parrot got a name?

The parrot man started, a small movement that nonetheless shook his entire body. You know what, he said, and his eyes grew limpid and sad like the rainwashed windows of an abandoned house. You know what, I never call him a goddamn thing. I just talk to him. I don't call him nothing at all.

When he reached the stairs down to the street Grant looked back at the game stand. The parrot man still stood at the counter, staring off at the starlit outline of the sea. Grant raised a hand to him, but the parrot man never turned.

He worked several weeks as the parrot's keeper, feeding it the seed the parrot man had provided and leaves off a head of lettuce he'd bought from a grocery. He was reluctant to ask the landlady to refrigerate the lettuce so he kept it on the floor of his closet, where it got increasingly limp and discolored. The parrot did not seem to mind. Mostly it slept under its cloth but at least once each night woke up and spoke in an unfamiliar language. Whether it was a foreign language or one of the parrot's own devising Grant could not tell. At these times he spoke back to the parrot, and it listened to what he said. In the daytime he worked at the stand wiping up the parrot's droppings and sorting its coins at the day's end. The parrot man allowed him breaks, which he spent exploring the boardwalk. There was a hotel for rich people that looked like a wedding cake and a place where cars of the future could be seen and touched. And of course there was the horse, which as promised jumped into the ocean hourly with a girl on its bare back. The girl wore a bathing suit and smiled all the way down, even as the water came up to engulf her. Grant thought she must be brave and dreamed of meeting her, but he could not imagine how to approach her or what to say if he did. The horse, on the other hand, though it possessed a beauty flying through the air, up close proved old and tired, its coat coarsened by the salt water.

Grant did not feel that his job was secure. When he returned with the parrot that first day the parrot man grabbed it from him, as if he had been holding it for ransom. After that the parrot man seemed more confident in Grant, at least for a short while. But the next week he appeared morose and sometimes took over Grant's work for him with a kind of gruff impatience. Some nights he said the parrot looked sick, and he prevented Grant from taking it back to his room. Grant saw no evidence of any illness but reasoned that he wouldn't know a sick parrot if he saw one anyhow. The parrot man paid him regardless.

After one September night without the parrot, Grant woke earlier than usual and left his room to sit on the beach and plan or at least imagine what he might do next. Although it was before ten in the morning, hundreds of people were out in the cool air, standing on the sand in their street shoes. There were no bathers at this hour. Grant walked through the crowd listening for clues to their purpose here, but learned only that something was expected to happen, some kind of show, and that it would happen out at sea. The presence of these people on what he had come to think of as his beach irritated him, and he found their proximity unnerving. Still he chose a spot and waited.

Pretty soon a dot appeared out on the water and resolved into the shape of a boat. The static of conversation became a thrum and dropped off entirely as more boats bulged onto the horizon and laved into clear view, as if brought by the tide. From newspaper photographs he'd seen, Grant was able to identify these as transports. It was in one like them that Thornton was killed. The ship had not been attacked but suffered an explosion on board and sunk. It was easy to imagine what this must have been like. After all, this death belonged to Grant and had simply been lent to his idiot brother, who gratefully wrapped it around himself like a poisoned blanket. He imagined Thornton hunkered in his tiny cabin, straining to assemble in his mind all the evidence of danger, the deadened blast and the rushing water and the sudden darkness, the slide of objects from their customary places. And finally the ocean's blind hungry clench.

Just offshore now, the ships yawned open to frenetic applause, and from the guts of them came soldiers who knelt in the surf and fired upon the onlookers, and got up and ran, heavy with seawater, onto the hard wet sand and fired again. Women screamed and a few fainted dead away. Soldiers pulled up short and theatrically dropped, writhing in mock death. And Grant knew genuine pain as the bullets entered him, even as he understood them to be imaginary; they found his heart and pierced it, tore the breath out of his lungs, swept his legs out from under him. They glowed inside him like irons. He was branded from within: the destruction his brothers had claimed was also his, was Max's and their mother's and father's. It waited for him back home like a once loved dog turned rabid and fierce.

He lay contorted in the sand forcing sobs from his body, oblivious to the sympathetic shadows falling across him, to the hands on his arms and back and head. But he would not be helped. He wanted instead to fill this ground with his tears and claim it as his own. He wanted to make himself an impossible promise, one he would sooner die than break but which he knew was already as good as broken, that he was never going to go back.

Allan Gurganus

He's at the Office

From *The New Yorker*

Till the Japanese bombed Pearl Harbor, most American men wore hats to work. What happened? Did our guys—suddenly scouting overhead for worse Sunday raids—come to fear their hatbrims' interference? My unsuspecting father wore his till yesterday. He owned three. A gray, a brown, and a summer straw one, whose maroon-striped rayon band could only have been woven in America in the nineteen-forties.

Last month, I lured him from his self-imposed office hours for a walk around our block. My father insisted on bringing his briefcase. "You never know," he said. We soon passed a huge young hipster, creaking in black leather. The kid's pierced face flashed more silver than most bait shops sell. His jeans, half down, exposed hatracks of white hipbone; the haircut arched high over jug ears. He was scouting Father's shoes. Long before fashion joined him, Dad favored an under-evolved antique form of orthopedic Doc Martens. These impressed a punk now scanning the Sherman tank of a cowhide briefcase with chromium corner braces. The camel-hair overcoat was cut to resemble some boxy-backed 1947 Packard. And, of course, up top sat "the gray."

Pointing to it, the boy smiled. "Way bad look on you, guy."

My father, seeking interpretation, stared at me. I simply shook my head no. I could not explain Dad to himself in terms of tidal fashion trends. All I said was "I think he likes you."

Dad's face folded. "Uh-oh."

By the end, my father, the fifty-two-year veteran of Integrity Office Supplier, Unlimited, had become quite cool again, way.

We couldn't vacation for more than three full days. He'd veer our Plymouth toward some way-station pay phone. We soon laughed as Dad, in the glass booth, commenced to wave his arms, shake his head, shift his weight from foot to foot. We knew Miss Green must be telling him of botched orders, delivery mistakes. We were nearly to Gettysburg. I'd been studying battle maps. Now I knew we'd never make it.

My father bounded back to the car and smiled in. "Terrible mixup with the Wilmington school system's carbon paper for next year. Major goof, but typical. Guy's got to do it all himself. Young Green didn't insist I come back, but she sure hinted."

We U-turned southward, and my father briefly became the most charming man on earth. He now seemed to be selling something we needed, whatever we needed. Travelling north into a holiday—the very curse of leisure—he had kept as silent as some fellow with toothaches. Now he was our tour guide, interviewing us, telling and retelling his joke. Passing a cemetery, he said (over his family's dry carbon-paper unison), "I hear they're dying to get in there!" "Look on the bright side," I told myself: "we'll arrive home and escape him as he runs—literally runs—to the office."

Dad was, like me, an early riser. Six days a week, Mom sealed his single-sandwich lunch into its Tupperware jacket; this fit accidentally yet exactly within the lid compartment of his durable briefcase. He would then pull on his overcoat—bulky, war-efficient, strong-seamed, four buttons big as silver dollars and carved from actual shell. He'd place the cake-sized hat in place, nod in our general direction, and set off hurrying. Dad faced each day as one more worthy enemy. If he had been Dwight Eisenhower saving the Western world, or Jonas Salk freeing kids our age from crutches, O.K. But yellow Eagle pencils? Utility paperweights in park-bench green?

Once a year, Mom told my brother and me how much the war had darkened her young husband; he'd enlisted with three other guys from Falls; he alone came back alive with all his limbs. "Before that," she smiled, "your father was funnier, funny. And smarter. Great dancer. You can't blame mustard gas, not this time. It's more what Dick saw. He came home and he was all business. Before that, he'd been mischievous and talkative and strange. He was always playing around with words. Very entertaining. Eyelashes out to here. For years, I figured that in time he'd come back to being whole. But since June of '45 it's been All Work and No Play Makes Jack."

Mom remembered their fourth anniversary. "I hired an overnight sitter for you two. We drove to an inn near Asheville. It had the state's best restaurant, candlelight, a real string quartet. I'd made myself a green velvet dress. I was twenty-eight and never in my whole life have I ever looked better. You just know it. Dick recognized some man who'd bought two adding machines. Dick invited him to join us. Then I saw how much his work was going to have to mean to him. Don't be too hard on him, please. He feeds us, he puts aside real savings for you boys' college. Dick pays our taxes. Dick has no secrets. He's not hurting anyone." Brother and I gave each other a look Mom recognized and understood but refused to return.

The office seemed to tap some part of him that was either off limits to us or simply did not otherwise exist. My brother and I griped that he'd never attended our Little League games (not that we ever made the starting lineup). He missed our father-son Cub Scout banquet; it conflicted with a major envelope convention in Newport News. Mother neutrally said he loved us as much as he could. She was a funny, energetic person—all that wasted good will. And even as kids, we knew not to blame her.

Ignored, Mom created a small sewing room. Economizing needlessly, she stayed busy stitching all our school clothes, cowboy motifs galore. For a while, each shirtpocket bristled with Mom-designed embroidered cacti. But Simplicity patterns were never going to engage a mind as complex as hers. Soon Mom was spending most mornings playing vicious duplicate bridge. Our toothbrush glasses briefly broke out in rashes of red hearts, black clubs. Mom's new pals were society ladies respectful of her brainy speed, her impenitent wit; she never bothered introducing them to her husband. She laughed more now. She started wearing rouge.

We lived a short walk from both our school and his wholesale office. Dad sometimes left the Plymouth parked all night outside the workplace, his desk lamp the last one burning on the whole third floor. Integrity's president, passing headquarters late, always fell for it. "Dick, what do you do up there all night, son?" My father's shrug became his finest boast. The raises kept pace; Integrity Office Supplier was still considered quite a comer. And R. Richard Markham, Sr.—handsome as a collar ad, a hat ad, forever at the office—was the heir apparent.

Dad's was Integrity's flagship office: "Maker of World's Highest Quality Clerical Supplies." No other schoolboys had sturdier pastel subject dividers, more clip-in see-through three-ring pen caddies. The night before school started, Dad would be up late at our kitchen table, swilling coffee, "getting you boys set." Zippered leather cases, English slide rules, folders more suitable for treaties than for book reports (" 'Skipper, A Dog of the Pyrenees,' by Marjorie Hopgood Purling"). Our notebooks soon proved too heavy to carry far; we secretly stripped them, swapping gear for lunchbox treats more exotic than Mom's hard-boiled eggs and Sun-Maid raisin packs.

Twenty years ago, Dad's Integrity got bought out by a German firm. The business's vitality proved somewhat hobbled by computers' onslaught. "A fad," my father called computers in 1976. "Let others retool. We'll stand firm with our yellow legals, erasers, Parker ink, fountain pens. Don't worry, our regulars'll come back. True vision always lets you act kind in the end, boys. Remember."

Yeah, right.

My father postponed his retirement. Mom encouraged that and felt relieved; she could not imagine him at home all day. As Integrity's market share dwindled, Dad spent more time at the office, as if to compensate with his own body for the course of modern life.

His secretary, the admired Miss Green, had once been what Pop still called "something of a bombshell." (He stuck with a Second World War terminology that had, like the hat, served him too well to ever leave behind.)

Still favoring shoulder pads, dressed in unyielding woollen Joan Crawford solids, Green wore an auburn pageboy that looked burned by decades of ungrateful dyes. She kicked off her shoes beneath her desk, revealing feet that told the tale of high heels' worthless weekday brutality. She'd quit college to tend an ailing mother, who proved demanding, then immortal. Brother and I teased Mom: poor Green appeared to worship her longtime boss, a guy whose face was as smooth and wedged and classic as his hat. Into Dick Markham's blunted constancy she read actual "moods."

He still viewed Green, now past sixty, as a promising virginal girl. In their small adjoining offices, these two thrived within a fond impersonality that permeated the ads of the period.

Integrity's flagship headquarters remained enamelled a flavorless mint green, unaltered for five decades. The dark Mission coatrack was made by Limbert—quite a good piece. One ashtray—upright, floor model, brushed chromium—proved the size and shape of some landlocked torpedo. Moored to walls, dented metal desks were gray as battleships. A series of forest-green filing cabinets seemed banished, patient as a family of trolls, to one shaming little closet all their own. Dad's office might've been decorated by a firm called Edward Hopper & Sam Spade, Unlimited.

For more than half a century, he walked in each day at seven-oh-nine sharp, as Miss Green forever said, "Morning, Mr. Markham. I left your appointments written on your desk pad, can I get you your coffee? Is now good, sir?" And Dad said, "Yes, why, thanks, Miss Green, how's your mother, don't mind if I do."

Four years ago, I received a panicked phone call: "You the junior to a guy about eighty, guy in a hat?"

"Probably." I was working at home. I pressed my computer's "Save" function. This, I sensed, might take a while. "Save."

"Exit? No? Yes?"

"Yes."

"Mister, your dad thinks we're camped out in his office and he's been banging against our door. He's convinced we've evicted his files and what he calls his Green. 'What have you done with young Green?' Get down here A.S.A.P. Get him out of our hair or it's 911 in three minutes, swear to God."

From my car, I phoned home. Mom must have been off somewhere playing bridge with the mayor's blond wife and his blond ex-wife; they'd sensibly become excellent friends. The best women are the best people on earth; and the worst men the very worst. Mother, overlooked by Dad for years, had continued finding what she called "certain outlets."

When I arrived, Dad was still heaving himself against an office door, deadbolt-locked from within. Since its upper panel was frosted glass, I could make out the colors of the clothes of three or four people pressing from their side. They'd used masking tape to crosshatch the glass, as if bracing for a hurricane. The old man held his briefcase, wore his gray hat, the tan boxy coat.

"Dad?" He stopped with a mechanical cartoon verve, jumped my way, and smiled so hard it warmed my heart and scared me witless. My father had never acted so glad to see me—not when I graduated summa cum laude, not at my wedding, not after the birth of my son—and I felt joy in the presence of such joy from him.

"Reinforcements. Good man. We've got quite a hostage situation here. Let's put our shoulders to it, shall we?"

"Dad?" I grabbed the padded shoulders of his overcoat. These crumpled to reveal a man far sketchier hiding in there somewhere—a guy only twenty years from a hundred, after all.

"Dad? Dad. We have a good-news, bad-news setup here today. It's this. You found the right building, Dad. Wrong floor."

I led him back to the clattering, oil-smelling elevator. I thought to return, tap on the barricaded door, explain. But, in time, hey, they'd peek, they'd figure out the coast was clear. That they hadn't recognized him, after his fifty-two years of long days in this very building, said something. New people, everywhere.

I saw at once that Miss Green had been crying. Her face was caked with so much powder it looked like calamine. "Little mixup," I said.

"Mr. Markham? We got three calls about those gum erasers," she said, faking a frontal normality. "I think they're putting sawdust in them these days, sir. They leave skid marks, apparently. I put the information on your desk. With your day's appointments. Like your coffee? Like it now? Sir?"

I hung his hat on the hat tree; I slid his coat onto its one wooden Deco hanger that could, at any flea market today, bring thirty-five dollars easy, two tones of wood, inlaid.

I wanted to have a heart-to-heart. I was so disoriented as to feel half sane myself. But I overheard Father already returning his calls. He ignored me, and that seemed, within this radically altered gravitational field, a good sign. I sneaked back to Miss Green's desk and admitted, "I'll need to call his doctor. I want him seen today, Miss Green. He was up on four, trying to get into that new headhunting service. He told them his name. Mom was out. So they, clever, looked him up in the book and found his junior and phoned me to come help."

She sat forward, strenuously feigning surprise. She looked rigid, chained to this metal desk by both gnarled feet. "How long?" I somehow knew to ask.

Green appeared ecstatic, then relieved, then, suddenly, happily weeping, tears pouring down—small tears, lopsided, mascaraed grit. She blinked up at me with a spaniel's gratitude. Suddenly, if slowly, I began to understand. In mere seconds, she had caved about Dad's years-long caving-in. It was my turn now.

Miss Green now whispered certain of his mistakes. There were forgotten parking tickets by the dozen. There was his attempt to purchase a lake house on land already flooded for a dam. Quietly, she admitted years of covering.

From her purse, she lifted a page covered in Dad's stern Germanic cursive, blue ink fighting to stay isometrically between red lines.

"I found this one last week." Green's voice seemed steadied by the joy of having told. "I fear this is about the worst, to date, we've been."

If they say "Hot enough for you?," it means recent weather. "Yes indeed" still a good comeback. Order forms pink. Requisition yellow. Miss green's birthday June 12. She work with you fifty-one years. Is still unmarried. Mother now dead, since '76, so stop asking about Mother, health of. Home address, 712 Marigold Street: Left at Oak, can always walk there. After last week, never go near car again. Unfair to others. Take second left at biggest tree. Your new Butcher's name is: Al. Wife: Betty. Sons: Matthew and Dick Junior. Grandson Richie (your name with a III added on it). List of credit cards, licnse etc. below in case you lose walet agn, you big dope. Put copies somewhere safe, 3 places, write down, hide many. You are 80, yes, eighty.

And yet, as we now eavesdropped, Dick Markham dealt with a complaining customer. He sounded practiced, jokey, conversant, exact.

"Dad, you have an unexpected doctor's appointment." I handed Dad his hat. I'd phoned our family physician from Miss Green's extension.

For once, they were ready for us. The nurses kept calling him by name, smiling, overinsistent, as if hinting at answers for a kid about to take his make-or-break college exam. I could see they'd always liked him. In a town this small, they'd maybe heard about his trouble earlier today.

As Dad got ushered in for tests, he glowered accusations back at me as if I had just dragged him to a Nazi medical experiment. He finally reemerged, scarily pale, pressing a bit of gauze into the crook of his bare arm, its long veins the exact blue of Parker's washable ink. They directed him toward the lobby bathroom. They gave him a cup for his urine specimen. He held it before him with two hands like some Magi's treasure.

His hat, briefcase, and overcoat remained behind, resting on an orange plastic chair all their own. Toward these I could display a permissible tenderness. I lightly set my hand on each item. Call it superstition. I now lifted the hat and sniffed it. It smelled like Dad. It smelled like rope. Physical intimacy has never been a possibility. My brother and I, half drunk, once tried to picture the improbable, the sexual conjunction of our parents. Brother said, "Well, he probably pretends he's at the office, unsealing her like a good manila envelope that requires a rubber stamp— legible, yes, keep it legible, *legible,* now speed-mail!"

I had flipped through four stale magazines before I saw the nurses peeking from their crudely cut window. "He has been quite a while, Mr. Markham. Going on thirty minutes."

"Shall I?" I rose and knocked. No answer. "Would you come stand behind me?" Cowardly, I signalled to an older nurse.

The door proved unlocked. I opened it. I saw one old man aimed the other way and trembling with hesitation. Before him, a white toilet, a white sink, and a white enamel trash can, the three aligned—each its own insistent invitation. In one hand, the old man held an empty specimen cup. In the other hand, his dick.

Turning my way, grateful, unashamed to be caught sobbing, he cried, "Which one, son? Fill which one?"

Forcibly retired, my father lived at home in his pajamas. Mom made him wear the slippers and robe to help with his morale. "Think 'Thin Man.' Think William Powell." But the poor guy literally hung his head with shame. That phrase took on new meaning now that his routine and dignity proved so reduced. Dad's mopey presence clogged every outlet she'd perfected to avoid him. The two of them were driving each other crazy.

Lacking the cash for live-in help, she was forced to cut way back on her bridge game and female company. She lost ten pounds—it showed in her neck and face—and then she gave up rouge. You could see Mom missed her fancy friends. I soon pitied her nearly as much as I pitied him—no, more. At least he allowed himself to be distracted. She couldn't forget.

Mom kept urging him to get dressed. She said they needed to go to the zoo. She had to get out and "do" something. One morning, she was trying to force Dad into his dress pants when he struck her. She fell right over the back of an armchair. The whole left side of her head stayed a rubber-stamp pad's blue-black for one whole week. Odd, this made it easier for both of them to stay home. Now two people hung their heads in shame.

At a window overlooking the busy street, Dad would stand staring out, one way. On the window glass, his forehead left a persistent oval of human oil. His pajama knees pressed against the radiator. He silently second-guessed parallel parkers. He studied westerly-moving traffic. Sometimes he'd stand guard there for six uninterrupted hours. Did he await some detained patriotic parade? I pictured poor Green on a passing float—hoisting his coffee mug and the black phone receiver, waving him back down to street level, reality, use.

One December morning, Mom—library book in lap, trying to reinterest herself in Daphne du Maurier, in anything—smelled scorching. Like Campbell's mushroom soup left far too long on simmer. Twice she checked their stove and toaster-oven. Finally, around his nap time, she pulled Dad away from the radiator: his shins had cooked. "Didn't it hurt you, Dick? Darling, didn't you ever feel anything?"

Next morning at six-thirty, I got her call. Mom's husky tone sounded too jolly for the hour. She described bandaging both legs. "As you kids say, I don't think this is working for us. This might be beyond me. Integrity's fleabag insurance won't provide him with that good a home. We have just enough to go on living here as usual. Now, I'll maybe shock you and you might find me weak or, worse, disloyal. But would you consider someday checking out some nice retreats or facilities in driving distance? Even if it uses up the savings. Your father is the love of my life—one per customer. I just hate to get any more afraid of him!"

I said I'd phone all good local places, adding, giddy, "I hear they're dying to get in there."

This drew a silence as cold as his. "Your dad's been home from the office—what, seven months? Most men lean toward their leisure years, but who ever hated leisure more than Dick? When I think of everything he gave Integrity and how little he's getting back . . . I'm not strong enough to *keep* him, but I can't bear to *put* him anywhere. Still, at this rate, all I'll want for Christmas is a nice white padded cell for two."

I wished my mother belonged to our generation, where the women work. She could've done anything. And now to be saddled with a man who'd known nothing but enslavement to one so-so office. The workaholic, tabled. He still refused to dress; she focussed on the sight of his pajamas. My folks now argued with the energy of newlyweds; then she felt ashamed of herself and he forgot to do whatever he'd just promised.

On Christmas Eve, she was determined to put up a tree for him. But Dad, somehow frightened by the ladder and all the unfamiliar boxes everywhere, got her into such a lethal headlock she had to scream for help. Now the neighbors were involved. People I barely knew interrupted my work hours, saying, "Something's got to be done. It took three of us to pull him off of her. He's still strong as a horse. It's getting dangerous over there. He could escape."

Sometimes, at two in the morning, she'd find him standing in their closet, wearing his p.j.s and the season's correct hat. He'd be looking at his business suits. The right hand would be filing, "walking," back and forth across creased pant legs, as if seeking the . . . exact . . . right . . . pair . . . for . . . the office . . . today.

I tried to keep Miss Green informed. She'd sold her duplex and moved into our town's most stylish old-age home. When she swept downstairs to greet me, I didn't recognize her. "God, you look fifteen years younger." I checked her smile for hints of a possible lift.

She just laughed, giving her torso one mild shimmy. "Look, Ma. No shoulder pads."

Her forties hairdo, with its banked, rolled edges, had softened into pretty little curls around her face. She'd let its color go her natural silvery blond. Green gave me a slow look. If I didn't know her better, I'd have sworn she was flirting.

She appeared shorter in flats. I now understood: her toes had been so mangled by wearing those forties quonset-huts of high heels, ones she'd probably owned since age eighteen. Her feet had grown, but she'd stayed true to the old shoes, part of some illusion she felt my dad required.

Others in the lobby perked up at her fond greeting; I saw she'd already become the belle of this place. She let me admire her updated charms.

"No," she smiled simply, "it's that I tried to keep it all somewhat familiar for him. How I looked and all. We got to where Mr. Markham found any change a kind of danger, so . . . I mean, it wasn't as if a dozen other suitors were beating down my door. What with Mother being moody and sick that long. And so, day to day, well . . ." She shrugged.

Now, in my life I've had very few inspired ideas. Much of me, like Pop, is helplessly a company man. So forgive my boasting of this.

Leaving Miss Green's, I stopped by a huge Salvation Army store. It was a good one. Over the years, I've found a few fine Federal side chairs here and many a great tweed jacket. Browsing through the used-furniture room, I wandered beneath a cardboard placard hand-lettered "The World of Early American." Ladder-back deacon's chairs and plaid upholstered things rested knee to knee, like sad and separate families.

I chanced to notice a homeless man, asleep, a toothless white fellow. His overcoat looked filthy. His belongings were bunched around him in six rubber-banded shoeboxes. His feet, in paint-stained shoes, rested on an ordinary school administrator's putty-colored desk. "The Wonderful World of Work" hung over hand-me-down waiting rooms still waiting. Business furniture sat parlored—forlorn as any gray-green Irish wake. There was something about the sight of this old guy's midday snoring in so safe a fluorescent make-work cubicle.

Mom now used her sewing room only for those few overnight third cousins willing to endure its lumpy foldout couch. The room'd become a catchall, cold storage, since about 1970. We waited for Dad's longest nap of the day. Then, in a crazed burst of energy, we cleared her lair, purging it of boxes, photo albums, four unused exercise machines. I paint-rolled its walls in record time, the ugliest latex junior-high-school green that Sherwin-Williams sells (there's still quite a range). The Salvation Army delivers: within two days, I had arranged this new-used-junk to resemble Integrity's workspace, familiarly anonymous. A gray desk nuzzled one wall—the window wasted behind. Three green file cabinets made a glum herd. One swivel wooden chair rode squeaky casters. The hatrack antlered upright over a dented tin wastebasket. The ashtray looked big enough to serve an entire cancer ward. Wire shelves predicted a neutral "in," a far more optimistic "out." I stuffed desk drawers with Parker ink, cheap fountain pens, yellow legal pads, four dozen paper clips. I'd bought a big black rotary phone, and Mom got him his own line.

Against her wishes, I'd saved most of Dad's old account ledgers. Yellowed already, they could've come from a barrister's desk in a Dickens novel. I scattered "1959–62." In one corner I piled all Dad's boxed records, back taxes, old Christmas cards from customers. The man saved everything.

The evening before we planned introducing him to his new quarters, I disarranged the place a bit. I tossed a dozen pages on the floor near his chair. I left the desk lamp lit all night. It gave this small room a strange hot smell, overworked. The lamp was made of nubbly brown cast metal (recast war surplus?), its red button indicating "on." Black meant "off."

That morning I was there to help him dress. Mom made us a hearty oatmeal breakfast, packed his lunch, and snapped the Tupperware insert into his briefcase.

"And where am *I* going?" he asked us in a dead voice.

"To the office," I said. "Where else do you go this time of day?"

He appeared sour, puffy, skeptical. Soon as I could, I glanced at Mom. This was not going to be as easy as we'd hoped.

I got Dad's coat and hat. He looked gray and dubious. He would never believe in this new space if I simply squired him down the hall to it. So, after handing him his briefcase, I led Dad back along our corridor and out onto the street.

Some of the old-timers, recognizing him, called, "Looking good, Mr. Markham," or "Cold enough for you?" Arm in arm, we nodded past them.

My grammar school had been one block from his office. Forty years back, we'd set out on foot like this together. The nearer Dad drew to Integrity, the livelier he became; the closer I got to school, the more withdrawn I acted. But today I kept up a mindless over-plentiful patter. My tone neither cheered nor deflected him. One block before his office building, I swerved back down an alley toward the house. As we approached, I saw that Mom had been imaginative enough to leave our front door wide open. She'd removed a bird print that had hung in our foyer hall unloved forever. A mere shape, it still always marked this as our hall, our home.

"Here we are!" I threw open his office door. I took his hat and placed it on its hook. I helped him free of his coat. Just as his face had grown bored, then irked, and finally enraged at our deception, the phone rang. From where I stood—half in the office, half in the hall—I could see Mom holding the white phone in the kitchen.

My father paused—since when did he answer the phone?—and, finally, flushed, reached for it himself. "Dick?" Mom said. "You'll hate me, I'm getting so absent-minded. But you did take your lunch along today, right? I mean, go check. Be patient with me, O.K.?" Phone cradled between his head and shoulder, he lifted his briefcase and snapped it open— his efficiency still water-clear, and scary. Dad then said to the receiver, "Lunch is definitely here, per usual. But, honey, haven't I told you about these personal calls at the office?"

Then I saw him bend to pick up scattered pages. I saw him touch one yellow legal pad and start to square all desk-top pens at sharp right angles. As he pulled the chair two inches forward I slowly shut his door behind me. Then Mother and I, hidden in the kitchen, held each other and, not expecting it, cried, if very, very silently.

When we peeked in two hours later, he was filing.

Every morning, Sundays included, Dad walked to the office. Even our ruse of walking him around the block was relaxed. Mom simply set a straw hat atop him (after Labor Day, she knew to switch to his gray). With his packed lunch, he would stride nine paces from the kitchen table, step in, and pull the door shut, muttering complaints of overwork, no rest ever.

Dad spent a lot of time on the phone. Long-distance directory-assistance charges constituted a large part of his monthly bill. But he "came home" for supper with the weary sense of blurred accomplishment we recalled from olden times.

Once, having dinner with them, I asked Dad how he was. He sighed. "Well, July is peak for getting their school supplies ordered. So the pressure is on. My heart's not what it was, heart's not completely in it lately, I admit. They downsized Green. Terrible loss to me. With its being crunch season, I get a certain shortness of breath. Suppliers aren't where they were, the gear is often second-rate, little of it any longer American-made.

But you keep going, because it's what you know and because your clients count on you. I may be beat, but, hey—it's still a job."

"Aha," I said.

Mom received a call on her own line. It was from some kindergarten owner. Dad—plundering his old red address book—had somehow made himself a go-between, arranging sales, but working freelance now. He appeared to be doing it unsalaried, not for whole school systems but for small local outfits like day-care centers. This teacher had to let Mom know that he'd sent too much of the paste. No invoice with it, a pallet of free jarred white school paste waiting out under the swing sets. Whom to thank?

Once, I tiptoed in and saw a long list of figures he kept meaning to add up. I noticed that, in his desperate daily fight to keep his desk top clear, he'd placed seven separate five-inch piles of papers at evened intervals along the far wall. I found such ankle-level filing sad till slowly I recognized a pattern—oh, yeah, "The Pile System." It was my own technique for maintaining provisional emergency order, and one which I now rejudged to be quite sane.

Inked directly into the wooden bottom of his top desk drawer was this:

Check Green's sick leave ridic. long. Nazis still soundly defeated. Double enter all new receipts, nincompoop. Yes, you . . . eighty-one. Old Woman roommate is: "Betty."

Mom felt safe holding bridge parties at the house again, telling friends that Dad was in there writing letters and doing paperwork, and who could say he wasn't? Days Mom could now shop or attend master-point tournaments at good-driving-distance hotels. In her own little kitchen-corner office, she entered bridge chat rooms, E-mailing game-theory arcana to well-known French and Russian players. She'd regained some weight and her face was fuller, and prettier for that. She bought herself a bottle-green velvet suit. "It's just a cheap Chanel knockoff, but these ol' legs still ain't that bad, hmm?" She looked more rested than I'd seen her in a year or two.

I cut a mail slot in Dad's office door, and around eleven Mom would slip in his today's *Wall Street Journal.* You'd hear him fall upon it like a zoo animal, fed.

. . .

Since Dad had tried to break down the headhunters' door I hadn't dared go on vacation myself. But Mother encouraged me to take my family to Hawaii. She laughed. "Go ahead, enjoy yourself, for Pete's sake. Everything under control. I'm playing what friends swear is my best bridge ever, and Dick's sure working good long hours again. By now I should know the drill, hunh?"

I was just getting into my bathing suit when the hotel phone rang. I could see my wife and son down there on the white beach.

"Honey? Me. There's news about your father."

Mom's voice sounded vexed but contained. Her businesslike tone seemed assigned. It let me understand.

"When?"

"This afternoon around six-thirty our time. Maybe it happened earlier, I don't know. I found him. First I convinced myself he was just asleep. But I guess, even earlier, I knew."

I stood here against glass, on holiday. I pictured my father facedown at his desk. The tie still perfectly knotted, his hat yet safe on its hook. I imagined Dad's head at rest atop those forty pages of figures he kept meaning to add up.

I told Mom I was sorry; I said we'd fly right back.

"No, please," she said. "I've put everything off till next week. It's just us now. Why hurry? And, son? Along with the bad news, I think there's something good. He died at the office."

Nathan Englander

The Gilgul of Park Avenue

From *The Atlantic Monthly*

THE JEWISH day begins in the calm of evening, when it won't shock the system with its arrival. That was when, three stars visible in the Manhattan sky and a new day fallen, Charles Morton Luger understood that he was the bearer of a Jewish soul.

Ping! Like that it came. Like a knife against a glass.

Charles Luger knew, if he knew anything at all, that a Yiddishe *neshama* was functioning inside him.

He was not one to engage taxicab drivers in conversation, but such a thing as this he felt obligated to share. A New York story of the first order, like a woman giving birth in an elevator, or a hot-dog vendor performing open-heart surgery with a pocketknife and a Bic pen. Was not this a re-birth in itself? It was something, he was sure. So he leaned forward in his seat, raised a fist, and knocked on the Plexiglas divider.

The driver looked into his rearview mirror.

"Jewish," Charles said. "Jewish, here in the back."

The driver reached up and slid the partition open so that it hit its groove loudly.

"Oddly, it seems that I'm Jewish. Jewish in your cab."

"No problem here. Meter ticks the same for all creeds." The driver pointed at the digital display.

Charles thought about it. A positive experience—or at least benign. Yes, benign. What had he expected?

He looked out the window at Park Avenue, a Jew looking out at the world. Colors were no brighter or darker, though he was, he admitted, already searching for someone with a beanie, a landsman who might look his way, wink, confirm what he already knew.

The cab slowed to a halt outside his building, and Petey, the doorman, stepped toward the curb. Charles removed his money clip and peeled off a fifty. He reached over the seat, holding on to the bill.

"Jewish," Charles said, pressing the fifty into the driver's hand. "Jewish right here in your cab."

Charles hung his coat and placed his briefcase next to the stand filled with ornate canes and umbrellas that Sue—who had carefully scouted them out around the city—would not let him touch. Sue had redone the foyer, the living room, and the dining room all in chintz, an overwhelming number of flora-and-fauna patterns, creating a vast slippery-looking expanse. Charles rushed through it to the kitchen, where Sue was removing dinner from the refrigerator.

She read the note the maid had left, lighting burners and turning dials accordingly. Charles came up behind her. He inhaled the scent of perfume and the faint odor of cigarettes laced underneath. Sue turned, and they kissed, more passionate than friendly, which was neither an everyday occurrence nor altogether rare. She was still wearing her contacts; her eyes were a radiant blue.

"You won't believe it," Charles said, surprised to find himself elated. He was a level-headed man, not often victim to extremes of mood.

"What won't I believe?" Sue said. She separated herself from him and slipped a pan into the oven.

Sue was the art director of a glossy magazine, her professional life comparatively glamorous. The daily doings of a financial analyst, Charles felt, did not even merit polite attention. He never told her anything she wouldn't believe.

"Well, what is it, Charles?" She held a glass against the recessed ice machine in the refrigerator. "Damn," she said. Charles, at breakfast, had left it set on "crushed."

"You wouldn't believe my taxi ride," he said, suddenly aware that a person disappointed by ice chips wouldn't take well to his discovery.

"Your face," she said, noting his odd expression.

"Nothing—just remembering. A heck of a ride. A maniac. Taxi driver running lights. Up on the sidewalk."

The maid had prepared creamed chicken. When they sat down to dinner, Charles stared at his plate. Half an hour Jewish and already he felt obliged. He knew there were dietary laws, milk and meat forbidden to touch, but he didn't know if chicken was considered meat and didn't dare ask Sue and chance a confrontation—not until he'd formulated a plan. He would call Dr. Birnbaum, his psychologist, in the morning. Or maybe he'd find a rabbi. Who better to guide him in such matters?

And so, a marrano in modern times, Charles ate his chicken like a gentile—all the while a Jew in his heart.

At work the next morning Charles got right on it. He pulled out the Yellow Pages, referenced and cross-referenced, following the "see" list throughout the phone book. More than one listing under "Zion" put him in touch with a home for the aged. "Redemption" led him further off course. Finally he came upon an organization that seemed frighteningly appropriate. For one thing, it had a number in Royal Hills, a neighborhood thick with Jews.

The listing was for the Royal Hills Mystical Jewish Reclamation Center, or, as the recorded voice said, "the R-HMJRC"—just like that, with a pause after the first "R." It was a sort of clearinghouse for the Judeo-supernatural: "Press one for messianic time clock, two for dream interpretation and counseling, three for numerology, and four for a retreat schedule." The "and four" took the wind out of his sails. A bad sign. Recordings never said "and four" and then "and five." But the message went on. A small miracle. "For all gilgulim, cases of possible reincarnation, or recovered memory, please call Rabbi Zalman Meintz at the following number."

Charles took it down, elated. This was exactly why he had moved to New York from Idaho so many years before. Exactly the reason. Because you could find anything in the Manhattan Yellow Pages. Anything. A book as thick as a cinder block.

The R-HMJRC was a beautifully renovated Gothic-looking brownstone in the heart of Royal Hills. The front steps had been widened to the width of the building, and the whole façade of the first two floors had been torn off and replaced by a stone arch with a glass wall behind it. The entry hall was marble, and Charles was impressed. There is money in the God business, he told himself, making a mental note.

This is how it went: Standing in the middle of the marble floor, feeling the cold space, the only thing familiar being his unfamiliar self. And then it was back. *Ping!* Once again, understanding.

Only yesterday his whole life had been his life—familiar, totally his own. Something he lived in like an old wool sweater. Today: Brooklyn, an archway, white marble.

"Over here, over here. Follow my voice. Come to the light."

Charles had taken the stairs until they ended, and he entered what appeared to be an attic, slanted ceilings and dust, overflowing with attic stuff—chairs and a rocking horse, a croquet set, and boxes, everywhere boxes—as if all the remnants of the brownstone's former life had been driven upward.

"Take the path on your right. Make your way. It's possible; I got here." The speech was punctuated with something like laughter. It was vocalized joy, a happy stutter.

The path led to the front of the building and a clearing demarcated by an oriental screen. The rabbi sat in a leather armchair across from a battered couch—both clearly salvaged from the spoils that cluttered the room.

"Zalman," the man said, jumping up and shaking Charles's hand. "Rabbi Zalman Meintz."

"Charles Luger," Charles said, taking off his coat.

The couch, though it had seen brighter days, was clean. Charles had expected dust to rise when he sat. As soon as he touched the fabric, he got depressed. More chintz. Sun-dulled flowers crawled all over it.

"Just moved in," Zalman said. "New space. Much bigger. But haven't organized, as you can see." He pointed at specific things: a mirror, a china hutch. "Please excuse, or forgive—please excuse our appearance. More important matters come first. Very busy lately, very busy." As if to illustrate, a phone perched on a dollhouse set to ringing. "You see," Zalman said. He reached over and shut off the ringer. "Like that all day. At night, too. Busier even at night."

The surroundings didn't inspire confidence, but Zalman did. He couldn't have been much more than thirty, but he looked to Charles like a real Jew: long black beard, black suit, black hat at his side, and a nice big caricaturish nose, like Fagin's but friendlier.

"Well, then, Mr. Luger. What brings you to my lair?"

Charles was unready to talk. He turned his attention to a painted seascape on the wall. "That the Galilee?"

"Oh, no." Zalman laughed and, sitting back, crossed his legs. For the first time Charles noticed that he was sporting heavy wool socks and suede sandals. "That's Bolinas. My old stomping grounds."

"Bolinas?" Charles said. "California?"

"I see what's happening here. Very obvious." Zalman uncrossed his legs, reached out, and put a hand on Charles's knee. "Don't be shy," he said. "You've made it this far. Searched me out in a bright corner of a Brooklyn attic. If such a meeting has been ordained, which by its very nature it has been, then let's make the most of it."

"I'm Jewish," Charles said. He said it with all the force, the excitement, and the relief of any of life's great admissions. Zalman was silent. He was smiling, listening intently, and, apparently, waiting.

"Yes," he said, maintaining the smile. "And?"

"Since yesterday," Charles said. "In a cab."

"Oh," Zalman said. "Oh! Now I get it."

"It just came over me."

"Wild," Zalman said. He clapped his hands together, looked up at the ceiling, and laughed. "Miraculous."

"Unbelievable," Charles added.

"No!" Zalman said, his smile gone, a single finger held up in Charles's face. "No, it's not unbelievable. That it is not. I believe you. Knew before you said—exactly why I didn't respond. A Jew sits in front of me and tells me he's Jewish. This is no surprise. To see a man so Jewish, a person who could be my brother, who *is* my brother, tell me he has only now discovered he's Jewish—that, my friend, that is truly miraculous." During his speech he had slowly moved his finger back; now he thrust it into Charles's face anew. "But not unbelievable. I see cases of this all the time."

"Then it's possible? That it's true?"

"Already so Jewish," Zalman said with a laugh, "asking questions you've already answered. You know the truth better than I do. You're the one who came to the discovery. How do you feel?"

"Fine," Charles said. "Different but fine."

"Well, don't you think you'd be upset if it was wrong what you knew? Don't you think you'd be less than fine if this were a nightmare? Somehow suffering if you'd gone crazy?"

"Who said anything about crazy?" Charles asked. Crazy he was not.

"Did I?" Zalman said. He grabbed at his chest. "An accident, purely. Slip of the tongue. So many who come have trouble with the news at home. Their families doubt."

Charles shifted. "I haven't told her."

Zalman raised an eyebrow, turning his head to favor the accusing eye. "A wife who doesn't know?"

"That's why I'm here. For guidance." Charles put his feet up on the couch and lay down, as at Dr. Birnbaum's. "I need to tell her, to figure out how. I need also to know what to do. I ate milk and meat last night."

"First, history," Zalman said. He slipped off a sandal. "Your mother's not Jewish?"

"No, no one. Ever. Not that I know."

"This is also possible," Zalman said. "It may be only that your soul was at Sinai. Maybe an Egyptian slave that came along. But once the soul witnessed the miracles at Sinai, accepted there the word, well, it became a Jewish soul. Do you believe in the soul, Mr. Luger?"

"I'm beginning to."

"All I'm saying is, the soul doesn't live or die. It's not an organic thing, like the body. It is there. And it has a history."

"And mine belonged to a Jew?"

"No, no. That's exactly the point. Jew, non-Jew, doesn't matter. The body doesn't matter. It is the soul itself that is Jewish."

They talked for more than an hour. Zalman gave him books: *The Chosen, A Hedge of Roses,* and *The Code of Jewish Law.* Charles agreed to cancel his shrink appointment for the next day; Zalman would come to his office to study with him. A payment would be required, of course: a minor fee, expenses, some for charity and to ensure good luck. The money was not the important thing, Zalman assured him. The crucial thing was having a guide to help him through his transformation. And who better than Zalman, a man who had come to Judaism the same way? Miserable in Bolinas, addicted to sorrow and drugs, he was on the brink when he discovered his Jewish soul.

"And you never needed a formal conversion?" Charles asked, astounded.

"No," Zalman said. "Such things are for others, for the litigious and stiff-minded. Such rituals are not needed for those who are called by their souls."

"Tell me, then," Charles said. He spoke out of the side of his mouth, feeling confident and chummy. "Where'd you get the shtick from? You look Jewish, you talk Jewish—the authentic article. I turn Jewish and get nothing. You come from Bolinas and sound like you've never been out of Brooklyn."

"And if I had discovered I was Italian, I'd play bocce like a pro. Such is my nature, Mr. Luger. I am most open to letting take form that which is truly inside."

This was, of course, a matter of personal experience. Zalman's own. Charles's would inevitably be different. Unique. If the change was slower, then let it be so. After all, Zalman counseled, the laws were not to be devoured like bonbons but to be embraced as he was ready. Hadn't it taken him fifty-five years to learn he was Jewish? Yes, everything in good time.

"Except," Zalman said, standing up, "you must tell your wife first thing. Kosher can wait. Tefillin can wait. But there is one thing the tender soul can't bear—the sacrifice of Jewish pride."

Sue had a root canal after work. She came home late, carrying a pint of ice cream. Charles had already set the table and served dinner, on the off chance she might be able to eat.

"How was it?" he asked. He lit a candle and poured the wine. He did not tease her, did not say a word about her slurred speech or sagging face. He pretended it was a permanent injury, nerve damage, acted as if this were a business dinner and Sue a client with a crippled lip.

She approached the table and lifted the bottle. "Well, you're not leaving me, I can tell that much. You'd never have opened your precious Haut-Brion to tell me you were running off to Greece with your secretary."

"True," he said. "I'd have saved it to drink on our verandah in Mykonos."

"Glad to see," she said, standing on her toes and planting a wet and pitifully slack kiss on his cheek, "that the fantasy has already gotten that far."

"The wine's actually a feeble attempt at topic broaching."

Sue pried the top off her ice cream and placed the carton in the center of her plate. They both sat down.

"Do tell," she said.

"I'm Jewish." That easy. It was not, after all, the first time.

"Is there a punch line?" she asked. "Or am I supposed to supply one?" He said nothing.

"Okay. Let's try it again. I'll play along. Go—give me your line."

"In the cab yesterday. I just knew. I understood, felt it for real. And—" He looked at her face, contorted, dead with anesthesia. A surreal expression in return for surreal news. "And it hasn't caused me any grief. Except for my fear of telling you. Otherwise, I actually feel sort of good about it. Different. But as if things, big things, were finally right."

"Let's get something out of the way first." She made a face, a horrible face. Charles thought maybe she was trying to bite her lip—or scowl. "Okay?"

"Shoot."

"What you're really trying to tell me is, Honey, I'm having a nervous breakdown, and this is the best way to tell you. Correct?" She plunged a spoon into the ice cream and came up with a heaping spoonful. "If it's not a nervous breakdown, I want to know if you feel like you're clinically insane."

"I didn't expect this to go smoothly," Charles said.

"You pretend that you knew I'd react badly." Sue spoke quickly and (Charles tried not to notice) drooled. "Really, though, with your tireless optimism, you thought I would smile and tell you to be Jewish. That's what you thought, Charles." She jammed her spoon back into the carton and left it buried. "Let me tell you, this time you were way off. Wrong in your heart and right in your head. It couldn't have gone smoothly. Do you know why? Do you know?"

"Why?" he asked.

"Because what you're telling me, out of the blue, out of nowhere—because what you're telling me is, inherently, crazy."

Charles nodded his head repeatedly, as if a bitter truth was confirmed. "He said you would say that."

"Who said, Charles?"

"The rabbi."

"You've started with rabbis?" She pressed at her sleeping lip.

"Of course rabbis. Who else gives advice to a Jew?"

Charles read the books at work the next day and filled his legal pad with notes. When his secretary buzzed with Dr. Birnbaum on the line, inquiring about the sudden cancellation, Charles, for the first time since he'd begun his treatment, $15,000 before, did not take the doctor's call. He didn't take any calls; he was absorbed in reading *A Hedge of Roses,* the definitive guide to a healthy marriage through ritual purity, and waiting for Rabbi Zalman.

When Charles heard Zalman outside his office, he buzzed his secretary. This was a first as well. Charles never buzzed her until she had buzzed him first. A protocol governed entry to his office. Visitors should hear buzz and counterbuzz. It set a tone.

"So," Zalman said, seating himself. "Did you tell her?"

Charles placed his fountain pen back in its holder. He straightened the base with two hands. "She sort of half believes me. Enough to worry. Not enough to tear my head off. But she knows I'm not kidding. And she does think I'm crazy."

"And how do you feel?"

"Content." Charles leaned back in his swivel chair, his arms dangling over the sides. "Jewish and content. Excited. Still excited. The whole thing's ludicrous. I was one thing and now I'm another. Neither holds any real meaning. But when I discovered I was Jewish, I think I also discovered God."

"Like Abraham," Zalman said, with a worshipful look at the ceiling. "Now it's time to smash some idols." He pulled out a serious-looking book, leather-bound and gold-embossed. A book full of secrets, Charles was sure. They studied until Charles told Zalman he had to get back to work. "No fifty-minute hour here," Zalman said, blushing and taking a swipe at the psychologist. They agreed to meet daily and shook hands twice before Zalman left.

He wasn't gone long enough to have reached the elevators before Walter, the CEO, barged into Charles's office, stopping immediately inside the door.

"Who's the fiddler on the roof?" Walter said.

"Broker."

"Of what?" Walter tapped his wedding band against the nameplate on the door.

"Commodities," Charles said. "Metals."

"Metals." Another tap of the ring. A knowing wink. "Promise me something, Charley. This guy tries to sell you the steel out of the Brooklyn Bridge, at least bargain with the man."

They had a few nights of relative quiet and a string of dinners with non-confrontational foods, among them a risotto and then a blackened trout, a spaghetti squash with an eye-watering vegetable marinara, and—in response to a craving of Sue's—a red snapper with tomato and those little bits of caramelized garlic that the maid did so well.

Sue had for all intents and purposes ignored Charles's admission and, mostly, ignored Charles. Charles spent his time in the study, reading the books Zalman had given him. This was how the couple functioned until the day the maid left a pot of boeuf bourguignon.

"The meat isn't kosher, and neither is the wine," Charles said, referring to the wine both in and out of his dinner. "And this bourguignon has a pound of bacon fat in it. I'm not complaining, only letting you know. Really. Bread will do me fine." He reached over and took a few slices from the basket.

Sue glared at him. "You're not complaining?"

"No," he said, and reached for the butter.

"Well, I'm complaining! I'm complaining right now!" She slammed a fist down so hard that her glass tipped over, spilling wine onto the table-cloth she loved. They both watched the tablecloth soak up the wine; the lace and the stitching fattened and swelled, the color spreading along the workmanship as if through a series of veins. Neither moved.

"Sue, your tablecloth."

"Fuck my tablecloth," she said.

"Oh, my." He took a sip of water.

" 'Oh, my' is right. You bet, mister." She made a noise that Charles considered to be a growl. His wife of twenty-seven years had growled at him.

"If you think I'll ever forgive you for starting this when I was crippled with Novocain. Attacking me when I could hardly talk. If you think," she said, "if you think I'm going to start paying twelve-fifty for a roast chicken, you are terribly, terribly wrong."

"What is this about chickens?" Charles did not raise his voice.

"The religious lady at work. She puts in orders on Wednesday. Every week she orders the same Goddamn meal. A twelve-dollar-and-fifty-cent roast chicken." Sue shook her head. "You should have married an airline chef if you wanted kosher meals."

"Different fight, Sue. We're due for a fight, but I think you're veering toward the wrong one."

"Why don't you tell me, then?" she said. "Since all has been revealed to you, why don't you enlighten me as to the nature of the conflict?"

"Honestly, I think you're threatened. So I want you to know I still love you. You're still my wife. This should make you happy for me. I've found God."

"Exactly the problem. You didn't find our God. I'd have been good about it if you'd found *our* God—or even a less demanding one." She scanned the table again, as if to find one of his transgressions left out absentmindedly, like house keys. "Today the cheese is gone. You threw out all the cheese, Charles. How could God hate cheese?"

"A woman who thinks peaches are too suggestive for the fruit bowl could give in on a quirk or two."

"You think I don't notice what's going on—that I don't notice you making ablutions in the morning?" She dipped her napkin into her water glass. "I've been waiting for your midlife crisis. But I expected something I could handle—a small test. An imposition. Something to rise above, to prove my love for you in a grand display of resilience. Why couldn't you have turned into a vegan? Or a liberal Democrat? Slept with your secretary for real?" She dabbed at the wine stain. "Any of those, and I would've made do."

Charles scrutinized her. "So essentially you're saying it would be okay if I changed into a West Side Jew. Like if we suddenly lived in the Apthorp."

Sue thought about it. "Well, if you have to be Jewish, why *so* Jewish? Why not like the Browns, in 6K? Their kid goes to Haverford. Why," she said, closing her eyes and pressing two fingers to her temple, "why do people who find religion always have to be so Goddamn extreme?"

"Extreme," Charles felt, was too extreme a word considering all he had to learn and all the laws he had yet to implement. He hadn't been to synagogue. He hadn't yet observed the Sabbath. He had only changed his diet and said a few prayers.

For this he'd been driven from his own bedroom.

Occasionally Sue sought him out, always with impeccable timing. She came into the den the first morning he donned prayer shawl and phylacteries, which even to Charles looked especially strange. The leather box and the strap twirled tightly around his arm, another box planted squarely in the center of his head. He was in the midst of the Eighteen Benedictions when Sue entered, and was forced to listen to her tirade in silence.

"My Charley, always topping them all," she said, watching as he rocked back and forth, his lips moving. "I've heard of wolf men and people being possessed. I've even seen modern vampires on TV. Real people who drink blood. But this beats all." She left him and then returned with a mug of coffee in hand.

"I spoke to Dr. Birnbaum. I was going to call him myself, to see how he was dealing with your change." She blew on her coffee. "Guess what, Charley. He calls me first. Apologizes for crossing boundaries, and tells me you've stopped coming, that you won't take his calls. Oh, I say, that's because Charley's Jewish and is very busy meeting with the rabbi. He's good, your shrink. Remains calm. And then, completely deadpan, he asks me—as if it makes any difference—what kind of rabbi. I told him what you told me, word for word. The kind from Bolinas. The kind who doesn't need to be ordained, because he's been a rabbi in his past nine lives. And what, I asked him, does one man, one man himself ten generations a rabbi, what does he need with anyone's diploma?" She put the mug down on a lampstand.

"Dr. Birnbaum's coming to dinner next week. On Monday. I even ordered kosher food, paper plates, the whole deal. You'll be able to eat in your own house like a human being. An evening free of antagonism, when we can discuss this like adults. His idea. He said to order kosher food once before leaving you. So I placed an order." She smoothed down her eyebrows, waiting for a response. "You can stop your praying, Charles." She turned to leave. "Your chickens are on the way."

Charles had no suits left. *Shatnez,* the mixing of linen and wool, is strictly forbidden. On Zalman's recommendation, he sent his wardrobe to Royal

Hills for testing and was forced to go to work the next day wearing slacks and suspenders, white shirt and tie. Walter hadn't left him alone since he'd arrived. "It ain't Friday, Charley," he said. "Casual day is only once a week." This he followed with "Why go to so much trouble, Charley? A nicely pressed bathrobe would be fine."

Charles had worked himself into a funk by the time Zalman entered his office. He'd accomplished nothing all morning.

"I am weakening," Charles said. "The revelation lasts about a second, comes and goes, a hot flash in the back of a taxi. But the headache it leaves you with, a whopper of a headache—that persists."

Zalman scratched at his nostril with a pinkie, a sort of refined form of picking. "Were you in a fraternity in college?"

"Of course," Charles said.

"Then consider this pledging. You've been tapped, given a bid, and now is the hard part before all the good stuff. Now's when you buy the letters on the sly and try them on at home in front of the mirror."

"Wonderful, Zalman. Well put. But not so simple. I've got to tell my boss something soon. And tensions have risen at home. We're having dinner on Monday, my wife and my shrink versus me. She's even ordered kosher food, trying to be friendly about it."

"Kosher food." A knee slap, a big laugh. "The first step. Doesn't sound anything but positive to me. By any chance has she gone to the ritual bath yet?"

Charles spun his chair around, looked out the window, and then slowly spun back.

"Zalman," he said, "that's a tough one. And it sort of makes me think you're not following. Sue refuses to go for a couple of reasons. One, because she hates me and our marriage is falling apart. And two, she maintains—and it's a valid point, a fairly good argument—that she's not Jewish."

"I see."

"I want you to come on Monday, Zalman. A voice of reason will come in handy after the weekend. I'm going to keep my first Shabbos. And if Sue remains true to form, I'm in for a doozy."

"Find out where the food is from. If it's really kosher catered, I'll be there."

· · ·

The clocks had not changed for the season, and Shabbos still came early. Charles put on the one suit jacket that had been deemed kosher and his coat and went home without explanation. He didn't touch the candlesticks on the mantlepiece, didn't risk raising Sue's ire. Instead he dug a pair, dented and tarnished, from a low cabinet in the overstuffed and unused butler's pantry. The maid passed, saying nothing. She took her pocketbook and the day's garbage into the service hall.

In the absence of wife or daughter, the honor of ushering in the Sabbath goes to the lone man. Charles cleared a space on the windowsill in the study and, covering his eyes before the lighted candles, made the blessing. He paused at the place where the woman is permitted to petition the Lord with wishes and private blessings and stood, palms cool against his eyes, picturing Sue.

The candles flickered next to the window, burning lopsided and fast.

Charles extended the footrest on his recliner. He closed his eyes and thought back to his first night away from home, sleeping on a mattress next to his cousin's bed. He was four or five, and his cousin, older, slept with the bedroom door shut tight, not even a crack of light from the hallway. That was the closest to this experience he could think of—the closest he could remember to losing and gaining a world.

The candles were out when Charles heard Sue pass on her way to the bedroom. He tried to come up with a topic of conversation, friendly and day-to-day. He came up with nothing, couldn't remember what they'd talked about over their life together. What had they said to each other when nothing was pressing? What had they chatted about for twenty-seven years?

He got up and went to her.

Sue was sitting at the far window on a petite antique chair that was intended only to be admired. She held a cigarette and flicked ash into a small porcelain dish resting on her knee. In half silhouette against the electric dusk of the city, Sue appeared as relaxed as Charles had seen her since long before his revelation. He could tell, or thought he could, that she was concentrating on ignoring his presence. She would not have her moment of peace compromised.

This was his wife. A woman who, if she preferred, could pretend he was not there. A woman always able to live two realities at once. She could spend a day at work slamming down phones and storming down hallways with layouts she'd torn in half, and then come home to entertain, serve dinner, pass teacups, in a way that hushed a room.

How was he to explain his own lack of versatility? Here was a woman who lived in two realities simultaneously. How was he to make clear his struggle living in one? And how to tell the woman of two lives that he had invited over Zalman, who carried in his soul a full ten?

On Sunday, Charles was reading a copy of Leon Uris's *QB VII* when Sue ran—truly ran—into the study and grabbed him by the arm. He was shocked and made the awkward movements of someone who is both dumbfounded and manhandled at the same time, like a tourist mistakenly seized by the police.

"Sue, what are you doing?"

"I could kill you," she said. Though smaller, she had already pulled him to his feet. He followed her to the foyer.

"What is this?" she yelled, slamming open the door.

"A mezuzah," he said. "If you mean that." He pointed at the small metal casing nailed to the doorpost. "I need it," he said. "I have to kiss it."

"Oh, my God," she said, slamming the door closed, giving the neighbors no more than a taste. "My God!" She steadied herself, putting a hand against the wall. "Well, where did it come from? It's got blue paint on it. Where does one buy a used mezuzah?"

"I don't know where to get one. I pried it off 11D with a letter opener. They don't even use it. Steve Fraiman had me in to see their Christmas tree last year. Their daughter is dating a black man."

"Are you insane? Five years on the waiting list to get into this building, and now you're vandalizing the halls. You think anyone but me will believe your cockamamie story? Oh, I'm not a Nazi, Mrs. Fraiman, just a middle-aged man who woke up a Jew."

"It happened in a cab. I didn't wake up anything."

Sue put her other hand against the wall and let her head hang.

"I've invited the rabbi," Charles said.

"You think that's going to upset me? You think I didn't know you'd drag him into this? Good, bring him. Maybe they have a double open at Bellevue."

"This is very intolerant, Sue." He reached out to touch her.

"Go back to the study," she said. "Go paw one of your books."

. . .

They considered the table. Charles and Sue stood at opposite ends, appraising the job the maid had done. It was admirable.

On a paper tablecloth were paper cups and plastic wine glasses with snap-on bases, patterned paper napkins that matched the pattern on the plates, plastic forks and plastic spoons, and a few other things—cheap but not disposable. Knives, for instance. The knives were real, new, wooden-handled steak knives. Sue had even gone to the trouble of finding a decent bottle of kosher wine. One bottle. The other was a blackberry. Charles wondered if the blackberry was a warning of what continued religiosity might do to the refined palate. Screw-top wine. Sugary plonk. He was going to comment, but looking again at the lavish spread, both leaves inserted into the table, the polished silver on the credenza, he reconsidered. This was more than a truce. It was an attempt to be open—or at least a request that the maid make an effort.

"Mortifying," Sue said. "Like a child's birthday party. We've got everything except for a paper donkey tacked to the wall."

"I appreciate it, Sue. I really, really do." He had sweetness in his voice, real love for the first time since he'd made his announcement.

"Eighty-eight dollars' worth of the blandest food you've ever had. The soup is inedible, pure salt. I had a spoonful and needed to take an extra high-blood-pressure pill. I'll probably die before dinner's over, and then we'll have no problems."

"More and more," Charles said, taking a yarmulke from his pocket and fastening it to his head, "more and more, you're the one who sounds like a Jew."

When Charles answered the knock on the study door, he was surprised to find Zalman standing there, surprised that Sue hadn't come to get him.

"She is very nice, your wife," Zalman said. "A sensible woman, it appears."

"Appearances are important," Charles said.

Zalman brightened, and exuded joy as he did. "It will be fine," he said. He hooked Charles's arm into his own and led him down the hall.

Sue and Dr. Birnbaum—sporting a yellow sweater—were already seated. Charles sat at the head of the table, and Zalman stood behind his chair.

The most painful silence Charles had ever experienced ensued. He was aware of his breathing, his pulse and temperature. He could feel the contents of his intestines, the blood in his head, the air settling on his eardrums, lake-smooth without sound.

Zalman spoke. "Is there a place where I can wash?" he asked.

Before eating bread, Charles knew. "Yes," Charles said. "I'll come too."

He looked at Sue as he got up. Charles knew what she was thinking. Say it, he wanted to tell her. Point it out to Dr. Birnbaum. You're right. It's true.

Ablutions.

Ablutions all the time.

Rabbi Zalman made a blessing over the bread, and Dr. Birnbaum muttered, "Amen." Sue just stared. A man with a beard, a long black beard and sidelocks, was sitting in her house. Charles wanted to tell her she was staring, but he stopped himself with "Sue."

"What!" she said. "What, Charles?"

"Shall we eat?"

"Yes," Zalman said, his smile broad, his teeth bright white and Californian. "Let's eat first. We can discuss better on full stomachs." Reaching first one way and then the other, Zalman picked up a bottle and poured himself a brimming glass of blackberry wine.

They ate in a lesser but still oppressive silence. All showed it in their countenances except for Zalman, who was deeply involved in the process of eating and paused only once, to say, "Jewish name—Birnbaum," before going back to his food. The other three took turns looking from one to the other and back to their plates. They stared at Zalman when they could think of nowhere to put their eyes.

"The barley is delicious." Dr. Birnbaum smiled as if Sue had cooked the food.

"Thank you," she said, snatching the empty container from next to Zalman and heading to the kitchen for another. Dr. Birnbaum took that opportunity to broach the topic with Charles.

"I don't think it's unfair to say I was startled by your news."

"Just your everyday revelation, nothing special."

"Even so, I would have hoped you'd feel comfortable discussing it with me. After all this time."

Sue returned with a quart container of barley, the plastic top in her hand. Charles cleared his throat, and no one said a word. Sue cocked her head. A slight tilt, an inquisitive look. Had such silence ever occurred at one of her dinner parties? Had her presence ever brought conversation to an abrupt end?

She slammed the container onto the table, startling Zalman. He looked up at her and removed a bit of barley from his beard.

"I was about to explain my presence," Dr. Birnbaum said. "Let Charles know that I have no secret agenda. This isn't a competency hearing. And I'm not packing a syringe full of Thorazine."

"That was before," Sue said. "Last week, before your patient started pilfering Judaica. Before he started mortifying me in this building. Do you know that on Friday night he rode the elevator up and down like an idiot, waiting for someone to press our floor? Like a retarded child. He gets in the elevator and keeps explaining it to everyone. 'Can't press the button on my Sabbath, ha ha.' He can't ask people outright, because you're only allowed to *hint.*"

"Very good," Zalman said. "A fine student."

"You," she said to Zalman. "Interloper!" And then, turning back to Dr. Birnbaum, "I heard it from old Mrs. Dallal. She's the one who pressed the button. Our poor old next-door neighbor, forced to ride the elevator with this maniac. She told me she was talking to Petey, the doorman, and couldn't figure out why the elevator door kept opening and Charley wouldn't come out. She told me that she actually asked him, 'Do you want to come out?' Now, is that insane, Doctor, or is it not? Do sane people need to be invited out of elevators, or do they just get out on their own?"

Charles spoke first. "She turned the light off in the bathroom on Friday night. She knows I can't touch the lights. I had to go in the dark. She's being malicious."

"We are at the table, Charles. Paper plates or not. A man who holds his fork like an animal or not, we shall have some manners."

Zalman laughed out loud at Sue's insult.

"Those are manners—embarrassing a guest?" Now Charles yelled. "And a rabbi, yet."

"He, Charley, is not even Jewish. And neither are you. One need not be polite to the insane. As long as you don't hose them down, all is in good taste."

"She's malicious, Doctor. She brought you here to watch her insult me."

"If I'm supposed to put my two cents in," Dr. Birnbaum said, "I suppose now is the time."

"Two cents?" Zalman said. "What does that come out to for you—a consonant?"

"Thank you," the doctor said. "A perfect example of the inane kind of aggression that can turn a conversation into a brawl."

"It's because you're not wearing a tie," Charles said. "How can you control people without a tie?"

"I'm not trying to control anyone."

"It's true," Zalman said. "I went to a shrink for twelve years. Started in seventh grade. They don't control. They absolve. Like atheist priests. No responsibility for your actions, no one to answer to. Anarchists with advanced degrees." Zalman spoke right to the doctor. "You can't give people permission to ignore God. It is not your right."

"Sir," Dr. Birnbaum said. "Rabbi. I invite you, as Charles's spiritual adviser, to join me in trying to help the situation."

"Exactly why I'm here," Zalman said. He pushed his chair back and rested his elbows on the table. "One way to help would be to give Charles your blessing, or whatever you call it. Shrinks always say it's okay, so tell him it's okay, tell her it's okay, and then all will be better."

"I can't do that—don't, in fact, do that," the doctor said. He addressed his patient. "Should we go into another room and talk?"

"If I wanted that, I'd have come to our sessions. All the therapy in the world could not bring the simple comfort that I've found in worshipping God."

"Listen to this," Sue said. "Do you hear the kind of thing I have to endure? Palaver!" The doctor looked at Sue, raised his hand, and patted the air.

"I'm listening," he said. "I actually *do* want to hear it. But from him. That Charles has gone from Christian nonbeliever to Orthodox Jew is clear. It is also perplexing." He spoke in sensible rhythms. The others listened, all primed to interrupt. "I came to dinner to hear from Charles why he changed."

"Because of his soul," Zalman said, throwing his arms up in frustration. "He's always had this soul. His way of thinking has always been agreeable, but now God has let him know He wasn't pleased with the way Charley was acting."

"It's true," Charles said. "That's how it feels—like it was always in me, but now it's time for me to do God-pleasing work."

Sue didn't speak but clenched her whole body, fists and shoulders and teeth.

"And God-pleasing work is living the life of the Orthodox Jew?" The doctor was all softness. "Are you sure it might not be something else—like gardening or meditation? Have you considered philanthropy, Charley—I mean, as a for instance?"

"Do you not see what he is doing?" Zalman said. "The sharp tongue of the philosopher." Zalman jumped to his feet, still leaning heavily on the table, which shook under his weight, though silently, devoid of the usual collection of silver and crystal and robbing him of some drama. "Tell him what the King of the Khazars told his own sharp-tongued philosopher five hundred years ago." He pointed an accusing finger. "Thy words are convincing, yet they do not correspond to what I wish to find."

"Just shut up. Would you, please?" Sue said.

"It's all right, Zalman," Charles said. Zalman sat. "That's not how I would have put it," Charles said, "but it's how I feel. You see, Doctor—with your eyes, I mean. You see how I look, how I'm acting. No different from before. Different rituals, maybe. Different foods. But the same man. Only I feel peaceful, fulfilled."

As Charles spoke, Sue slipped from her chair and slid to the floor, as might a drunk. She did not fall over but rested on her knees, interlocking her fingers and bowing her head. She rested in the traditional Christian pose of prayer. His wife, who was mortified by a white purse after Labor Day, was on her knees in front of company.

"Sue, what are you doing? Get up off the floor."

She raised her chin but kept her eyes shut.

"What?" she said. "Do you have a monopoly on God? Are you the only one who can pray?"

"Point taken. Your point is taken."

"I'm making no point," she said. "I understand now. You were as desperate as I've become. God is for the desperate. For when there is nothing left to do."

"There is always something," Zalman said. No one acknowledged him.

"There are options, Sue." Charles was perspiring through his shirt.

Sue opened her eyes and sat leaning on an arm, her legs at her side.

"No," she said. She did not cry, but all could tell that if she hit the wrong note, the wrong word, if she was in any way agitated further, she would lose her composure completely. "You don't seem to understand, Charles. Because you don't want to. But I do not have any idea what to do."

If there was one sacrifice Charles had thought she would not be able to make, it was this—to be open in front of outsiders, to look tired and overworked in front of a table set with paper plates.

"Is that what you want to hear, Charles? I'm not resigned to a Goddamn thing. I'm not going to kill you or have you committed or dragged up to the summer house for deprogramming." Charles was at once relieved and frightened—for she had clearly considered her options. "But I will, Charley, be thinking and waiting. You can't stop me from that. I'm going to hope and pray. I'll even pray to your God—beg Him to make you forget Him. To cast you out."

"That's wrong, Sue." It sounded wrong.

"No, Charles. It's fair. More fair than you've been to me. You have an epiphany and want everyone else to have the same one. Well, if we did, even if it was the best, greatest, holiest thing in the world, if every person had the same one, the most you would be left with is a bright idea."

"I don't know if that's theologically sound," Zalman said, twisting the pointed ends of his beard.

"It's wonderful," the doctor said. His face was full of pride.

Charles got down on the floor and sat cross-legged in front of Sue. "What does that mean, Sue? What does it mean for me?"

"It means that your moment of grace has passed. Real or not. It's gone now. You are left with life—daily life. I'm only letting you know that as much as you worry about staying in God's favor, you should worry about staying in mine. It's like taking a new lover, Charles. You're as dizzy as a schoolgirl. But remember which one of us dropped into your life and which of us has been in for the long haul. I *am* going to try and stick it out. But let me warn you: as quickly as God came into your life, I might one day be gone."

"I can't live that way," Charles said.

"That is what I go to sleep hoping."

From the corner of his eye Charles caught Dr. Birnbaum trying to slip out of the room without interrupting the conversation's flow. He watched the doctor recede, backing away with quiet steps, and then turned to Sue. He turned to her and let all the resentment he felt come into his face. He let the muscles go, felt his eyelids drop and harden, spoke to her as intimately as if Zalman were not there.

"The biggest thing that ever happened to me, and you make me feel that I should have kept it to myself."

She considered. "True. It would have been better. I would much rather have found a box after you were gone—prayer books and skullcaps, used needles and women's underwear. At this point, at my age, I'd have had an easier time finding it all after you were gone."

Charles looked to Zalman, who was, like the doctor, slowly making an exit. "You're leaving me too?"

"Not as elegant as the doctor, but not so stupid as to miss when it's time to go."

"One minute," Charles said to his wife. "One minute and I'll be back," he pleaded, untucking his legs. "I'll walk him to the door. Our guest."

Charles followed the rabbi down the front hallway. Zalman put on his coat and tilted his hat forward, an extra edge against the city below.

"This is a crucial time," Charles said.

They were by the umbrella stand. Zalman pulled out a cane. He scratched at his nose with a pinkie. "It's an age-old problem. To all the great ones tests are given. I wouldn't be surprised if the King of the Khazars faced the same one."

"What happened to the King?" Charles asked. "How does it turn out for the great ones?"

Zalman leaned the cane against the wall. "It doesn't matter. The point is they all had God. They knew in their hearts God."

Charles put a hand on Zalman's shoulder. "I'm only asking for you to tell me."

"You already know," Zalman said. The joy drained from his face. "You know but want me to lie."

"Is that so bad?"

The rabbi's face looked long and soft; the rapture did not return. "No hope, Mr. Luger. I tell you this from one Jew to another. There is no hope for the pious."

. . .

Charles made his way back to the table only to find Sue gone, the table clean, and the chairs in place. Could more than a minute have passed? He saw the pantry garbage can in the middle of the kitchen, the paper table-cloth sticking out the top. A disposable dinner, the dining room as if un-touched.

He started toward the bedroom and stopped at the study door. Sue was standing at the window beside the tarnished candlesticks, which were fused in place where wax had run off the bases. She picked at the hard-ened formations, forcing her nail underneath and lifting them away from the painted wood of the sill.

"It's not sacrilegious, I hope?" She picked at the wax that ran over the silver necks in braids.

"No," Charles said. "I don't believe it is."

He crossed the room to stand beside Sue. He reached for the hand that scratched at the fine layers of wax on the sill. "So it'll stay there," he said. "So what?"

"It will ruin the paint," she said.

"It will make the window frame look real. Like someone lives in the apartment and uses this room."

Charles looked around the study, at the lamp and the bookcase, and then out the window at the buildings and the sky. He had not read far into the Bible, and still thought that God might orchestrate his rescue.

He took hold of Sue's other hand and held them both in place. He wanted her to understand that a change of magnitude had indeed oc-curred, but the mark it left was not great. The real difference was con-tained in his soul, after all.

Sue's gaze fell past him before meeting his eyes.

He tried to appear open before her, to allow Sue to observe him with the profound clarity he had only so recently come to know. Charles was desperate with willingness. He struggled to stand without judgment, to be only for Sue, to be wholly seen, wanting her to love him changed.

Andrea Barrett

Theories of Rain

From *The Southern Review*

Kingsessing, on the Schuylkill
September 8, 1810

HE RODE past earlier, that slip of a Sophie at his side: James. If you knew what I feel when I see him . . . but why shouldn't you know? If I can imagine you, not your face or your gestures perhaps but your mind and your heart, why not imagine you capable of feeling all I feel? I picture us on the bank of the river here, near the fieldstone bench, exchanging confidences. I think how, when at last I find you, I will hand you these lines and you will know me.

The aunts do not even look up as he passes. The hayfields surrounding us, north and west, belong to James; the lush pastures to the south, the oats and rye and cattle and sheep, the fine stand of timber between our wedge of riverfront land and the ramble of the Bartrams' botanic gardens—his, all his. He is nearing thirty, not yet married though rumored to be looking for a wife. Wealthy, now that he's come into his grandfather's estate. And favored in all the other ways as well. About him there is a kind of sheen, the golden skin of good fortune.

In the room below me the aunts ignore him as they work on their *Manual of Geography*, a book for schoolgirls; they have such high hopes. Lessons composed of questions and answers, which a classroom of girls with scraped-back hair may murmur in unison:

Q. What is the climate of the Torrid Zone?
A. *It is very hot.*

Q. What is the climate of the Frigid Zone?
A. *It is very cold.*

Q. What is the climate of the Temperate Zone?
A. *It is mild or moderate; the heat being not so great as in the Torrid Zone, nor the cold so severe as in the Frigid Zone.*

Aunt Daphne, Aunt Jane. If they knew what I think. If they were to step outside and hail James, and if he were ill-mannered enough (which he's never been in his five years as our neighbor) to inquire about our unusual family, they would say they are cousins; they are not. That they are my aunts, which they are not. Not looking at his broad shoulders, the strength of his hand on his horse's reins; not looking at the planes of his jaw or the shape of his brow, because they care for the minds but not the bodies of men, they would point out the charms of our small stone house. Three women, and everything just so. They would not say that I was born on a farm near Chester, to a family with two parents, two sisters, three brothers—all but one dead of the yellow fever when I was an infant, and the surviving brother torn from my side while a few pigs and chickens wandered bewildered through the dirt. The aunts took me in; I belong to them. They think I will live here forever with them, sharing their studies, caring for them: I will not.

Their book is to have a section on meteorology. Why there is weather. What it is. From the papers and books their friends have loaned us, I am to collate the theories of rain. What will be left of all my work, after they simplify it? Something like this, which they wrote today:

Q. What surrounds the Earth?
A. *The Atmosphere; composed of air, vapor, and other gases.*

Q. What can you say of the Atmosphere?
A. *It is thinner or less dense the farther it is from the Earth.*

Q. When water dries up, where does it go?
A. *It rises into the air.*

Q. How can water rise into the air?
A. *It is turned to vapor, and then it is lighter than the air.*

Q. When vapors rise and become condensed, what are they called?
A. *Clouds.*

Anaximenes, I tell the aunts—offering this scrap much as our cat, Cassandra, brings moles to the kitchen door and lays them at my feet— Anaximenes thought air might condense first to cloud, then to water, then to earth, and finally to stone. Why not include, I asked Aunt Daphne, this:

Q. Why are raindrops round?
A. *One theory is this: Because the corners get rubbed off as they fall side by side; and because the round shape overcomes the resistance of the air; and because even the smallest parts of the world are obliged to represent and mirror the round image of the universe.*

But the aunts are no more interested in these old theories than in the question of why Cassandra has extra toes. Aunt Daphne said, "Lavinia. When will you learn to keep in mind our audience?"

Yet why would the girls who will someday sit in a hot schoolroom, bored and weary with reciting these lessons, not feel the longings I feel? For the tantalizing theory, the mysterious fact—Descartes's assumption that water is composed of eel-shaped particles, easily separated; Urbano d'Aviso's proposition that vapor is bubbles of water filled with fire, ascending through the air so long as it is heavier than they are, stopping when they arrive at a place where the air is equally light. Why must all we write be *practical?*

September 13, 1810

He comes, he goes, he comes, he goes. The other one I would tell you about: Mr. Frank Wells. He is well enough favored, tall and slim, thinning brown hair, a nose as long and sensitive as a greyhound's. A bit older than James, with printer's hands. He has his own business and has built a house, upriver from us, which I have never seen. Unlike James, he likes the way I look. He comes, he goes, along with the others—botanists and geologists; a Frenchman named Rafinesque, fat about the waist, whose shirt escapes from his pantaloons and shows bare flesh as he lectures us; a shy and friendly entomologist named Thomas Say. They admire the aunts and their work and the way they have raised me. Our house of three virgins, so studious. So neat. Every hour occupied by something useful. We rise, cook, sweep and wash, tend to the gardens, and then study and study, always useful things. The aunts wear spectacles; their eyes are weary. At night they ask me to read to them. Their spirits are weary as well. Aunt Jane has spells.

"It is all too much for me," she says. April, often. Or September, like now. When everything around us is lush and damp and hot and fertile and florid. The box hedges send out a powerful smell, and the vines trying to strangle the trees send out another, even stronger; the mockingbirds sit on the roof and sing all night, a sound you would like, as I do. Aunt Jane takes to her bed, her skin muddy and cold and her limbs unmoving, with a cloth on her eyes and tufts of cotton blocking her ears from the birdsong. She gets sick for no reason, well for no reason. One day she rises, resumes her duties, declares she is better. In a few months it will all be too much for her again. Her friends, those studious men, shake their heads in sympathy and whisper, *Melancholia.*

The aunts are Quakers and have raised me the same. On our day of rest we go to Meeting; we sit in silence, we wait with the sun streaming through the windows for the spirit to enter and move us. In that calm, still place I struggle not to leap from my bench and shout—but what is the use of talking about this, when you are not here to advise me? What is the use?

September 24, 1810

James again. He nods as he rides by, once more on his way to visit Sophie. The slip of a Sophie, in her house on the hill. Half my weight and half my brains and half my wit; and a hundred times my fortune and a father who's a banker. Around her neck, a fine gold chain. Little rings on little fingers, little kid shoes on little feet. James could pick her up the way I might a spaniel, if we had a spaniel: the aunts do not like dogs. No doubt he has lifted her lightly into a carriage, or onto a saddle. I hear she plays the piano beautifully. In the garden I watch him passing by; I stand so he can see me, and he nods. He rides on, lovely, taken.

If the aunts knew what I think. If the aunts knew what I dream. Aunt Daphne has her room and Aunt Jane hers, but they bundle at night in the same bed—for comfort, they say, for warmth—and they think I will settle for this.

September 8, September 13; October 1, 2, 3—what is the point of dating these words as I write them? They are for you, and when I find you, dates will mean nothing to us. You are in Ecuador, or in Cleveland; in England or Boston, the Rocky Mountains; or perhaps you are a few miles away, stripped as I was of our family name. Perhaps we have met without knowing whom we met.

I have but the faintest memory of our last day. The aunts said the plague left only two of us alive: a little boy, almost four years old, and me, not yet turned two. Did you cry when the wagons came? When everything inside our home was burned, the bedding and furniture piled and torched but the things outside, uncontaminated, prudently saved and divided? The aunts took me, some hoes and hay rakes, two pigs, a horse, a cart. Whoever took you, said the aunts—and how could they lose the name of that family who stopped on their journey to someplace else and, out of pity and charity, left with an extra, orphaned child?—whoever took you, also took the cow.

On September 13 I turned twenty: I am grown, and what I write is mine; I may write whatever I want in any fashion. Wherever you are—perhaps you have headed out West?—you are now twenty-two. On an arid plain you may have picked up a glossopetra, shaped like the tongue of a man or a snake or a duck, and wondered if it rained from the sky on a moonless night. If you were here I would lift that triangular stone from your hand and say: this has nothing to do with the rain; this is the tooth of a shark.

A few times I have been alone with James. Once he arrived with a side of venison, a gift for the aunts, who were out. I was still a girl, perhaps sixteen. He arrived without servants and wouldn't let me touch the meat or help him convey it to the smokehouse. As if I were a young lady, as if I had never prepared a meal or handled a bloody bundle of ribs. Even then

I felt something like lightning pass between us. It has nothing to do with who we are, who we think we are; he knows nothing of me, and I know only what I can see of him, his actions and possessions. The mysterious current leaping between us comes from someplace deeper. Our bodies speaking. Or maybe our souls; it has nothing to do with our minds.

Once we met in the woods, his woods, he out marking trees for felling and I walking furiously away from the aunts, filling my lungs with air; around me the wild profusion of tulip trees and witch hazel and honeysuckle, the beeches and myrtle and sugar maples, magnolias and pitcher plants. He asked if I was enjoying myself, and when I stopped to answer I blushed and broke into a sweat, the hollows of my armpits weeping: all this from the sight of him, standing like a tree himself in the cool, dark shadows.

And once—it is this that wakes me at night—once we were together a little longer. The aunts keep bees, not just for the honey but for what they represent. Our visitors are trotted out to the hives, shown their neatness and order, subjected to Aunt Daphne's monologues about the virtues of bee civilization. How the bees work as one, for a common goal; how they aid and nurture each other, raise their young, store up food for the winter; a community of females, the epitome of order. Into this model of virtue come the kingbirds, who love above all else to eat bees. Once, last August, the aunts appealed to James for help, and he came with a shotgun and slaughtered twenty birds. The aunts fled from the carnage, but I stayed. One bird, James said, was leading all the others; he pointed out a beautiful creature that snapped with great determination at a line of bees returning from the clover. This bird he brought down with a single shot, then retrieved it and laid it at my feet.

"May I show you something?" he said. "You're not frightened of blood?"

"I am not," I said.

He knelt with a penknife and slit the bird from throat to vent, plunging his hand in the craw. On a bit of smooth grass he laid handfuls of bees, shaking his head at their number. The sun was blazing bright, the air heavy with the scents of grass and clover; in that syrupy atmosphere, the blanket of bees began to stir. To my astonishment, half of them rose like Jonah from the whale, licked clean their rumpled golden down, and flew back to their hives apparently undamaged.

"All those," he said with satisfaction. "In that single bird."

I couldn't say a word. I think he knew what I felt. A cloud passed over the sun as the bees vanished into their hive; the sky darkened, and mosquitoes rose from the pond and arrowed toward us. I was looking at James, watching hypnotized as he lifted his arm and reached in my direction. Gently, firmly, he pressed his palm against my forearm, flattening the creature that had already penetrated my skin. When he lifted his hand we both stared at the streak of blood, so red against my whiteness. He was the one who blushed that time; he picked up his gun and bowed. "I am glad I could be of use to your aunts," he said, and then he left. I wanted to lick the blood from my arm; I wanted to lick his arm. Oh, what use is this?

Mr. Wells again today.

He sat with us; we all drank tea. The aunts showed him what we have so far done on the *Manual*. "And Lavinia?" he inquired. His hands on the papers were long and intelligent.

"She helps with every step," said Aunt Jane.

"But also," I said, "also I am working on something of my own."

Aunt Daphne sniffed; Cassandra entered, bearing a grasshopper, and busied herself in tearing it apart.

"What is it that interests you?" Mr. Wells said. Which no one ever asks me.

"What you would expect," I replied, and told him what I would tell you, if you were here. "How a cloud floats, when water is much heavier than air. How cloud particles form from vapor, and how raindrops grow from those particles. Whether the winds drive the particles together, coalescing them."

He looked puzzled, yet also, I thought, interested. "There are rains of manna and quails in the Bible," he said. "And in Pliny the Elder, rains of milk and blood and birds and wool."

What I wanted to say was this: *It was raining the day they took us from each other.*

Q. What kind of rain?
A. *A light rain, a drizzling rain.*

Q. You remember that?
A. *It is almost all I remember. On the muddy ground our household*

*burns without flame, the smoke rising up through the fine rain falling
down. You have no face. Your figure, clad in damp homespun, disappears into
a cloud.*

What I said was, "Rains of fish." The aunts, who don't remember the
rain, have no idea what asking me to collate these theories has meant.
"And of frogs and hay and grain and bricks," I continued. "But almost
everyone agrees that those result from whirlwinds."

Mr. Wells bent down to Cassandra, meaning I think to rescue the
grasshopper; too late—she had left nothing but the wings. He straightened with these in his right hand. "Rains of stone," he said, augmenting
our list. "Do you know the theory of the lapidifying juice?" Aunt Daphne
struggled to maintain the expression of deferential interest she feels is
proper with such men.

"Through the earth's crust moves a fluid body, or juice, that can turn
various substances into stone," said Mr. Wells, nodding in the aunts' direction but addressing me. Really his face is very kind, almost handsome
in its way. His linen is clean, his hands as well, but on the middle finger
of his right hand is a callus always stained with ink. "It is also found in
the sea, and in the atmosphere, in a gaseous form: moving through these
layers as blood moves through the body. In the air this lapidifying juice
makes pebbles, which fall to earth."

"I have never heard of this," I said.

"A sixteenth-century theory," he said, setting down the broken wings.
"An attempt to account for the generation of stones, and a distinct ad-
vance on the theory of the petrific seed."

Another phrase I had never heard. The aunts turned the conversation
toward their textbook before Mr. Wells could finish his thought, but later
I was able to thank him for teaching me something new.

"It's nothing," he said. "Do you investigate the theories of snow and
hail and dew, as well as rain?"

When I told him I was interested in all the hydrometeors, he made me
spell and define the word. "It's just as you would expect," I said. "If 'meteor' is any atmospheric phenomenon—think of *meteorology*—so we
speak of the aerial meteors, or the winds; the luminous meteors, such as
rainbows and haloes; the igneous or fiery meteors, such as lightning and
shooting stars. Among the watery or hydrometeors are all those things
you mentioned."

"Now we have made a fair trade," he said. "You have taught *me* something new."

He is kind enough, smart enough. If you were here, would you tell me what to do?

Q. What is it I feel for James?

Q. What is it James feels for me?

Q. What theory accounts for these feelings, which can come to nothing?

Q. What?

In the garden Mr. Wells held out a sheaf of papers. "From my Charleston cousin, William Wells," he said. "He practices medicine in London now, and in his spare time studies nature. He is writing an essay on the dew."

Perhaps you are in London as well; perhaps you are leading the life I long for, rich in friends and good conversation, the universe unfolding before you. I smoothed my skirts against the bench, aware that Mr. Wells was watching me as he talked about dew as rain that falls very slowly, particles of water moving toward the objects that attract them. He stuttered and looked down at the papers in his lap.

"Does dew come from the earth, or from the air?" he read from his cousin's notes. "Does it rise or fall? What is the source of the cold that condenses the vapor? At first I thought the deposition of the dew might cause the cold we observe on those objects. But I have come to realize that the cold *precedes* the dew."

He turned to another page. "My cousin did an experiment," he said. "Which we might try to repeat."

We gathered uncarded wool from the aunts' stores, and on the balance they use to weigh mordants and pigments for dyeing, we weighed out two equal amounts. One sample we spread in a loose circle on the grass. Inside a long, thick-walled piece of clay drainage pipe, set on end so it was open to the darkening sky, we spread the other sample in a circle the same size. The aunts watched, unimpressed but polite. They have borrowed many books from Mr. Wells.

"I'll return in the morning," he said. "Quite early, if you don't mind."

When the aunts didn't offer him a bed, he rode off to his home, seven miles upriver. His horse's legs disappeared in the mist, then the horse's head, and then his own, leaving only the silver rays of the moon and the clear, cold air. Aunt Daphne made me come inside, but then she and Aunt Jane kept me awake, arguing in the fierce, airy whispers they think I can't hear through the wall between our rooms. Their words were lost but not their tone, and I knew they had settled into their favorite topic:

Q. What shall we do with Lavinia?
A. *Is there an answer to this?*

I slept, and dreamed of you. In the morning Mr. Wells arrived, and we gathered and reweighed the samples. Just as his cousin had found, the sample on the grass had collected more dew.

"Which it would not," I said, "if dew fell from the sky like rain; an equal amount should have fallen within the cylinder as without."

"My cousin's point exactly," said Mr. Wells. "He contends that the cooling of the earth's surface causes water vapor to condense from the air. What matters is how much heat is radiated into the atmosphere. What matters is the exposure of the objects to the air. The sheltering walls of the drainage pipe lessened the radiation to the sky; it was colder outside the pipe than within, hence there was more dew outside."

My skirt was wet; our hands and arms were drenched; there was damp wool everywhere and the smell of sheep. "I'll borrow some thermometers from my friends," he said. "We'll set them around and see if the dew is heaviest where they read lowest."

As I spread my arms, pointing out a sheltered hollow and a promising rise, I caught him looking at me. I forget sometimes how long my limbs are, how fleshy I am in the shoulders and bust. You are built the same, I expect, tall and strong and capable, like James. Mr. Wells looked me over shyly and said, "Forgive me, I don't mean to stare. But you have such *amplitude.* You are very different from your aunts in this way."

They are not my aunts, I wanted to say. Instead I reached over to brush off the bits of wool on his coat, which caused him to color up to the roots of his soft brown hair.

A rain that moves in swirls and gusts, pushing the leaves against the limbs, pushing my hair away from my face; then a rain hardly more than a mist, seeming simply to condense on my skin: it is raining today. And though you disappeared in the rain, perhaps because I last saw you in it, I love the rain. In it I am sleek and slender and smooth, attractive as Sophie is attractive, a woman someone might love. The wide span of my hips reduced, the thick mat between my legs tamed and trimmed, and my monthly bleeding dried to a few dainty drops—oh, forgive me for these thoughts. You will know what I mean by them.

Out of the rain stepped James. Behind him his wagon, and on it two boxes: two solid, well-made wooden hives. Gifts for the aunts. But once more they were absent. "I thought they might like to enlarge their apiary," James said.

When I told him they had gone to consult a printer about their book, he murmured something about their industriousness. "A pleasure," he said. He smelled of wood and wool and leather harness, of honey, and himself. "To have such neighbors."

"I'm sure they'll be grateful," I replied.

He nodded and stood at the door for a moment, before hoisting the first of the boxes and hauling it past the barn and the sheds, to join the others among the apple trees. A second trip and he was done, back before me, sweat slipping down beneath his heavy hair. He did not refuse the glass of water I offered. He drank slowly, steadily, the muscles moving in waves beneath the smooth skin of his throat. After he passed me the empty glass, he stepped back. "Why are you looking at me like that?" he asked.

"There is something," I said faintly. "A little spot of something, on your cheekbone."

The gesture with which he raised his hand—index and little fingers spread, ring and middle fingers together, the whole strong, shapely hand displayed—was that of a beautiful woman. Two fingertips brushed his cheekbone, where I would place my tongue. He knew that, knew there was nothing to brush away but a few drops of sweat. That was pity passing over his face, and fear at the hunger in my gaze, and pleasure, just a little, at being so sharply admired. He started to say something, stopped, shook his head and left.

I cannot have James. This is perfectly clear. In my mind I know he belongs to the slip of a Sophie, and I accept this, I understand it. In my mind. Still, my heart lags behind. Though even if my heart wants to be broken, if part of me wants me to be brought to my knees, it is not to be my choice. For James I will never be more than one of the three virgins he passes daily.

The aunts have no idea of this, but it is from the likes of James that they have wished to preserve me. From that giving in, that going under, they would preserve me as they have themselves. Not the children born every year, half or more of them to die; not the daily bowing down, the loss of my own thoughts and my independence; not the loss of my mind nor (the thing the aunts can't envision) the loss of that clear, separate place in me where I dream of you, and long for you. Through that channel of longing, the world enters me.

Yesterday Mr. Wells took me to visit our elderly neighbor, William Bartram, who has grown so reclusive. We've met before; when I was a girl, still in short skirts with my hair in a braid, the aunts occasionally trotted me over to him. Great man, they said, introducing him to me. Then me to him: our niece, whom we are raising. She is very studious. A few questions they would put to me, so Mr. Bartram might see how well I answered. After those I was expected to be silent.

Mr. Wells brought me there as someone like an equal. On a seat in the garden, near the giant cypress Mr. Bartram's father brought back from Georgia, with Mr. Bartram's menagerie disporting about us, snakes and frogs and salamanders, two dogs, a possum, a crow named Virgil—there, Mr. Wells had me describe our experiment with the dew.

Mr. Bartram listened attentively, Virgil perched on his shoulder and pecking at his spectacles. "This is most interesting," he said. Then he rose and beckoned us to follow him down the gentle slope from the house to the river, touring us through the persimmons and walnuts, the odd vines tangled high in the chestnuts, the cider press perched above the water, and the pond he'd deepened and banked with stone.

As we walked round the pond, something went plop and plop and plop. "My little green frogs," Mr. Bartram said fondly. "At night their croaking keeps us awake." When he waved his arms about, fending off the mosquitoes and gnats, the strands of white hair left on his head rose and danced in the sun. The grasshoppers rose and danced in the fields—it is still very warm for October—and in the orchard the ground beneath the trees was thick with foxgloves and asters and goldenrod. He walked quickly for such an old man, but I kept up with him, delighted with the black calf boots Mr. Wells had given me as a belated birthday gift. At the peach grove Virgil leapt down from Mr. Bartram's shoulder and pecked inquisitively at my boot buttons. "Was he hard to train?" I asked.

"Not at all," Mr. Bartram said. "His wit is prodigious. The first time he saw me pulling weeds from the vegetable garden, he watched for a while and then hopped over and began plucking blades of grass from the ground with his beak. When I am writing, and he would rather I came outside, he pulls the pen from my hands. You might train a crow yourself, if you desired a companion."

"My aunts," I said. "I think they would not . . ."

Mr. Bartram nodded. "Worthy women," he said. "But very . . . tidy." He gestured toward his specimens, which live in a tangle that might seem chaotic had he not explained it. For each plant he'd made a place imitating its natural home; a split rock if he'd found it in a mountain cranny, a moist spot under briars if it lived under briars in the woods.

"When those ladies used to visit," he said, "they always suggested I might want to *neaten* things a bit. I'm glad they haven't wholly neatened you." His gaze on me was clear and straight; I think that, like our other older neighbors, he has always known that the aunts are not my aunts. If he knows too that they're not kin to each other, he hasn't betrayed this to me—though who knows what he'll say to Mr. Wells. Perhaps, when they next meet, they'll speculate over a glass of whiskey. What do men think when they see women living together? Do they imagine the aunts sleeping side by side, wrapped in flannel, untouched?

Back in the garden, cool glasses of cider before us, Mr. Wells complimented Mr. Bartram. "The riches you and your father have gathered—such a marvelous array of species," he said. "No visitor can fail to be impressed."

"I've had good company," Mr. Bartram said. "Men from Russia and France and England and Germany have all honored me with their visits, even Peter Kalm from Sweden. This has been a great pleasure."

Virgil flew past us, carrying something bright, and landed beneath the cypress. With his beak he tossed scraps of bark over his toy, until it was hidden.

"What Kalm wrote about Niagara Falls," Mr. Wells said. "Such a powerful description—the blinding fog and the cascading water, the birds losing their way in the cloud of vapor rising from the rocks. Ducks and geese and swans, their wings weighed down by the mist until they drop from the air and tip over the cataract. . . ."

"Feathers," Mr. Bartram said dreamily.

They can't imagine the aunts: or not the aunts young and caught together in a current. What binds these two men is a shared understanding and love of the world. They converse as if jointly creating the falling birds and the rising water; where is the theory, I wanted to ask, that might make sense of this?

"When Kalm visited," Mr. Bartram continued, "he said he found below the falls each morning enough feathers to stuff many beds. And fish, all broken and writhing, and sometimes deer, once a bear."

They weren't ignoring me; they were talking to each other but also to me, perhaps in part for me; they were so happy that I felt happy too. From the table I slipped a little knife, which Mr. Bartram had used to sever the stems of the grapes. Virgil, who'd been creeping closer while the men spoke, was staring beseechingly at my boots. From the left one I cut the topmost button, which I never use, and held it out to him. He bent his head, and his beak grazed my hand; the button disappeared. At the base of the cypress he tossed it up in the air, again and again, until he tired and buried it near his other treasures.

When we rose to go, Mr. Bartram asked us to wait and went into the house for a minute. He returned with a book, his own famous *Travels*. Mr. Wells rested his hand on my arm and looked at Mr. Bartram; I saw Mr. Bartram nod. "A small gift," he said. "In return for the pleasure of your company, and for what you gave Virgil."

I had thought myself unobserved. Inside the front cover Mr. Bartram had written: *For my new friend, who can listen to the birds.*

Another of Aunt Jane's spells. She took to her bed, pale and damp; when I brought a tray with her supper, she turned her face and said she couldn't eat. "I have no appetite," she sighed. "Not for food, not for work. Not for anything." I looked at her and wondered what I am *except* appetite.

"Shall I read to you?" I asked. What I should have done was smooth her hair and say I loved her. Say I would live my life like hers, that I am grateful for all she has taught me and do not judge her.

"Read," she said. "Please."

And softly, so she could hardly hear, I read about the wonders of the planetary system, the perfections of the Deity, and the plurality of worlds. I read about igneous meteors. "Another species of phenomena, on which a great mystery still hangs," I read, "is the singular but not well-attested fact of large masses of solid matter falling from the higher regions of the atmosphere, or what are termed meteoric stones. Few things have puzzled philosophers more than to account for the large fragments of compact rocks proceeding from regions beyond the clouds, and falling to the earth with great velocity."

"Oh," Aunt Jane moaned. "What has this to do with anything?"

Beneath the counterpane her body made barely a ridge. I wondered what she was like at my age, what she longed for and couldn't have.

"Listen," I said.

It was you I was reading to. I read about luminous meteors over Benares, a large ball of fire followed by falling stones. About a huge stone that fell in Yorkshire, burying itself deep in the ground; about an extraordinary shower of stones in Normandy. "In the whole district," I read, "there was heard a hissing noise like that of a stone discharged from a sling, and a great many mineral masses, exactly similar to those distinguished by the name of meteor stones, were seen to fall."

Outside her window the frogs were singing. "These stones," I read— but I had done something good after all; she had closed her eyes and entered the dead sleep from which she'd emerge, twelve hours later, washed clean and a little stupid. "These stones," I read, "have a peculiar and striking analogy with each other. They have been found at places very remote from each other, and at very distant periods. They appear to have fallen from various points of the heavens, at all periods, in all seasons of the year, at all hours both of day and night, in all countries of the world, on mountains and on plains, and in places remote from any volcano. The luminous meteor which generally precedes their fall is carried along in no fixed or invariable direction; and as their descent usually takes place in a calm and serene sky, and frequently in cloudless weather, their origin cannot be traced to the causes which operate in the production of rain."

Here I paused and closed the book. Into the still night air I said:

Q. But what are the causes that operate in the production of rain?

A. *We do not understand even those; how should we understand a rain of stones?*

I was talking to you. I was asking you. Lapidifying juice, petrific seed, volcanic spume, the tears of the moon—somewhere, wherever you are, do you look at the world and ask question after question?

You have no face, but sometimes I can hear you. Not as a human voice but as a pulsing hum, lower in pitch than the tree frogs' note, higher than the cicadas—pure intonation, no information. When I think about Mr. Wells, I hear the hum deepen, as if with pleasure, while I imagine a life: sons and daughters and a large, airy house, a garden soft with ferns and herbs, and a long drive bordered by peonies. His work—he works hard, he will not be home much—and mine. Much of mine the education of children; but *my* children, not the children of strangers. At night a hand on my breasts, a thigh between mine; and if that body doesn't belong to James, if it is not James who bends to me, if it is not James . . .

While Aunt Jane slept, I leaned out the window, looking at the cloudless sky and the ring around the moon. Looking up, I grew dizzy. All that is there, all that hangs suspended in air, suspended above the air: rain and hail and fire and stone; the mind of God, if there is a God; the stars and planets and comets and our fates. Sleep well, my dear. Wherever you are.

"What makes you happy?" Mr. Wells asked. We were in the garden again. This is a question no one has ever asked me. The question you might have asked, might someday still ask.

"To be out here at night," I told him. "On a clear, cold night when the dew is heavy, to walk on the grass between the marigolds and the Brussels sprouts and feel my skirts grow heavy with the moisture. Or to go farther, into the hayfield, where the mist hangs above the ground, rising nearly to my waist. . . ."

I should not have said that; he looked startled. But though it was burning hot and the sun was shining, I could feel myself in that field, timothy and clover and young wild grasses knee-high and soaking wet, my skirts clinging to my legs, and before me the low cloud spreading and spreading, white in the light of the moon and the stars above. On a ridge in the distance a white house is shining; this is the house where James lives. At night, long after the aunts are asleep, I have stood in the field, sopping wet, gazing across the sea of mist to a porch set with tall columns. Behind the columns are rows of windows, two of them softly lit; and in the golden slots a chair is outlined, a rocking chair with a wooden back and a woven rush seat. Sometimes the chair is empty. Sometimes the chair holds James. I stand in the cloud, invisible to him, moving through the damp green growth like a deer, my height and heaviness cut in half, suspended above the suspended water. As the mist rises to my waist, my shoulders, my head, I am standing in a kind of rain: and in that rain I am beautiful, at least to one man. Above me a meteor cuts the air and hot stones shower down. In that light, across the field, is all I will never have. Next to me is all I will.

"Will you marry me?" Mr. Wells asked.

I placed my hand in his and thought how I would say to you, how I would say . . . oh, my brother, where are you? In the hum that is you, or my longing for you, I heard an answer.

"I would be honored," I said.

Jeannette Bertles

Whileaway

From *The Gettysburg Review*

IN NOVEMBER of 1973, shortly before Mrs. Marjorie Major went to live in a depressed area in the inner city in a house she had inherited from her great aunt, she announced to her children—on postcards of long mountain views—that she had decided to change her name. "I have never had confidence in being Mrs. Marjorie Major, and it wasn't entirely those M's," wrote Mrs. Major. "And now that this thing with your father has happened, I will need a name I can trust. Love and kisses." Her children tried calling, but Mrs. Major had taken her phone off the hook; so they sent her night letters (cheaper than telegrams) to say this was nonsense, and how could she, their very own mother, just high-handedly dispose of their name? Mrs. Major pointed out—on postcards of birch trees—that they were adults and therefore could not complain of a thing she did, just as she could not complain of a thing they did. "That is the only advantage in having grown-up children," wrote Mrs. Major. "Otherwise there *is* no advantage." After some thought, Mrs. Major decided to call herself Miss Marjorie Ire, because, as she explained to her children on postcards of suburban shopping malls, the *Ire* part was what was left over when you took the Major out of Marjorie—and the *Miss* part was in one way a fact that went without saying, although in another it felt good once you did. Her children sent back night letters to assert their shock and to declare they would not come and see her for ages and ages, but she sent them leftover Christmas cards saying she had nursed them from tiny seeds, and therefore their not coming to see her would be unacceptable. "Although you must wait until I get the house fixed up," she added.

However, when she actually got to the house and stood with her suitcase outside its gate—into which the name *Whileaway* had been wreathed in confident, permanent, cast-iron announcement—Miss Ire realized that Whileaway was not something she could ever fix up: either she must live in it and take the consequences, or she must sell it and forget about it as fast as possible. *For the present,* she thought, *I will opt for the former. Then perhaps in the future I will let pure, blind necessity sneak up and leave me no choice—that will be for the best.*

It was clear that the house, which sat stuffed between more modest neighbors, had never been charming. But Miss Ire—lowering her suitcase, squinting her eyes, and backing away from the gate—tried to see whether Whileaway's sheer hulking size might help it to pass itself off as a former mansion. Instead she saw—she sensed—a churlish resistance of such an intensity that the mansion-dimensions were nullified. Whileaway was an ugly square brute of a building sheathed in crumbling brown stones, adorned with weighty bay windows in capricious and perilous spots, and topped with a slate mansard roof from which broken pieces shaped like arrowheads plunged murderously down. *I got what I didn't deserve, that's clear,* said Miss Ire to herself as she opened the gate. *And it's probably worse than it seems.*

Miss Ire's great aunt had left her not only the structure but its interior furnishings as well. When Miss Ire took her suitcase inside and walked through her new home—its back halls, front landings, and bedrooms with dressing compartments, its window-nooked studies and pantries—she found every inch of it weighted with gilt-framed oil paintings of desperate barques on midnight seas and freighted with serious brown furniture, with faded, brocaded pillows, with tasseled and beaded lamps, with purplish Sarouk stair carpets and frayed, muddied Isfahans—and the whole mess appended by a joke of a sooted, distended conservatory that clutched at the house on one side. Miss Ire saw at once that living such a siege of oppression would force her to lead her life in new, unaccustomed ways. She could not tell where these ways might begin, but the forcing— which she could already feel as a cold-poker pressure under her shoulder blades—pleased when it might have depressed her as it seemed the chief benefit of having such a terrible house. She was not superstitious, but she wondered if it wasn't the house, reaching out across all those miles of filthy city and boring suburbs and right into her glorious foothills, that had caused her to change her name.

Miss Ire immediately sent postcards of industrial sites to her children, saying that since she was not going to fix up the house, they had better not come to see her. "You would inevitably make comparisons between past and present," she wrote. "I could bear this as I am already different, but you are not." Then she added that if they had friends who needed a place to stay in the city, she would be willing to put them up—or at least put up with them. Miss Ire had heard that many young people found the depressed inner city challenging or attractive or whatever, and she thought she might do a good turn and have a little company at the same time. "After all, I am not a recluse, just a peculiar person," she said out loud—talking out loud was something she felt was required in her new abode, as a hedge against going totally mad.

When Miss Ire, in need of milk and eggs and Kleenex, ventured out into the neighborhood, she discovered it was inhabited by Blacks and Hispanics and Arabs. She could not think how they had all got in there together, but she saw that they seemed to be living in racially random arrangements in run-down houses which, although much smaller, still had an angry kinship with her own; and she saw that, although they bought strange things such as hog jowls and plantains and tahini, they also bought eggs and milk and Kleenex. She noticed too that the young men of the neighborhood carried huge, blaring radios clapped next to their ears, but the young women pushed strollers with placidly sleeping babies. "I will never be friends with my neighbors, I am not up to that," Miss Ire wrote to her children on postcards of the nearby waterfront reproduced from smoky 1890s photographs, "but any other relationship will be fine."

Miss Ire had barely unpacked her suitcase and dispersed her few things about in the bulky black wardrobe and in one of the two bulbous chests in the large front bedroom—she was sure it was meant to be called the green room even though its peau de soie draperies, its taffeta bedspread, its flocked wallpaper, its petit point cushions had faded toward yellow and brown—when the first friend of one of her children arrived. Actually, it was a friend and a friend of the friend. Sally—the friend—had round puppy eyes and strong, stubby legs in cutoff jeans. Barry—the friend of the friend (whom Sally called "my old man")—had a curly, blond beard, wore white carpenter's overalls covered with sawdust, and had clearly not ever washed his hair. "Wow, are you gutsy!" cried Sally, bouncing happily up and down on her toes. "How long can we stay? I mean, like we go with the flow, so we'll set up our tent wherever you say, like you won't even see us. Whoa, back stairs—neat!" "Please stay as long as you're welcome— and I *had* hoped to see you. I have given it some thought, and although I find young people wearing, I prefer that to being a lonely old lady, much less a recluse," said Miss Ire. "Hey, Barry, let's stake out the attic!" cried Sally, scrambling up the back stairs. "We're here first, so—" "Wait!" called Miss Ire. "I shall make a house rule, and you must obey it: if I hear a complaint—even one—we're finished, we're done!" "Gotcha," laughed Sally. "Nothing to it—right, Barry?" And she continued to charge up the stairs. Miss Ire turned toward Barry. "I give you free rein with this barn," she said. "Of course there's no money, but I *do* have tenacity, and I can wear earplugs. What I lack is ability, creativity, and propensity. Other than that, I'm fine." Barry didn't reply, but he went outside to their van and carried in first a sky blue nylon tent and then armfuls of tools. On one of his trips, an Irish setter with its tail between its legs followed him in. "Don't touch Wendy—she'll bite you," he said. These were the next to the last words Barry ever spoke to Miss Ire, but she always felt comforted at night when he played his guitar and sang the amazingly doleful cowboy songs that floated down from the blue nylon tent in the attic to where she lay in her frayed greenish-blanketed bed in her greenish front room. "Wendy looks hungry—may I feed her?" asked Miss Ire when Sally came skipping and leaping back down. "She's not hungry, she was beaten," Sally said. "We saved her, but she doesn't trust anyone." "She's entirely right," said Miss Ire, and she sat on the back stairs and tried to explain to Wendy— who scooted behind the pantry door—that they were birds of a feather and should flock together.

Miss Ire had barely pulled up the shades in the arctic kitchen when the next friend of one of her children arrived. His name was James. "I may not stay for long," he said the moment Miss Ire opened the door. "On the other hand, I may never leave." Miss Ire saw that he too had a van. "And do you have a dog?" she asked, for she did not want Wendy to feel threatened. "Are you crazy? I'm a painter," said James. "Dogs get in the way, they turn things over. I have Meow Zedong." "A cat?" said Miss Ire. "Well, that's up to Wendy. She's the one with the trauma, so her feelings come first." "You'd let a dog vote on my cat? The hell with you," said James. He was tall, with long, red hair in a braid and hands that were freckled and looked oddly aged. He walked about the first floor of Whileaway, with Miss Ire following and Wendy slinking at a good distance behind. He went up the stairs of the great, weighted house and opened the doors to the bedrooms; he stared in turn into the blue room, the gold room, the pink room, Miss Ire's green room. "You want my advice? Throw everything out. It's crap," he said. "How dare you!" cried Miss Ire. She stopped. "That's not quite what I meant—pay no attention," she said. "I wasn't," said James. He kept opening doors and closing them until finally he came to the nursery, which was a huge, icy room on the north side of the second floor. "This'll do for my studio," he said, "and I'll take the bedroom across from it. Whoever was nuts enough to put little kids on the frozen north side?" "Perhaps you should leave and go elsewhere. Perhaps," suggested Miss Ire, "Whileaway won't nurture the artist in you." "What the fuck, it'll do, it'll do," replied James. He went to his van and came back with a beautiful calico cat on his shoulder. "Meow Zedong, meet Miss Ire," he said. He brought in his canvases, all of them larger than he was—he made many trips—and stacked them wall to wall in two of the dressing compartments between the bedrooms. "Tomorrow I'll get rid of that shit in the nursery," he said. "You will certainly not!" cried Miss Ire. "You will make no decisions! I will brook no invasions! I will stand no . . ." She paused, then continued: "Incidentally, James, you must promise, come hell or high water, to obey my one rule—" "Forget it—artists and rules—incompatible. But don't worry, Spitfire. I dig your brand of insanity," said James. And he kissed Miss Ire on the top of her head and went into the pink bedroom and shut the door. "That one spells trouble," said Miss Ire out loud. Of course she already liked him best.

The third friend of the children's was Melissa, who arrived in the middle of a wet, black night a few days after James. She banged on the door until

Miss Ire pulled up her window and called out, "Yes? Who is it?" "It's me—it's Melissa. Let me in!" she cried. When Miss Ire opened the door, Melissa threw her arms around Miss Ire's neck and burst into tears. "God, it was rotten!" she sobbed. "That bastard! Who does he think he is? Could I have a cup of mint tea?" Miss Ire took Melissa back to the kitchen. She pulled the light cord, and the one bare bulb made a small cave of light in the huge, icy room. "Holy gee! Where's the butler?" cried Melissa. She and Miss Ire sat at the white enameled kitchen table while Melissa explained why women were not equal—"it's because of our pectorals"—and what she'd said to that bastard's mother—"I told her, *you* brought him up like that—where's your sisterhood? Aren't you ashamed?" Then Melissa—who was tall and thin and bit her nails with a furious energy and wore an Indian cotton dress (made from a bedspread) that swiped at her sandaled feet—said she had to crash out. Miss Ire showed her the gold bedroom and the blue bedroom. "Multo fantastico!" said Melissa, and she chose the gold room because good vibes came from the bed's lace canopy. "Melissa, I've invented a rule for this house," said Miss Ire. "So be warned: if I hear one complaint—even one—then it's finished, out, done." "Oh boy, what an ogress—no problem—sleep tight," said Melissa. "Where'd you get that awful hound?"

In the morning—actually it was noon when the house's new inmates got up—Miss Ire called a meeting. Barry, Sally, Melissa, and James lounged half-asleep on the purplish Sarouk stair carpet, while Miss Ire—protected by Wendy and Meow Zedong, who had already taken to sitting beside her like bookends—stood down below. "We are now the full complement, no one else may come in," said Miss Ire. "I am feeling impacted already. What you do inside Whileaway is up to you; I myself will do nothing but live here. I have called this meeting to fully and finally restate my one rule: while I draw breath in this house, there will be no complaints. If I hear even one, then it's finished, out, gone—which reminds me: always keep the phone off its hook." "That's two rules," said Sally. "Oh, no," said Miss Ire, "the second's an eccentricity; only the first is a rule. Melissa, why don't you retract what you said about Wendy last night?" "Boy, are you touchy. Someone's been screwing you over," said Melissa. "The language is foul, but the statement is fair," said Miss Ire. She looked at Melissa, then closed her eyes and tapped her forehead. "You remind me of someone I've always disliked," she said. "I wonder whom? I shall try not to think of it. Meeting adjourned."

Now that Whileaway had so many inhabitants, Miss Ire felt free to leave it alone, and she began to explore further into the neighborhood. The riverfront was only a few blocks away, and she walked cautiously along its filthy cobblestoned edge, looking up at abandoned brick warehouses, several of which sported mutilated signs that read: "Loft space available! Tax abatements! Courtesy, Your Mayor." "Hah—talk about wishful thinking," said Miss Ire out loud. Back from the river lay street after street of run-down houses, most of them glued to each other in terror, a few bravely separated by tiny alleys and yards. The yards were jungles of ailanthus and dead stalks of ragweed and boa-constricting vines, and the alleys had been made into concrete runways on which deep-chested, blue-gray pigeons steadily departed and arrived. At the street corners, Miss Ire came across small, separate clots of those musically inclined young male Blacks and Hispanics who were some of her neighbors. She immediately put her fingers into her ears, and sometimes she yelled at them—"What is the matter with you? Don't you know these are the very best years of your lives?"—not that they heard her over the blasts from their boom boxes. Miss Ire noticed that on some blocks there were houses outside of which stood pale blue vans and pickup trucks decorated with pastel rainbows or smiling dragons, from which purposeful, fair-faced, blue-jeaned young men and women came and went. *This is curious,* thought Miss Ire. *Do I have the overflow? Why have these nice, middle-class American children chosen to live in this dreadful, dispirited place?*

When Miss Ire returned from her neighborhood walks, she would glance apprehensively up at Whileaway, which edged forward as if barely chained to its lot, its wicked slate arrows dropping, its far-hung bays waiting to crush some passerby. She stared at the stinging green roof of the sooted conservatory and winced at its cracked and splattered panes. "You had better not ruin what's left of me," she said on one of those days, and shook her fist at the house. She opened the gate with its cast-iron announcement and went up the brownstone steps. She yanked at the stubborn oak doors and slipped into the black-and-white marble-tiled vestibule. There stood a small young man neatly dressed in a tight black suit. He had neatly trimmed black hair, heavy-rimmed black glasses, and behind them the yellow eyes of a fox. "Your bell doesn't work and your sidewalk's uneven, you're gonna be sued if somebody trips—you should pray it won't happen—pleased to meet you, I'm Getz," he said. He held out his hand, and when Miss Ire didn't raise hers, he reached down and took it and shook and patted and lowered it for her. "Oh, no you don't, not on your life, we are oversubscribed!" cried Miss Ire. "Ah, but wait 'til you hear: I'm a law student—I'm poor but I'm smart—thank God I'm so smart. You need a good tax man?" said Getz. "For nothing I'll do 'em. The garbage, the city, they're headaches?—believe me, I'll fix 'em. Then soon as I graduate, soon as I've beaten the bar exam, I can start making you rich. The taxes are just a beginning. But right now I need you, I'm down to rock-bottom, and from two days of watching this house, believe me, you're needing me too. As for hippies and setters and calico cats," Getz shrugged, "life's a compromise—so what do you say—I mean, how can you lose?" Miss Ire looked carefully at Getz's yellow fox eyes. "Do you have any pets?" she said. "Only my secretary," said Getz, "but she eats like a mouse, and she sleeps in my bed. She'll file your papers, balance your checkbook—believe me, you got a good deal." He pulled up her hand again, patted it, lowered it, and Miss Ire sighed. "You and your secretary can have the blue bedroom—if Wendy approves," she said. And she went up to her own green bedroom and shut the door. "This is too much," she said out loud. "Now it turns out I'm a weak-willed pushover."

The next noon Miss Ire called another house meeting. Barry had started a fire in the grate in the smaller back parlor, Sally and Melissa lay on their stomachs on the frayed but freshly washed Isfahan, Wendy peeked out from under a chair, Miss Ire sat wrapped in a moth-eaten paisley shawl on the black horsehair sofa, James hung about near the door with Meow Zedong on his shoulder, and Getz and his secretary stood before one of the desperate barques on midnight seas. "I didn't want this," said Miss Ire, indicating Getz and his secretary, "but some people are born salesmen. Getz has offered to take over my mental stress. This is his secretary, Stanya. She will do the paperwork. They will inhabit the blue room." "Miss Ire, this is not a complaint," said Melissa, "but we've got a serious problem with your eccentricity—you know, the phone off the hook—I mean, what are you scared of? It's cramping everyone's style." "It's this way," said Miss Ire. "I don't want to be on the qui vive ever again. Take it or leave it." She looked at Stanya, who was a tiny, dark girl—even smaller than Getz—and, like him, dressed in black. "Stanya, what do you think of Wendy?" she asked. "Believe me," said Getz very quickly, "Stanya loves Wendy, believe me." "Another silent partner? Let her say it herself," said Miss Ire. "To be truthful," said Getz, "right this moment Stanya speaks only Russian. We got her out just in time." "Your secretary—who's to balance my checkbook—speaks only Russian? Am I hearing that right?" said Miss Ire. "Sure, that's why she's my secretary, not somebody else's," said Getz; at which point Sally jumped up and said, "Necessity is the mother of a second language, Miss Ire!" and Melissa called out, "The hand learns faster than the mouth, Miss Ire!" Miss Ire looked at Getz's yellow fox eyes. "Congratulations, you make your connections fast," she said. "Why wait?" said Getz, and James, from the doorway, said, "Christ, this is my last meeting *ever*. I don't have time to waste on this crap." He reached out his hand toward Miss Ire and said, "Come on, Irish, pose for me." "For one of your paintings? Pose for a blob? There's nothing in them: no faces, no places, no things," said Miss Ire. "That's okay, you'll inspire me." Placing his hand over his heart, James sang in a high, mocking voice, "Miss Ire, inspire, desire, require, misfire, mistrial, mystery—" He dropped his voice. "See how it goes?" he said. "Yuck—a head!" exclaimed Melissa. "Me, an artist's model? The fulfillment of all my childhood dreams?" said Miss Ire, with a smile. But she got up and followed James. "Melissa," she said at the door, "explain to Getz so he can explain to Stanya—make sure it sinks in: if I hear a complaint—even one—then it's finished, out, done. That's an absolute."

She went along to the nursery, where James's great looming paintings stood about in place of the rocking horse and the white gabled doll house and the two little white cribs he had dragged to the basement. "James, please tell me, exactly what is a 'head'—my children never divulged anything," she said as he seated her on a low stool so that she faced the cold, north windows. James walked around her and looked at her from all sides. "It's someone who freaks out on drugs—I'm a prime suspect. You could have modeled for Modigliani," said James. "When you freak out, will you harm anyone?" asked Miss Ire. "Not Wendy and not those idiot flower children," said James as he stared at her and arranged her shawl. "Don't worry—the one who's in danger is me." "Do you know," said Miss Ire, "when I was young, I had long golden tresses and was spoken of as a beauty?" "Too bad—but are you surprised? That's why I paint," said James. He lay down on his side and continued to stare at her. "And what did you mean by that ridiculous string of rhyming words?" asked Miss Ire. "I only meant that the dumbest connections, the most mundane inventions, pay off—but you never know which, so you just keep them moving," said James. "Well," said Miss Ire, "I'm a very mundane person at heart, no one knows that better than I—I suppose it will show in my portrait." But James didn't answer; he had fallen asleep on the freezing cold floor. Miss Ire got up and tiptoed out; however, a minute later she tiptoed back in and left him a note on a blank page that she tore from his sketchbook: "Thank you for asking me to pose for you—I can hardly believe it. I thought I was finished," it said. That evening she found a note under her bedroom door, scribbled on the reverse side of *her* note. "Don't you *ever* touch my sketchbook again!" his said.

Miss Ire now tried to live quietly on the periphery of the small world she had created. It should have been restful out there, but it wasn't. And—since she didn't care to prove herself the exception—she couldn't complain. But, even out there on the periphery, she was aware of a constant static that bounced off the brown walls of Whileaway and smote her and pinched her as she edged around formerly spiderwebbed corners and coasted down newly vacuumed Sarouk stair carpeting. *Could all of this free-floating energy emanate from those six young people?* she thought. *Not that it matters, but it's exhausting, whatever it is.* She couldn't complain, and the free-floating energy didn't seem harmful, but her kitchen was taken over by Sally and Melissa, who were now getting up early and baking cookies and cakes for private parties and for gourmet shops downtown. And although the banging in the attic had long ago stopped, Barry seemed to be out on the roof or in some other remote space all day. "Strictly maintenance, Miss Ire, don't worry," said Sally when Miss Ire indicated she might want to ask. Getz, when he wasn't at law school, was dictating to Stanya in the library—although she still didn't speak English, Getz, in some mysterious way, had trained her to transcribe it. One day Getz said to Miss Ire, "Listen, we got to get you incorporated, or I'm thinking maybe foundation? I mean, a big old wreck in a run-down neighborhood with a bunch of wacky inhabitants—let's call them artists—especially James: I think I could swing it." "Do whatever you like, so long as it's none of my business. And speaking of neighborhoods," said Miss Ire, "there's a new sign down by that stinking waterfront. It says, 'Chemical waste cleanup! Beautification! Signed, Your Governor.' How's that for madness? Couldn't you fall down laughing?" She went and sat in the nursery and watched James work. She took Meow Zedong on her lap and stroked the cat's shining fur. "I wish I could understand what's going on in this room," she said. "Melissa and Sally and Barry and Getz and possibly even Stanya make sense to me. But when I come up here, things get blurred." "Next week I'll do you with the cat on your lap," said James. "For instance," she asked, "how do you make the decisions—I mean, which color and where, and cat or no cat?" "Do me a favor: either shut up or get out," said James. "I wish you were a little less interesting to me," said Miss Ire.

In the middle of the worst weather, James began making the rounds of the galleries. Night after night he came back to Whileaway wet and exhausted. "Well, how did it go?" asked Miss Ire as James stormed into her bedroom. "Fuck them—fuck everybody. Screw out of here, Wendy!" he bellowed, then threw himself onto the greenish taffeta spread on Miss Ire's bed. "I do not understand you, James. Why don't you like Wendy?" said Miss Ire. "Jealousy, pure and simple," replied James. He took a small bag and some filter paper from his pocket and began to roll a little mess of a cigarette. Miss Ire watched with interest. "It's amazing how much I don't know—is that a lesser evil? My children hung out in the woods," she said and pointed to the cigarette. "This is a nothing, Misfire; that I guarantee," said James. "Listen James, couldn't you be creative without all the pain? It would be so much better for all of us," suggested Miss Ire. "No, I couldn't," said James. "Nobody can." Suddenly he thrashed up off Miss Ire's bed. "And stop bugging me—missile, reptile, senile!" he shouted at her. He kicked at Wendy and stormed off to his room. Miss Ire poked her head out of her door. "You're wonderfully verbal for a painter!" she shouted after him. At midnight Miss Ire, who could not sleep, got up and slipped a note under James's door. "I believe in you," the note said. The next morning she found a note under *her* door. "That makes two of us," it said.

. . .

"You're so easy to live with—do you know that, Miss Ire?" said Sally one day. "I'm easy to live with because I live by myself," said Miss Ire. "What do you mean? You live here with *us*!" said Sally, smiling and cocking her head. "I do not live with you, I live beside you," answered Miss Ire. "If I had to live *with* you I should probably go insane." "Barry says do you want to see what he's done with the attic?—I mean, you've never been up there, have you?" asked Sally. "Tell Barry I'm grateful—I'm sure the attic's wonderful. But as for seeing more of this great gray elephant, I can hardly stand what I've already seen—does Barry actually talk to you?" "Well, sort of. Like, if I ask him a question, he grunts yes or no," said Sally. "On the other hand, if I give him coffee instead of red zinger, he goes sort of ba- nanas and words pour out of him like out of a fountain and we end up at four A.M.—wow!" "That shows you—inside human bodies there really are people. Isn't life odd," said Miss Ire. "Basically, Barry talks with his hands," said Sally. "Like, we're in bed and I'm almost asleep and he—" "Stop!" cried Miss Ire, covering her ears. "I have flushed all that out of my life. Don't remind me." "Stephanie and Pete and Marianne say you don't want them to come here, they say you don't love them, you've even stopped sending them postcards. Like, what happened, Miss Ire?" said Sally. "I mean, is it true?" Miss Ire turned startled eyes toward Sally. "You see," she said, "those particular young people belong to my past—and I prefer them to stay there. That is, I can't have my past turning up here and sucking me down into intimation and remonstrance and indebtedness and sorrow and migraines. Now can I?"

"Guess what, Miss Ire? We're going to the movies!" exclaimed Melissa as everyone except James passed her on the stairs. "Good luck—there isn't a decent movie house within a million miles," said Miss Ire. "Oh, sure there is: they've renovated that wrecked-up Plaza and made it into a place that shows these great old movies—why don't you come, it's neat!" said Sally. "Thank you, but I've already seen that show, whatever it is," replied Miss Ire. "Miss Ire, what's your all-time favorite movie?" asked Melissa. "At the moment it's *The Gay Divorcée*—ha-ha," said Miss Ire grimly, continuing up the stairs. But when she reached the top, she folded her left arm lightly across her waist, raised her right arm out to the side, and then began to

hum and to rotate with slow and elegant steps about the long, dark upstairs hall. "What the hell are you doing?" barked James, coming out of
his nursery studio. "I'm being Ginger Rogers, can't you tell?" said Miss Ire
as—without losing a step—she continued her airy, elegant, partnerless
dance.

One gray and rainy afternoon when James had gone out with his slides to
pester the galleries, Miss Ire opened the door to the nursery and went in.
There was *Portrait of Miss Ire with Cat,* finished and resting against the
wall. The painting looked exactly like all of James's paintings, except that
when Miss Ire peered closely at it she could see—caught in the swirls and
whorls of color—little lines fanned out like whiskers and neat, tied-to-
gether parcels of letters that spelled *mistrial, desire, Irish, missile, inspire,*
empire, senile, reptile: "I sat all those hours on a tiny stool in this cold nursery for *that*?" said Miss Ire out loud. Nevertheless, she went downstairs
and took Getz aside. "You will never believe this—I certainly don't—but
James is going to be famous, not to say worth a fortune. Shouldn't you do
something?" she said. "So what can I do? James hates me," said Getz. "He
thinks I'm a snake in the grass, an asp in your bosom, a dog in the
manger—you know, like that." Miss Ire smiled. "That certainly sounds
like James," she said. "And by the way, although there's no such thing as
yet, I'm appointing you trustee of my estate." "Trustee, huh? You want me
creative or honest—I can work either way," said Getz. "Honest is fine,"
said Miss Ire. Getz shrugged his shoulders. "There are pluses both sides,"
he said. Miss Ire looked at Getz very carefully. "You know, in spite of your
double standards and your slapdash morals, I sense an internal recti-
tude—tell me if I'm wrong," she said. Getz frowned. "I was never bar
mitzvahed," he said doubtfully. "It's your lovely fox eyes that confuse me,
Getz," said Miss Ire. "I can almost imagine—" "Why are you plaguing
me?" Getz cried out suddenly, and tears began to run down his cheeks.
"And why does James call me a snake in the grass? And what makes everyone think it's a snap to act like a hardened cheat at twenty-five? And what,
oh God, am I guilty of that I should feel such guilt?" And Getz began to
bawl without reservation, whereupon Stanya, who had sneaked into the
room, threw her strong little arms around him and boomed in an amazingly deep, vibrant voice: "Paragraph One: Effects of acceptance of defec-
tive performance upon subsequent enforceability of full rights under

contract—" "Hey, come on, you noodle!" cried Getz. But he put his arms around Stanya and smiled proudly through his tears, while Miss Ire stuck her head out the study door and called, "Yoo-hoo, everybody! Stanya's just said her first words!"

"Has anyone in here seen James?" asked Miss Ire. She looked through the kitchen door at the children's friends, who were seated around the big white enameled table, eating Sally's and Melissa's freshly made bread and jam. A soft warmth permeated the kitchen, and there were layers of cooking smells: the bacon for quiche, the yeasty bread, the pies and cookies and muffins still baking. A small bunch of bittersweet fell angularly out from a marmalade jar on the table, which was laid with a blue homespun cloth. Plants hung by the windows, Wendy lay next to the stove, and Meow Zedong was curled up on top of it. "We hardly ever see James—*you* see him, Miss Ire," said Melissa. "James can't stand the rest of us." "Well, I haven't seen him—not today, not yesterday. And the weather's so bad, and he keeps making the rounds—he's awfully persistent. Getz, come check his studio with me, maybe he fell or he's sick," said Miss Ire. "Like, Getz is allergic to James and vice versa," Sally said, "so you'd better take Barry." "I can't explain this," said Miss Ire, "so please don't laugh, but somehow I'm very afraid." She started up the stairs with Barry following her and Wendy slinking along after them both. It seemed to Miss Ire that Whileaway was darker than ever this morning, more threatening, more terrible. She wanted to tell Barry it was grinding her nerves all raw, but she felt that might be an intrusion on what Sally had warned her was Barry's space. She looked first into James's bedroom: the pink taffeta spread was wadded into a ball on the floor, the pink damask curtains had been yanked from the windows, the pink overstuffed chair was turned upside down, but James wasn't there. She knocked on the nursery door. "James! James!" she called. "I want to talk to you!" Nothing stirred, but Wendy sniffed at the bottom of the door, then slunk away downstairs. "That's a bad sign, Barry. You'd better break down the door," she said. Barry shook his head, disappeared up the attic stairs, came back with some tools, and proceeded to work at the lock until it gave. They stepped into the nursery, which was bitterly cold and full of James's huge swirly paintings. There was a low couch in the far corner, and James was lying on it. "Oh, thank heaven!" cried Miss Ire, and she rushed toward it.

"James," she began—but there was something about James's position on the couch that caused her to stop. "Barry," she said, "I think James has permanently, has permanently—freaked out." Barry stepped toward the couch and touched James's face and hands. There was a single sheet of paper from his sketchbook lying on James's chest, and Barry folded it and tucked it into his pocket. He bent over, picked up one of the paint-soaked pink damask curtains that was lying nearby and covered James's body with it; then he and Miss Ire descended to the kitchen. "Well," said Melissa, "what's the genius of the paint pots up to now?" "James is no longer with us," said Miss Ire, in a choked-up voice. "No good, Miss Ire—like his van's out front," said Sally. "I mean," said Miss Ire, "he's no longer among us—he has permanently retired from the fray." The children's friends looked at Barry, who drew his finger slowly across his neck. "Getz," said Miss Ire, "this is not my dish of tea. I leave the police and the sordid details to you. Barry, give Getz that piece of paper." Barry took the piece of paper out of his pocket and handed it to Getz. "Now don't any of the rest of you get such ideas," said Miss Ire. "I want to say that James's demise is as close to an outright complaint—which all of you know is against every rule of this house—and I made only one—" and she fled from the room.

Miss Ire carried the little container. She walked with the others to the waterfront. Melissa held Meow Zedong in her arms, and Sally had Wendy on a leash made from a strip of pink damask curtain. The smell coming up off the water was foul, but there were new large signs all along the stone dock that said, "Coming soon! Shops! Cafes! 200-Room Holiday Inn! Congratulations to the Citizens of This Fair City! Signed, Your Governor." Miss Ire unscrewed the top of the container and scattered James's ashes into the water. "Ugh, this is the most gruesome thing ever," said Melissa. Barry in his overalls, Sally in her cutoff jeans, Getz and Stanya in black, and Melissa in a long Indian dress, sat down in a circle on the cold stones, and Miss Ire, huddled in the moth-eaten paisley shawl, stood slightly outside the circle. Barry unslung his guitar from his shoulder and started to sing: *"He was just a lone-some cow-boy/With a heart so brave and true. But he learned to love a mai-den/With eyes of heaven's own blue."* Stanya and Melissa and Sally began to cry. "That song has ten verses; how much losing is good for me?" murmured Miss Ire. *"They had learned to love each o-ther/And had named their wed-ding day,"* sang Barry.

Miss Ire took Meow Zedong from Melissa and Wendy from Sally, then left the little circle. *"When a quar-rel came be-tween them—"* Holding the cat in her arms and leading the dog on its pink damask leash, Miss Ire walked slowly back toward Whileaway. The house loomed toward her, straining and struggling to get at her. "Perhaps I lack tenacity after all. Too bad—that was my one good quality," she said out loud and took herself off to her green room.

When she got up for breakfast two days later, Miss Ire said to Getz, "By the way, what was that piece of paper Barry gave to you?" "It was James's will—neat and witnessed and totally legal. He had no family: you get the whole schmeer," said Getz. "Look here, Getz," said Miss Ire, "I have not exerted myself since I came to this rotten place, I have just floated with the current. Now I want to do one thing—of course you will do it for me. Find a gallery to show James's paintings." "Easy, a snap, I could have done it anytime. James knew I had this uncle," said Getz. "Why didn't he ask me?" "He couldn't ask you because he hated you—remember?" said Melissa. "And he wouldn't talk to the rest of us, just to Miss Ire. He loved her." "He did *not*!" cried Miss Ire, turning furiously upon Melissa. "James did *not* love me. I will *not* shoulder that burden!" "Why don't you see a shrink, Miss Ire? Why don't you try T.A.? Honestly, you don't know anything—that's not a complaint," said Melissa. Miss Ire drew herself up. "I'd like you to know, Melissa," she said in a dignified manner, "that I am the central figure in my life. And I've got to hold on to that—otherwise what have I?"

"Well, how is your English coming?" Miss Ire said to Stanya one Saturday morning. Stanya was lying on an old Heriz in the study, in front of a tiny black-and-white television Getz had bought for her. She was wearing a pair of Sally's cutoff jeans and an Indian shirt of Melissa's. One hand moved steadily between her mouth and a bag of Fritos; with the other, she pointed toward Bugs Bunny and Elmer Fudd—who were engaged in a battle using cabbages as ammunition—and said in her deep, stentorian voice, "Is directing summary judgment against defendant subsequent to and as result of action by plaintiff." There was a noise of thwacking cabbages, and Stanya clapped her hands: "Beep, beep!" she cried. "What's up, Doc? Deponent, find dat wascally wabbit!" Miss Ire went off and buttonholed Getz. "Don't you think," she said, "that perhaps Stanya should mix with the world a little more? Let her start cooking with Sally—or she could hang around with Melissa." "Sometimes she sleeps with Melissa," said Getz. "She and Melissa—" Miss Ire reached out and covered Getz's mouth with her hand. "No!" she said. "Not now! I can adjust, but it takes time."

The next morning Miss Ire dropped into the kitchen to see Melissa, who was designing new wrappings for Sally's cakes and cookies. "I am trying to adjust to something: Getz says that you and Stanya, that is, sometimes you sleep together—how am I to take that? What am I to think?" asked Miss Ire. "You are to think," replied Melissa, "that I am learning Russian and Stanya is learning English. Actually, it's great; we snuggle down into our sleeping bags, we say things to each other in both languages, and then we sleep on it. In the morning we check to see what we've remembered— *Pero moyei tyoti na stole*—" "That's all you do? That's it?" cried Miss Ire. "Oh, how lovely! I didn't know life could still be that innocent!" "The trouble with old people," said Melissa, "is they're always digging up dirt where it doesn't exist." "You watch your tongue," replied Miss Ire. "Old people—I could probably still have a child if I wanted." And she began to laugh insanely.

Miss Ire called a meeting. "All right, Getz, let's have an update," she said. "Okay, it's like this," said Getz, and he began ticking things off on his fingers. "To begin, there's James's show—I gave them only a few of his paintings, but already they've sold every one and they're hinting for more: those blobs—now he's dead—have become a hot item. Then there's the Whileaway Foundation, we got to be patient with that, it's just getting off the ground. Also—now that this area's a historic district—I managed a T-51. And last but not least, there's the Ire Fund, about that you better just trust me." Sally spoke next. "Miss Ire," she said, "Melissa and I—we want to open a restaurant in the conservatory. See, it has a separate entrance, and Barry says you've not even noticed how long he's been working in there and the things he's been doing—" "Barry said all that?" murmured Miss Ire. "—and Getz says he'll do our accounts in exchange for free meals, and Stanya has memorized medium-rare, sauce on the side, coffee or tea, American Express or Mastercharge—so is that okay?" Miss

Ire looked carefully from one to another of the children's friends. It was appalling: how had she let it slip by her? They all looked so serious and businesslike, and she noticed that Sally had on a pair of tailored black slacks, and Melissa was wearing a gray flannel suit. "I wonder if I spend too much time ruminating? This will have to be done over my dead body—but go ahead anyway," she said faintly. "Oh, good! And can we take a couple of James's paintings to hang on the inside wall?" asked Sally. "Like, now that he's practically famous, it would give the place clout." "I never thought I'd hear the word 'clout' coming from you, Sally—on the other hand, I cannot hold back Stanya's language development," said Miss Ire. "However, you must promise you'll never ask me to dine there—I couldn't choke down even one bite. And if your restaurant's a failure, just keep in mind I am a limited woman, so expect no compassion from me. Naturally you cannot take phone reservations."

Another meeting was called—but not by Miss Ire. "Time's of the essence, Miss Ire—I'll come straight to the point," said Melissa as she looked at her watch. "You see, we've really tried hard. But Getz's contacts, your business interests, our social life, and now the restaurant—everything suffers. So, both individually and as a group, we're lodging a formal, official complaint: Miss Ire, as of this moment, we want the phone put back on its hook." Miss Ire looked at the group assembled about her. There was Getz in khaki pants, tasseled loafers, and a new Harris tweed jacket; Stanya in her blue-and-white waitress uniform; Sally in her neat white slacks with a chef's apron over them; Melissa in an elegant black suit; and Barry in his old carpenters' overalls—but with hair that was short and clean and shining. She was sure they must be the same people underneath, and yet—"There were times when I used to think this was just a costume party," said Miss Ire. "But now the scales have fallen. And speaking of that, it's odd, but all of you—even Getz—have developed eyes like bits of sharp, falling slate." "We want you to know, Miss Ire, we're really grateful," said Sally. "Yes, really we are," added Melissa. "I mean, you've done so much for us. And if you'll just do this one more tiny thing—" "This one more tiny—" Miss Ire laughed. "Do you know what I've done?" she said. "I've changed my name, and I've sat in this frozen and terrible house, and I've made my one rule, which of course you broke. Well, you know what that means: it means gone, finished, out." She got up, went to her room, and wrote her final postcards to her children. "I adored your friends; they saved my life. Love and kisses, and don't think you weren't helpful—now we are even," she wrote to each one. The postcards were blanks she had bought—in case of necessity—from the U.S. Post Office.

In the early morning, when she came down, Miss Ire was muffled in her coat and hat, and she carried her suitcase in one hand. The children's friends were already up and stationed in ludicrously offhand positions about the great, dark front hall, while Wendy and Meow Zedong were curled on the purplish Sarouk at the foot of the stairs. "Is that all you got?" asked Getz, pointing to Miss Ire's one suitcase. "I once had two houses and two cars," said Miss Ire. "And in the houses there were Sheraton breakfronts and Steuben glasses and Waring blenders and floor to ceiling windows and around the houses there were beautiful gardens and behind one of the houses there was an ocean and behind the other house there was a pool; and the cars were always lemons and the houses were full of dogs and the gardens were full of bugs and the pool was full of guests and yet each of them—and not excepting my husband and my children—was kept in perfect order by me." Miss Ire put her hand on her one suitcase. "You can never in a million years imagine what that meant," she said. "Miss Ire, will you, like, know anyone where you're going?" asked Sally. "Once I knew someone—actually he was my husband—for over twenty years," said Miss Ire, "and that was enough." "Miss Ire," said Getz, "when you warned us, 'finished, done, out,' we just assumed"—he began to snuffle and wipe his eyes—"we didn't know *you'd* be the one." "Are you sure of that, Getz?" asked Miss Ire. "Will you please leave a forwarding address?" he said. "I will," said Miss Ire, "when I've found one worth forwarding—and Getz, there's no need to snuffle. I've been ready to leave since the moment I came. I was just waiting for pure, blind necessity—" "Does this mean you'll go back to your beautiful hills?" asked Sally. "—and who would have guessed," went on Miss Ire, "that pure, blind necessity would turn out to be a complaint." Miss Ire held out her hand, and Getz grabbed it and shook it and patted it and lowered it to her side. "Thank you, Getz. I hope you all like postcards," Miss Ire said. She walked from the house and opened the gate. She put down her suitcase, turned, and looked back at Whileaway. "Good luck with this horror; it certainly takes guts," she said. "But Miss Ire, wait a minute—how about

Wendy? She loves you! You love her!" cried Melissa, and she came running down the steps. Miss Ire's lids trembled. "Don't I know that," she said. "Oh, and by the way, Getz, I might want to call you sometime—strictly business, of course—so please put the telephone back on its hook." "Unfair!" cried Melissa. "Unfair to the last!" And she threw her arms around Miss Ire and burst into tears; and Barry, crouched down on the steps, holding back Wendy, suddenly shouted, "You know what you are? You're a crazy old bitch!" "Well, Barry, two sentences—*bravo!*—you sound just like James!" cried Miss Ire. And she picked up her suitcase and departed.

At first the postcards came in droves. They fluttered through the mail slot like bright homing pigeons, and the children's friends cradled them in their hands and hurried to warm them in the kitchen. At first there were pictures of airplanes and highways and bridges and buses; at first there were messages that said, "Dear Friends: It is all right for you, you can ignore the decay and disorder and concentrate on what is important. I could not." "Dear Sally: You were all wonderful—of course James was the most wonderful, but perhaps at some point that doesn't pay." "Dear Melissa: Wasn't it lucky I never remembered whom you reminded me of?" "Dear Stanya: Look, look! See the bus, see the bridge, see the highway! Oh-oh, says the woman, wherever is this leading me?" "Dear Barry: 'Things as they are/Are changed upon the blue guitar.' Look that up." "Dear Getz: Make a rule—any rule. Having a rule will give cohesion." All of the postcards were signed: Miss Ire. Gradually, however, the postcards changed: there were fewer of them; they came less frequently; their tone seemed at once more fragile and more dense. There was one group of three that came together: the first showed a picture of the Dismal Swamp. "Dear Friends:" it said, "I am either incognito or an echo of my former self." It was signed: Irish. The second showed a shipwreck off the barrier reefs. It said: "Dear Friends: I will either peter out, or parthenogenesis will occur. That all depends." The third postcard showed an unending expanse of trailer courts. It said: "The defendant becomes the protagonist; the moth enters the flame; the loony looks for her bin." These last two were signed Mistrial and Misfire. After a while, one postcard came by itself. It showed a picture of Mickey Mouse and Minnie Mouse with their arms around each other. The card said: "Guess where I am?" and was signed: Margie. Then for a long time no postcards came. But one day, when the children's friends had stopped expecting, a huge picture post-card packet was stuffed through the mail slot. Stanya, passing by in white slacks, a red sweater, and a gray flannel jacket, ran with it to the kitchen, where Whileaway's occupants were seated around the table, eating coq au vin. The kitchen was newly painted a strong, glazed yellow, and there was a new stove, a forest of hanging plants, new double-glazed windows, and a new puppy named Charlemagne. Stanya tore open the seal on the post-card packet, and as the children's friends watched, a cascade of postcards, each linked to the other and printed on both sides with pictures of conch shells and beaches, of blue sky and palm trees, of red sunsets and flowers, of tanned men and bikinied women, unfolded and flopped down before their eyes. At the top there was space for a message, and Stanya, in her deep-throbbing, deeply accented voice, read it out: "Dear Melissa and Sally and Barry: Hi folks," it said. "Have undergone a sea change—every-thing marvelous—no desperate barques in sight. Dear Stanya: See the Sun! See the beach! See the people! Oh-oh, the lady vanishes—what fun! Dear Getz: Send money—lots of it." The postcard was signed: Mrs. Desirée Major, Your Gay Divorcée. The message was written in purple ink, and the *i*s were dotted with little circles. After that, no more post-cards came.

John Biguenet

Rose

From *Esquire*

"IT MUST have been, I think she said, two years after the kidnapping when your wife first came by." The voice on the phone sounded young. "What was that, '83, '84?"

"Kidnapping?"

"Yeah, she told me all about it, how it was for the private detective you hired after the police gave up."

"You mean the picture?"

"Right, the age progression. You had to write your own code back then. But once we had the algorithms for stuff like teeth displacement of the lips, cartilage development in the nose and ears, stuff like that, all you had to do was add fat-to-tissue ratios by age and you wound up with a fairly decent picture of what the face probably looked like. I mean, after you tried a couple different haircuts and cleaned up the image—the printers were a joke in those days."

"And you kept updating Kevin's age progression?"

"Every year, like clockwork, on October 20. Of course, the new ones, it's no comparison. Onscreen, we're 3-D now; the whole head can rotate. And if you've got a tape of the kid talking or singing, there's even a program to age the voice and sync it with the lips. You sort of teach it to talk, and then it can say anything you want, the head." The voice paused.

"I mean, we thought it was cool, Mr. Grierson, the way you two didn't lose hope you'd find your boy one day. Even after all these years."

He hung up while the man was still talking. On the kitchen table, the photo album Emily had used to bind the pictures, the age progressions, lay open to one that had the logo and phone number of Crescent Compu-Graphics printed along its border. His son looked fifteen, maybe sixteen, in the picture.

He had found the red album the night before, after his wife's funeral. Indulging his grief after the desolate service and the miserly reception of chips and soft drinks at her sister's, he had sunk to his knees before Emily's hope chest at the foot of their bed, fingering the silk negligee bruised brown with age, inhaling the distant scent of gardenias on the bodice of an old evening gown, burying his arms in all the tenderly folded velvet and satin. It was his burrowing hand that discovered the album at the bottom of the trunk.

At first, he did not know who it was, the face growing younger and younger with each page. But soon enough, he began to suspect. And then, on the very last leaf of the red binder, he recognized the combed hair and fragile smile of the little boy who returned his gaze from a school photograph.

As he thought of Emily secretly thumbing through the age progressions, each year on Kevin's birthday adding a new portrait on top of the one from the year before, he felt the nausea rising in his throat and took a deep breath. It's just another kind of memory, he told himself, defending her.

He, for example, still could not forget the green clock on the kitchen wall that had first reminded him his son should be home from school already. Nor could he forget the pitiless clack of the dead bolt as he had unlocked the door to see if the boy was dawdling down the sidewalk. And he would always remember stepping onto the front porch and catching, just at the periphery of his vision, the first glimpse of the pulsing red light, like a flower bobbing in and out of shadow.

In fact, turning his head in that small moment of uncertainty, he took the light to be just that: a red rose tantalized by the afternoon's late sun but already crosshatched with the low shadows of the molting elms that lined the street. And he remembered that as he turned toward the flashing light, lifting his eyes over the roses trellised along the fence—the hybrid Blue Girl that would not survive the season, twined among the thick canes and velvet blossoms of the Don Juan—and even as he started down the wooden steps toward the front gate, slowly, deliberately, as if the people running toward the house, shouting his name, had nothing to do with him, he continued to think rose, rose, rose.

Kate Walbert

The Gardens of Kyoto

for Charles Webster, 1926–1945

From *DoubleTake*

I HAD a cousin, Randall, killed on Iwo Jima. Have I told you?
The last man killed on the island, they said; killed after the fighting
had ceased and the rest of the soldiers had already been transported away
to hospitals or to body bags. Killed mopping up. That's what they called
it. A mopping-up operation.

I remember Mother sat down at the kitchen table when she read the
news. It came in the form of a letter from Randall's father, Great-uncle
Sterling, written in hard dark ink, the letters slanted and angry as if they
were aware of the meaning of the words they formed. I was in the kitchen
when Mother opened it and I took the letter and read it myself. It said
that Randall was presumed dead, though they had no information of the
whereabouts of his body; that he had reported to whomever he was intended to report to after the surrender of the Japanese, that he had, from
all accounts, disappeared.

I didn't know him too well but had visited him as a young girl. They
lived near Baltimore, across the bay outside Sudlersville. No town, really,
just a crossroads and a post office and farms hemmed in by cornfields.
Theirs was a large brick house set far back from the road, entirely wrong
for that landscape, like it had been hauled up from Savannah or Louisville
to prove a point. It stood in constant shadow at the end of an oak-lined
drive and I remember our first visit, how we drove through that tunnel of

oak slowly, the day blustery, cool. Sterling was not what we in those days called jovial. His wife had died years before, leaving him, old enough to be a grandfather, alone to care for his only child. He had long rebuked Mother's invitations but for some reason had scrawled a note in his Christmas card that year—this was before the war, '40 or '41—asking us to join them for Easter dinner.

Mother wore the same Easter hat and spring coat she kept in tissue in the back of the hallway linen closet, but she had sewed each of us a new Easter dress and insisted Daddy wear a clean shirt and tie. For him this was nothing short of sacrifice. Cynthia said he acted like those clothes might shatter if he breathed.

Daddy turned off the engine and we all sat, listening to the motor ticking. If Mother had lost her determination and suggested we back out then and there, we would have agreed. "Well," she said, smoothing out the lap of her dress. It was what she did to buy time. We girls weren't moving anyway. We were tired enough; it was a long drive from Pennsylvania.

"Wake me up when it's over," Cynthia said. She always had a line like that. She curled up and thrust her long legs across Betty and me, picking a fight. Betty grabbed her foot and twisted it until Cynthia shrieked *For the love of Pete.* Mother ignored them, reapplying the lipstick she kept tucked up the sleeve of her spring coat. I looked out the window. I'm not sure about Daddy. No one wanted to make the first move, Betty twisting Cynthia's foot harder and Cynthia shrieking *For the love of Pete get your gosh darn hands off me* and Mother jerking around and telling Cynthia to stop using that language and to act her age.

The last reprimand struck Cynthia to the core. She sat up quickly and yanked the door open.

Did I say oak? It might have been walnut. I believe at that point, standing outside the car, we heard the comforting thwack of a walnut on a tin roof, the sound popping the balloon Cynthia had inflated, releasing us to walk, like a family, to the front door, where Randall already stood, waiting.

He had some sort of sweet-smelling water brushed into his hair. This I remember. It was the first thing you would have noticed. He also had red hair, red as mine, and freckles over most of his face. He stood there, swallowed by the doorway, his hand out in greeting. His were the most delicate fingers I had ever seen on a boy, though he was a teenager by then. I have wondered since whether he polished his nails, since they were shiny, almost wet. Remember he was a son without a mother, which is a terrible thing to be, and that Great-uncle Sterling was as hard as his name.

Anyway, Cynthia and Betty paid him little mind. They followed Mother and Daddy in to find Sterling and we were left, quite suddenly, alone. Randall shrugged as if I had proposed a game of cards and asked if I wanted to see his room. No one seemed much concerned about us, so I said sure. We went down a water-stained hallway he called the Gallery of Maps. It was after some hallway he had read about in the Vatican, one that has frescoes of maps from before the world was round. Anyway, he stood there showing me the various countries, pointing out what he called trouble spots.

I can still picture those fingers, tapering some, and the palest white at the tips, as if he had spent too long in the bath.

We continued, passing one of those old-fashioned intercom contraptions they used to have to ring servants. Randall worked a few of the mysterious oiled levers and then spoke, gravely, into the mouthpiece. "I have nothing to offer but blood, toil, tears, and sweat," he said. Churchill, of course, though at the time I had no idea. I simply stood there waiting, watching as Randall hung up the mouthpiece, shrugged again, and opened a door to a back staircase so narrow we had to turn sideways to make the corner.

"They were smaller in the old days," Randall said, and then, perhaps because I didn't respond, he stopped and turned toward me.

"Who?" I said.

"People," he said.

"Oh," I said, waiting. I had never been in the dark with a boy his age.

"Carry on," he said.

We reached a narrow door and pushed out, onto another landing, continuing down a second, longer hallway. The house seemed comprised of a hundred little boxes, each with tiny doors and passages, eaves to duck under, one-flight stairways to climb. Gloomy, all of it, though Randall didn't seem to notice. He talked all the while of how slaves had traveled the underground railway from Louisiana here, and how one family had lived in this house behind a false wall he was still trying to find. He said he knew this not from words but from knowing. He said he saw their ghosts sometimes—there were five of them—a mother and a father and three children, he couldn't tell what. But he'd find their hiding place, he said. He had the instinct.

I'm not sure whether I was more interested in hearing about slaves in secret rooms or hearing about their ghosts. This was Maryland, remember, the east side. At that time, if you took the ferry to Annapolis, the colored sat starboard, the whites port, and docking felt like the flow of two rivers, neither feeding the other. In Pennsylvania colored people were colored people, and one of your grandfather's best friends was a colored doctor named Tate Williams, who everybody called Tate Billy, which always made me laugh, since I'd never heard of a nickname for a surname.

Anyway, Randall finally pushed on what looked like just another of the doors leading to the next stairway and there we were: his room, a big square box of a room filled with books on shelves and stacked high on the floor. Beyond this a line of dormer windows looked out to the oaks, or walnuts. I could hear my sisters' muffled shouts below and went to see, but we were too high up and the windows were filthy, besides. Words were written in the grime. *Copacetic,* I still recall. *Epistemological, belie.*

"What are these?" I said.

"Words to learn," Randall said. He stood behind me.

"Oh," I said. This wasn't at all what I had expected. It felt as if I had climbed a mountain only to reach a summit enshrouded in fog. Randall seemed oblivious; he began digging through his stacks of books. I watched him for a while, then spelled out H*E*L*P on the glass. I asked Randall what he was doing, and he told me to be patient. He was looking for the exact right passage, he said. He planned to teach me the art of "dramatic presentation."

Isn't it funny? I have no recollection of what he finally found. And though I can still hear him telling me they were smaller then, ask me what we recited in the hours before we were called to the table, legs up, in his window seat, our dusty view that of the old trees, their leaves a fuzzy new green of spring, of Easter, and I will say I have no idea. I know I must have read my lines with the teacher's sternness I have never been able to keep from my voice; he with his natural tenderness, as if he were presenting a gift to the very words he read by speaking them aloud. I know that sometimes our knees touched and that we pulled away from one another, or we did not. I wish I had a picture. We must have been beautiful with the weak light coming through those old dormers, our knees up and backs against either side of the window seat, an awkward *W,* books in our hands.

It became our habit to write letters. Randall wrote every first Sunday of the month. He would tell me what new book he was reading, what he'd marked to show me. I might describe a particular day, such as the time Daddy flooded the backyard with water to make an ice skating pond, though we told Mother the pump had broken and it was all we could do to turn the thing off before the rain cellar flooded. Of course, once the sun wore down our imagined rink and we found ourselves blade-sunk and stranded in your grandmother's peony bed, Daddy had to tell her the truth.

She loved her peonies, as you may remember, and fretted all that winter that we had somehow damaged the roots, that spring would come and the pinks she had ordered, the ones with the name that rhymed with Frank Sinatra, would have no company. But everything grew and blossomed on schedule, and we ended up calling the peony bed our lake and threatening to flood it every winter.

Randall sent me back a letter about a book he had found on the gardens of Kyoto, how the gardens were made of sand, gravel, and rock. No flowers, he said. No pinks. Once in a while they use moss, but even their moss isn't green like we know green. No grass green or leaf green but a kind of grayish, he wrote. You can't even walk in these gardens because they're more like paintings. You view them from a distance, he wrote, their fragments in relation.

That line I can still recall, though at the time I was baffled. I knew we were at war with the Japanese; we were repeatedly given classroom instruction on the failings of the Japanese character. We had learned of crucifixions and tortures; we understood the Japanese to be evil—not only did they speak a language no one could decipher, but they engaged in acts of moral deprivation our teachers deemed too shocking to repeat. I understood them to be a secret, somehow, a secret we shouldn't hear. Now, oddly, I knew something of their gardens.

The last time I saw him was the Easter of 1944. He was not yet seventeen—can you imagine? the age of enlistment—but would soon be, and he understood that it would be best if he went to war, that Sterling expected him to, that there were certain things that boys did without question. He never spoke of this to me; I learned it all later. Instead, his letters that winter were filled with some tremendous discovery he had made, a surprise he intended to share that Easter, not beforehand. You can imagine my guesses. Daddy had barely shut off the engine when I opened the door and sprung out. I might have bypassed all those narrow rooms and passageways altogether, scaled the tree and banged on one of those filthy windows, but I could feel Mother's eyes. She wanted me to slow down, to stay a part of them. In truth, the drive had been a sad one—Cynthia newly married and stationed with Roger in California, Betty oddly silent. Our first visit seemed light-years past, an adventure far more pleasant than it had actually been, a family outing when we were still family. We had grown into something altogether different: guests at a party with little in common.

I stood, waiting for everyone to get out of the car, waiting until Mother opened the door and yelled, Hello. Then I ran to Randall's room. I knew the way, could find it blindfolded—through the passageways and up the flights of stairs. I touched the countries in the Gallery of Maps, the danger spots, the capital cities. I picked up the mouthpiece and recited my Roosevelt impression—"I hate war, Eleanor hates war, and our dog Fala hates war"—just in case anyone was listening.

When I got to Randall's door I saw that it was just ajar, so I went in without knocking. He stood facing the line of dormers, his back to me, something so entirely unfamiliar, so adult, in his stance that for an instant I thought I might have barged in to the wrong room, that for all this time a second, older Randall had lived just next door.

"Boo," I said. I was that kind of girl.

He turned, startled, and I saw he had been writing my name on the window grime.

Have I told you he was thin? Rail thin, we called it. A beanpole. Just legs and arms and wrists and neck. I imagine if he had been permitted to live his life, he might have married someone who would have worried about this, who would have cooked him certain foods and seen that his scarves were wrapped tight in winter. No matter. He crossed the room to me.

"Any guesses?" he said.

"None," I said, blushing. Of course, this was the age of movie star magazines, of starlets discovered at soda fountains. I had plenty of guesses, each sillier than the next, but I knew enough to keep them to myself.

He marched me out of his room to the cook's stairway, a long narrow corridor down to the foyer, then pushed on a second door I'd always assumed led to the pantry. It took us back to the Gallery of Maps, where he paused, as if expecting me to react. "So?" I said. He ignored me, taking my hand and leading me to the darkest continent in the Gallery—an hourglass stain near the far end tucked behind the door to the musty unused parlor.

Randall swung the door shut and pointed to a few shredded cobwebs collected in the corner, where Antarctica would have been.

"Look," Randall said. And then I saw: a tiny black thread, horizontal, a hairline fracture dividing time remaining from time spent unlike the other cracks in the walls, the vein-like fissures that ran through that old house. "A *clue,"* Randall said.

Sometimes, when I think about it, I see the two of us there, Randall and me, from a different perspective, as if I were Mother walking through the door to call us for supper, finding us alone, red-haired cousins, twins sketched quickly: bones, hair, shoes, buttons. Look at us, we seem to say. One will never grow old, never marry. One will never plant tomatoes, drive automobiles, go to dances. One will never drink too much, disappoint his children, sit alone, wishing, in the dark.

No matter. Randall knocked on the wall and I heard a strange hollowness. "Right here," he said. "Right beneath my nose."

He pushed and the wall flattened down from its base like a punching bag. He held it there and got down on all fours, then he crawled in. I followed, no doubt oblivious to the white bloomers Mother still insisted I wear with every Easter dress.

The wall snapped shut, throwing us into instant black. It was difficult to breathe, the sudden frenzied dark unbearable. And cold! As if the chill from all those other rooms had been absorbed by this tiny cave, the dirt floor damp beneath my hands, my knees.

"Randall?" I said.

"Here," he said. Then, again. "Here."

His voice seemed flung, untethered; it came from every direction and I began to feel the panic you know I feel in enclosed places. I would have cried had Randall not chosen that moment to strike a match. He was right there beside me, touchable, close. I sat as he held the match to a candle on the floor. It wasn't a cave at all, just a tiny room, its walls papered with yellowed newspaper, the words buried by numbers. Literally hundreds of numbers had been scrawled across the walls, the ceiling. Everywhere you looked. The strangest thing. Some written in pencil, others in what looked like orange crayon, smeared or faint, deep enough to tear the newsprint. There seemed to be no order, no system to them. Just numbers on top of numbers on top of numbers.

I could hear Randall breathing. "What do you think they were counting?" I said.

"Heartbeats," he said.

It was the slaves' hiding place, of course. I crawled to the far corner, my palm catching on something hard: a spool of thread. Red, I remember, its color intact. There were other things to look at. Randall had collected them, and now he showed me, piece by piece: a rusted needle, a strand of red thread still through its eye, knotted at the end; a leather button; a tin box in which were cards with strange figures printed on them, an ancient tarot, perhaps; a yellow tooth; a handkerchief—the initials BBP embroidered in blue thread on its hem; a folded piece of paper. Randall unfolded it slowly, and I believed, for an instant, that the slaves' story would be written there. Another clue. But there was nothing to read, simply more numbers, a counting gone haywire.

Randall held the paper out to me and I took it, feeling, when I did, the brush of his soft fingers. "It must have been the only thing they knew," I said, staring at the numbered paper, my own fingers burning.

"Or had to learn," Randall said.

"Right," I said, not fully understanding.

"Look," he said. He held a comb, its wooden teeth spaced unevenly. "I bet they played it," he said.

"I bet they did," I said. Even then I knew I sounded stupid. I wanted to say something important, something that might match his discovery. But all I could think of was the dark, and the way the candlelight made us long shadows. I pulled my legs beneath me, still cold, and pretended to read the numbers. After a while, aware of his inattention, I looked up. He was bent over, holding the needle close to the candlelight, sewing, it appeared, the hem of his pant leg with a concentration I had only witnessed in his reading.

I leaned in to see. *BB,* he had embroidered, and now he stitched the straight tail of the *P.*

He startled. I'm not sure we had ever been that close to one another, eye-to-eye, my breath his breath. The candlelight made us look much older than ourselves, eternal, somehow, stand-ins for gods. "I thought I'd take him along," he said, by way of explanation.

We remained in the slaves' hiding place until supper, sitting knee-to-knee, trying to count the numbers. We gave up. Randall read some advertisement for Doctor something-or-other's cure-all, which worked on pigs and people, and we laughed, then he took the stub of a pencil he always kept knotted in his shoelaces and wrote three numbers across the advertisement—5, 23, 1927—the date and year of his birth. He stared at the numbers a minute, and then drew a dash after them, in the way you sometimes see in books after an author's name and birthdate, the dash like the scythe of the grim reaper.

"Don't," I said, licking my finger and reaching to erase the line. I may have smeared it a bit, I don't know. I know at this point Randall grabbed my wrist, surprising me with the strength in those fingers. It was the most wonderful of gestures. He brought my hand to his cheek and kissed my palm, no doubt filthy from crawling around on that floor. He seemed not to care. He kept his lips there for a very long time, and I, as terrified to pull away as I was to allow him to continue, held my breath, listening to my own heart beat stronger.

There was one other, actually. Visit, I mean. The morning Randall came through Philadelphia on his way out. He was going to ride the Union Pacific, in those days a tunnel on wheels chock full of soldiers stretching from one end of the country to the other—some heading east to Europe, others heading west to the Pacific. Your grandmother would tell me stories of worse times, during the Depression, when she said that same train took children from families who could no longer feed them. She said she remembered a black-haired boy walking by their farmhouse, stopping with his parents for a drink of water. They were on their way to the train, the orphan train, they called it, sending the boy east, where someone from an agency would pick him up and find him a new place to live. She said it was a terrible thing to see, far worse than boys in bright uniforms heading out to save the world from disaster. She said children in trains, sitting high on their cardboard suitcases to get a view out the window, their eyes big as quarters, their pockets weighted down with nothing but the few treasures their parents had to give them—first curls, nickels, a shark's tooth, ribbons—things they no doubt lost along the way. That, she'd say the few times I tried talking to her of Randall, is the worst thing of all. Children given up for good.

But I don't know. I remember the look of Randall stepping off the train. His uniform indeed bright, his leather shoes polished to a gleam shiny as those fingernails. It was a terrible sight I can tell you. Mother and I had driven to meet him at the station. I believe it was the only time I ever saw him when I wasn't in an Easter dress. You would have laughed. I wore a pink wool skirt and a pink cashmere button-down, my initials embroidered on the heart. A gift from Cynthia. I was so proud of those clothes, and the lipstick, Mother's shade, that I'd dab with a perfumed handkerchief I kept in my coat pocket.

But the look of Randall stepping off the train. He had grown that year even taller, and we could see his thin, worried face above the pack of other soldiers. The morning was blustery, and it felt like there might be snow. Other girls were on the platform slapping their hands together, standing with brothers, boyfriends. It seemed we were a collection of women and boys. Mother stepped forward a bit and called out to him, and Randall turned and smiled and rushed over to us, his hand extended.

But that was for Mother. When I went to shake it, he pulled me into a hug. He wore the regulation wool coat, and a scarf, red, knotted at his neck, and I tasted that scarf and smelled the cold, and the lilac water, and the tobacco smoke all at once.

"Look at you," he said, and squeezed me tighter.

Mother knew of a coffee shop nearby, and we went, though we had to stand some time waiting for a table, the room swamped with boys in uniform. I became aware of Randall watching me, though I pretended not to notice. I had come in to that girl age of boys finding me pretty, and I felt always as if I walked on a stage, lighted to an audience somewhere out in the dark. Mother chattered, clearly nervous in that big room with all those soldiers, waiters racing to and fro, splashing coffee on the linoleum floor, wiping their foreheads with the dishrags that hung from their waists, writing checks, shouting orders to the cooks. Yet all the while I felt Randall's gaze, as if there were something he needed to tell me, and that all I had to do was turn to him to find the clue.

But I don't know. There wasn't much time. Too soon there came upon the place that feeling of leaving. Soldiers scraped back their chairs, stood in line to pay their checks. Everyone had the same train to catch. Mother smoothed her skirt out and said she believed we should be heading back ourselves. Then she excused herself, saying she'd rather use the ladies' room there than at the train station.

Randall and I watched her weave her way around the other tables, some empty, others full. We were, quite suddenly, alone.

Have I told you he was handsome? I didn't know him well, but he had red hair, red as mine, and a kind, thin face. He might have had the most beautiful thin face I have ever seen. I should have told him that then, but I was too shy. This is what I've been thinking about: maybe he wasn't waiting to tell me anything, but waiting to hear something from me. No matter. I may have taken another sip of coffee, then. I know I did anything not to have to look at him directly.

"On the train up I sat next to a guy from Louisville," he finally said. "His name was Hog Phelps."

"Hog?" I said.

"Said he wasn't the only Hog in his family, said he was from a long line of Hogs."

I looked at Randall and he shrugged. Then he laughed and I did, too. It seemed like such a funny thing to say.

I received only one letter from Randall after that. It was written the day before he sailed for the Far East, mailed from San Francisco. I remember that the stamp on the envelope was a common one from that time— Teddy Roosevelt leading his Rough Riders up San Juan Hill—and that Randall had drawn a bubble of speech coming from his mouth that said, "Carry on!" I opened the letter with a mixture of trepidation and excitement. I was too young and too stupid to understand what Randall was about to do. I imagined his thoughts had been solely of me, that the letter would be filled with love sonnets, that it would gush with the same romantic pablum I devoured from those movie star magazines. Instead, it described San Francisco—the fog that rolled in early afternoons across the bay, the Golden Gate Bridge, and how the barking sea lions could be heard from so many streets, and the vistas that he found, as if painted solely for him, on the long solitary walks he took daily through the city. He wrote how he seemed to have lost interest in books, that he no longer had the patience. There was no *time*, he wrote, to sit. He wanted to walk, to never stop walking. If he could, he would walk all the way to Japan by way of China. Hell, he wrote (and I remember the look of that word, how Randall seemed to be trying out a different, fiercer Randall), when I'm finished with this I'm going to walk around the entire world.

I tried to picture him writing it, sitting at a large metal desk in the middle of a barracks, like something I might have seen in *Life*. I pictured him stooped over, with a reader's concentration, digging the pen into the regulation paper in the way he would have, if we were face-to-face talking, stressed a word. I saw him in civilian clothes, in the dress pants he wore every Easter. The same ones, as far as I could tell—a light gray wool, each year hitched up a little higher and now, leg crossed across one knee, entirely ill-fitting, the *BBP* far above the ankle. He might have, from time to time, put the pen down and leaned back to think of a particular description, fingering those initials he had stitched in red. It was clear to me even then that he had worked on the letter like a boy who wants to be a writer. Certain words broke his true voice, were tried on, tested for fit. They were a hat too big for him—the Randall I knew interrupted again and again by the Randall Randall might have become. The *Hell*, as I have mentioned. A line from some dead poet—*I would think of a thousand things, lovely and durable, and taste them slowly*—I had heard him recite in his room a hundred times, and other words I recognized as words still left to learn. It seemed he wanted to cram everything in.

Still, it is a beautiful letter. I have saved it for years. It finds its way into my hands at the oddest times, and when it does I always hold it for a while, rereading the envelope. Teddy shouts, Carry on!, and I curse him. All of them. Then I pull out the paper, one folded sheath, and unfold it as slowly as I would a gift I'd never opened. My fear is that somehow in my absence, his words have come undone, been shaken loose, rearranged, so that what I will find is no more than a page of randomness, letters shuffled into forms with no meaning, indecipherable, foreign.

But there! My name in salutation, the sweetness of the attendant *Dear*. I'm again as I was, as he may have pictured me—writing at that desk beneath the window, the metal newly polished, the air fresh, eucalyptus-scented, the sea lions barking—when he signed *Love, Randall*, and underlined it with a flourish as elegant as a bow.

Tim Gautreaux

Easy Pickings

From *GQ*

HE DROVE into Louisiana from Texas in the stolen sedan, taking the minor roads, the cracked and grass-lined blacktop where houses showed up one to the mile. The land was overrun with low crops he did not recognize and was absolutely flat, which he liked because he could see a police car from a long way off. He was a short man, small of frame, tattooed on the neck and arms with crabs and scorpions, which fit his grabbing occupation of thief. In the hollow of his throat was a small blue lobster, one of its claws holding a hand-rolled cigarette. He thought of the woman in Houston he'd terrorized the day before, coming into her kitchen and pulling his scary knife, a discount bowie he'd bought at the KKK table at a local gun show, and putting it to her throat. She'd wept and trembled, giving him her rings, leading him to her husband's little stash of poker money. The day before that, he'd spotted an old woman in Victoria returning alone from the grocery, and he followed her into the house, taking her jewelry, showing the knife when she balked and getting the cash from her wallet. He'd robbed only these two women, but it seemed that he'd been doing it all his life, like walking and breathing, even though he'd just got out of jail the week before after doing two years for stealing welfare checks. He looked through the windshield at the poor, watery country. Anyone who would live out here would be simple, he thought, real stupid and easy pickings.

His name was Marvin, but he called himself Big Blade because the name made him feel other than what he was: small, petty and dull.

He noticed a white frame house ahead on the right side of the road, sitting at the edge of a flooded field, clothes on the line out back. Big Blade had been raised in a run-down Houston subdivision and had never seen clothes dried out in the open. At first he thought the laundry was part of some type of yard sale, but after he stopped on the shoulder and studied the limp dresses and aprons, he figured it out. Across the road and 200 yards away was a similar house, an asbestos-sided rectangle with a tin roof, and after that nothing but blacktop. Big Blade noticed that there were no men's clothes on the line, and he moved the car toward the driveway.

Mrs. Arceneaux was eighty-five years old and spoke Acadian French to her chickens because nearly everyone else who could speak it was dead. She came out into the yard with a plastic bowl of feed and was met at the back steps by Marvin, who pulled out his big knife, his eyes gleaming. Mrs. Arceneaux's vision was not sharp enough to see the evil eye, but she saw the tattoos and she saw the knife.

"Baby, who wrote all over you? And what you want, you, wit' that big cane cutter you got? If you hungry, all I got is them chicken *là-bas,* and if you cut off a head, throw it in the bushes at the back of my lot and pluck them feather over there because the wind is blowin' west today and . . ."

"Shut up and get inside," Big Blade growled, giving the old woman a push toward her screen door. "I want your money."

Mrs. Arceneaux narrowed her eyes at the man and then hobbled up the back steps into her kitchen. "Well, I be damn. Ain't you got nobody better to rob than a ol' lady whose husband died twenty-nine years ago of a heart attack in a bourrée game holding ace, king, queen of trumps? The priest told me . . ."

Big Blade began to seethe, his voice low and aspirated, "I will kill you if you don't give me your jewelry and money. I'll gut you like one of your chickens." The old lady stopped speaking for just a second to bring him into focus.

"You, wit' the crawfish drew on your throat, you trying to scare me wit' a knife? Like I ain't use to death? I break a chicken neck three times a week, and my brother, he got shot dead next to me at the Saint Landry

Parish fair in 1936, and all my husband's brother got killed in that German war, and that Lodrigue boy died with his head in my apron the day the tractor run over him, 'course he was putting on the plow with the damn thing in gear, and even the priest said it wasn't too bright to get plowed under by your own plow, and . . ."

"They call me Big Blade," Marvin thundered.

"My name's Doris Arceneaux. I used to be a Boudreaux before . . ."

Marvin slapped the old woman, and her upper plate landed on the Formica dinette table. With no hesitation, she picked up her teeth and walked to the sink to rinse them off. Grabbing the incisors, she slid her dentures back in place. "Hurt?" she yelled. "You want to hurt a ol' lady what had seven children, one come out arm-first? Look, I had eight major surgeries and a appendix that blowed up inside me when I was first marry, made me so sick I was throwing up pieces of gut and the priest gave me extreme unction nine time."

"Shut up," Marvin yelled, raising his hand over her puff of hair.

"Oh, you kin hit me again, yeah, and then I'm gonna drop on the floor and what you gonna do with me then?"

"I can kill you," Marvin hollered.

"But you can't eat me," Mrs. Arceneaux shrilled back, wagging a knobby finger in Big Blade's befuddled face.

In the other house on that stretch of road, old Mrs. Breaux realized with a gasp that she was not going to take a trick in a bourrée game and would have to match an $18 pot. After the third trick had been raked off the table, Mrs. Breaux turned up her hearing aid with a twist of her forefinger and began begging, "Oh, please, somebody, don't drop you biggest trump so I can save myself."

"I can't hold back, *chère*," Sadie LaLonde told her. "I got to play to win. That's the rules." Mrs. LaLonde's upper arms jiggled as she slapped down a trump ace.

Mrs. Breaux's eyes got as small as a bat's, and her mouth turned into a raisin. "You done killed my jack," she yelled, following suit with her card. "I'm bourrée'd."

Mr. Alvin crossed his legs and sniffed. "You bourrée'd yourself, girl. You should know better to come in a game with the jack dry." Mr. Alvin shook a pouf of white hair out of his florid face and carefully led off with a four trump, followed by Mrs. LaLonde's ten and a stray diamond by Mrs. Breaux, whose little cigarette-stained mustache began to quiver as she watched the money get raked off the table.

"You done it," Mrs. Breaux hollered. She shrank back in her wooden chair and searched over her ninety years of evil-tempered earthly existence for the vilest curse words she'd ever heard, and none of them packed the power she wanted. Finally she said, "I hope you get diabetes of the blow-hole!"

The other three widows and one never-married man laughed aloud at her exasperation and fidgeted with the coins in their little money piles, digging for the next ante. Mrs. Guidroz pulled her aluminum cane off the back of her chair to get up for a glass of tap water.

"There's ice water in the fridge," Mrs. LaLonde offered.

Mrs. Guidroz shook her tight blue curls. "I wasn't raised to drink cold water. That stuff hurts my mout'." As she drew a glassful from the singing tap, she looked out the window and down the road. "Hey. Doris, she got herself some company."

"If it's a red truck, it must be her son Nelson," Mrs. LaLonde said. "Today's Tuesday, when he comes around."

"Non, this is a li'l white car."

"Maybe it's the power company," Mr. Alvin suggested.

"Non, this is too little for a 'lectric-company car. Where would they put their pliers and wire in that thing?"

Sadie LaLonde hoisted herself off the two chairs she was sitting on and wobbled to the window, putting her face next to Mrs. Guidroz's. "That's either a Dodge or a Plimmit."

"What's the difference?"

"I think they the same car, but they label the ones with ugly paint Plimmets." Mrs. LaLonde looked over her glasses. "Doris don't know no-body drives a car like that."

Mr. Alvin came to the window and wedged himself between the women. "You sure it ain't a Tyota? One of her two dozen granddaughters drives one like that."

"Nanette. I think she sold that, though."

Mr. Alvin shook his head. "Oh no, she wouldn't. You know, them lit-tle yellow fingers make them Tyotas, and they don't never wear out." He looked through the window. "But that's one of them little Freons."

"Is that a Chevrolet?"

"No, it's a cheap Dodge with a rubber-band motor. Only a Jehovah Witness would drive something like that."

"Aw, no." Mrs. Guidroz stamped her cane on the linoleum. "You think we ought to call over there and see if she needs help runnin' them off. Them Jehovah Witness like cockleburs on corduroy."

From the card table behind the group at the sink rose Beverly Perrilloux's voice. She had lit up a Camel and was talking out the smoke. "Y'all come back and play some cards before Mrs. Breaux catches herself a little stroke." She took another intense drag, all the tiny warts on her face moving into the center.

"Damn right," Mrs. Breaux complained. "I got to win my $18 back."

Mr. Alvin dusted off his chair and sat down, and Mrs. Guidroz gulped two swallows of water while Sadie LaLonde reached for her wall phone.

Big Blade looked around Mrs. Arceneaux's kitchen at the plywood cabinets, at the swirling linoleum that popped when he stepped on it, at a plastic toaster that was a clock and out of which a piece of plastic toast slowly arose every thirty seconds. It occurred to him that he was trying to rob the wrong woman.

"I want your wedding ring," he announced.

She held her hand out toward him. "I stopped wearin' one when Arthur told me to."

Big Blade wiggled his knife. "Arthur?"

"Yah. Arthur-itis."

"Where is it?"

"It wasn't but a little silver circle, and I gave it to a grandbaby to wear on her necklace. Oh, I had a diamond up on some prongs, too, but it used to get plugged up with grandbaby shit when I'd change diapers, so I gave that away, too."

The phone rang and Big Blade stepped toward it. "Answer and act normal. One false word and I'll cut you open."

Mrs. Arceneaux gathered her arms vertically in front of her, her fists under her chin, feigning fright, and tiptoed to the wall phone.

"Hallo," she yelled. Then, turning to Big Blade, she said, "It's Sadie LaLonde from down the road." Speaking back into the receiver, she said,

"No, it ain't no Holy Rolly; it's some boy with a sword trying to rob me like the government."

Big Blade reached out and cut the phone cord with a swipe. "I ought to kill you where you stand," he said.

Mrs. Arceneaux grabbed the swinging cord and gave him a savage look. "And then what would you have?"

He blinked. "Whoever called better not cause no trouble."

Mrs. Arceneaux put a thumb over her shoulder. "Sadie and that gang playing bourrée. You couldn't blow 'em out that house with dynamite."

The man looked around as if he considered gathering up the worn-out contents of her kitchen and packing them into the stolen car he'd left idling out front on the grass. "You got to have some money around here somewhere. Go get it."

She raised a hand above her head and toddled off toward the hall. "If that's all it takes to get you out my hair, you kin have it, yeah." Abruptly she turned around and walked toward the stove. "I almos' forgot my chicken stew heatin' on the burner."

"Never mind that," he growled.

Mrs. Arceneaux rolled up an eye toward him. "You hungry, you?" She lifted a lid, and a nimbus laden with smells of onion, garlic, bell pepper and a medium–nut-brown roux rose like a spirit out of the cast-iron pot.

"What's that?" Big Blade sniffed toward the stove, his knife drifting.

"Chicken stew. You eat that over some rice and with potato salad and hot sweet peas." She looked at the boy's eyes and stirred the rich gravy seductively. "You burglars take time to eat or what?"

"Oh, Jesus, Mary and Joseph," Mrs. LaLonde sang, holding the dead receiver to her ear and looking out of her little kitchen window with the four other card players. "I don't know what to think."

"She's probably being nasty to us," Mrs. Guidroz said, tapping her cane against Mr. Alvin's big, soft leg. "She wants us to worry."

"That woman says some crazy things," Mrs. Perrilloux called, her warty elbows propped on the card table. "She spends so much time cooking, I think she's got natural gas on the brain."

Mrs. Breaux lit up a Picayune with her creaky Zippo. "Hot damn, let's play cards. Ain't nobody can put nothin' over on Doris Arceneaux."

"Somebody's over there intrudin'," Mrs. LaLonde protested.

Mrs. Breaux sniffed. "She'll talk the intrudin' parts off their body, that's for true."

"Well, her phone won't answer back. Somebody ought to go over and see who's there with her."

The old women turned toward Mr. Alvin, a tall, jiggly old man built like an eggplant and with pale, fine-textured skin. His pleated gray trousers hung on him like a skirt on a fat convent-school girl. "Why me?"

"You a man," Mrs. Guidroz exclaimed.

Mr. Alvin's eyes expanded as though the information were a surprise. *"Mais,* what you want me to do?"

Mrs. LaLonde turned him toward the screen door. "Just go look in her kitchen window and see if everything is all right."

"I shouldn't knock on the door?"

Mrs. Guidroz shook her tiny head. "If there's a bad man in there, you gonna tip him off."

Mr. Alvin hung back from the door. "I don't know."

"Dammit, Alvin," Mrs. Guidroz said, "I'd go myself, but it's been raining, and last time I walked to Doris's from here, my stick went down in her lawn a foot deep, yeah, and I couldn't get it unstuck, and Doris wasn't there, so I had to limp all the way back and call my son to come pull it out."

"Go on, Alvin," Mrs. LaLonde said, putting a shoulder to his back and nudging him out the door.

Mr. Alvin looked down the road to Mrs. Arceneaux's house as he walked the clamshell shoulder, trying to seem inconspicuous. An old pickup truck passed, driven by what seemed to be a twelve-year-old boy, and Mr. Alvin did not return the child's wave. He walked the grassy edge of Mrs. Arceneaux's driveway and took to the spongy lawn, circling around to her kitchen window. He stooped and walked under it, the way he had seen detectives do in the movies. When he raised his eyes slowly past the window ledge, he saw a strange man at Mrs. Arceneaux's table waving a murderous-looking knife at the old woman while chewing a big mouthful of chicken stew.

"You don't watch out, I'm gonna put you in that stew pot," the man said, and Mr. Alvin lowered himself as slow as a clock's hand and began to slog through the deep grass toward the highway, where he heard something like a steam engine puffing as he walked along, then realized it was his own breath. He thought about running and tried to remember how to do it, but his heart was pounding so hard, all he could do was swing his arms faster and paddle the air back to Mrs. LaLonde's house.

The women were at the window watching him hurry back. "Oh, *mon Dieu,*" Mrs. Guidroz sang, "look how fast Alvin's moving. What's it mean?"

Mrs. Breaux cackled. "It's probably just his Ex-Lax working."

They opened the door and pulled him into the room by his flabby arms.

"There's someone there holding a knife on Doris," Mr. Alvin gasped.

"Eie, yaie, yaie," Mrs. LaLonde shouted.

"Call Deputy Sid," Mrs. Perrilloux announced from the card table, where she was refilling her butane lighter from a miniature canister of gas.

Mrs. LaLonde shook her head. "It'll take him a half hour to get out here." She straightened up and looked around. "Maybe one of us ought to go over there with a gun."

Mr. Alvin put up his big hands. "Oh no, I went already." He walked over to the phone and dialed the sheriff's office.

Mrs. Breaux threw down a pack of cards in disgust. "What kind of gun you got?"

Mrs. LaLonde reached into the next room to a little space between an armoire and the wall, retrieving a double-barreled shotgun with exposed hammers. "This was Lester's daddy's gun."

Mrs. Breaux walked over and figured out how to open the action. "They ain't no bullets in this thing."

Mrs. LaLonde walked over to her dresser, her perfume and lotion bottles clinking against one another on the vanity, and pulled open the top drawer. "Does this fit?" She handed Mrs. Breaux a tarnished .38-caliber cartridge. She dropped it into the gun, but it rattled down the barrel and tumbled out onto the linoleum.

"It's not the right size," Mrs. Breaux complained, peering into Mrs. LaLonde's outstretched hand and plucking two high-brass cardboard shells labeled with double O's. "Here you go." She plunked in the shells and snapped the action shut.

· · · ·

The parish had only one settlement to the south, Grand Crapaud, and south of that a few miles, the highway came to an end. The center line of the road led up to the steps of a twelve-by-twelve-foot asbestos-sided building on piers, the office of the South End deputy.

Deputy Sid was a tall black man who wore a cowboy hat with a gold badge on the crown and an immaculate, freshly ironed uniform. He sat at his little desk, filling out a report about Minos Blanchard letting his Dodge Dart roll overboard at the boat ramp next door. The phone rang, and it was the dispatcher from the parish seat.

"Sid, you there?"

"I'm here all right."

"Mrs. LaLonde out by Prairie Amer called in that Doris Arceneaux has an intruder in her house right now."

"That's those peoples always playin' cards?"

"And the one that's always cookin'."

"How does Mrs. LaLonde know they's somebody in there?"

"There's a strange car in the yard."

"Did she say what kind it was?"

"She said it was a Freon."

"They ain't no such thing."

"I know that. Mr. Alvin looked in the window and saw the intruder."

Deputy Sid pushed back his hat. "What's Mr. Alvin doing looking in a *woman's* window?"

"Can you get out there?"

"Sho." He hung up and in one step was at the door.

Mrs. Arceneaux watched Big Blade finish one overflowing plate of chicken stew, and then she fixed him another, providing him all the while with French dripped coffee laced with brandy. "You better think where you put your money," Big Blade said through a mouthful of potato salad.

"You ain't had some dessert yet," Mrs. Arceneaux cooed. "Look, I foun' some bread pudding with whiskey sauce in the fridge."

Big Blade took a tentative taste of the dessert, then a spoonful, eating slowly and with one eye closed. By the time he'd finished everything on the table, he was stunned with food, drowsy, dim-witted with food. He had been eating for a half hour. When he saw movement at the back screen door, he ignored it for a moment, but when the form of a uniformed black man imprinted itself on his consciousness, he jumped up holding his knife in one hand and the old lady's bony arm in the other.

Deputy Sid stepped in smiling, moving easily, as though he'd lived in the kitchen all his life and was walking through his own house. "How you doin', Mrs. Arceneaux?"

"Hey, yourself, Deputy Sid. They's fresh coffee on the stove."

"Freeze," Blade barked.

Deputy Sid stopped the motion of his hand above the range. "I can't have no coffee?"

The little plastic slice of toast peeked out of the clock, and Blade jumped. "Ahhh."

"What?" Deputy Sid looked to the windowsill.

"It's that damn clock," Mrs. Arceneaux said. "That crazy thing scares the hell out of me too, but my sister give it to me, and what can you do? I come in here at night sometime, and that little toast rises up like a rat sticking its head out a cracker can and . . ."

"Never mind." Big Blade was looking at the deputy's staghorn-gripped, nickel-plated revolver. It was angled toward him on the policeman's narrow hip. "Give me your gun or I'll cut the old lady's throat."

Deputy Sid considered this for a moment. "OK, man. But hold on to Misres Doris, 'cause she fixin' to take off." The deputy popped his safety strap, lifted his revolver with two fingers and placed it on the table. Blade held on to the old lady with one hand, reached to the table and realized that he would have to let go of his knife to retrieve the gun. The second he set it down and put his finger into the trigger guard of the pistol, Deputy Sid moved his hand over and picked up the knife.

"Hey," Blade told him, pointing the shiny weapon at his head.

"You don't need this no more." Deputy Sid dropped the knife behind the refrigerator.

"I want my knife."

"You better get on out of here while you got the upper hand."

Big Blade glanced through the screen door. "Yeah. I bet you got buddies outside just waiting."

Deputy Sid shook his head. "No, man. It's just me. But let me give you some advice. You on a dead-end parish highway. The open end got a roadblock right now. South here is marsh and alligators."

"And then what?"

Deputy Sid screwed up an eye to think. "Cuba, I guess."

"Shit. What about north?"

"Rice fields for five miles."

"That little car I got will get me through the roadblock?"

"I don't know. You left the motor running and it idled out of gas. You can get in it, but it won't go nowhere."

Big Blade's eyeballs bounced back and forth for a few seconds. He waved the gun. "Handcuff yourself to that oven door and give me the keys."

Mrs. Arceneaux pointed. "Careful you don't scratch nothin'. The last thing my husband did before he died is buy me that stove, and it got to last me a long time. He told me . . ."

"I'm taking her with me. So if you got partners outside, you better call to them."

"I'm the onliest one back here."

"Is your cruiser idling?" Big Blade asked with a wicked smile.

The deputy nodded slowly.

"Hah, you people are dumb as dirt," he said, backing out of the kitchen with the old lady in tow.

Deputy Sid watched them walk out of his line of vision. He looked at the stove, reached and felt the side of the coffeepot with his free hand, and then stretched to the cabinet to get himself a cup.

The cruiser was eight years old, and Big Blade had to clean out clipboards, digital adding machines, dog-eared manuals on report writing, apples, candy bars, chewing gum, magazines and empty cans of Mace before Mrs. Arceneaux would fit into the front seat. She buckled her safety harness, and he climbed in on the driver's side. The old white Dodge's transmission slipped so badly, it would hardly back out onto the road, but soon they were spinning along the highway, going west. After five miles, he could see one police car in the distance parked across the flat road, and he knew he could make the escape work. All he had to do was hold the pistol to her head and let the officers see this. They would let him roll through like a tourist. Just then Mrs. Arceneaux crossed her hands over her breastbone and announced in a strangled voice, "I'm having me another heart attack." Big Blade stopped the car and watched the old woman's face turn red. She coughed once, and her arms fell limp at her side, her upper plate tumbling from her mouth and bouncing onto the floor mat. He looked ahead to what he could now see were two police cars waiting with their flashers swatting the flat light rolling off the rice fields. Feeling with great dread the flesh of the woman's neck, he could find no pulse, and suddenly everything changed. He imagined himself strapped to a gurney in a Louisiana prison waiting for the fatal injection to come along the tube into his arm. He looked into his rearview and then turned the car around, the old woman's head rolling right. Maybe there would be a boat at the end of the road and he could escape in that.

The Dodge stuttered and groaned up to thirty, forty, forty-five as he headed in the other direction. Soon Doris Arceneaux's house was rolling up on the right, and on the left he watched the only other house in the area, with a mailbox out front and a bushy cedar growing next to it. As soon as he passed that mailbox, his peripheral vision snapped a picture of five old people crouching in a line, hiding behind the cedar. At once he heard a huge detonation, and the car began a drunken spin, metal grinding on the blacktop, the tires howling until the cruiser stopped sideways in the road. Big Blade shook his head and fell out of the front seat, holding Deputy Sid's revolver. He saw a skinny old woman in a print dress walking up and holding a shotgun toward his midsection. One hammer on the gun was down, and the other was up like a fang ready to drop. He stood and raised the nickel-plated revolver and pulled the trigger, aiming at her legs, but all the weapon did was go *tik-tik-tik-tik-tik-tik*.

"Get on the damn ground," Mrs. Breaux hollered in her creaky voice, "or I'll let the air out of you like I did that tire, yeah."

As Big Blade lay down in the road, he heard a cackle from the front seat of the cruiser as Mrs. Arceneaux unbuckled herself and climbed out with her upper plate in her hand. "Ha, haaaa, I foolt him good. He tought I was dead and ran from them other cops."

Along the shoulder of the road came Deputy Sid, a sea green oven door under his arm. He bent down, retrieved his revolver and loaded it with six shells dug out of his pocket. "I got him now, ladies, Mr. Al."

Mrs. Arceneaux sidled up to him. "You got some more police coming?"

"Yeah. I called 'em from your bedroom phone. Then I called your neighbors here. Told 'em to be on the lookout."

Mrs. Breaux lowered the hammer on the shotgun. "Hot damn. Now we can get back to the game. Doris, you want to play?"

She waved her hand above her white hair as if chasing a fly. "Naw, me, I got to go clean up my kitchen."

"What about you, Deputy Sid?"

He looked at his blasted front tire and the pellet holes in the fender. He let the bottom of the oven door rest on the asphalt. "It gon' take me a week to write all this up. Maybe next time ya'll play you can give me a call."

Mrs. LaLonde lumbered up out of the grass, followed by Mr. Alvin. "Don't bring that gun into the house loaded," she said.

Mrs. Breaux opened the action and plucked out the good shell, chucking the empty into a roadside ditch. She handed the weapon to Mr. Alvin, who took it from her with his fingertips, as though it might be red-hot. Mrs. Breaux grabbed a handful of the old man's shirt and let him tow her off the road and across the soft lawn. Suddenly, she wheeled around. "Hey, you with no bullets," she called to Big Blade, who was squirming under the barrel of Deputy Sid's revolver.

"What?" He had to look through the window of the oven door to see her.

"If you ever get out of jail, I want you to come play cards with us." She threw back her head and laughed.

"Why's that?" He twisted his head up. "What you mean?"

"Just bring lots of money, boy," Mrs. Breaux called as she turned to look down the road toward an approaching parade of flashers and the warbling laugh of a siren sailing high over the simple rice fields.

Michael Byers

The Beautiful Days

From *Ploughshares*

IN THE days of his youth, Aldo often found himself—as many of us did—in a state of grace, and the sensation in his boundless filling heart resembled, to his mind, the transports of love. His Midwestern college, set down in the middle of a cornfield and isolated from any big city by fifty miles of empty, cold-roughened highway, seemed a basin of happiness in which he had been permitted, by some heavenly dispensation, to swim. Elms, dead elsewhere, had somehow survived in this town, pointing their great forked limbs at the sky. The quarry south of campus, hidden in its fringe of college-owned forest, echoed with the autumn shouts of naked swimmers; and in the frigid winters, skaters hiked the long way through the trees and picked their way carefully down to the ice. The rural sky was a comforting black infested with stars, and though he bruised himself when he skated, the cold Ohio air acted as a sort of balm, or at any rate it numbed him until later, when, in the heat of the town's one diner, he could examine his empurpled knees, not without some pride. ·

Small towns were new to him. The daily goodness of the Ben Franklin on College Street, offering its yarn and Bic lighters and artificial plants to whomever happened to walk through the swinging glass doors, swelled his soul. The tiny bank employed two tellers, both named Marie. The movie theater with its red velvet seats ran only the most second-rate films, and the screen was stained near the upper-left-hand corner; but this became visible only in outdoor scenes, when the stain resembled a small rain cloud. Despite the bad acting and ridiculous, juvenile plots, Aldo usually left the theater in a haze of goodwill, while around him the town disappeared into darkness down its two main streets, streets which carried their heavy freight of brick and ironwork as they had for a hundred and sixty years. He loved the town and the college, both lit with a stage-set perfection. Naturally, like many other students, he was often tired and fretted over his schoolwork, and his romances were only middlingly satisfying. He was poor, and had grown chubby on dormitory food. But even when he least expected it, he would be visited with a new gust of this unnamable generosity of spirit, when the world seemed nearly Platonic in its perfection. At these times he loved the world with such a passion that he worried he would one day lose his way to this grace, that its sources were more mysterious than the town around him: the pharmacy, its Valentine hearts illuminated in the window display; the dense tarry air in the Army-Navy store. The sensation that he was one among many—and yet still one, an individual being set loose on the planet—and that so much beauty abounded, on all sides, in every form, for him to encounter—all this combined to lift his heart above the ordinary, and made him, when it came, inexpressibly joyful. He was not religious, but such moments drove him to believe that something indefinite stood behind the bright curtain of the world—some great moral idea, some brilliant distillation of planetary consciousness that ringed the earth like a second atmosphere—something. It had come on him slowly in his three years here, this feeling, but now he sensed it defined him, and if he lost it, he feared, it would be like dying. Superstitiously he avoided thinking of it, as much as he could. Grace examined was—he suspected—grace denied.

His apartment off-campus Aldo shared with two relative strangers: a woman pianist named Eleanor, who used her long fingers as leverage to open difficult jars; and Bram, a dull, thick-chested economics major. Eleanor the pianist was taller than he, with a great pianist's wingspan, and irritatingly left behind in the shower's drain trap her short brown hairs. Though pretty she was a poor housekeeper, and her dirtied knives and half-eaten lunches lingered on the brown Formica counters for days. Beneath the window of her long bedroom she kept a sleek Japanese keyboard, futuristically black and technological; wearing headphones, she tamped its keys with great passion. Bram, who had an almost perfectly cylindrical head—except for his jutting nose, it looked as though it had been painstakingly lathed—strenuously lifted barbells in his small room beneath the eaves, filling the hallway with a sweaty stink. Strutting to the shower after these sessions, he wore bikini underwear, his blunt uncircumcised penis visible in outline beneath the fabric. A girlfriend could be heard in his room late at night, though she never stayed till morning. As for Aldo he had his metal shelves and rickety desk, his Greek and Latin dictionaries—he was a classics major—and his shoeboxes full of vocabulary flashcards. In the mirror he was a plumpish, curly-headed version of his father, shorter by three inches and with his mother's large sorrowful Italian eyes fastened, somewhat incongruously, above his father's looming, cavernous nose. While not vain exactly, he liked his own looks, and was bothered only by the troublesome way his eyebrows met in the middle, giving him a sort of primitive appearance. He had slept with four girls— women—since his freshman year, when he had lost his virginity to a slim and fragile-feeling poetess who had since dropped out of school and gone home to Columbus. Such were the facts of Aldo Gorman's life at twenty: sexually adequate, though unremarkable; interesting-looking, and handsome in the manner of most youths; periodically filled with an inexplicable grace which, when it faded under some daily pressure, he feared would never come again; and, not unimportantly, devoted to two dead languages, great sloppy tubs of vocabulary and syntax he hefted alternately—Greek four times a week, Latin five. And also, that winter, there was a girl he loved who did not love him back. Her name was Miranda Lowe.

She sat beside him one day in his glaciology class—a gut, to complete his science requirements—and she had forgotten to bring her book; would he mind if she looked on at his? "Oh—no," he said, surprised.

"You'd think, with all this snow," she said, almost whispering, "we wouldn't need a class on glaciers."

"You'd think," he agreed. "I felt like Amundsen this morning."

She smiled. "I know what you mean."

"Without the dogs."

"I don't think he used dogs," she said. "I think he used ponies."

"Oh," he said. "Really? Ponies?"

"One of them did."

"Actual ponies?"

"I think so," she said, glancing at him shyly, "and then I think they ate them."

"Oh," he said again. In the cold classroom full of melting boots and wet wool, she wore only a thin-looking white cotton sweater imprinted with black dots, as though her own heat were enough to keep her warm. Brown hair, brown eyes, pretty, with a fine long nose: in many ways she was a conventional sort of beauty, but what seemed to be shyness—she wouldn't meet his eyes—distinguished her from any of a hundred beautiful girls, as did, seen this close, the ghostly blond mustache on her upper lip, which he imagined another girl might have eradicated in some way. She seemed, like him, mostly innocent, and it was this that twanged at his heart, producing not love but its disreputable cousin, desire. "Okay?" he asked, before turning the page. "Mm-hm," she answered. A tiny feather, released from his puffy down jacket, lifted into the air between them.

But she would not have him. She was from New Mexico, and was already engaged—unusual in their generation, but she had the ring to prove it. In the library she held it out, where, under the fluorescent lights, it seemed a pale, fragile thing. "Two years ago," she said.

The news disappointed him, but it wasn't exactly a surprise. "You see him much?"

"At breaks."

"What's his name?"

"Oh . . . I'll tell you, but you can't laugh."

"All right."

"It's *Elmer*. But he's not what you think!" A flush of embarrassment colored her cheeks, and the sight weakened Aldo's heart. "He's very tall, and he doesn't hunt rabbits. And he talks like a normal person."

"He in school?"

"He's doing his residency now."

"He's a doctor?"

"Yes." She hesitated. "Or—almost. He's got a year still."

"And he's back in New Mexico?"

"No," she said. "He's at Harvard."

"Oh."

"He's going back to New Mexico when he finishes, to work on the reservations." She touched his arm, laughing. "He's not at all snobby."

"I didn't say anything."

"The way you said 'Oh.' It was suspicious."

"Elmer."

"Yes: Elmer Grand," Miranda said. And she pronounced the name with such firmness and resolution that Aldo understood at once he had no chance at her. The name as she spoke it seemed a brand of fine paint, or an excellent, old-fashioned toothpaste—something common, decent, thoroughly goodhearted. Like the glue, he thought.

A junior, Aldo was the only student studying Herodotus that year, under the direction of Larry Feingold—a short, skinny man in his seventies whose two front teeth rested endearingly on his lower lip, like a rabbit's. He seemed happy among his decades of books, with the radiator ticking cozily under the snowy window, and despite his age Feingold had a round, childish head and a great shrubbery of curly black hair; settled back in his worn chair, with his tiny brown shoes propped nimbly on the desktop, he looked more like a boy than anything. When Aldo stumbled, Feingold corrected him with a high cackling giggle—it was meant to be encouraging—and then, with a flourish that seemed showy from so small a man, he would lean forward and take over, speaking first one language and then the other, as though playing tennis with a second, equally agile version of himself.

By January they were skipping around in Book Two and had reached the material on Egypt. "When an Egyptian committed a crime," Feingold said, "*adikema*, it was not the custom of Sabacos to punish him with death, *thanatou*, but instead of the death penalty he compelled the offender, see that? Compelled, in the aorist"—he rolled his eyes with the pleasure of it—"to *raise the level of the soil* in the neighborhood, *geitoniai*, dative of location, of his native town, yes, or home, or—well, yes, *native town*, let's say, for simplicity."

"Raise the soil?"

"Yes," said Feingold. "Hm. I think, in other words, to build a levee. Against the Nile."

This seemed plausible. But down the page, an entire town had somehow been lifted high above the river, houses and all. Had the buildings been somehow propped on jacks, and soil shoveled beneath them? Or were they collapsible structures that one could take down and put up at will, like tents? And where did the extra soil come from? "No," said Feingold, puzzling, "it's just a levee. See? *In the neighborhood* of his native town." He chewed with his rabbity teeth on his lower lip. "But, hmm. The temple stands in the center of the city, *tou polou,* and, since the level of the buildings everywhere else has been raised, *anaskanomai,* one can look down and get a fine view of it from all around. Now that seems to say . . ."

"But the temple's on the river."

"Oh, that must be it. So, the temple is down *there,* on an island essentially in the middle of the river. The town is up *here* on the riverbanks. They look down on the temple."

"But they did raise the buildings, he says."

"Yes . . . well, fanciful, maybe. It's hearsay, at least. He gets it from the priests, after all. Or maybe he doesn't mean *buildings* really." Feingold read on. "Oh, but look at this, here. The road is lined, *grammatos,* yes, *lined* on both sides with immense trees, so tall that they seem to touch the sky."

"So . . . ?"

"Oh, nothing," said Feingold. "Just those trees. Ancient ancient trees that were *there* once, on the road to the temple. Dead twenty-five hundred years, and yet there they stand. God bless the man for that."

Grace was to be found in the library as well, in the long free weekend mornings, when the sun was out over the snowy fields. From the top-floor windows the little town could be seen huddled under a Saturday morning's icy calm—Aldo might be in the library as early as eight—while light, the cleanest, brightest illumination he had ever seen, poured down from the tiny, wintry sun and, after caroming off the snowy lawns, went flooding back into the empty sky, to fill it more with light. The world, though cold, was illuminated as though by the gods, in a way that seemed somehow removed from time; and the leathery odor of the hundreds of thousands of books—among them his own Greek lexicon, the paper soft with wear—gave even this modern concrete building a gratifying, antique atmosphere, as though he had sat here for a hundred years, and would sit here a hundred more, until the winter's light consumed him.

But he could not forget Miranda Lowe, and she seemed unable, for her part, to leave him alone. Without meaning to, he had become something of a companion to her. They studied together. She was an English major, and he watched as she beat her way faithfully through *Pamela,* the book's polished black cover becoming creased and scuffed and its spine acquiring a series of white cracks. She *used* the book, writing in it heedlessly, while he, beside her, filled notebooks with long columns of writing, leaving his texts clean, unblemished, as though they had never been read at all. Necrophilic, he supposed. Orderly, at any rate. This contrast between them pleased him, though he couldn't say why, exactly. He enjoyed her teasing, maybe. Pacing restlessly the night before an exam she read the dictionary, folding back page after page. "Megrims," she said. And then after a pause, "Mephitic."

Spending so much time with Miranda allowed him to watch her move around in the world. She had long graceful arms, and though her legs were unremarkable, her feet, when she slid her shoes onto the checkered carpet, were shapely and even-toed. Small, compact breasts. He was not alone in thinking her beautiful. She had dozens and dozens of friends, far more than Aldo, and many of them were admiring men who, after talking with Miranda, would look him over querulously. He permitted himself to feel some pride at such times, though he knew she considered him a sort of eunuch, not to be feared. This was wounding; but there she was, sitting with him, while the other men had to drift away into the stacks. She did talk endlessly about Elmer, which grew tiring; but to her credit she knew it. "I don't want to," she said, "but he's all I think about sometimes."

"It's understandable."

"You'd like him, I think."

"I think maybe I would."

"Maybe. Listen to you. He's such a good guy."

"If he's so good, what's he doing away from you?"

"Oh, stop, he is good. He's always talking about *helping* people. Which is, you know—it's good. But he can actually *do* it, and it's what he wants." She touched his books. "Unlike the rest of us. Like me. I'm so *not* good it's not even funny."

He didn't know what to say to this. "You could teach."

"But I don't like kids. I don't know *what* I'll do, I'm so selfish. He's just so *good,* just categorically good. At least in that particular way."

"Good is good."

"But the thing is, he's *too* good sometimes. In that way. *Socially* good. It's like an act sometimes. Especially . . ."

He waited. "Well, badness is good, too, now and then."

"For a change," she said.

"Exactly."

"Mostly he *is* good," she insisted, "and he can't help it. So don't make fun of him."

"I'm not."

"Yes, you are. You always do. It's because of his silly name."

"Like I'm one to talk."

"I like your name. It's exotic. Not like *Elmer.*"

"Forget his name for once."

"But I can't!" she cried. "Elmer Grand!"

Neither had a car, but when a friend of hers drove to Cleveland after Valentine's Day, Aldo came along, squished in the back seat beside Miranda, their arms mashed together and their legs touching from the hip down. For comfort's sake he extended his arm along the back of the seat. They could almost have been a couple. And her beauty, despite his familiarity with it, had not faded. In fact, under the red neon of the Flats bars, he could hardly look at her. But she talked constantly of Elmer, and her frail ring darted in and out of the light. She irritated him. And he wondered what he was doing here, in the racket of the bar—what he hoped for. Nothing, plainly, would come of any of this. It was foolish to think otherwise. She got up to dance, and Aldo, unable to watch, stayed at the table.

But she sat happily beside him on the way back, smelling of cigarettes. "I forgot to tell you," she whispered, her mouth close to his ear, "Elmer's coming to visit."

"Good," he said. "Have a good time." Outside, the flat, frozen landscape sped past in darkness, and the warm air in the car had taken on a beery, hopeless sort of stink. Drunk, he began to feel a little sick. Jacqueline, on the other side of Miranda, slept, her skull rolling against the window.

"I want you to meet him. You've got a lot in common."

At least one thing, he thought. "I'll look forward to it."

"You'd like him."

"Okay."

"You sound reluctant."

"Let me know when he's coming."

"Why? So you can get sick, I guess."

"No, so I can leave town." Daringly he added, "And take you with me."

In the darkness she said, "Very funny."

"I mean it."

"If you really meant it," she said, "you wouldn't be sitting here."

"I wouldn't?"

"No. You'd be somewhere else. Alone with me."

"I've always figured that was impossible."

"I know you have." She put a hand on his leg. "That's what I like about you."

"No, what you like," he said, "is that I hang around and adore you, and don't make things awkward by making passes at you, which you would be duty-bound to deflect."

"Oh, duty," she said. Spitefully she removed her hand from his thigh. " 'New occasions teach new duties.' "

"You can keep that there."

She turned to look at him, her face dark in the darkened car. Her lips were close to his. "I thought I was duty-bound."

"You've always thought so until now."

"How do you know what I've thought?"

"I know what you tell me," he said.

"Oh—you won't get far that way. Being good." She leaned and kissed him carefully, just once, and sat back again, hand on his leg. Then she took her hand back. No one had noticed. The car motored on dumbly into the night.

"I—" he began.

"No, I'm sorry. I won't do that again," she said, her face turned away.

He leaned to kiss her, but caught only the side of her cheek.

"Please don't," she said. "Please."

He tried again.

"Please, Aldo. I'm sorry."

Touching from hip to calf, they rode the rest of the way home in silence. Drunk, he thought. But still, this was unfair. When he climbed alone from the car, the first to get out, he called his good-nights to everyone, but Miranda said nothing: she merely slid over away from Jacqueline, glanced up at him with her apologetic, beautiful eyes, and closed the door.

After this, she stopped returning his calls. When he encountered her by chance in the library, she seemed always to be idling—killing time. She was still as lovely as ever, but she appeared, to his eyes, preoccupied, as though she had been caught in the dragging middle of one of her gigantic novels. He felt he had missed some opportunity—that had he been more forceful earlier, been more daring, he might have won her, and he regretted his weeks of inaction. But he had only been behaving decently, he told himself, and no one could blame him for that. On the other hand, hadn't he been waiting, vulture-like, for the engagement to be miraculously broken off, so he could snatch Miranda before she touched the earth? And how could that be considered decent behavior? In fact, wasn't he both timid and sleazy—and who would ever bother over a man like that?

By the middle of April the winter had rounded nicely into an early spring, and the elms, so long dormant, had begun again to bud, acquiring a faint green haze. Elmer Grand had come and gone sometime in March, or so Aldo heard: he had fallen that quickly from her circle. He continued to avoid Eleanor and Bram, and in the meantime Cambyses invaded Egypt from Persia, crossing the Arabian desert to engage Psammenitus at the mouth of the Nile. Years after the battle had been fought, Herodotus walked the battlefield, the dry bones of the fallen still divided, as the bodies had been, into Persian and Egyptian camps. "Yes," said Feingold, "the *skulls,* exactly, of the Persians, are so thin that the merest touch, *epaphes,* with a pebble will pierce them, but the skulls of the Egyptians are so tough . . ."

". . . that it is hardly possible . . ."

Feingold put a narrow hand on the back of his head. "Wait," he said. A look of concern crossed his face. "The skulls . . ."

"That it is hardly possible," Aldo continued, "to break them with a blow from a stone."

"Yes," said Feingold, puzzled.

"Right?"

"Oh—yes," he said again. "Do you know what I was thinking? How much I would like a drink just now."

"Now?"

"And I don't drink," said Feingold. "I haven't for years. I quit twenty years ago, and since then I've been clean. And now suddenly I need a gin and tonic. Out of the blue." He laid his text gently on his desk. "I was a terrible drunk, you know."

"No."

"Oh, I was. Terrible. I stopped because I nearly killed myself. My liver was calcifying, or whatever it is that happens to livers. Lithifying. And I was just careening all over the country." A look of great distance had entered Feingold's eyes. "I never thought I'd get to be this old. I'm seventy-one." He narrowed his expression. "You're a calm boy."

"Calm," said Aldo. "I guess so."

"No, that's good. I don't mean to put you on the spot. I *wasn't* calm, is what I mean."

"But here you are."

Feingold nodded, once. "Yes, here I am. And almost dead, anyway."

"No getting around it."

"No. A cruel thought, but true. Are you a Jew?"

"Me? No," said Aldo. "I'm not."

"No? I thought you and I . . ." Feingold in his sky-blue jacket shrugged. "A Christian?"

"No."

"Nothing at all?"

"I guess not," said Aldo.

"Do you believe in an afterlife?"

"Not really."

"But maybe a little bit?"

"I would like to," he said, "but it seems a little delusional."

"Awfully attractive, though, isn't it? Imagine."

Aldo hesitated. "I believe in grace."

"Oh: grace. Are you Catholic?"

"No, just"—it was inexpressible—"happiness."

"Oh. Well, good. Happiness is good."

"But not *only* happiness . . . *grace,*" he said, ferociously. But worryingly he had not felt it in weeks, and it felt like bad luck mentioning it out loud. "It's the only word. When you know your place in the world."

"Yes; I remember the feeling."

"The beauty," said Aldo. "Something about all . . ." He gestured. But it was eluding him. "Everything being *where* it is, in *time,* in the right proportions. *Beauty.* When things are perfect."

"That which is immortal in us."

"Well—"

"That's grace. And then you get to sin: the sullying of that goodness. But to begin with, starting out, *now,* say, for you, that which is immortal is inherently good, by definition."

"But not all goodness is immortal."

Feingold picked up his book again. "I believe in an afterlife," he said, "because it gives me solace, and because so many people have believed in it before me. If it is a delusion then it is an old and very decent delusion. But people are starting to come back now, with this new technology." He looked away. "That tunnel of light."

"I've heard there's a biological explanation for it."

"Well."

"Dopamine, or something."

"Well, go fuck yourself, Aldo," said Feingold, mildly, "if you can't let an old man believe what he needs to."

"Sorry. That's what I've read. It's all biological."

"Well, go fuck yourself, anyway," said Feingold, with more force. He closed his book. "Just wait till you're my age. Then you'll be happy? I don't think so."

"I'm sorry."

"You should be." Feingold reclined, looked away. "There are other people in the universe, Aldo," he said. "Pay attention."

That afternoon, feeling guilty and ashamed, and sickened by Bram's grunting, Aldo called Miranda. She picked up immediately. "Why, it's Aldo," she said, surprised. "The long-lost stranger."

"Ha," he said.

"Why haven't you been calling me?"

With some irritation he said, "I have been." And he had: once a week at least. Never home. Always got her housemates. "I've left messages."

She sighed. "I don't always check the machine."

"Well, I've been calling."

"I've got something to tell you, actually, Aldo. A little surprise."

"You do?" She'd broken it off, he thought. "What?"

"I think it's better said in person."

"Okay," he said. "There's a movie tonight."

"Fine."

"I won't do anything," he said. "Scout's honor."

"Oh, I wouldn't know a Boy Scout if I stepped on one."

"Really. I won't do anything."

"Fine," she said.

"Just so you know."

"I know, all right?"

"Good."

"So stop talking about it."

"I can't just not bring it up."

"Look," she said, "I'm sorry I didn't call."

"I was wondering about that."

"It was a stupid thing to do," she said. "I mean in the car. But I do like you."

"I know you do."

"Christ almighty," she said, and laughed. "You're so *somber.*"

Though he knew he had no right to be hopeful, he couldn't help it. With great devotion he shaved the smooth planes of his face in the befogged mirror. Flecks of white foam dotted his earlobes. Cowardly, he was. It was cowardly to see Miranda again, rather than forget about her. Or, if not cowardly, then indulgent. He was purposefully fooling himself. Lying.

But he lied all the time. Despite his protestations to Feingold he did believe—didn't he?—in something like an afterlife; but what an embarrassment to admit to it! Though if he believed in the soul, as he thought he did, then why not? The soul takes nothing with it into the next world, said Plato, except its education and culture. That was a gratifying thought. Silly and unscientific, but gratifying. The springy air puffed through the bathroom window, drying his hair. On the twilit walk across campus through the daffodils, he felt a little shimmering—a faint suggestion of the old feeling—though by the time he met her at the theater it had gone away again. He didn't mind, really. She was lovely, as she always was, waiting for him under the marquee in a yellow dress, holding a magazine, and abruptly he had the sensation that he was exchanging something—trading in, somehow, the ineffable for the tangible. The loose weave of her dress. "This won't be very good," she said.

"I suppose," he said, "we could go elsewhere."

"Like?"

"I don't know. Valentine's? No."

"So, look." She held out a hand. "I have a new ring."

It took a moment to understand. "You're married."

"We did it when he came in March. Downtown."

"Oh. Congratulations." A bitter disappointment rose in him. "That's the surprise."

She smiled. "I didn't want to tell you over the phone."

"He's a lucky man."

"I tell him that, too. We're doing the ceremony this summer, if you'd like to come."

"Maybe I would."

"You and your maybes. *Maybe* you would." They bought tickets.

"It might tear my heart out."

"Oh, Aldo, don't say that."

"You know it would. I don't think that's a secret."

"Well," she said, "I need my friends to be my friends."

"I'll do my best." He followed her down to their seats.

"You did promise."

"I know I did."

Her eyes were weak, and she disliked wearing glasses, so they sat near the front, leaning back in their seats to watch. The movie was bad, and to pass the time Aldo watched the lit-up clock over one of the exits, the second hand patiently sweeping the minutes away. The stain on the screen appeared and disappeared, and he watched it idly. Now and then their arms brushed. Her lovely arms, bare, shone in the white cinematic light. At last, hopelessly, he took her hand. Married, he thought, guiltily. But she allowed it. In the dark he studied the architecture of her fingers. Each one was long and finely articulated—like Eleanor's, he realized. The knuckles were boxy, like dice under the skin. The palm was slender. He heard her breathing beside him, little puffs through her nose. She whispered: "You promised."

"You don't mind," he replied.

"You're being bad."

"Yes I am."

"So am I, I guess."

He clasped her hand more tightly. He touched her wrist: his fingertips against the soft skin.

"I'm married," she told him.

"Big deal." He put his hand on her thigh. "This doesn't count."

"It doesn't?"

"No. We're just friends." He leaned and kissed her ear. "Doesn't count," he said. He had a terrific erection which pushed uncomfortably against his fly. He kissed her again. "Doesn't count."

"No," she said. She kissed him back, her lips narrow and firm.

When the movie ended they sat together and watched the credits. He counted names: three hundred sixty, and he could stand up and in the darkness rearrange himself without much embarrassment. Then she took his arm and led him through the rear exit, which opened onto the brick-walled alley. Against the wall they began kissing again. That he should be this close to her lovely face—that she should allow it—that she allowed his hands to travel unimpeded over her hips—all this was wonderful to him. At the same time he knew it was a crappy thing to do, and could lead to no good. In fact it was a very bad thing: but he didn't care.

"Miranda—"

"We shouldn't be doing this," she said.

"But you want to," he said, kissing her throat, "and I do, too."

"I almost told him no," she said.

"Don't talk."

"This is why I never called you."

"Good thing I called *you.*"

"I can't do this," she said, and kissed him again.

Presently they separated and walked hand-in-hand down the alley; when they reached the sidewalk they let go and walked hurriedly through town. It was balmy still, and though the sky was clear the horizon flashed with heat lightning, and the elm trees moved their limbs about in the warm wind.

"Come back to my place," he suggested. "It's a nice night."

"I shouldn't." She clasped her bare arms to her sides. "I shouldn't be doing any of this."

"But you want to," he said.

"All right. But we can't do anything."

"Fine," he said, blithely, "we won't."

"We will." She clasped his elbow. "I know we will."

"Not if you don't want to."

"It's not that," she said, "it's not that at all. Obviously."

They kept walking. As they reached the dark side streets, she took his arm again.

"So," he said.

She stopped abruptly. "I left my magazine back there."

"You want to go back?"

"Yes—no," she said. "Never mind."

Three blocks down they came to his little house sitting on its sloppy lawn. Lights were on inside. "People are home," he said.

She had grown momentarily timid. "That's all right."

He lifted the creaking screen door open. Upstairs, Bram had filled the hall with his sweaty stink, and Eleanor could be heard tamping away at her keyboard. "My housemates," he said, and ducked with her into his bedroom, and locked the door.

"What are their names?"

He told her. "Hear that?" He tipped his head at the wall. "He's lifting weights."

"So neat," she said, glancing around. "It's like a guest room."

"He does it all the time," he said.

"Who?"

"Bram."

"Why doesn't he go to the gym?"

"I don't know. They're actually both sort of gross."

She examined his bookshelf. "That's not very nice of you."

"I mean—I was late with the housing thing. I wouldn't have chosen them."

"That's not very nice, either."

"I'm being bad."

"No," she said, "you're *not* being *nice*. It's different."

He came up behind her and spoke into her ear. "It's not so different," he said. He put his hands on her hips.

"This is the only time this is going to happen," she said, turning to him. "We'll just get it out of our systems."

Bram set down something heavy on the floor. The screws in the book-case jingled.

She reached behind him to turn out the light. He opened the buttons on the back of her dress: the material was a light cotton, warmed by her skin. He took down her shoulder straps and the dress settled to the car-pet. In her white underwear she was much slimmer than he had imagined: the points of her pelvis rose in little knobs. He helped her with his shirt, which slid off him easily, like a jacket off a book. A shaft of orange light from the street entered through the uncurtained window and marked a square on the wall.

"You're so quiet," she said.

"So are you."

"I'm just—I feel like—" She threw out her arms. "Ta daa." Her little breasts bounced in her brassiere. "Such a performance this is."

"Well."

"So I'm proving something," she whispered, "and I know it, and after this it's forget it, right?" She set her jaw and peered at him. "Right?"

"Right."

Abruptly she reached behind her, unfastened her bra, then stepped out of her underpants. "Okay," she said, and stood naked. "You like this?"

He found it difficult to speak.

"So somber," she said again.

"I," he said.

She took off her ring, set it on the dresser. "Is that better?"

They climbed into bed together. He kissed her and took her breast in one hand, the nipple firm in his palm.

"What if I told you I wasn't married?"

"It wouldn't matter to me." Not true, exactly.

She was disappointed. "Not at all?"

"No. Maybe. I don't think so."

"Isn't it more fun if we're—if I am?"

"We should be quiet," he said, and turned on the radio. "The room-mates."

"You care about them?"

"No—"

Her nakedness had surprised him with its loveliness, the sweetness of the curve beneath her little white breasts, the inward dip of her flat, pale stomach, the fine wiry hair in unexpected abundance between her legs and across her lower belly. Beside him it tufted pleasantly against his leg.

"Well," she said, "your move."

"It matters to me that you're married," he said, "because I can't marry you."

"No, you can't."

"But that's all."

"He made me," she said, kissing his throat. "He said he'd leave me if I didn't do it. But this is showing him."

He didn't believe her; it didn't much matter. Still. "Don't do this for me."

"I wouldn't."

"You wouldn't?"

"No. This is for me."

"What if you weren't with—? Would you—would I—"

"Oh, don't ask me that," she said. "Please."

Hesitantly, he asked, "Do you use any—are you on—?"

"Yes," she said, blinking. "Yes, yes, yes."

Stupidly he felt as though he might cry; but he stopped it, and turned up the radio, which crackled with the approaching lightning. Shifting his weight, he moved atop her. "Just—?" he asked.

"Aldo," she said.

His name in her mouth thrilled him. "What?"

"Nothing."

"What?"

"No," she said, "I just wanted to say it."

"Say it again."

She did, and he slid easily into her. Smooth and easy, all the way to the bottom.

"There." She smiled up at him from her tousle of hair. "Feel better?"

"You do. Don't lie."

"Yes, I do," she said, *"Aldo."*

"Don't—" He felt himself letting go, pulled back.

"Your own name," she said. "What narcissism."

"Let's not talk."

"My voice?" she asked. "Or is it just your name?"

"No."

"Which one?"

"It's neither."

She laughed, "Aldo!" Loud enough to be heard.

He would make her stop, he thought. "Elmer," he said.

"Okay," she said, wincing. "Don't."

"Don't? Elmer Grand."

"Oh—truce."

"Elmer Grand."

"Truce!"

"Truce," he said.

"You're terrible." She shifted beneath him, locked her legs at the backs of his knees, and pressed upward. "You're so terrible—so bad."

He supposed he was. And if that was what she wanted, then he would say so. "Both of us. You're bad, too," he said. "You're so bad."

"I am?"

"So bad," he said.

"Oh, yes—yes." She grimaced menacingly, eyes shut. "Fuck," she said, "fuck, fuck, fuck—"

Slipping in and out of Miranda he felt—as he had felt before, with other women—that he was exploring a city, an ancient clay-walled town, through the narrow streets, where various flags were hung out . . . She was very firm, and he fit her with a great precision. They sweated a good deal, and their bodies, in the humid room, smacked together like fish hitting a countertop. If it was really to be only one night—and he did not believe this, either—then they were making the most of it. The storm that had stood on the horizon hours ago had come across the countryside and now walked slowly through town, delivering five or six great crashing bolts of lightning which illuminated the room—enough to see Miranda, above him, working in a pose of great determination, gazing down not at his face but at some spot near his sternum. Why, he wondered, had she agreed to this? What did she want to prove? That she was desirable?—but no, that was only too plain. That she was unpredictable? This was closer; but he didn't know, and to his surprise he found he didn't know her well enough to guess.

"Let's do something," she told him, past two, "you've always wanted to do."

"This is about it," he said.

"Something else."

"Oh—"

She propped herself up on an elbow. In the darkness the whites of her eyes flashed. "Think," she said. "Out of our systems."

"Well—"

"That's the deal," she said. "We agreed."

"I know."

She sighed, lay back. "Do you want to tie me up?"

He laughed. "No."

"Do you want me to tie you up?"

"Not really."

"A little bit?"

"No," he said.

"What, then?"

"I don't know."

"I won't tell anyone," she said.

"How about—just—" he motioned, downward.

"Except that," she said.

"Not bad enough?"

"No, it's not bad at all," she said, "I just don't like it."

"Just a little," he said.

"I don't like it."

He said, "You should have said so."

"Maybe."

"Just a little."

She said, "A little."

"Okay, a little."

"Just once," she said.

"Okay."

Grimacing, she made her way down his abdomen. He was sore, slightly, and he flinched when she began, taking him half-erect into her mouth. And he felt it *was* dirty—particularly since she didn't like it. The thought excited him, very suddenly. He held her head. She twisted once, stopped. Quickly he came in her mouth. Extracting himself, he pressed his hand over her lips, over her nose. "Swallow," he said.

She twisted again.

"That's what I want," he said. It was. He knew it as he said it.

She made a sound. Spitting, she bit his hand. "Asshole," she said, hitting him.

"That's what I want."

"Asshole," she repeated. Freeing herself, she spat at him, wiped her mouth on his discarded shirt. "Fucking shithole asshole." Spat again, wiped.

He sat up. "I just thought of it then," he said.

"You incredible fucking asshole." She dressed, retrieved her ring. "Fucking shithole. Jesus."

"I just realized it," he said. What had compelled him? He put on his underwear.

"Don't say anything." She pulled her dress over her shoulders. "I can't believe you."

"That was—"

"Don't say anything."

"I'm sorry—"

"You're supposed to *know,*" she said, "how to *behave.*"

"Stay."

"Oh, you fucking asshole," she said, loudly. "You unbelievable fucking asshole."

"Don't—they'll hear—"

"He hates you," she shouted, "he hates you both." She swung, hit him with the sole of her shoe. "Prick," she said. Barefoot, she walked downstairs. The screen door creaked and slammed.

After a moment Bram appeared in the hallway, dressed in his bikini underwear. He filled the corridor, huge.

"Sorry," said Aldo.

"Friend of yours?"

Aldo stepped back into his bedroom, closed the door.

Bram knocked. "Sounded bad," he said, through the door. "Woke me up."

"Sorry."

"Guys were loud."

"What about you and your weights?"

"You should try it. Lose that chub."

"Thanks."

Bram opened the door a crack. "Want to borrow them?"

"Not right this second."

"Whenever," said Bram. "You want a beer?"

"No."

"They're half Eleanor's," he whispered.

"No thanks."

"Say the word."

"Goodnight," said Aldo.

"Okay," said Bram, "goodnight."

It was essentially the last he saw of Miranda. He was ashamed of what he had done, and he was happy to avoid her when he could. He caught glimpses of her around campus, but they never spoke. Her friends eyed him unpleasantly. For the second time, she vanished from his life. Embarrassed and contrite, Aldo kept to himself. It was a terrible thing to have done, and he had done it, and couldn't forget it. All the talk about goodness, and *things being right,* and grace, seemed so much crap. And Feingold, though still genial, also withdrew.

After graduation Aldo moved back to Portland, believing he was only taking time off from his studies, that he would return soon enough, but he landed a job teaching Latin at a boys' school in town, and the pleasures of this, and a certain lassitude, kept him from leaving. The corridors smelled of wax and the heated air that came forced through vents in the floor. His classes, full of the sons of the rich and happy, were sedate, and the boys were, as a rule, at least well-informed about things, if not always interested or original. When he turned them loose at vacations, Aldo was sorry to see them go. "Goodbye, Fitch," he said, standing at the door, "and Gerard, and Lumber, and Poole, and Regent, and Franklin, and Vinton, and Chillingham," and they would ceremoniously shake his hand as they went out, loosening their ties. He was liked. The custodial staff knew his name, and Mike seemed genuinely affectionate when he arrived in the afternoon to sweep and empty the trash.

"Mr. Gorman."

"Mike."

"Not bad weather."

"Little sun," said Aldo.

"Oh, a little sun, not bad. Not bad at all."

But it was nothing like the grace he had known: no, that had gone, seemingly for good. He was essentially friendless in the dark, gloomy city, and he remembered his college days with a mixture of nostalgia and shame, a complicated shame that had to do with, first, not going on with his education, and second, with the way he had behaved that night with Miranda. He was not civilized, not at heart. No, he was not at heart a good person, and he had proved that. And as if in punishment he had been shunted onto this side track, a track occupied by others like him: Mr. Toobman, who taught history, a sour, balding homosexual who smelled of his lemony soap; Mrs. Graven, the shy, aged mathematics instructor whose throat was peppered with protuberant moles. Even Aldo, old before his time, had grown a gut and developed a persistent phlegmy cough. He was sick all the time. Some weeks he was mostly well, other times the cough racked him, and he would run a fever, which gave him harrowing dreams in which he grew to a terrific size, then shrank away to nothing. His heart raced, then beat lopsidedly, as though on three legs. Hacking into his handkerchief, he graded his exercises: *That friendly king did not remain there a long time. Our mothers had not understood the nature of that place.* He began to drink more, and thought of Feingold when he did. If this was his punishment, it was not the worst he could imagine; and at any rate he felt he deserved it. And at the same time he knew he was being stupid: that holding on to a little guilt in this way was a waste of time. Forget it, he told himself. But he didn't.

His cough worsened that spring, grew painful, and one weekend the fever knocked him down entirely. In his chilly Saturday apartment he poured sweat terribly into his sheets. From bed he watched the sky change through its stages of gray, one layer of cloud sliding aside sluggishly to reveal another, each darker than the last. It seemed a vision of terrible unhealth, and he grew afraid. Sleep came abruptly around noon, and he woke in darkness, in what felt like the middle of the night, with his heart racing. A gurgling escaped his lungs. He had no one to call. Next door his neighbor was hammering a nail into the plaster. Sitting up in bed he gasped for breath. It was just past dinnertime. Teetering against his dresser, he buttoned his pants with trembling hands. Outside in the parking lot the wind had picked up and blew through his hair, wind that smelled pleasantly of the river. It would not be so bad—he could take a week off. And he was not all that sick, really. But his fingernails on the steering wheel were so purple they looked bruised—and this frightened him—as though he had grasped too eagerly at something, and had it snatched away.

The clinic was empty, and he was seen almost at once by a doctor whose large masculine hands, covered with red hair, pressed the glands in his throat, his armpits, his groin. The doctor looked young, not yet thirty: Dr. Grieve. "Harvard," said Aldo, sighting the diploma.

"Yes."

"What're you doing here?"

"This is where I live." He peered into Aldo's eyes. "Do any drugs?"

"No."

"Drink?"

"Not much."

The doctor sighed. "Why do you ask? You know someone there?"

"Elmer Grand."

"Oh—Elmer Grand," said Dr. Grieve. "I know Elmer Grand."

"Really?"

The doctor peered into his ears. "Friend of yours?"

"No—I don't know him. I used to know his wife."

"Miranda?"

Startled, Aldo croaked, "Yes."

"Miranda. Breathe. In. Now hold it." He applied the stethoscope to Aldo's sternum. "Quite a girl."

He nodded.

"Out." There came a long pause. "Bronchitis," he said at last, "and sounds like pneumonia."

"How is Miranda?"

"Oh, well, fine," said the doctor. "Last I heard."

"No news?"

"Not that I know of. It's only a Christmas card sort of thing."

"Not—they're still together?"

"They were at Christmas."

"No children?"

"I don't know. I don't think so."

"Well," said Aldo.

Ruefully, Dr. Grieve said, "Elmer was a hound. Anything that walked."

Aldo said, "Really."

"Really. And I imagine she must have known."

"She never—I don't remember her mentioning it," he said.

"You knew her well, then."

"Pretty well. For a while."

"You're pretty sick," said Dr. Grieve. "This cough, how long?"

"I don't know. Months."

"Months? Two? Eight?"

"Six."

"Any blood?"

"No."

"What about your heart?"

"My heart?"

"This kind of long-term infection, it can get lodged in the heart valves. We see that now and then."

"It's been fine," he said.

"No palpitations? No irregularities?"

"Oh—" he said, "no." A current of dread moved through him.

"You're lucky, then."

"Okay," said Aldo. "Good."

"So: Elmer Grand."

"How many—" Aldo stopped. "He did it a lot, then."

"Slept around? Oh, all the time, Jesus. Sleep-deprived and still he'd be after it."

"But—"

"That's what he liked. Likes, still. Probably."

"So," said Aldo.

"You should take a week off. Keep warm. Get these filled. You'll feel better."

He hesitated. "And the heart—?"

"If anything unusual comes up, come back." He helped Aldo off the table. "Okay? All better."

And he did get better, more quickly than he imagined possible. His lungs cleared. His heart beat normally again, in sequence. His sleep, for the first time in months, was seamless. And by Thursday he was back at school. *"Copia?"* he asked.

"Abundance," said the class.

"Yes; *ratio?*"

"Judgment," they said.

"Yes; *duco?*"

"To lead," they said.

Well, it was something, these voices. Always answering. They hardly asked anything of you; and what they did ask, you could give. It was not the life he had wanted; but it was close, in some ways. He had his languages, and he had the afternoons to himself. He thought of Miranda now and then, but less often as time went on. He had lost his way to grace, that was true. Sometimes—driving over a high bridge, say, or waking up early on a bright Saturday—he felt a sort of echo, from what might have been his soul, and then he was sorry for what he had lost. But more often he felt sorry for that old figure of himself, waiting for grace to descend, afraid when it left him. No one could live that way, not forever. It was too much to expect of life. Always waiting. No; but he could work. A cedar tree outside the classroom window broke the sunlight, and the confetti of broken light played on the back wall of the room, where he could watch it in the afternoons. Doors closed, here and there, in the empty cavern of the school. The waxing machines murmured up and down the hallways. When Mike put down the trash can, it made a nice, hollow bonging sound; always he put it down on the wrong side of the door, and Aldo, before he left for the night, would put it back where it belonged.

Alice Elliott Dark

Watch the Animals

From *Harper's Magazine*

WE HAD a trying relationship with Diana Frick. She was a moneyed blue blood, the descendant of a signer, who could have been one of our old guard except that she spurned the role. Instead, she was interested in animals to the point of obsession, which in our part of the country was saying a lot. There were few among us who hadn't mourned a loyal dog or put out scraps for a stray cat or developed a smooth working relationship with a horse. Animals had a place in our lives, to be sure, and we took seriously our responsibilities toward them. But Diana went further and always had.

For decades she'd chosen the company of other species over companionship with her own kind, a preference we naturally took as a rejection. So after she was diagnosed with lung cancer and she began to seek homes for her menagerie in the event of her death, we didn't line up at her door. Why should we? We owed her nothing. Yet the woman was fading, and we'd known her all our lives. On the telephone, in the clubs, shops, and churchyards, we tried to decide what to do.

She first came around to plead her case in autumn, when the lanes swelled with bright leaves. We couldn't help but examine her for signs of the illness, but nothing much showed; she'd always been spare. Her eyes shone blue as ever, that was the main thing. She appeared without calling first, the way we used to do when we were liable to be having tea or drinks in the afternoon and could easily accommodate company. Now we were busy, but we didn't turn her away. Years of curiosity assured her a vigorous welcome.

"Let's sit outside," she said. "I've got the dogs, and I need a smoke." She noticed our raised eyebrows. "Well, I've got no reason not to smoke anymore, do I? I was planning to start again anyway when I turned eighty, but my schedule has been moved up a bit."

That was typical of her sense of humor—black, direct, laced with a stubbornly nonconformist aroma. We didn't smile, but she didn't care. "Where are your bird feeders?" she asked as we walked around to the back. "It's going to get cold soon."

Her voice rasped now rather than boomed, but it was still forceful. "You put the porch furniture away already? But it's only October! Oh, all right then, we'll sit on the grass."

She always brought along at least two of her dog pack and spoke to them in a high whine, to which they responded with a great deal of tongue-wagging enthusiasm. "Stop smiling!" she'd command. They'd shiver with pleasure. Often, she kissed them on their mouths.

When we were all settled and mugs of tea had been handed around, she made her play.

"I'm leaving money to cover their expenses," she told us. The days were over when it was considered impolite to talk about money, but she made her offer sound like a bribe. It was yet another example of how clumsy she was with people.

"I'll need a promise in return," she continued. "I don't want to have to look up from where I'll no doubt be burning to see them shunted around. If you take them, you keep them for the duration."

We said we'd think it over, then changed the subject. When would she begin treatments? we wondered.

"Statistically, my chances aren't much better with chemo and cutting than they are just twiddling my thumbs, so I'm not going to let them touch me." She shook her head in a manner that conveyed her through disapproval of standard medical remedies. Good old Diana. It was a conversation stopper. We fumbled to pat the dogs.

"They're incredible, aren't they?" She grinned at our attention to them. "I've got all the dogs working as therapy animals in nursing homes. They can relate to anybody. What heart they have, considering how they were treated. We should all be more like dogs when we grow up."

When we compared notes on these visits, we couldn't help but bristle. It wasn't that it was unheard of to put conditions on a request, or to shore up a good deed with a financial benefit, but to do so successfully required finesse and subtlety. People want to believe they are high-minded and generous, not greedy and bought. A good monger could have offered us the same deal in terms that would have us not only clamoring to agree to it but also feeling grateful she'd come to us.

Diana created no such feeling. The only positive we could find in her pitch was that at least she understood that her animals required incentives to make them palatable. Most of them were not pure breeds or even respectable mutts. She collected creatures that others had thrown away, the beasts left on the side of the highway or confiscated from horrific existences by her contacts at the ASPCA; the maimed sprung from labs; the exhausted retired from dog tracks; the unlucky blamed for the sins of the household and made to pay with their bodies, appetites, well-being. Immigrants from hell, she called them, and made a mission of acknowledging these crimes, beginning with naming them for their misfortunes. Thus a cat who'd been paralyzed by a motorcycle was called Harley; a dog whose leg had been chopped off by its owner earned the name Beaver Cleaver; a kitten whose eyes had been sewn shut as part of a research grant went by Kitty Wonder; and so on.

She took these animals that otherwise would have ended up euthanized at best, and she trained them and groomed them and nursed them and fed them home-cooked foods until—we had to admit—they bore a resemblance to the more fortunate of their species. They behaved, as far as we could tell. But from a practical standpoint, could they ever be considered truly trustworthy? Who knew what might set them off?

We had our children and grandchildren to consider, and guests, and pets of our own. It was not a commitment that could be made in a hurry. We told one another pretty much what we'd told her—that we'd think about it. That seemed a reasonable approach, everything considered. What else could she expect?

For a while we didn't see her much, but she became the central topic of conversation, a level of attention she'd earned several times before, usually when her books came out and we'd read or hear in interviews about her anti-hierarchical theories of nature, her view of animals that countered the harsh interpretations science ascribed to their behavior, and her sorrow at the ways of the world—i.e., *our* world. She wasn't as contentious now, but we didn't believe she'd softened underneath; perhaps she was finally being a little smart, that was all. She wanted a favor, and she knew that she wasn't likely to get it if she didn't participate to some degree in normal human relations.

For the benefit of younger generations and those new to town, at dinner parties and on Sunday walks, we repeated her story—that is, how her early years had seemed to us. Her childhood didn't offer much. Her parents were jolly enough, if often absent, but so were a lot of ours. She went to Miss Dictor's, also like a lot of us, and she rode, skated, danced. In fact, she was popular—with the boys, naturally, because of her looks, but also with the girls, among whom she was known as a good egg. Her coming-out party was of the spare-no-expense variety, and she shone even in the requisite ivory, a hard color to wear; but she overcame it with tan arms, the radical touch of a bracelet clasped high on her bicep, and her thick brown hair worn long and loose.

We assumed she'd follow the path we all walked: marriage to someone like-minded, a house of her own but similar to her parents', children raised with the traditions that she remembered fondly, all the little habits that connect one generation to the next. Nothing we could see in her indicated she was headed anywhere but in that direction. Then her brother, the heir, died in a sailing accident, and her direction changed.

Her parents had no other children, so her father had to face the prospect of leaving all that money, albeit in trust, to a woman. He let it be known far and wide that he was not happy about this. He never said a word about losing his son, but the death of the line and his name—his hand strayed north to massage his aching heart when he spoke of it.

"Don't be ridiculous," we told him. "Diana will have children, and they'll be your descendants."

"But they won't be Fricks," he said dolefully.

We felt sorry for Caroline, his wife, and could only imagine the style of second-class citizenship in which she must live. Our efforts to bring his thinking into the modern world made no dent, however. He died only a few years later, full of self-pity to the end. We hoped Caroline would then become a merry widow, but as often happens, she followed him shortly to the grave.

Diana got everything.

She had suitors, of course; beauty and money are an attractive combination. Every so often a fellow would say he believed he was getting somewhere with her, but it never panned out. When an interviewer later asked why she'd never married, she replied that from childhood she knew she had a vocation and couldn't afford the distraction of human love—spoken as if she were a nun. But her calling was low rather than high, down at the level of the animals, and we couldn't help but think it a delusion and a waste.

She was in her early twenties when her first book appeared, an anthropomorphic children's tale, simply yet effectively illustrated, that caught on well enough to lead to another, and more after that, until the series was a standard in every nursery, a basic christening gift. The world loved them; we alone were ambivalent. How could we not be? The characters were a barnyard of familiar types, replete with our habits and belittled by suggestions of inbreeding and snobbery. We saw ourselves drawn with a harsh, loveless pen and felt stung by her portrayal, especially as we were *proud* of her.

We never spoke to her about our sense of injury, however. As we did with our own children, we showed what support we could while we waited for the day when she'd come to us offering thanks or forgiveness or perhaps a smaller token of reconciliation—a recognition, in any case.

Meantime, she bought a piece of land close to town and made it into a gentleman's farm, pruning the trees away until she had rolling vistas and putting in a pond and an off-limits strip of sod next to it to accommodate the nesting habits of Canadian geese. In her forties, she took in a series of foster children and brought them to the club for swims. If she thought we'd complain, we disappointed her; instead, we offered to make calls for them to the schools, but she turned us down flat.

"I believe in public education," she scolded, as if we didn't.

We sighed and went back to waiting, though with diminishing hope.

Perhaps if she'd been average we might not have been so bothered by her hostility. Diana was marvelous, however, in exactly the way we admired most. Hers was an artless, natural beauty that managed to get by the envy of other women while arousing in the men a filial pride—a desire for her success and happiness, as well as for her. We admired her

work, too; the spirit of it if not the letter. We looked at her and saw ourselves at our best. She was the sum of our efforts over the last four hundred years in this country, and back into the past to Britain and the continent, Normandy, Saxony, the high, clear springs of our culture. We
wanted to be able to trot her out at our ceremonies, to have her bend her
long neck to the yoke of our charities and bow before our altars, cut ribbons at our dedication ceremonies, and stand side by side with us at our
weddings and confirmations and graduations.

That she cared so little about such gatherings was irksome, to say the
least. People scrabbled all their lives for just a fraction of what was hers
from the start, yet she didn't feel fortunate or grateful or privileged. She
preferred to be in her barn prying stones out of her horses' hooves or sitting motionless by a closet door watching a new litter of kittens pump
blindly at their mother. Those things were fine, in moderation. It was her
excess that we didn't understand. Or maybe it was the opposite; we understood it all too well and were afraid of it.

We'd taken to heart the often repeated caveat from our childhoods that
the elders applied to all manner of deviance—*think what would happen if
everyone behaved like that!* The consequence was never exactly specified;
for most of us, the implication of chaos and breakdown was enough. We
knew our own bad thoughts, after all, knew what we had to suppress. We
understood why we couldn't indulge our baser natures or the full range of
our whims; we might lose what we had if we did. How had it happened
that Diana didn't understand what was at stake?

The final straw came when Diana published her autobiography. At last
we learned her gripes about us, and they cast a wide net. She recounted
various instances of cruelty she'd observed as a child, among which were
incidents that had bothered us, too. None of us had applauded Harold
Johnson's shooting of his dog for eating the Thanksgiving turkey, nor were
we amused when someone nailed a cat through its feet to a plank of
wood. Yet did she extend to us any credit for empathy and shock? No. We
were a town without pity, a callous bunch who didn't realize, as she did,
that animals have feelings and souls. Would we get rid of one of our children for taking a long time to be toilet trained or shedding too much?
Would we call the police on a stranger for asking directions? Yet we per-
petrated these evil deeds on animals without thinking twice.

Her arguments were silly, but the book became a hit. Souls, she claimed. That was the crux of what she had to tell the world. As always, she pushed it beyond the beyond.

The next foray in her campaign consisted of a mailing, eight double-sided pages of pictures and descriptions of her menagerie. The cover page sported the title "Full Disclosure," and, as usual, Diana meant what she said. She was certainly no mistress of persuasion—we already knew that. Yet these pages set a new standard in their complete refusal to make even the smallest nod to the principles of salesmanship. Beneath a grainy picture of each animal she described their routines in detail—ear cleanings, pillings, and other noxious chores—as well as offered predictions as to what health problems they were likely to suffer in the future. Then there were their habits and eccentricities: this one had to drink from the tap in the kitchen, that one slept under the covers by Diana's knees, and on and on. For the armchair behaviorists among us, the document offered interesting anecdotal evidence of how creatures adapt to hardship and abuse versus luxury and pampering—not to mention what it revealed about Diana. No wonder she never went out!

After receiving these pages, we called to ask how she was. "Not bad, with the minor complication of stage four lung cancer," she replied.

Wasn't she doing anything at all?

"I'm killing the pain. Of course, they're queer about that, never want to give you enough. What difference does it make if you become addicted to opiates when you're riddled with the big C? I have my sources, though. Veterinary drugs are easy to come by."

We told her we knew lots of doctors and had ins at the university hospital if she'd like us to make a few calls. She responded by lecturing us on birds and their need of water in the winter; we could buy solar-heated birdbaths from such-and-such catalogues.

"So no decision yet?" she prompted.

Not yet, we replied.

"Don't wait too long, or I won't be around to hear it. But no pressure!" Ha ha ha.

Then she surprised us. We were at church for the children's choir service on Christmas Eve afternoon and were settling ourselves to the tune of the organist's prelude when Diana walked in and took a place on the aisle two-thirds of the way back. For the next few moments the old fieldstone nave rippled with elbowings and turnings around and head tiltings; immediately we began to compose comments for later about how she was the second-to-last person we expected to see there, as the old joke went— the last being Jesus. The organist struck the chord for the processional, but we took a beat longer to stand than was customary as we watched her kneel all the way to the ground to say her private prayer. How beautiful she was—the picture of devotion, like Jennifer Jones in *The Song of Bernadette*. Then we stood, and she disappeared beneath taller heads as the children came up the aisle clad in the garb of the ancient Israelites à la Italian medieval painting: drapes, drapes, drapes. They made faces and batted at the frankincense that one of the kings swung dramatically in a censer, and we gave them the usual pleased, encouraging smiles as they passed.

We loved them best, better than anything, but at that moment we were grateful when they were finally all up front posed in the familiar tableau so that we could gawk at Diana. It appeared that she'd bought a new suit for the occasion; we hadn't seen her legs in years. She participated fully in the service and afterward joined the crowd in the narthex who were waiting for children and grandchildren to drop backstage the raiments and contraints of their holy personae. We assumed she wanted to congratulate them on their performances, to play the village eccentric by speaking to them exclusively, but she turned quite amiably to us. "Such wonderful music," she said.

"We have a new organist," we informed her, though in fact he may have been well down the line since she was last there.

"Lovely," she said. Then the children appeared and loudly gave their insiders' versions of the pageant. Diana was lost in the mayhem as we walked outside.

Dark had fallen by then, but the day was strangely balmy; there was a low moon in the purple sky. It wasn't the Currier & Ives Christmas we all held as the ideal, but it was Christmas nonetheless. Our church was built of fieldstone. In the precincts of the churchyard, we may as well have been in the home counties. Even the graveyard did not betray us; the dates went back far enough to afford us a claim to a history and a past. We knew that the teenagers sometimes went there at night to try to spook themselves—but that seemed an impulse the flip side of Sunday morning, and the rector ignored them as long as they did no harm.

Many of us took a detour before going to our cars and walked for a few moments down the narrow pathways among the markers. Here were our parents, grandparents, ancestors. In spite of our tacit assumption that the here and now was the end of it, we found ourselves addressing them in our minds. "It's Christmas Eve again," we informed them, "and, as always, everything and nothing has changed." We didn't go in much for putting flowers on the graves, but it was seemly to stop for a moment of acknowledgment. It was a moment of calm before the revels, part of our yearly ritual.

Then Diana walked past us and made her way to the Frick family plot. We saw her bow her head and her hands rise to her face. We winced. We'd all had the thought when standing by those graves that we'd be there soon enough ourselves, but for Diana the time was imminent. She wasn't toying with history, as we were, but staring directly at her own extinction. It was natural, yes, but still awful. When she rejoined us, we could see the disease in her. Without benefit of the flattering church light, she appeared emaciated, her skin thin and gray.

"We're having cocktails at the Gardeners'. Why don't you come?" We didn't like the idea of her going home to an empty house. Not on Christmas. Even by choice.

She smelled like our adolescent girls who put vanilla on their pulse points in the summer.

"I thank you very much," she said, "but I have mouths to feed."

She said this plainly, imbuing it with no hint. Yet the spirit of the day was in us, and the favor she'd asked seemed logical rather than an imposing chore.

Laddie Phillips spoke first. "Look," he said. "I'll take that greyhound. Rescued from a dog track, was he?"

Mina Jones, never one to be outdone, instantly said she'd take two cats—*at least,* she added, affording her room to maneuver in case anyone displayed a more impressive generosity.

Ben Knowlton, home from college, asked for the pit bull.

"The Staffordshire terrier," Diana instructed. Then, as if coaching herself to be agreeable, she gave a shake of her head that ended in a softening of her expression. "But perhaps it's a good thing to say pit bull. You and she can be ambassadors for the breed."

And so it went until nearly every animal was spoken for and promises made to find placements for the rest.

"So how about that drink?" we offered again. There was a pause. How could she refuse? She couldn't, and, finally, she understood that. She followed us out of the parking lot.

The next morning, after all the presents had been opened and the wrapping paper was blazing in the fireplace, we felt the usual letdown, not the smallest part of which was regret for having acted so impulsively with Diana. By lunchtime, however, we felt ourselves again and glad of our gesture. We'd opened a door that had been locked for decades. It seemed a good omen for the new year.

After that, we began calling to ask how she was. Soon, without calling first, we stopped by to drop off leftovers. We offered to take her dogs for a walk so she didn't have to go out in the rain. In other words, we did all in our power to show her that even if she had never taken our side, we were nevertheless on hers.

At first, predictably, she declined, and when we wouldn't hear of it, she flat-out refused our ministrations.

"Go away," she'd shout when we knocked on her windows. It was quite a picture, seeing this frail shrinking creature waving her bird arms at us, as if she could keep us out. We no longer took it personally. She was dying, and there was no time to dwell on slights or insults, no room for the luxuries of holding grudges and taking offense. She needed us at last, and her need was as good as an apology. We took her keys to the hardware store and made copies, then set up a schedule of rotating shifts so that except for at night after we'd tucked her into bed she was never alone. It was a lot of work, but it was what we'd do for any sister or mother or aunt; it was simply right.

The one difficulty was her habit of sleeping with all the dogs in her bedroom. We didn't think it was safe; if any one of them knocked her over, her bones would surely shatter. Before we left we put them in their cages, but when we arrived the next morning there they were, on her bed and all along the walls like wainscoting. No matter how patiently we explained the danger to her, she persisted in sneaking downstairs at night and letting them up.

"We're going to have to put you in a nursing home if you don't take care of yourself," we told her. We said it out of exasperation, the way we told the children that Santa wouldn't come if they were bad.

"Dogs go off on their own to die," she said.

"You're not a dog." It was like talking to a child, and we became child-ish ourselves, doing it. We wanted to wring her skinny neck.

"Leave me alone," she said.

We were tempted, but we couldn't. She had no one else.

One early spring morning the house seemed unnaturally quiet. Usually Diana had let the dogs out by the time we arrived. It was the one part of her old routine she maintained even after she'd become too weak to man-age their heavy bowls of food and water anymore. In our experience, she'd never kept them waiting past seven. And so we knew.

We weren't squeamish, yet we tiptoed up the stairs and approached her room with trepidation. We needn't have worried, though. The scene, when we finally faced it, was peaceful. Diana had that mythic look of death that apes sleep, while the absence of her singular spirit made the room feel empty. The only disturbing note was that the dogs were still with her—the large ones in their customary spots along the walls and the smaller creatures arrayed around her on the bed like a wreath. When we entered, they eyed us lugubriously.

"Out!" we commanded, but they didn't move.

Then we forgot them for some time as we began to piece together de-tails we'd overlooked at first glance. We pulled the curtains and, in the early light, saw that a crust of powder ringed her lips, and scattered on the bedside table and the floor below lay dozens of gelatin capsules, all of them opened and empty. How typical of Diana to do things her way, re-gardless of any constraints of law or ethics. Yet we didn't disapprove of her for it. It was her choice, we decided, as we would want it to be for our-selves. There was no reason for anyone else to know, however. The world at large isn't always as understanding as one's own kind, and we feared they might judge her weak or criminal. We cleaned up the pill bottles, washed out the glass, and tucked the note she'd left in a pocket for dis-posal at home. She hadn't written much anyway, just three words: *Watch the dogs.* It was an odd exhortation, as we'd already agreed to it. It re-minded us, though, that they were still in the room.

"Shoo!" we ordered, with no luck. Then someone recalled the ironic command Diana used when she wanted them to hop in their crates. It might at least get them downstairs, where we could deal with them more easily.

"Prison time!" we said, imitating her singsong way of speaking to them. The phrase got *some* results; they stood and walked to the door. Then they stopped, though, and simply stared. Was there another command we should be giving? We racked our brains. Meanwhile, it was eerie how they looked at us. It was as if they understood they'd never see her again, and that within the day they'd be in strange houses, separated from one another, adjusting to new circumstances and people and demands.

"Prison time!" we said again.

This time they seemed ready to obey, but not before taking what appeared to be a last look back at Diana. Was it possible they had an inkling of what was happening? No doubt they recognized death; but the idea that they might feel grief was another matter. That was a notion from Diana's realm, not ours. We'd interpret the dogs' baleful behavior as consternation at a disruption in their routine. Diana would say they were bereft. Who was right? It occurred to us that the greatest tribute we could pay her would be to give her, for once, the benefit of the doubt. (Perhaps the only tribute, for she'd always said she wouldn't be caught dead having a funeral.) And why not? What could we lose by extending them our empathy; what would we gain by holding back? We afforded them a moment of silence. What went on during that time we would never know. The way they looked at us afterward, though: we didn't believe in an afterlife, not a corporeal one at least, but in spite of ourselves, we hoped she could see.

Finally we coaxed them outside and began to notify everyone. The man at the *New York Times* had a file on Diana already and rang back to verify the details.

"Name of hospital?" he asked.

Oh no, we said, no hospital, none of that. On the contrary, the end was quite soulful, what we'd all like when the time comes—to die at home, during sleep, surrounded by friends.

Raymond Carver

Kindling

From *Esquire*

IT WAS the middle of August and Myers was between lives. The only thing different about this time from the other times was that this time he was sober. He'd just spent twenty-eight days at a drying-out facility. But during this period his wife took it into her head to go down the road with another drunk, a friend of theirs. The man had recently come into some money and had been talking about buying into a bar and restaurant in the eastern part of the state.

Myers called his wife, but she hung up on him. She wouldn't even talk to him, let alone have him anywhere near the house. She had a lawyer and a restraining order. So he took a few things, boarded a bus, and went to live near the ocean in a room in a house owned by a man named Sol who had run an ad in the paper.

Sol was wearing jeans and a red T-shirt when he opened the door. It was about ten o'clock at night and Myers had just gotten out of a cab. Under the porch light Myers could see that Sol's right arm was shorter than his other arm, and the hand and fingers of the right arm were withered. He didn't offer either his good left hand or his withered hand for Myers to shake, and this was fine with Myers. Myers felt plenty rattled as it was.

You just called, right? Sol said. You're here to see the room. Come on in.

Myers gripped his suitcase and stepped inside.

This is my wife. This is Bonnie, Sol said.

Bonnie was watching TV, but she moved her eyes to see who it was coming inside. She muted the TV with the remote, then turned it off altogether. Then she got up off the sofa onto her feet. She was a fat girl. She was fat all over and she huffed when she breathed.

I'm sorry it's so late, Myers said. Nice to meet you.

It's all right, Bonnie said. Did my husband tell you on the phone what we're asking?

Myers nodded. He was still holding the suitcase.

Well, this is the living room, Sol said, as you can see for yourself. He shook his head and brought the fingers of his good hand up to his chin. I may as well tell you that we're new at this. We never rented a room to anybody before. But it's just back there not being used, and we thought what the hell. A person can always use a little extra.

I don't blame you a bit, Myers said.

Where are you from? Bonnie said. You're not from anywhere around town.

My wife wants to be a writer, Sol said. Who, what, where, why, and how much?

I just got here, Myers said. He moved the suitcase to his other hand. I got off the bus about an hour ago, read your ad in the paper, and called up.

What sort of work do you do? Bonnie wanted to know.

I've done everything, Myers said. He set the suitcase down and opened and closed his fingers. Then he picked up the suitcase again.

Bonnie didn't pursue it. Sol didn't either, though Myers could see he was curious.

Myers took in a photograph of Elvis Presley on top of the TV. Elvis's signature ran across the breast of his white sequined jacket. He moved a step closer.

The King, Bonnie said.

Myers nodded but didn't say anything. Alongside the picture of Elvis was a wedding picture of Sol and Bonnie. In the picture Sol was dressed up in a suit and tie. Sol's good strong left arm reached around Bonnie's waist as far as it would go. Sol's right hand and Bonnie's right hand were joined over Sol's belt buckle. Bonnie wasn't going anywhere if Sol had anything to say about it. Bonnie didn't mind. In the picture Bonnie wore a hat and was all smiles.

I love her, Sol said, as if Myers had said something to the contrary.

How about that room you were going to show me? Myers said.

I knew there was something we were forgetting, Sol said.

They moved out of the living room into the kitchen, Sol first, then Myers, carrying his suitcase, then Bonnie. They passed through the kitchen and turned left just before the back door. There were some open cupboards along the wall, and a washer and dryer. Sol opened a door at the end of the little corridor and turned on the light in the bathroom.

Bonnie moved up and huffed and said, This is your private bathroom. That door in the kitchen is your own entrance. Sol opened the door to the other side of the bathroom and turned on another light.

This is the room, Sol said.

I made up the bed with clean sheets, Bonnie said. But if you take the room you'll have to be responsible from here on out.

Like my wife says, this is not a hotel, Sol said. But you're welcome, if you want to stay.

There was a double bed against one wall, along with a nightstand and lamp, a chest of drawers, and a pinochle table with a metal chair. A big window gave out onto the backyard. Myers put his suitcase on the bed and moved to the window. He raised the shade and looked out. A moon rode high in the sky. In the distance he could see a forested valley and mountain peaks. Was it his imagination, or did he hear a stream or a river?

I hear water, Myers said.

That's the Little Quilcene River you hear, Sol said. That river has the fastest per-foot drop to it of any river in the country.

Well, what do you think? Bonnie said. She went over and turned down the covers on the bed, and this simple gesture almost caused Myers to weep.

I'll take it, Myers said.

I'm glad, Sol said. My wife's glad, too, I can tell. I'll have them pull that ad out of the paper tomorrow. You want to move in right now, don't you?

That's what I hoped, Myers said.

We'll let you get settled, Bonnie said. I gave you two pillows, and there's an extra quilt in that closet.

Myers could only nod.

Well, good night, Sol said.

Good night, Bonnie said.

Good night, Myers said. And thank you.

Sol and Bonnie went through his bathroom and into the kitchen. They closed the door, but not before Myers heard Bonnie say, He seems okay.

Pretty quiet, Sol said.

I think I'll fix buttered popcorn.

I'll eat some with you, Sol said.

Pretty soon Myers heard the TV come on again in the living room, but it was a very faint sound and he didn't think it would bother him. He opened the window all the way and heard the sound of the river as it raced through the valley on its way to the ocean.

He took his things out of the suitcase and put them away in the drawers. Then he used the bathroom and brushed his teeth. He moved the table so that it sat directly in front of the window. Then he looked at where she'd turned the covers down. He drew out the metal chair and sat down and took a ballpoint out of his pocket. He thought for a minute, then opened the notebook, and at the top of a blank white page he wrote the words *Emptiness is the beginning of all things*. He stared at this, and then he laughed. Jesus, what rubbish! He shook his head. He closed the notebook, undressed, and turned off the light. He stood for a moment looking out the window and listening to the river. Then he moved to get into bed.

Bonnie fixed the popcorn, salted it and poured butter over it, and took it in a big bowl to where Sol was watching TV. She let him help himself to some first. He used his left hand to good effect and then he reached his little hand over for the paper towel she offered. She took a little popcorn for herself.

What do you make of him? she wanted to know. Our new roomer.

Sol shook his head and went on watching TV and eating popcorn. Then, as if he'd been thinking about her question, he said, I like him all right. He's okay. But I think he's on the run from something.

What?

I don't know that. I'm just guessing. He isn't dangerous and he isn't going to make any trouble.

His eyes, Bonnie said.

What about his eyes?

They're sad eyes. Saddest eyes I ever saw on a man.

Sol didn't say anything for a minute. He finished his popcorn. He wiped his fingers and dabbed his chin with the paper towel. He's okay. He's just had some trouble along the way, that's all. No disgrace attached to that. Give me a sip of that, will you? He reached over for the glass of orange drink that she was holding and took some. You know, I forgot to collect the rent from him tonight. I'll have to get it in the morning, if he's up. And I should have asked him how long he intends to stay. Damn, what's wrong with me? I don't want to turn this place into a hotel.

You couldn't think of everything. Besides, we're new at this. We never rented a room out before.

Bonnie decided she was going to write about the man in the notebook she was filling up. She closed her eyes and thought about what she was going to write. *This tall, stooped—but handsome!—curly headed stranger with sad eyes walked into our house one fateful night in August.* She leaned into Sol's left arm and tried to write some more. Sol squeezed her shoulder, which brought her back to the present moment. She opened her eyes and closed them, but she couldn't think of anything else to write about him. Time will tell, she thought. She was glad he was here.

This show's for the birds, Sol said. Let's go to bed. We have to get up in the morning.

In bed, Sol loved her up and she took him and held him and loved him back, but all the time she was doing it she was thinking about the big, curly headed man in the back room. What if he suddenly opened the bedroom door and looked in on them?

Sol, she said, is this bedroom door locked?

What? Be still, Sol said. Then he finished and rolled off, but he kept his little arm on her breast. She lay on her back and thought for a minute, then she patted his fingers, let air out through her mouth, and went off to sleep thinking about blasting caps, which is what had gone off in Sol's hand when he was a teenager, severing nerves and causing his arm and fingers to wither.

Bonnie began to snore. Sol took her arm and shook it until she turned over on her side, away from him.

In a minute, he got up and put on his underwear. He went into the living room. He didn't turn on the light. He didn't need a light—the moon was out, and he didn't want a light. He went from the living room into the kitchen. He checked to make sure the back door was locked, and then he stood for a while outside the bathroom door listening, but he couldn't hear anything out of the ordinary. The faucet dripped—it needed a washer, but then, it always dripped. He went back through the house and closed and locked their bedroom door. He checked the clock and made sure the stem was pulled. He got into bed and moved right up against Bonnie. He put his leg over her leg, and in that way he finally went to sleep.

These three people slept and dreamed, while outside the house the moon grew large and seemed to move across the sky until it was out over the ocean and growing smaller and paler. In his dream, someone is offering Myers a glass of Scotch, but just as he is about to take it, reluctantly, he wakes up in a sweat, his heart racing.

Sol dreams that he is changing a tire on a truck and that he has the use of both of his arms.

Bonnie dreams that she is taking two—no, three—children to the park. She even has names for the children. She's named them just before the trip to the park. Millicent, Dionne, and Randy. Randy keeps wanting to pull away from her and go his own way.

Soon, the sun breaks over the horizon and birds begin calling to each other. The Little Quilcene River rushes down through the valley, shoots under the highway bridge, rushes another hundred yards over sand and sharp rocks, and pours into the ocean. An eagle flies down from the valley and over the bridge and begins to pass up and down the beach. A dog barks.

At this minute, Sol's alarm goes off.

Myers stayed in his room that morning until he heard them leave. Then he went out and made instant coffee. He looked in the fridge and saw that one of the shelves had been cleared for him. A little sign was scotch-taped to the shelf: MR. MYERS SHELF.

Later, he walked a mile toward town to a little service station he remembered from the night before that sold a few groceries. He bought milk, cheese, bread, and tomatoes. That afternoon, before it was time for them to come home, he left the rent money in cash on the table and went back into his own room. Late that night, before going to bed, he opened his notebook and on a clean page he wrote, *Nothing*.

He adjusted his schedule to theirs. Mornings he'd stay in the room until he heard Sol in the kitchen making coffee and getting his breakfast. Then he would hear Sol calling Bonnie to get up and then they'd have breakfast, but they wouldn't talk much. Then Sol would go out to the garage and start the pickup, back out, and drive away. In a little while, Bonnie's ride would pull up in front of the house, a horn would toot, and Bonnie would say, every time, I'm coming.

It was then that Myers would go out to the kitchen, put on water for coffee, and eat a bowl of cereal. But he didn't have much of an appetite. The cereal and coffee would keep him for most of the day until the afternoon, when he knew they would arrive home. He'd eat something else, a sandwich, then stay out of the kitchen for the rest of the time when they might be in there or in the living room watching TV. He didn't want any conversation.

She'd go into the kitchen for a snack the first thing after she got in from work. Then she'd turn on the TV and wait until Sol came in, and then she'd get up and fix something for the two of them to eat. They might talk on the telephone to friends, or else go sit outside in the backyard between the garage and Myers's bedroom window and talk about their day and drink iced tea until it was time to go inside and turn on the TV. Once he heard Bonnie say to someone on the telephone, How'd she expect me to pay any attention to Elvis Presley's weight when my own weight was out of control at the time?

They'd said he was welcome anytime to sit in the living room with them and watch TV. He'd thanked them but said, No, television hurt his eyes.

They were curious about him. Especially Bonnie, who'd asked him one day, when she came home early and surprised him in the kitchen, if he'd been married and if he had any kids. Myers had nodded. Bonnie had looked at him and waited for him to go on, but he hadn't.

Sol was curious, too. What kind of work do you do? he wanted to know. I'm just curious. This is a small town and I know people. I grade lumber at the mill myself. Only need one good arm to do that. But sometimes there are openings. I could put in a word, maybe. What's your regular line of work?

Do you play any instruments? Bonnie asked. Sol has a guitar, she said.

But I don't know how to play a guitar, Sol said. I wish I did.

Myers kept to his room, where he was writing a letter to his wife. It was a long letter and, he felt, an important letter. Perhaps the most important letter he'd ever written in his life. In the letter he was attempting to tell his wife that he was *sorry* for everything that had happened and that he hoped someday she would forgive him. *I would get down on my knees and ask forgiveness if that would help.*

After Sol and Bonnie had both left for the day, he sat in the living room with his feet on the coffee table and drank instant coffee while he read the newspaper from the evening before. Once in a while his hands trembled and the newspaper began rattling in the empty house. Now and then the telephone rang, but he never made a move to answer it. It wasn't for him, because nobody knew he was here.

Through his window at the rear of the house he could see up the valley to a series of steep mountain peaks whose tops were covered with snow, even though it was August. Lower down on the mountains, timber covered the slopes and the sides of the valley. The river coursed down the valley, frothing and boiling over rocks and under granite embankments until it burst out of its confines at the mouth of the valley, slowed a little, as if it had spent itself, then picked up strength again and plunged into the ocean. Days when Sol and Bonnie were gone, Myers sat in the sun in a lawn chair out back and looked up the valley toward the peaks. Once he saw an eagle soaring down the valley, and on another occasion he saw a deer picking its way along the riverbank.

He was sitting out there like that one afternoon when a big flatbed truck pulled up in the drive with a load of wood.

You must be Sol's roomer, the driver of the truck said. He was talking out the truck window.

Myers nodded.

Sol said to just dump this wood in the backyard and he'd take care of it from there, the driver said.

I'll move out of your way, Myers said. He took the chair and moved to the back step, where he stood and watched the driver of the truck back it up onto the lawn, then push something inside the cab until the truck bed began to elevate. In a minute, the six-foot logs began to slide off the truck bed and pile up on the ground. The bed rose even higher, and all of the logs rolled with a loud bang down onto the lawn.

The driver touched the lever again and the truck bed went back to its normal place. Then the driver revved his engine, honked, and drove away.

What are you going to do with that wood out there? Myers asked Sol that night. Sol was standing at the stove frying smelt when Myers surprised him by coming into the kitchen. Bonnie was in the shower—Myers could hear the water running.

Why, I'm going to saw it up and stack it, if I can find the time between now and September. I'd like to do it before the rain starts.

Maybe I could do it for you, Myers said.

You ever cut wood before? Sol said. He'd taken the frying pan off the stove and was wiping the fingers of his left hand with a paper towel.

I couldn't pay you anything for doing it, Sol said. It's something I was going to do anyway. Just as soon as I get a weekend to my name.

I'll do it, Myers said. I can use the exercise.

You know how to use a power saw? And an ax and an awl?

You can show me, Myers said. I learn fast. It was important to him that he cut the wood.

Sol put the pan of smelt back on the burner. Then he said, Okay, I'll show you after supper. You had anything to eat yet? Why don't you have a bite to eat with us?

I ate something already, Myers said.

Sol nodded. Let me get this grub on the table for Bonnie and me then, and after we eat I'll show you.

I'll be out back, Myers said.

Sol didn't say anything more. He nodded to himself, as if he was thinking about something else.

Myers took one of the folding chairs that was out back and sat down on it. He looked at the pile of wood and then up the valley at the mountain peaks that had the sun shining off the snow. It was nearly evening. The tops of the mountains thrust up into some clouds. Mist seemed to be falling from the clouds. He could hear the river crashing through the undergrowth down in the valley.

I heard talking, Myers overheard Bonnie say to Sol in the kitchen.

It's the roomer, Sol said. He asked me if he could cut up that load of wood out back.

How much does he want to do it? Bonnie wanted to know. Did you tell him we can't pay much?

I told him we can't pay anything. He wants to do it for nothing. That's what he said, anyway.

Nothing? She didn't say anything for a time. Then Myers heard her say, I guess he doesn't have anything else to do.

Later, Sol came outside and said, I guess we can get started now, if you're still game.

Myers got up out of the lawn chair and followed Sol over to the garage. Sol brought out two sawhorses and set them up on the lawn. Then he brought out a power saw. The sun had dropped behind the town. In another thirty minutes it would be dark. Myers rolled down the sleeves of his shirt and buttoned the cuffs. Sol worked without saying anything. He grunted as he lifted one of the six-foot logs and positioned it on the sawhorses. Then he began to use the saw, working steadily for a while. Sawdust flew. Finally he stopped sawing and stepped back.

You get the idea, he said.

Myers took the saw and nosed the blade into a length where Sol had left off. He found a rhythm and stayed with it. He kept pressing, leaning into the saw. In a few minutes, he had sawed through several logs, which dropped in sections onto the ground.

That's the idea, Sol said. You'll do, he said. He picked up two blocks of wood, carried them over, and put them alongside the garage.

Every so often—not every piece of wood, but maybe every fifth or sixth piece—you'll want to split it with the ax down the middle, Sol said. Don't worry about making kindling—I'll take care of that later. Just split about every fifth or sixth chunk. I'll show you. He propped the chunk up and, with a blow of the ax, split the wood into two pieces. You try it now, he said.

Myers stood the block on its end, just as Sol had done, and he brought the ax down and split the wood.

That's good, Sol said. He placed the chunks of wood alongside the garage. Stack them up about so high, and then come out this way with your stack. I'll lay some plastic sheeting over it once it's all finished. But you don't have to do this, you know.

It's all right, Myers said. I want to, or I wouldn't have asked.

Sol shrugged. Then he turned and went back to the house. Bonnie was standing in the doorway, watching, and Sol stopped in the doorway, too, reached his arm around Bonnie, and they both looked at Myers.

Myers picked up the saw and looked at them. He felt good suddenly, and he grinned. Sol and Bonnie were taken by surprise at first. Sol grinned back, and then Bonnie. Then she and Sol went back inside.

Myers put another piece of wood on the sawhorses and worked awhile, sawing, until the sweat on his forehead began to feel chill and the sun had gone down. The porch light came on. Myers kept on working until he'd finished the piece he was on. He carried the two pieces over to the garage and then he went in, used his bathroom to wash up, then sat at the table in his room and wrote in his notebook. *I have sawdust in my shirt sleeves tonight,* he wrote. *It's a sweet smell.*

That night he lay awake for a long time. Once he got out of bed and looked out the window at the mound of wood which lay in the backyard, and then his eyes were drawn up the valley to the mountains. The moon was partially obscured by clouds, but he could see the peaks and the white snow, and when he raised his window, the sweet, cool air poured in, and farther off he could hear the river coursing down the valley.

The next morning it was all he could do to wait until they'd left the house before he went out back to begin work. He found a pair of gloves on the back step that Sol must have left for him. He started up the saw and went back and forth sawing and splitting wood until the sun was directly over his head. Then he went inside and ate a sandwich and drank some milk.

When he went back outside and began again, he noticed that his shoulders hurt and his fingers were sore. In spite of the gloves, he'd picked up a few splinters and could feel blisters rising, but he kept on. He decided that he would cut this wood and split it and stack it before sunset, and that it was a matter of life and death that he do so. I must finish this job, he thought, or else . . . He stopped to wipe his sleeve over his face.

By the time Sol and Bonnie came in from work that night—first Bonnie, as usual, and then Sol—Myers was nearly through. A thick pile of sawdust lay between the sawhorses, and, except for two or three blocks of wood still in the yard, all of the wood lay stacked in tiers against the garage. Sol and Bonnie stood in the doorway without saying anything. Myers looked up from his work for a minute and nodded, and Sol nodded back. Bonnie just stood there looking, breathing through her mouth. Myers kept on.

Sol and Bonnie went back inside and began their supper. Afterwards, Sol turned on the porch light, as he'd done the evening before. Just as the sun went down and the moon appeared over the mountains, Myers split the last chunk and gathered up the two pieces and carried the wood over to the garage. He put away the sawhorses, the power saw, the ax, a steel splitting wedge, and the awl. Then he went inside.

Sol and Bonnie sat still at their table, but they hadn't begun on their food.

You better sit down and eat with us, Sol said.

Sit down, Bonnie said.

I'm not hungry just yet, Myers said.

Sol didn't say anything. He nodded. Bonnie waited a minute and then reached for a platter.

You got it all, I'll bet, Sol said.

Myers said, I'll clean up that sawdust tomorrow.

Sol moved his knife back and forth over his plate as if to say, Forget it.

I'll be leaving in a day or two, Myers said.

Somehow I figured you would be, Sol said. I don't know why I felt that, but I didn't think somehow when you moved in you'd be here all that long.

No refunds on the rent, Bonnie said.

Hey, Bonnie, Sol said.

It's okay, Myers said.

No, it isn't, Sol said.

It's all right, Myers said. He opened the door to the bathroom, stepped inside, then shut the door. As he ran water into the sink he could hear them talking out there, but he couldn't hear what they were saying.

He showered, washed his hair, and put on clean clothes. He looked at the things of his in the room that had come out of his suitcase just a few days ago, a week ago, and figured it would take him about ten minutes to pack up and be gone. He could hear the TV start up on the other side of the house. He went to the window and raised it and looked again at the mountains, with the moon lying over them—no clouds now, just the moon, and the snowcapped mountains. He looked at the pile of sawdust out in back and at the wood stacked against the shadowy recesses of the garage. He listened to the river for a while. Then he went over to the table and sat down and opened the notebook and began to write.

The country I'm in is very exotic. It reminds me of someplace I've read about but never traveled to before now. Outside my window I can hear a river of fast-moving water, and in the valley behind the house there is a forest and precipices and mountain peaks covered with snow. Today I saw a wild eagle, and a deer, and I cut and chopped two cords of wood.

Then he put the pen down and held his head in his hands for a moment. Pretty soon he got up and undressed and turned off the light. After he'd gotten into bed he realized he'd left the window open. But he didn't get up. It was okay like that.

Contributors' Notes

RUSSELL BANKS is the author most recently of the novels *Cloudsplitter* and *Rule of the Bone* and a collection of new and selected stories, *The Angel on the Roof: The Stories of Russell Banks*. He was born in 1940, grew up in New Hampshire and eastern Massachusetts, attended Colgate University, and graduated Phi Beta Kappa from the University of North Carolina at Chapel Hill. He worked at various jobs over the years, including plumber, shoe salesman, and display artist, has taught at a number of colleges and universities, and recently retired from the Creative Writing Program at Princeton University, where he is the Howard G. B. Clark University Professor in the Humanities, Emeritus.

"I began writing short stories in the early 1960s, my early twenties, and over the years published four book-length collections, usually between novels, writing them a batch at a time as a respite, maybe, from the ordeal of a two- or three-year stint of novel-writing. Then, from the late 1980s until last year, for reasons unknown, I stopped writing stories altogether and instead wrote one novel after another, obsessive, submerged labor, until a year ago, when I came up exhausted and remembered the clear-running pleasure of writing short stories. I happily returned to the form, and this story, 'Plains of Abraham,' is the first of the batch that emerged from that return. It's set in the northeast corner of New York State, where I've lived since 1987, and the catastrophe at the center of the story is based loosely on an actual catastrophe endured by my father and his ex-wife (not my mother) years ago in New Hampshire. In fiction as in dreams, however, the dreamer is every character dreamed; and thus this story is more mine than my father's or his ex-wife's, and at bottom it feels to me like a story that dramatizes the ancient conflict between love and work, home and the territory ahead, family life and solitude—the oldest divide in the American male psyche, there at the beginning and still hanging around to clobber us these three centuries later."

KEITH BANNER: "I was born in Anderson, Indiana, grew up there, spent a bunch of years working in fast-food restaurants, and finally went to college, then to graduate school in creative writing. Once out, with my M.A. in hand, I stumbled into a job as a social worker for people with disabilities, here in Cincinnati, where I continue to live and work and write. My first novel, *The Life I Lead,* was published last year by Alfred A. Knopf.

"I wrote 'The Smallest People Alive' because I wanted to come up with a love story that's both absurdly tragic and somehow sweet and pure. I also wanted to come up with two main characters who are 'disabled' (both literally and figuratively), but who find a way to be triumphant in the end. When I first sat down to write the story, I was afraid it was too tragic, too bleak, but then I found Mike's voice, and then I found the three family albums under Ben's bed. The story started to push itself forward after these discoveries, and I realized that tragedy and comedy must work in tandem, love and sorrow too.

"I want to thank these people for their kindness and encouragement: David Bergman, Nancy Zafris, David Lynn, Marianne Merola, Gail Hochman, Terri Chenault, Vicki Sluss, Mary Beth Shepherd, Victoria Wilson, and Bill Ross."

ANDREA BARRETT is the author of five novels, most recently *The Voyage of the Narwhal,* and of a collection of short fiction, *Ship Fever,* which received the 1996 National Book Award. She lives in Rochester, New York.

"Several years ago my dear friend, Sarah Stone, gave me an antique *Manual of Geography,* which was used as a school-text in the nineteenth century. The book's catechetical form—it's composed entirely of questions and answers—intrigued me even more than the maps and the subject matter of the text. Later, when I was trying to envision the character of a young nineteenth-century woman, Lavinia, before she was transformed into the guise in which I'd first known her—as the dead mother of Erasmus Darwin Wells, the protagonist of *The Voyage of the Narwhal*—it was through that form that I found her."

JEANNETTE BERTLES "When I was at Bennington I thought I might be a composer, but lacked the talent. Next I thought I might be a fiction writer, but found I had nothing to say. I then graduated and was married and had children all in one big bite—I was of that generation. When my children were in school I got an M.A. in teaching, thinking I could salvage hundreds of little minds; this turned out not to be a good idea. By the time I was in my forties I *did* have something to say, and I started taking courses in fiction writing at the New School with a series of amazingly helpful teachers.

"I have published in *Artful Dodge, Epoch, The New Renaissance,* and *North American Review,* among others. In a year when I publish a story I tell people I am a writer. Otherwise I tell them I am a housewife.

"The exterior of the house in 'Whileaway' comes from the ten years I lived in brownstone Brooklyn. The interior comes from the huge houses of impoverished widows whom my mother and I visited often in my childhood in Greenwich, Connecticut. The waterfront comes from Savannah, Georgia. I am a compulsive rewriter, partly because I care about the aural or musical aspects of storytelling. 'Whileaway,' my longest story, was saved from the wastebasket only because I changed from typewriter, scissors, and carbon paper to the computer."

JOHN BIGUENET's stories have appeared in journals such as *Esquire, Granta, Story,* and *The Southern Review* and have been cited in *The Best American Short Stories* for the last three years. His collection of short fiction, *The Torturer's Apprentice,* is due out in early 2001 from the Ecco Press, an imprint of HarperCollins Publishers. He is also editor-in-chief of *The Encyclopedia of Translation,* forthcoming from Academic Press. He teaches English at Loyola University in New Orleans.

"I think of my very brief story as a kind of meditation on Faulkner's 'A Rose for Emily,' even though it must necessarily come to understand loss, grief, and memory in its own terms. I hope readers will forgive the inexorably sad subject of 'Rose': I have done my best to use not a single word more than I needed to tell this story."

KEVIN BROCKMEIER was raised in Little Rock, Arkansas, and attended Southwest Missouri State University and the University of Iowa. He has received a James Michener–Paul Engle Fellowship, and his stories have appeared in *The Georgia Review, The Carolina Quarterly, Crazyhorse, The Chicago Tribune,* and *Writing on the Edge.* He currently teaches creative writing at the University of Arkansas at Little Rock.

"This story came very slowly for me. I was afraid that if I made a single wrong decision, the whole thing would turn sour, and I remember telling people this as I was writing it. The only note of (almost) autobiography is the passage where Lewis talks about how his older brother could understand his gabbling when he was first learning to speak: this is true, except that I was the older brother, and my brother Jeff was the younger brother. What else? A friend of mine told me that when she read a certain passage in the story—it's on page six of my copy—she immediately went to the kitchen to examine her reflection in a spoon. This delighted me."

JUDY BUDNITZ is the author of a story collection, *Flying Leap,* and a novel, *If I Told You Once.* Her stories have appeared in *McSweeney's, The Paris Review, Story, Glimmer Train,* and the anthologies *Seeing and Writing* and *25 and Under/Fiction.* She lives in New York City.

"In this story, as in most of my stories, I was trying to write about something that can't be summed up neatly in a sentence. I was thinking about: the intertwinedness of families, the blurring of borders, the way people withhold crucial information from the ones they care about most *because it would only upset them,* and the kind of self-sacrifice and devotion that can turn out to be so oppressive and even destructive to the person you're professing to help.

"My clumsiness in trying to explain what I was doing just illustrates my point that stories should say something that cannot be expressed in any other way.

"I almost never revise stories. If a story doesn't work I usually throw it away, I don't try to fix it. This one is an exception, and I'm indebted to the editors of *McSweeney's* for their patience in helping me beat it into shape."

MICHAEL BYERS grew up in Seattle, where he now lives. He is the author of *The Coast of Good Intentions,* which won the 1999 Sue Kaufman Prize from the American Academy of Arts and Letters. He received a Whiting Award in 1998.

" 'The Beautiful Days' surprised me in a couple ways: first by being so long, and second by taking such an ugly turn. Who knows where stories come from, really? This one started with that town in Ohio—I wanted to write about those feelings Aldo has at the beginning of the story, feelings engendered by being in that particular place, and by having a certain cast of mind. As for the rest of it, I'm not sure. It sometimes felt like a logic problem—given X, then Y, but probably not Z—and though this isn't the way I usually work, it seemed to do the trick here."

RAYMOND CARVER was born in Clatskanie, Oregon, in 1938. His first collection of stories, *Will You Please Be Quiet, Please* (a National Book Award nominee in 1977), was followed by *What We Talk About When We Talk About Love, Cathedral* (nominated for the Pulitzer Prize in 1984), and *Where I'm Calling From* in 1988, when he was inducted into the American Academy of Arts and Letters. He died in August of that year, shortly after completing the poems of *A New Path to the Waterfall*. His collected poems, *All of Us*, were published in 1988. *Call If You Need Me*, Carver's uncollected works, including five recently discovered stories, will be published in January of 2001.

According to his wife and literary executor, Tess Gallagher, the story "Kindling" is similar in theme and setting to a poem of Carver's, "To Begin With," which was first included in his 1985 collection, *Where Water Comes Together with Other Water*, and later collected in *All of Us*. She writes:

> Both the poem "To Begin With" and the story "Kindling" are about a man who has left his wife and is renting a room temporarily from another couple. He is trying to begin again, after a seeming escape from domestic turmoil. In the poem he seems to be more a voyeur of the couple's odd relationship (the husband sleeps on the floor next to his wife's bed), whereas in the story the narrator rather tries to avoid the couple and to simply maintain some solitude in the room he is renting, in order to gather himself for going forth again into his life. There is a freshness in "Kindling" by its conclusion, as if the main character, a writer who is also recovering from alcoholism, has performed some inner alchemy (by chopping a load of

wood for his landlords) by which he is enabled to go forward again, spiritually renewed. This story seems to correspond to the renewal Ray himself found after his recovery from three near death collapses from alcoholism. He had several sources of renewal, of which one was likely his life with me here in the Pacific Northwest, although he never rented a room here! That happened elsewhere, so it seems he has transported that event (I believe it happened in Iowa City initially) to the Northwest where the chopping of wood really does help many on-the-fringe people maintain hope and keep some semblance of work-clarity available when jobs give out, as they have here in our mills and timber industry. There is a beautiful decisiveness and determination and fragility acting all at once in "Kindling" which gains power as the story moves toward its very quiet ending. I think Ray was trying to give a portrait of the solitude necessary to make a boundary between lives. It's hard to find. But, by the end of the story, it makes all the difference to this man's life.

ALICE ELLIOTT DARK is the author of the story collections *In the Gloaming* (2000), and *Naked to the Waist* (1991). Her work has been published in *Harper's, Redbook, The New Yorker, Book, Five Points, Double Take,* and others. One story, "In the Gloaming," was adapted into two films, by HBO and Trinity Playhouse, and has been chosen for many anthologies, including *Best American Short Stories* and *Best American Short Stories of the Century,* selected by John Updike. She has received a grant from the National Endowment for the Arts. A novel, *Think of England,* will be published in 2001.

" 'Watch the Animals' is a combo of several images and ideas that have meaning for me: Christmas Eve at the church I attended as a child; the question of whether or not the other animals (let's not forget that we're in that category) have souls; fall; and a great friend of mine who saves animals from horrible places and fates. It took a while for me to decide on the point of view. As I fooled around with scenes, though, the story became more about the community than Diana, and its voice emerged. Diana, in turn, got more fabulous and contrary and eccentric. I worked on the ending until it was both a transcendent moment for the group and a funny portrayal of how quickly people revert to type after they've been generous—if *The New York Times* wanted to believe they were Diana's friends, that was okay by them! The original title was 'In Dogs We Trust,' which I still like."

KIANA DAVENPORT is *hapa haole,* half Native Hawaiian, half Anglo-American. She is the author of the novels *Shark Dialogues,* which has been translated into six languages, and most recently, the best-selling *Song of the Exile* (Ballantine, July 1999). Her short fiction has been published world-wide.

Davenport's short story "The Lipstick Tree" was selected for *Prize Stories 1997: The O. Henry Awards,* and *Pushcart Prize Stories XXI,* 1998. "Fork Used in Eating Reverend Baker" was selected for *Prize Stories 1999: The O. Henry Awards.* Recipient of a Fiction Grant from the NEA, Davenport was also a 1992–93 Fiction Fellow at Harvard-Radcliffe's Bunting Institute, and the 1997–98 Visiting Writer at Wesleyan University. She lives in Boston and Hawaii.

"This is my third inclusion in the *O. Henry Awards: Prize Stories.* I am deeply honored. I think every family is an automatic piece of fiction. But some stories we don't want to tell. We want to outrun them. With 'Bones of the Inner Ear,' the past finally came banging on my door at 2 A.M., demanding to be let in.

"This story was harder to write than anything I have ever undertaken. Cutting it down from ninety pages, struggling with it month after month, reinforced my love for writing fiction. We hide behind fiction. We embellish. We vanish. I wrote 'Bones of the Inner Ear' hoping no one will believe it's true."

NATHAN ENGLANDER is the author of the collection *For the Relief of Unbearable Urges* (Alfred A. Knopf, 1999). His stories have appeared in *The Atlantic Monthly, The New Yorker, Story, The Best American Short Stories 1999,* and *The Pushcart Prize XXII.* Born and raised in New York, he has been living in Jerusalem for the past four years.

"My own transformation from religious to secular was slow and studied and utterly unspontaneous. In 'The Gilgul of Park Avenue' I wanted to explore the opposite kind of transformation. Not the journey from secular to religious, but the inspired moment, the instantaneous (and purely emotional) understanding that a person is other than what he or she has always known him- or herself to be. I always liked the notion of the gilgul—the Jewish equivalent to reincarnation. I thought this a suitable vehicle for the story, or, more exactly, that the character Charles Luger was the proper vehicle for such a soul."

TIM GAUTREAUX was born and raised in south Louisiana. He has a Ph.D. in English from the University of South Carolina and has published two collections of short stories *(Same Place, Same Things* and *Welding with Children)* and one novel, *The Next Step in the Dance,* all with St. Martin's Press/Picador. The novel won the Southeastern Bookseller's Award for best novel of 1998. His stories have appeared in *Atlantic, Harper's, GQ, Zoetrope, Story,* and others. He is writer in residence at Southeastern Louisiana University.

"I grew up around tough older south Louisiana women who liked to gamble, smoke, and cook. The ones I knew always outlived their husbands by many years. 'Easy Pickings' is a tribute to them, and to the culture that produced them. No matter what their shortcomings were, they knew how to have a good time and how to help each other out."

MARY GORDON's novels have been best-sellers—*Final Payments, The Company of Women, Men and Angels, The Other Side, Spending,* and a memoir, *The Shadow Man.* She has published a book of novellas, *The Rest of Life;* a collection of stories, *Temporary Shelter;* and two books of essays, *Good Boys and Dead Girls* and *Seeing Through Places.* Her most recent work is the biography *Joan of Arc.* She has received the Lila Acheson Wallace Reader's Digest Award and a Guggenheim Fellowship. Mary is a professor of English at Barnard College.

" 'The Deacon' is one of those stories that comes to you if you live in New York and open your eyes and ears."

ALLAN GURGANUS says his family has been "shabby genteel over-explainers for five generations." He was born in Rocky Mount, North Carolina, in 1947, and after serving in the Navy during the Vietnam War, after teaching at Stanford, the Iowa Writers' Workshop, and Sarah Lawrence College, he returned to live in his native state. Gurganus's novels include *Oldest Living Confederate Widow Tells All* and *Plays Well with Others.* His story collection, *White People,* will be followed by a group of novellas, *The Practical Heart.* His novel in progress is called *Saint Monster.*

About the enclosed story "He's at the Office," Gurganus writes: "Everybody's worst fear must be the death of memory. What physical pain can compare to having Outer Space where your innermost thoughts should dwell? For writers, a jeopardized memory means the loss both of private dignity and of professional value. Some close friends of mine are now all in their eighties. They've known each other their whole lives and their histories are mutual, loving, dense. They now speak mostly of the past; so whenever one person's factual grasp wavers, another rushes in to help. 'Who'll ever forget the party we had in Rome for . . . that great diva, Greek-American? with all the temperament? . . .' 'Maria Callas.' 'And at that party for Callas, a fight broke out between some young boy hustler and . . . the brilliant Italian director eventually beaten to death? by street thugs? . . .' 'Pasolinni.' 'Precisely. Well then . . .' In my friends' splendid company, I'm reminded that the finest memories all eventually become communal, a minuet among necessary partners. In 'He's at the Office,' I try imagining how one family might help its failing leader 'save face.' To remember decency despite the loss of memory—that, in art and life, seems to me a goal impossibly difficult. Though not impossible. It seemed therefore—as the subject for a story—at least stubbornly memorable."

J. ROBERT LENNON is the author of two novels, *The Funnies* and *The Light of Falling Stars.* He lives in Ithaca, New York. A version of "The Fool's Proxy" serves as the first chapter of a third novel, just completed.

"This story was inspired by the parrot, which was apparently real, as was the horse. These details, and others of mid-century Atlantic City, were provided by my uncle, Jim Lennon.

"I'm grateful to Ben Metcalf at *Harper's* for his close editing, and to Larry Dark for choosing to include 'The Fool's Proxy' in this anthology."

BETH LORDAN "In the spring of 1998, through the generosity of the Irish and Irish Immigration Studies program at Southern Illinois University at Carbondale (where I teach), my husband, daughter, and I spent four months in Ireland. I had every intention of not writing about Ireland: although I'd never been abroad before, I knew enough about the complexity of place to know that in four months I'd know nothing about that one. However, near the end of our time there, having written nothing to justify my existence, I set myself an exercise: write a story like John

McGahern's stories, which I admire a great deal. I discovered that I couldn't write like McGahern (I'd blown it in the first sentence), but also that, while I couldn't write an Irish story, I might write one about the deep and disturbing experience of being foreign, and about the peculiar place of language (maybe especially in a country where mine is spoken, but differently) in that experience. For reasons that will probably be obvious to others but remain mysterious to me, this experience seemed to find its natural form in stories about marriage. (In my last book of stories, *And Both Shall Row,* I rarely managed to get a living married couple to inhabit the same page, much less the same landscape.) I believe I'll have a bookful of stories about Lyle and Mary and Laura and Mark, all worrying about foreignness, language, marriage, and the peculiar relationship between America and Ireland. As the title 'The Man with the Lapdog' implies, there's another thing afoot as well—something about the connection between contemporary stories and previous literature. I'm imagining the new book will be called *But Come Ye Back,* and that it'll really be a novel in stories. I'm also imagining I'll get all those stories written."

MELISSA PRITCHARD is the author of two story collections, *Spirit Seizures,* which received the Flannery O'Connor Award, and *The Instinct for Bliss,* which received the Janet Heidinger Kafka Award, as well as two novels, *Phoenix* and *Selene of the Spirits.* "*Salve Regina*" is included in a new collection of stories, *The Disappearing Ingenue.* Her fiction has most recently appeared in *The Paris Review, Boulevard, The Gettysburg Review, The Southern Review,* and *Pushcart XX, Best of the Small Presses.* She teaches in the Creative Writing Program at Arizona State University.

"In 1997, I received a letter dated May 24 from Sister Georgiana Logan, a former classmate at the Convent of the Sacred Heart, a private girls' school in Menlo Park, California. In this letter, which began 'Dear Classmates,' I received news that Sister Marnie Dilling, a professor of ethnomusicology, had died of cancer on May 13 at the age of fifty-seven. On countless occasions, I had thought to write about this woman who had so profoundly affected my adolescent years at Sacred Heart. Always I balked, feeling I could not begin to do justice to the hidden richness of that time or to Marnie Dilling, a twenty-five-year-old nun whose exuberance and beauty could not, it seemed, be weighted by the volumes of black cloth she wore. With news of her premature death, I gave up hope of perfection and wrote what I could. I am grateful to Peter Stitt at *The Gettysburg*

Review for publishing 'Salve Regina,' and to Larry Dark for including it among so many extraordinary stories. This story is dedicated to Marnie Dilling—a woman more lovely, intelligent, and honorable than my character, Mother Fitzgerald—and thus strays the willful arrow of fiction to a place where memory, pierced by imagination, comes up with a surprise or two all its own."

KATE WALBERT's fiction has appeared in *The Paris Review, DoubleTake,* and *Fiction,* among other places. She is the author of *Where She Went,* a collection of stories, and the novel *The Gardens of Kyoto,* to be published in the spring of 2000 by Scribner. She lives in New York City with her husband and daughter and teaches fiction writing at Yale.

"My father's family were tenant farmers on the Eastern Shore of Maryland, a fact that for me has always suggested romantic scenes of men and women toiling away at the tough soil. I'm sure the truth is far more stark, though my father so rarely speaks of his childhood that when he does every detail feels charged and potent, precisely the starting place for fiction. In this way 'The Gardens of Kyoto' began with what little I know of my father's cousin, Charles Webster, to whom the story is dedicated. Charles was a few years older than my father, the sole boy of his beloved Aunt Maude—who lived about a mile down the road—and a surrogate brother since my father's own were off fighting in Europe. When Charles turned seventeen and enlisted I imagine everyone believed he would return home as those boys eventually did—veterans, heroes of sorts, soldiers who had done their duty. But Charles was killed on Iwo Jima, just weeks after he reached the Pacific.

"The story took me a very long time to write, but even after I had finished it and gone on to other things, the narrator kept her hold on me. And so I went back to hear more."

JOHN EDGAR WIDEMAN "The first line of this story came first. I thought the line was kind of funny and also intriguing so I wrote the story to discover what the first line was all about. Turns out it was about my whole life. More specifically about my relationship to the extraordinary woman whose womb was my first habitation (unless, as I sometimes believe, there is a reverse cascade of wombs tumbling backward and simultaneously forward into the infinity of Great Time).

"Mother love, of course, is a defining feature of African-American males. We are stone mama's boys. Utterly, hopelessly so. Mama's baby, daddy's maybe. You've heard *Hi Mom* from the lips of every colored sports star interviewed on TV. Mama worship a cliché amongst us maybe. As much from a guilty conscience, maybe, as from unencumbered adoration, maybe, since the trajectory of our male lives—chasing success, chasing women, chasing art and duty, chased by the racist wolves—often catapults us far from mama's nest. We're off and running, and when we look back, there she is. We owe her everything and know we do and know there's no way to pay her back. It's always too late. God bless the child who's got his own, she instructs us, and perhaps we get something but where's Mama? Why didn't she ever get hers? Except her babyboy is hers. Always.

"Pittsburgh public schools, University of Pennsylvania, Oxford University, Iowa Writers Workshop, Penn again, Wyoming, UMass-Amherst—some points defining my trajectory. Fifteen books along the way."

Jurors

MICHAEL CUNNINGHAM is the author of the novels *A Home at the End of the World, Flesh and Blood,* and *The Hours,* which won both the 1999 PEN/Faulkner Award and the 1999 Pulitzer Prize. His stories have appeared in *The New Yorker, DoubleTake, The Atlantic Monthly,* and *The Paris Review,* as well as *The Penguin Book of Gay Short Stories* and *The KGB Bar Reader.* He has received fellowships from the Guggenheim and Whiting foundations.

PAM HOUSTON is the author of two books of short stories, *Cowboys Are My Weakness* and *Waltzing the Cat,* as well as a book of essays, *A Little More About Me.* She lives at nine thousand feet above sea level in Colorado, near the headwaters of the Rio Grande.

GEORGE SAUNDERS is the author of the story collections *CivilWarLand in Bad Decline,* a finalist for the 1996 PEN/Hemingway Award and a *New York Times* Notable Book for that year, and *Pastoralia.* His work, which has appeared in *The New Yorker, Harper's,* and *Story,* has received three National Magazine Awards and three times been included in O. Henry Awards collections. He is also the author of *The Very Persistent Gappers of Frip,* a children's story, illustrated by Lane Smith. He teaches in the Creative Writing Program at Syracuse University.

Short-Listed Stories

ALEXIE, SHERMAN, "The Toughest Indian in the World,"
The New Yorker, June 21 & 28, 1999 ✗

A Native American newspaper reporter, who makes it a habit to pick up Indian hitchhikers, stops for a man who makes his living traveling from reservation to reservation to fight a tribe's toughest man for money. When they stop for the night, the reporter allows the fighter to share his hotel room with him, where they have an intimate encounter.

ALLEN, DWIGHT, "Succor," *The Georgia Review,* Vol. LII, No. 1

A husband and father encounters a seedy local character in the woods and meets up with him several times later around the small town where they live. The other man seems to bring out the worst in the man, yet he can't keep him away.

ANSAY, A. MANETTE, "Box," *The Nebraska Review,*
Vol. 27, No. 1

The anxious husband of a pregnant woman, who is weeks overdue, returns home after taking a stray cat she has adopted and its kittens and leaving them in a box by the side of a highway. After arguing with his wife, the husband feels guilty. He goes after his wife, who has fled to a nearby restaurant, buys her breakfast, and leads her to where he left the box, which is now gone.

BAKER, ALISON, "One Owner, Runs," *Story,* Spring 1999

A middle-aged car dealer begins to believe he is Jesus after the death of his father. He moves in with his mother and encounters the eager young pastor of a local church.

BERNTHAL, CRAIG, "A Small Parenthesis in Eternity,"
ZYZZYUVA, Vol. XV, No. 1

A group of geology students drives around mapping various rock formations near Lake Superior. One of them is a young woman who keeps to herself, but whose sketches are very skillful. A male student, who has a crush on her, asks her to join his group and learns the secret of her sadness.

BILLMAN, JOHN, "Becky Weed," *Esquire,* April 1999

A man who once crashed his father's plane in the front yard of a girl, to show off for her, finds the girl again many years later, now a married woman. Having been rejected by the Air Force, the man has become the pilot of a crop-dusting plane. The girl he liked has married a onetime football quarterback, now a banker. The pilot flies low over her house and dusts the fields around it.

BOBIER, MICHELLE, "The Goddess of the Moon,"
The Virginia Quarterly Review, Vol. 75, No. 4

A young woman who lives with a sculptor and runs a preschool struggles with memories of abuse during her childhood. She has never told her lover about her past and tries to maintain an orderly existence, but finds herself filled with grief when she learns of the breakup of a friend's marriage.

BOYLE, T. CORAGHESSAN, "All the Wrecks I've Crawled Out Of,"
Story Quarterly, No. 35

A young man takes a job as a bartender at a restaurant and moves in with one of the waitresses. His life is good, but he courts disaster through a series of outright accidents and near misses until he loses everything.

BRADFORD, ARTHUR, "Dogs," *Esquire,* July 1999

A man has sexual relations with a dog and spawns a litter that includes one human offspring in miniature. The father casts his child off, Moses-like, in a shoebox. Later the child returns, disguised as a singing muskrat, and is accidentally killed by one of the other dogs in his litter. But the little man has impregnated a woman in an iron lung who gives birth to a litter of singing pooches.

BROWN, SHARON MAY, "Kwek," *Mānoa,* Vol. 11, No. 1
The title character is an eight-year-old boy sent to a relocation camp by the Khmer Rouge for stealing food. He continues to steal in blatant fashion, seemingly to taunt the Khmer Rouge and despite the beatings he receives. The punishments worsen, but the boy's spirit cannot be broken, though his body can.

BROYARD, BLISS, "Snowed In," *Open City,* No. 7
A group of high school classmates left behind during spring break get together in the house of a student whose parents are away. They drink beer and play drinking games, and things begin to spin out of control as the day wears on.

BYERS, MICHAEL, "Roll on Columbia (1962),"
***DoubleTake,* No. 16**
A young man, recently appointed professor of geology at a college, has an embarrassing encounter with a group of nude bathers along the Columbia River. Later he runs into them again in a coffee shop. A young woman writes her name and phone number on his wrist in pen. He decides he is in love with her, but they never meet again.

DANTICAT, EDWIDGE, "The Book of the Dead," *The New Yorker,* June 21 & 28, 1999
A woman whose parents came to America from Haiti loses track of her father while the two are on a trip from New York to Florida to deliver a sculpture of hers to a famous actress of Haitian descent. Her father returns, having disposed of the statue, and confesses to her that he is not the heroic victim she had always thought he was.

DAVIES, PETER HO, "The Next Life," *Harper's Magazine,* March 1999
A man arranges for a traditional Chinese funeral for his father, a

West Coast Chinese-language newspaper publisher and a respected figure in Chinatown. The arrangements include paid mourners and paper effigies of money and possessions, which are burned at the ceremony so the father can take them with him to the next world.

DeNiro, Alan, "Skinny Dipping in the Lake of the Dead," *Fence,* Vol. 2, No. 2

A futuristic story told in the form of a college application essay by a young man living in Suddenly, part of the nation of Pittsburgh. The town is made up almost entirely of teenagers living by themselves. He meets a young woman who shows him another culture that exists at the bottom of a dead lake in the center of the town.

Devine, Maija Rhee, "Crane's Grace," *The Kenyon Review,* Vol. XXI, Nos. 3 & 4

A young Korean woman, rejected by her husband after he discovers a small flaw in her, is sent to be the concubine of a married man whose wife has been unable to conceive a child. In his house, she must learn to adapt to her role and find the right relationship to both the man and his wife.

Diaz, Junot, *"Otravida, Otravez,"* The New Yorker, June 21 & 28, 1999

A Dominican woman who works in a hospital laundry room is involved in a relationship with a married man who has left his wife behind in the Dominican Republic. They buy a house together, but still she fears he will return to his wife.

Finger, Anne, "Gloucester," *The Southern Review,* Vol. 35, No. 2

A middle-aged man from a well-known family is hospitalized with AIDS-related complications and finds he is going blind. He arranges for his money to go to his two sons, the more responsible one controlling the trust for the other. But it is the younger, more free-spirited son who proves to have the stronger bond with the father and ultimately to be more trustworthy.

FRANCIS, H. E., "The Playground," *Shenandoah,* **Vol. 49, No. 1**

Three adults, a woman with two children and her adult brothers, observe a woman along the beach near a playground in a resort town during the off-season. A group of eight or so children gather around this woman every afternoon and play a game of sorts, moving in response to her. She turns out to be a painter who is mute. One day the woman stops coming to the beach, leaving the children desolate in her absence.

FULTON, JOHN, "Rose," *The Southern Review,* **Vol. 35, No. 4**

At a dinner to celebrate a woman's seventy-seventh birthday, her husband, a Korean War veteran, has a stroke and dies. In those last moments, she recalls their life together.

HEMON, ALEKSANDAR, "Blind Josef Pronek," *The New Yorker,* **April 19, 1999**

A Slav from Bosnia comes to Chicago to visit an American woman he met in Ukraine just as hostilities were escalating in his homeland. He ends up staying in the States and gets a succession of menial jobs as, all the while, the situation in Bosnia gets worse.

HOFFMAN, ALICE, "The Boy Who Wrestled with Angels," *Five Points,* **Vol. III, No. 3**

A young man courts his own self-destruction through drug use and other forms of recklessness, despite a concerned sister, mother, and aunt.

HOLLADAY, CARY, "The Lost Pone," *Five Points,* **Vol. III, No. 2**

A woman recalls the spotted pony she'd won in a raffle, then lost three weeks later, and the small Virginia town of her youth.

HRBEK, GREG, "Green World," *Harper's Magazine,* **December 1999**

A thirteen-year-old tried as an adult and found guilty of murder awaits his execution and tells of his final days in a series of journal entries.

JACOBS, MARK, "Confidence in Izmir," *Southwest Review,*
Vol. 84, No. 1

An aging American hustler in Turkey spots a handsome young hustler just starting out and takes him under his wing. The older man is dying of cancer, and the younger man helps him, but partly to take advantage of him.

JIN, HA, "The Bridegroom," *Harper's Magazine,* July 1999

A childless couple in China takes in the daughter of a friend after he dies. The husband is surprised when a handsome young man proposes to the homely girl. Not only is the man handsome but he is also educated, has good manners, and is skilled at martial arts. After the couple has been married for eight months, the young man is arrested for homosexuality and sent to a state hospital for a cure that is doomed to failure.

KLAM, MATTHEW, "Issues I Dealt with in Therapy,"
The New Yorker, July 12, 1999

A man and his girlfriend go to an East Coast resort island for the wedding of his successful friend, who runs a political campaign. The narrator feels ambivalent about his friend and anxious about his relationship with his girlfriend. At a pre-wedding dinner, he makes a toast that turns into a roast of the groom-to-be.

KLEIN, RACHEL S., "Beatrice: The Sacrifice,"
The Literary Review, Vol. 42, No. 4

After joining a very strict order of monastic nuns, an intellectually gifted young Italian woman stops speaking. She is sent home by the Abbess, who fears the young woman is suffering an emotional collapse. Upon the young woman's return she levitates and has spells and visions. The young nun struggles with her faith and rails against the role assigned to women in monastic orders even as the Abbess tries to help find a place for her in the church.

KNIGHT, MICHAEL, "The Mesmerist," *Esquire,* March 1999

A hypnotist casts a spell over a young woman he sees on a train and takes her to live with him in the Midwest. An investigator comes

looking for her, but the hypnotist hypnotizes him and throws him off the trail.

LAHIRI, JHUMPA, "The Third and Final Continent," *The New Yorker,* June 21 & 28, 1999

An Indian man arrives in America in 1969, having taken a new job after an education in England and an arranged marriage in Calcutta. He rents a room from an eccentric old woman. After six weeks, the man's wife arrives and he moves with her to a furnished apartment. They have trouble getting used to one another until he takes her back to visit the old woman, an incident that somehow brings them closer together and paves the way for a life together in a new place.

LEWIS, TRUDY, "The Bones of Garbo," *New England Review,* Vol. 20, No. 1

Sections of narrative concerning a girl who wants to be an actress and who lands a role in a high school play are interspersed with the story of Greta Garbo, with whom the girl identifies. The girl lives with her mother, who recently left her father, and they take in a strange, theatrical girl the same age.

MACMILLAN, IAN, "Squid Eye," *Hawaii Pacific Review,* Vol. 13

A twelve-year-old native Hawaiian living with his unemployed father and mother in a van parked in a lot by a public beach discovers a talent for catching squid. This talent impresses acquaintances of his father, who pay him for the squid he catches and offer the father a job. The boy's parents, however, are content to spend the money on vodka and live in a stupor.

McNEELY, THOMAS H., "Sheep," *The Atlantic Monthly,* June 1999

A dim-witted man raised on a sheep ranch in the Texas panhandle and abused as a child is arrested for the murders of several young women. He can't remember committing the crimes, because he was often drunk and experienced blackouts, but he also feels uncomfortable with his defense lawyer's efforts to have him declared incompetent.

MENENDEZ, ANA, "In Cuba I Was a German Shepherd,"
Zoetrope: All-Story, **Vol. 3, No. 1**

A group of Latinos gather in a park in Miami to play dominoes, as they have for many years. Two of them are Cuban, two Dominican. One of the Cubans tells jokes about Cuba and Fidel Castro as they play. Tourists come and take their pictures. The man who tells the jokes was a college professor in Havana, but in Miami he ran a lunch truck and then a restaurant with his wife. Now he is a retired widower, longing for his past.

MUNRO, ALICE, "The Bear Came over the Mountain,"
The New Yorker, **December 27, 1999 & January 3, 2000**

A man notices that his wife is starting to slip. Eventually, her memory gets so bad that he places her in a home and is instructed not to visit for a month, so she can adjust to her new surroundings. When he returns, he finds that his wife has become attached to another man, whom she claims she knew when she was very young, and she seems barely to remember her husband. When the other man is sent back home, the wife becomes forlorn and the husband goes off to find the other man, to make his wife happy.

NELSON, ANTONYA, "Stitches," *The New Yorker,*
September 20, 1999

A woman is awakened in the middle of the night by a call from her daughter, a freshman at college. The daughter says she has been raped. The father immediately sets off for the college, a hundred miles away. While he drives there, the daughter tells the mother about what happened, which turns out to have resulted from consensual sex with a teaching assistant.

NYREN, RON, "The Yearbook," *The Paris Review,* **No. 150**

A young man forced to stay in his apartment for the summer because he can't sublet it to anyone else, works in the university inventory department and dreams of moving to Chicago and starting a new life. One day he finds a blue crate, left behind by a roommate-to-be. A young woman calls looking for the roommate, and the young man and she strike up a romance centered on a fascination with the absent roommate.

O'NAN, STEWART, "Please Help Find," *Ploughshares,*
Vol. 25, Nos. 2 & 3

A young woman recovering from a suicide attempt is driven to college by her mother, accompanied by the family's aging cocker spaniel. The dog becomes lost in the course of settling the young woman. The dog is later found at a fraternity house, and the mother drives off, leaving the daughter alone to face a losing battle with her despair.

OCHSNER, GINA, "Cartography of a Heart,"
Columbia: A Journal of Literature and Art, Issue 32

Doctors discover that a lifelong bachelor in need of a transplant has a very unusually shaped heart and only an organ of similar proportions will do. Eventually one is found and the transplant is a success. The new heart changes the man, and he decides to pursue romance with a waitress. She moves in with him for a while, but she leaves, accusing the man of not really loving her. He lets her go without a protest but then feels great pain in his new heart.

OLMSTEAD, ROBERT, "The Babes in the Woods," *Epoch,*
Vol. 47, Nos. 2 & 3

A married man and a married woman, not his wife, set off on a weekend together hiking in the woods and staying at the house of the woman's friend. They feel anxious about entering into an affair, though they have been building up to it for weeks, and there is as much discomfort between them as pleasure.

PEARLMAN, EDITH, *"Allog,"* *Ascent,* Vol. 24, No. 1

The lives of the residents of a building in Jerusalem, divided into five apartments, are changed by the arrival of an Asian man who has come to tend to the stroke-damaged husband of one of the women. The man is handy and kind, and everyone in the building grows to depend on him in different ways.

PROULX, ANNIE, "People in Hell Just Want a Drink of Water,"
GQ, April 1999

Two families in Laramie, Wyoming: one is made up of hardworking ranchers; the other is haunted by a tragedy. The son of the family haunted by tragedy leaves home at sixteen but returns years later, damaged and disfigured as the result of a car accident. He takes to riding around on horseback and exposing himself to women, until one of the boys from the other family takes matters into his own hands.

SHANE, THOMAS, "Bedtime Story," *Other Voices,* No. 31

The thoughts of a middle-aged husband and wife at bedtime. He is reading in bed when she comes home from an evening out, undresses, and bathes. He feels desire for her, but she is tired and goes to sleep.

SHERWOOD, FRANCES, "Basil the Dog," *The Atlantic Monthly,* September 1999

A boy growing up in Trinidad in 1950, half black and half Indian, believes that he sees a malevolent creature, he calls Basil, each time tragedy or near-tragedy strikes. He first spots the creature when he falls through a roof and nearly dies, then when his grandmother, aunt, and sister die.

WALBERT, KATE, "The Intervention," *The Paris Review,* No. 151

A group of affluent suburbanites decide to confront one of their number with an intervention, because of his self-destructive behavior. They meet several times and practice confronting him, but the intervention doesn't quite go as planned.

WALLACE, DAVID FOSTER, "On His Deathbed, Holding Your Hand, the Acclaimed New Young Off-Broadway Playwright's Father Begs a Boon," *Tin House,* Vol. 1, No. 1

A monologue in which a dying man talks of his lifelong hatred for his son, whom he sees as having destroyed his marriage and hastened the death of his wife, the boy's mother.

WELCH, NANCY, "Mental," *Prairie Schooner,* Vol. 73, No. 2

Two sisters commit their paranoid-schizophrenic brother to a mental hospital, hoping for a cure, but they learn that there is no cure, only medication and coping.

WING, BETSY, "Art History," *The Southern Review,* **Vol. 35, No. 2**

A mother and her young child wander into a strange house in Provence, which turns out to be a hospital Vincent van Gogh once stayed in. They are taken on a tour by a Frenchman who claims that he was a child when van Gogh stayed in the house and has some mementos of that time.

WOLFF, TOBIAS, "Kiss," *The New Yorker,* **March 29, 1999**

A man's mother shows him a clipping from a newspaper about a woman who died in a car accident. At the age of fifteen, he had been obsessed with this girl. He and she would make out anytime, anyplace. But then he blew the relationship, his father died, and his mother moved him away. The man has become a doctor, a husband, and a father, but he still can't shake the memory of those kisses.

YEAGER, LAURA, "Having Anne," *The Missouri Review,*
Vol. XXI, No. 3

A woman suffering from a bipolar condition and forced to stop taking Lithium during her pregnancy hires a baby-sitter to look after her and grows increasingly manic during the course of the nine months.

2000 Magazine Award:
The Atlantic Monthly

O N THE strength of three O. Henry Award–winning stories—the second-prize-winning "The Man with the Lapdog" by Beth Lordan, the third-prize-winning "The Deacon" by Mary Gordon, and "The Gilgul of Park Avenue" by Nathan Englander—*The Atlantic Monthly* is this year's winner of the O. Henry Award for the magazine publishing the best fiction during the course of the past year. *The Atlantic Monthly* also published two of the fifty stories short-listed for this year's volume.

Other strong contenders for the magazine honors this year included *Esquire,* with three prizewinning stories, and *Harper's Magazine* and *The Gettysburg Review,* both with two prizewinning stories. Congratulations are due to these magazines, as well as to *Callaloo, DoubleTake, The Georgia Review, GQ, The Kenyon Review, McSweeney's, The New Yorker, Ploughshares, The Southern Review,* and *Story,* each of which published an O. Henry Award–winning story in 1999.

The Atlantic Monthly, now in its 143rd year of publication, has, over the course of eighty volumes of *Prize Stories: The O. Henry Awards,* published 113 O. Henry Award–winning stories, tied with *Harper's Magazine* and second only to *The New Yorker,* with 160 prizewinners over the years. The first story ever to appear in the O. Henry Awards, Margaret Prescott Montague's first-prize-winning story in the 1919 volume, "England to America," was first published in the September 1918 issue of *The Atlantic Monthly.* The magazine's commitment to literary fiction is further underscored by its Web site, Atlantic Unbound, which, in addition to reprinting some of the contents of the print version, includes original short fiction and interviews with writers, among other Web-only material. Congratulations to editor Michael Kelly, Senior Editor C. Michael Curtis, and the other staff members involved in selecting, editing, and publishing the fiction in *The Atlantic Monthly.*

A&U

25 Monroe Street
Suite 205
Albany, NY 12210–2743
Christopher Hewitt, Literary
Editor
www.aumag.org
*Monthly. "America's AIDS
magazine."*

Acorn Whistle

907 Brewster Avenue
Beloit, WI 53511
Fred Burwell, Editor
Publishes one or two issues a year.

African American Review

Stalker Hall 213
Indiana State University
Terre Haute, IN 47809
Joe Weixlmann, Editor
web.indstate.edu/artsci/AAR
*Quarterly with a focus on
African American literature and
culture.*

Agni

236 Bay State Road
Boston University Writing
Program
Boston, MA 02215
Askold Melnyczuk, Editor
webdelsol.com/AGNI
Biannual.

AIM Magazine

P.O. Box 1174
Maywood, IL 60153
Myron Apilado, Editor
*"America's Intercultural
Magazine." Quarterly.*

Alabama Literary Review

Smith 253
Troy State University
Troy, AL 36082
Theron Montgomery, Chief
Editor
Published annually.

Alaska Quarterly Review

University of Alaska Anchorage
3211 Providence Drive
Anchorage, AK 99508
Ronald Spatz, Editor
www.uaa.alaska.edu/aqr

Alligator Juniper

Prescott College
220 Grove Avenue
Prescott, AZ 86301
Melanie Bishop, Managing
Editor
www.prescott.edu/news/aj.html
Annual.

Amelia

329 "E" Street
Bakersfield, CA 93304
Frederick A. Raborg Jr., Editor
amelia@lightspeed.net
*Quarterly. Includes two supple-
ments:* Cicada *and* SPSM&H.

**American Letters and
Commentary**

850 Park Avenue
Suite 5B
New York, NY 10021
Jeanne Marie Beaumont, Anna
Rabinowitz, Editors
www.amletters.org
Annual.

Magazines Consulted

ENTRIES ENTIRELY in boldface and with their titles in all-capital letters denote publications with prizewinning stories. Asterisks following titles denote magazines with short-listed stories. The information presented is up-to-date as of the time *Prize Stories 2000: The O. Henry Awards* went to press. For further information, including links to magazine Web sites, visit the O. Henry Awards Web site at:

www.boldtype.com/ohenry

Magazines that wish to be added to the list and to have the stories they publish considered for O. Henry Awards may send subscriptions or all issues containing fiction to the series editor at:

P.O. Box 739
Montclair, NJ 07042

All other correspondence should be sent care of Anchor Books or, via e-mail, to Ohenrypriz@aol.com.

Please note: It is the responsibility of the editors of each magazine to make sure that issues are sent to the series editor. If none are received during the course of the year, a publication will no longer be listed as a magazine consulted for the series.

American Literary Review
University of North Texas
P.O. Box 13827
Denton, TX 76203–1307
Lee Martin, Editor
www.engl.unt.edu/alr/images/
main.html
Biannual.

The American Voice
332 West Broadway
Suite 1215
Louisville, KY 40202
Frederick Smock, Editor
*Triannual publication. Ceased
publication in 1999.*

Another Chicago Magazine
Left Field Press
3709 North Kenmore
Chicago, IL 60613
Barry Silesky, Editor and
Publisher

Antietam Review
41 S. Potomac Street
Hagerstown, MD 21740
Susanne Kass, Executive Editor
www.wcarts@intrepid.net

The Antioch Review
P.O. Box 148
Yellow Springs, OH 45387
Robert S. Fogarty, Editor
www.antioch.edu/review/
home.html
Quarterly.

Apalachee Quarterly
P.O. Box 10469
Tallahassee, FL 32302
Barbara Hamby, Editor

Appalachian Heritage
Berea College
Berea, KY 40404
James Gage, Editor
*Quarterly magazine of Southern
Appalachian life and culture.*

Arkansas Review
Dept. of English and
Philosophy
Box 1890
Arkansas State University
State University, AR 72467
Norman Lavers, Editor
www.clt.astate.edu/arkreview
Formerly the Kansas Quarterly.
"A Journal of Delta Studies."
Triannual.

Ascent*
English Department
Concordia College
901 8th Street S
Moorhead, MN 56562
W. Scott Olsen, Editor
ascent@cord.edu
www.cord.edu/dept/english/
ascent
Triannual.

Atlanta Review
P.O. Box 8248
Atlanta, GA 31106
Daniel Veach, Editor and
Publisher
www.atlantareview.com
Biannual.

THE ATLANTIC MONTHLY*
77 N. Washington Street
Boston, MA 02114

C. Michael Curtis, Senior Editor
www.theatlantic.com
2000 O. Henry Award winner for magazines. The Atlantic Unbound site features stories from the magazine plus Web-only content, including interviews with authors, fiction not published in the print version, a reader forum, and more.

The Baffler
P.O. Box 378293
Chicago, IL 60637
Thomas Frank, Editor-in-Chief
thebaffler.org

The Baltimore Review
P.O. Box 410
Riderwood, MD 21139
Barbara Westwood Diehl, Editor
Biannual featuring the work of writers "from the Baltimore area and beyond."

Barnabe Mountain Review
P.O. Box 529
Lagunitas, CA 94938
Gerald Fleming, Editor
Annual, first published in 1995. Planned to cease publication after its fifth issue in 1999.

Bellowing Ark
P.O. Box 55564
Shoreline, WA 98155
Robert R. Ward, Editor
Bimonthly.

Beloit Fiction Journal
Box 11
Beloit College
700 College Street
Beloit, WI 53511
rotating editorship
www.beloit.edu/~libhome/
Archives/BO/Pub/Fict.html
Biannual.

Black Dirt: A Journal of Contemporary Writing
Elgin Community College
1700 Spartan Drive
Elgin, IL 60123–7193
Rachel Tecza, Fiction Editor
Biannual. Formerly known as Farmer's Market. Has ceased publication.

Black Warrior Review
University of Alabama
P.O. Box 862936
Tuscaloosa, AL 35486–0027
rotating editorship
www.sa.ua.edu/osm/bwr
Biannual.

Bomb
594 Broadway, 9th floor
New York, NY 10012
Betsy Sussler, Editor-in-Chief
bomb@echonyc.com
www.bombsite.com
Quarterly magazine profiling artists, writers, actors, directors, and musicians.

Book
4645 N. Rockwell Street
Chicago, IL 60625
Jerome V. Kramer, Editor

www.bookmagazine.com
"The Magazine for the Reading Life." Sometimes publishes fiction. Monthly.

Border Crossings

Y300–393 Portage Avenue
Winnipeg, Manitoba
R3B 3H6 Canada
Meeka Walsh, Editor
bordercr@escape.ca
bordercrossingsmag.com
Quarterly magazine of the arts with occasional fiction.

The Boston Book Review

30 Brattle Street, 4th Floor
Cambridge, MA 02138
Theoharis Constantine
Theoharis, Editor
BBR-Info@BostonBookReview.com
www.BostonBookReview.com
A book review that also publishes fiction, poetry, and essays. Published ten times a year—monthly with double issues in January and July.

Boston Review

E53–407, MIT
Cambridge, MA 02139
Joshua Cohen, Editor-in-Chief
bostonreview@mit.edu
bostonreview.mit.edu
"A political and literary forum." Published six times a year.

Boulevard

4579 Laclede Avenue
Suite 332
St. Louis, MO 63108–2103

Richard Burgin, Editor
Triannual.

The Briar Cliff Review

3303 Rebecca Street
P.O. Box 2100
Sioux City, IA 51104–2100
Tricia Currans-Sheehen, Editor

The Bridge

14050 Vernon Street
Oak Park, MI 48237
Jack Zucker, Editor
www.bridge.com/issues/currentissue.html
Biannual.

Button

Box 26
Lunenburg, MA 01462
Sally Cragin, Editor/Publisher
"New England's tiniest magazine of poetry, fiction, and gracious living." Biannual.

CALLALOO

**English Department
322 Bryan Hall
University of Virginia
Charlottesville, VA 22903
Charles H. Rowell, Editor
www.press.jhu.edu/press/journals/cal/cal.html**
A quarterly journal of African American and African arts and letters.

Calyx

P.O. Box B
Corvalis, OR 97339–0539
Editorial collective
calyx@proaxis.com
www.proaxis.com/~calyx

Triannual journal of art and literature by women.

Canadian Fiction
P.O. Box 1061
Kingston, Ontario
K7L 4Y5 Canada
Geoff Hancock and Rob Payne, Editors
Biannual.

The Carolina Quarterly
Greenlaw Hall CB#3520
University of North Carolina
Chapel Hill, NC 27599–3520
rotating editorship
cquarter@email.unc.edu
www.unc.edu/student/orgs/cquarter
Triannual.

The Chariton Review
Truman State University
Kirksville, MO 63501
Jim Barnes, Editor
Biannual.

Chattahoochee Review
2101 Womack Road
Dunwoody, Georgia
30338–4497
Lawrence Hetrick, Editor
www.gpc.peachnet.edu/~twadley/cr/index.htm
Quarterly.

Chelsea
P.O. Box 773
Cooper Station
New York, NY 10276–0773
Richard Foerster, Editor
Biannual.

Chicago Review
5801 South Kenwood Avenue
Chicago, Ill 60637–1794
Andrew Rathmann, Editor
humanities.uchicago.edu/humanities/review
Quarterly.

Cimarron Review
205 Morrill Hall
Oklahoma State University
Stillwater, OK 74078–0135
E. P. Walkiewicz, Editor
cimarronreview.okstate.edu
Quarterly.

City Primeval
P.O. Box 30064
Seattle, WA 98103
David Ross, Editor
Quarterly featuring "Narratives of Urban Reality."

Clackamas Literary Review
Clackamas Community College
19600 South Molalla Avenue
Oregon City, OR 97045
Jeff Knorr and Tim Schell, Editors
www.clackamas.cc.or.us/instruct/english/CLR/index.htm
Biannual.

Colorado Review
Colorado State University
English Dept.
Fort Collins, CO 80523
David Milofsky, Editor
www.colostate.edu/Depts/English/pubs/revie/review.htm
Biannual.

Columbia: A Journal of Literature and Art*
  415 Dodge Hall
  Columbia University
  New York, NY 10027–6902
  rotating editorship
  arts-litjournal@columbia.edu
  www.columbia.edu/cu/arts/
  writing/columbiajournal/
  columbia.html
  Biannual.

Commentary
  165 East 56th Street
  New York, NY 10022
  Neal Kozodoy, Editor
  editorial@commentary
  magazine.com
  www.commentarymagazine.com
  *Monthly, politically conservative
  Jewish magazine.*

Communities
  P.O. Box 169
  Masonville, CO 80541–0169
  Diana Leafe Christian, Editor
  communities@ic.org
  *Quarterly "Journal of
  Cooperative Living."*

Concho River Review
  English Department
  Angelo State University
  San Angelo, TX 76909
  James A. Moore, General
  Editor
  www.angelo.edu/dept/eng/river.
  htm
  Biannual.

Confrontation
  English Department
  C. W. Post Campus of Long
  Island University
  Brookville, NY 11548–1300
  Martin Tucker, Editor-in-Chief

Conjunctions
  21 East 10th Street
  New York, NY 10003
  Bradford Morrow, Editor
  www.conjunctions.com
  Biannual.

Cottonwood
  Box J, 400 Kansas Union
  University of Kansas
  Lawrence, KS 66045
  Tom Lorenz, Editor
  cottonwd@falcon.cc.ukans.edu
  www.falcon.cc.ukans.edu/
  ~cottonwd/index.html
  Biannual.

Crab Orchard Review
  Southern Illinois University at
  Carbondale
  Carbondale, IL 62901–4503
  Richard Peterson, Editor
  www.siu.edu/~crborchd
  Biannual.

Crazyhorse
  English Department
  University of Arkansas at Little
  Rock
  Little Rock, AR 72204
  Ralph Burns and Lisa Lewis,
  Editors
  www.ualr.edu/~english/chorse.
  htm
  Biannual.

The Cream City Review
University of Wisconsin-
Milwaukee
P.O. Box 413
Milwaukee, WI 53201
rotating editorship
www.uwm.edu/Dept/English/
CCR/about.html
Biannual.

The Crescent Review
Box 15069
Chevy Chase, MD
20825–5069
J. Timothy Holland, Editor
www.thecrescentreview.com
Triannual.

CutBank
English Department
University of Montana
Missoula, MT 59812
rotating editorship
cutbank@selway.umt.edu
www.umt.edu/cutbank
Biannual.

Dead Snake Apotheosis
87–3193 Road H
Captain Cook, HI 96704
Carol Greenhouse, Editor
DEAD Eds@aol.com
Published irregularly. Est. 1998.

Denver Quarterly
University of Denver
Denver, CO 80208
Bin Ramke, Editor
www.du.edu/english/
DQuarterly.htm

Dominion Review
Old Dominion University
English Dept., BAL 220
Norfolk, VA 23529–0078
rotating editorship
www.cais.net/aesir/fiction/dreview
Annual.

DOUBLETAKE*
55 Davis Square
Somerville, MA 02144
Robert Coles, Editor
dtmag@aol.com
www.doubletakemagazine.org
Beautifully produced quar-
terly devoted to photography
and literature.

Emu Review
400 Old Mill UVM
Burlington, VT 05405
rotating editors
uvmemu@zoo.uvm.edu
www.uvm.edu/~uvmemu/
emureview_index.html
Published irregularly.

Epoch*
251 Goldwin Smith Hall
Cornell University
Ithaca, NY 14853–3201
Michael Koch, Editor
*Triannual. 1997 O. Henry
Award Winner for Best Magazine.*

ESQUIRE*
250 West 55th Street
New York, NY 10019
Adrienne Miller, Literary Editor
www.esquiremag.com
Monthly with annual summer
reading issue.

Event
Douglas College
Box 2503
New Westminster, British
Columbia
V3L 5B2, Canada
Calvin Wharton, Editor
Triannual.

Fence*
14 Fifth Avenue, 1A
New York, NY 10011
Rebecca Wolff, Editor
rwolff@angel.net
www.fencemag.com
Biannual.

Fiction
English Department
The City College of New York
New York, NY 10031
Mark Jay Mirsky, Editor
www.ccny.cuny.edu/Fiction/
fiction.htm
All-fiction format.

Fiction International
Department of English and
Comparative Literature
San Diego State University
San Diego, CA 92182
Harold Jaffe, Editor
Annual.

The Fiddlehead
University of New Brunswick
P.O. Box 4400
Fredericton, New Brunswick
Canada E3B 5A3
Ross Leckie, Editor
Fid@nbnet.nb.ca
Quarterly.

Five Fingers Review
P.O. Box 12955
Berkeley, CA 94712–3955
Jaime Robles, Editor
vladstutu@aol.com

Five Points*
English Department
Georgia State University
University Plaza
Athens, GA 30303–3083
David Bottoms, Pam Durban,
Editors
www.gsu.edu/~wwweng/
fivepoints
Triannual.

The Florida Review
English Dept.
University of Central Florida
Orlando, FL 32816
Russell Kesler, Editor
pegasus.cc.ucf.edu/~english/
floridareview/home.htm
Biannual.

Flyway
203 Ross Hall
Iowa State University
Ames, IA 50011
Stephen Pett, Editor

Folio
Literature Department
The American University
Washington, DC 20016
Cynthia Lollar, Fiction Editor
Biannual.

Fourteen Hills
The Creative Writing
Department
San Francisco State University

1600 Holloway Avenue
San Francisco, CA 94132–1722
rotating editorship
hills@sfsu.edu
userwww.sfsu.edu/~hills
Biannual.

The Free Press
P.O. Box 581
Bronx, NY 10463
J. Rudolph Abate, Literary
Editor
MariaRaf@aol.com
Monthly New York City newspaper that occasionally publishes fiction.

Fugue
Brink Hall 200
University of Idaho
Moscow, ID 83844–1102
www.uidaho.edu/LS/Eng/Fugue
Biannual with rotating editorship.

Gargoyle
1508 U Street, NW
Washington, DC 20009
Richard Peabody, Lucinda
Ebersole, Editors
atticus@atticusbooks.com
www.atticusbooks.com/
gargoyle.html
Published irregularly.

Geist
1014 Homer Street #103
Vancouver, British Columbia
V6B 2W9 Canada
Stephen Osborne, Publisher
geist@geist.com
www.geist.com

"The Canadian Magazine of Ideas and Culture." Quarterly.

THE GEORGIA REVIEW*
The University of Georgia
Athens, GA 30602–9009
Stephen Corey, Acting Editor
www.uga.ed/garev
Quarterly.

THE GETTYSBURG REVIEW
Gettysburg College
Gettysburg, PA 17325
Peter Stitt, Editor
www.gettysburg.edu/
academics/gettysburg_review
Quarterly.

Glimmer Train Stories
710 SW Madison Street
Suite 504
Portland, OR 97205–2900
Linda Burmeister Davies, Susan
Burmeister-Brown, Editors
www.glimmertrain.com
Quarterly. Fiction and interviews.

Global City Review
Simon H. Rifkind Center for
the Humanities
The City College of New York
138th St. and Convent Ave.,
New York, NY 10031
Linsey Abrams, Editor
webdelsol.com/GlobalCity
Nifty, pocket-size format. Once again biannual.

GQ*
350 Madison Avenue
New York, NY 10017
www.gq.com

Swank monthly men's magazine.

Grain

Box 1154

Regina, Saskatchewan

Canada S4P 3B4

J. Jill Robinson, Editor

Quarterly.

Grand Street

131 Varick Street

Room 906

New York, NY 10013

Jean Stein, Editor

info@grandstreet.com

www.grandstreet.com

Quarterly artsy arts magazine.

The Green Hills Literary Lantern

Box 375

Trenton, MO 64683

Jack Smith, Ken Reger, Senior

Editors

Biannual.

Green Mountains Review

Box A 58

Johnson State College

Johnson, VT 05656

Tony Whedon, Fiction Editor

Biannual.

The Greensboro Review

English Department

University of North Carolina at

Greensboro

P.O. Box 26170

Greensboro, NC 27402–6170

Jim Clark, Editor

www.uncg.edu/eng/mfa/review/

Grhompage.htm

Biannual.

Gulf Stream

English Department

FIU-North Miami Campus

300 NE 151 Street

North Miami, FL 33181–3000

Lynn Barrett, Editor

barrettl@fiu.edu

as11s.fiu.edu/cwp/gulfstream.

htm

Biannual.

Habersham Review

Piedmont College

Demorest, GA 30535–0010

Frank Gannon, Editor

Biannual. Publication suspended.

Hampton Shorts

P.O. Box 1229

Water Mill, NY 11976

Barbara Stone, Editor-in-Chief

hamptonshorts@hamptons.com

"Fiction plus from the Hamptons and the East End."

Happy

240 East 35th Street

Suite 11A

New York, NY 10116

Bayard, Editor

Two words: offbeat quarterly.

HARPER'S MAGAZINE*

666 Broadway

New York, NY 10012

Lewis Lapham, Editor

www.harpers.org

150-year-old monthly.

Harrington Gay Men's Fiction Quarterly

2215-R Market Street

Suite 101

San Francisco, CA 94114
Brian Bouldrey, Editor

Hawaii Pacific Review*
Hawaii Pacific University
1060 Bishop Street
Honolulu, HI 96813
hpreview@hpu.edu
Annual.

Hayden's Ferry Review
Box 871502
Arizona State University
Tempe, AZ 85287–1502
rotating editorship
HFR@asu.edu
www.statepress.com/hfr
Beautifully produced biannual.

High Plains Literary Review
180 Adams Street
Suite 250
Denver, CO 80206
Robert O. Greer Jr., Editor-in-Chief
Triannual.

The Hudson Review
684 Park Avenue
New York, NY 10021
Paula Deitz, Editor
www.litline.org/HUDSON/home.html
Quarterly.

The Idaho Review
Boise State University
English Department
1910 University Drive
Boise, ID 83725
Mitch Wieland, Editor-in-Chief

english.boisestate.edu/idahoreview/
Annual, inaugurated in 1998.

Image
P.O. Box 674
Kennett Square, PA 19348
Gregory Wolfe, Publisher and Editor
image@imagejournal.org
www.imagejournal.org
"A Journal of the Arts and Religion." Quarterly.

Indiana Review
Ballantine Hall 465
1020 E. Kirkwood Avenue
Bloomington, IN 47405–7103
Brian Leung, Editor
inreview@indiana.edu
www.indiana.edu/~inreview/ir.html
Biannual.

Ink Magazine
P.O. Box 52558
264 Bloor Street West
Toronto, ON
M5S 1V0 Canada
John Degan, Editor
Quarterly.

Inkwell
Manhattanville College
Purchase, NY 10577
Rotating editorship
Biannual.

Interim
English Department
University of Nevada
Las Vegas, NV 89154

James Hazen, Editor
Biannual.

The Iowa Review
308 English/Philosophy
Building
University of Iowa
Iowa City, IA 52242–1492
David Hamilton, Editor
www.uiowa.edu/~iareview
Triannual.

Iowa Woman
P.O. Box 680
Iowa City, IA 52244–0680
Rebecca Childers, Editor

Joe
1271 Avenue of the Americas
Suite 2800
New York, NY 10020
Paula Champa, Associate Editor
*Produced in conjunction with the
Starbucks Coffee Company and
available in Starbucks outlets. No
longer published.*

The Journal
The Ohio State University
English Department
164 West 17th Avenue
Columbus, OH 43210
Michelle Herman, Fiction
Editor
thejournal05@postbox.acs.
ohio-state.edu
www.cohums.ohio-state.edu/
english/journals/the_journal/
Biannual.

Kalliope
Florida Community College at
Jacksonville
3939 Roosevelt Boulevard
Jacksonville, FL 32205
Mary Sue Koeppel, Editor
www.fccj.org/kalliope/
kalliope.htm
*Triannual journal of women's lit-
erature and art.*

Karamu
English Department
Eastern Illinois University
Charleston, IL 61920
Peggy Brayfield, Editor
Annual.

THE KENYON REVIEW*
Kenyon College
Gambier, OH 43022
David H. Lynn, Editor
kenyonreview@kenyon.edu
www.kenyonreview.com
Triannual.

Kiosk
State University of New York at
Buffalo
English Department
306 Clemens Hall
Buffalo, NY 14260
rotating editorship
eng-kiosk@acsu.buffalo.edu
wings.buffalo.edu/kiosk
Annual.

**Krater: College Workshop
Quarterly**
P.O. Box 1371
Lincoln Park, MI 48146

Leonard D. Fritz, Managing
Editor
*Quarterly. Features work by
writers currently enrolled in college writing workshops.*

The L.A. Weekly
6715 Sunset Boulevard
Los Angeles, CA 90028
Sue Horton, Editor
www.laweekly.com
*Publishes annual summer fiction
issue as part of its Weekly
Literary Supplement.*

The Laurel Review
English Dept.
Northwest Missouri State
University
Maryville, MO 64468
William Trowbridge, David
Slater, Beth Richards, Editors
Biannual.

Literal Latté
Suite 240
61 East 8th Street
New York, NY 10003
Jenine Gordon Bockman,
Publisher and Editor
Litlatte@aol.com
www.literal-latte.com
Bimonthly.

The Literary Review*
Fairleigh Dickinson University
285 Madison Avenue
Madison, NJ 07940
Walter Cummins, Editor-in-
Chief
tlr@fdu.edu

www.webdelsol.com/tlr/
Quarterly.

Louisiana Literature
SLA-792
Southeastern Louisiana
University
Hammond, LA 70402
Jack B. Bedell, Editor
Biannual.

Madison Magazine
126 S. Franklin Street
Madison, WI 53703
Brian Howell, Editor
www.madisonmag.com
*Monthly magazine of Madison,
Wisconsin. Has annual short fiction contest with winner published in the August issue.*

The Madison Review
University of Wisconsin
English Department, Helen C.
White Hall
600 North Park Street
Madison, WI 53706
rotating editorship
Biannual.

The Malahat Review
University of Victoria
P.O. Box 1700
Victoria, British Columbia
V8W 2Y2 Canada
Marlene Cookshaw, Acting
Editor
malahat@uvic.ca
web.uvic.ca/malahat
Quarterly.

Mānoa*
  English Dept.
  University of Hawai'I
  Honolulu, HI 96822
  Frank Stewart, Editor
  www.hawaii.edu/mjournal
  Biannual.
The Massachusetts Review
  South College
  University of Massachusetts
  Box 37140
  Amherst, MA 01003–7140
  Jules Chametzky, Mary Heath,
  Paul Jenkins, Editors
  wwwunix.oit.umass.edu/
  ~massrev
  Quarterly.
McSWEENEY'S
  394A Ninth Street
  Brooklyn, NY 11215
  David Eggers, Editor
  mcsweeneys@earthlink.net
  www.mcsweeneys.net
  Est. 1998. A heart-warming
  quarterly of staggering genius?
Meridian
  University of Virginia
  English Department
  Charlottesville, VA 22903
  rotating editorship
  meridian@virginia.edu
  www.engl.virginia.edu/meridian
  Biannual, student-run.
The Metropolitan Review
  1 Embarcadero Center
  P.O. Box 26470
  San Francisco, CA 94126–6470

Mary Claire Ray, Editor
www.metroreview.com
Biannual established in 1998.
Michigan Quarterly Review
  The University of Michigan
  3032 Rackham Building
  915 E. Washington Street
  Ann Arbor, MI 48109–1070
  Laurence Goldstein, Editor
  www.umich.edu/~mqr
Mid-American Review
  English Department
  Bowling Green State University
  Bowling Green, OH 43403
  Wendell Mayo, Editor-in-Chief
  www.bgsu.edu/
  midamericanreview
  Biannual.
Midstream
  633 Third Avenue, 21st floor
  New York, NY 10017–6706
  Joel Carmichael, Editor
  Published nine times a year.
  Focus on Jewish issues and
  Zionist concerns.
The Minnesota Review
  English Department
  University of
  Missouri–Columbia
  110 Tate Hall
  Columbia, MO 65211
  Jeffrey Williams, Editor
  Non-Minnesota-based biannual.
Mississippi Review
  Center for Writers
  University of Southern
  Mississippi

Box 5144
Hattiesburg, MS 39406–5144
Frederick Barthelme, Editor
rief@netdoor.com
orca.st.usm.edu/mrw
Biannual. Internet site publishes
full-text stories and poems
monthly, many of which are not
included in regular issues of the
magazine.

The Missouri Review*
1507 Hillcrest Hall
University of Missouri
Columbia, Missouri 65211
Speer Morgan, Editor
www.missourireview.org
Triannual.

Nassau Review
English Department
Nassau Community College
One Education Drive
Garden City, NY 11530–6793
Paul A. Doyle, Editor
Annual.

Natural Bridge
English Department
University of Missouri–St.
Louis
8001 Natural Bridge Road
St. Louis, MO 63121
Steven Schreiner, Editor
natural@jinx.umsl.edu
www.umsl.edu/~natural
Biannual. First issue published
in 1999.

The Nebraska Review*
Writers' Workshop
Fine Arts Building 212

University of Nebraska at
Omaha
Omaha, NE 68182–0324
James Reed, Fiction and
Managing Editor
unomaha.edu/~nereview
Biannual.

Neotrope
P.O. Box 172
Lawrence, KS 66044
Adam Powell and Paul Silvia,
Editors
apowell10@hotmail.com
www.brokenboulder.com
Annual featuring progressive fic-
tion, established in 1999.

New Delta Review
English Department
Lousiana State University
Baton Rouge, LA 70803–5001
rotating editorship
wwwndr@unix1.sncc.lsu.edu
www.lsu.edu:80/guests/wwwndr/
Biannual.

New England Review*
Middlebury College
Middlebury, VT 05753
Stephen Donadio, Editor
NEReview@middlebury.edu
www.middlebury.edu/~nereview
Quarterly.

New Letters
University of Missouri–Kansas
City
5100 Rockhill Road
Kansas City, MO 64110
James McKinley, Editor-in-
Chief

newletters@umkc.edu
umkc.edu/newletters
Quarterly.

New Millennium Writings
P.O. Box 2463
Knoxville, TN 37901
Don Williams, Editor
www.mach2.com/books/
williams/index.html
Biannual. Started in 1996.

New Orleans Review
P.O. Box 195
Loyola University
New Orleans, LA 70118
Ralph Adamo, Editor
noreview@beta.loyno.edu
www.loyno.edu/english/
noreview.htm
Quarterly.

The New Renaissance
26 Heath Road #11
Arlington, MA 02174–3614
Louise T. Reynolds, Editor-in-
Chief
wmichaud@gwi.net
Biannual.

New York Stories
English Department
La Guardia Community
College/CUNY
31–10 Thomson Avenue
Long Island City, NY 11101
Michael Blaine, Editor-in-Chief
Triannual. Inaugural issue in 1998.

THE NEW YORKER*
4 Times Square
New York, NY 10036
Bill Buford, Fiction Editor

www.newyorker.com
Esteemed weekly with fiction
double issues in June and
December. 1998 and 1999
O. Henry Award winner for
magazines. Note new address.

Nimrod
The University of Tulsa
600 South College
Tulsa, OK 74104–3189
Francine Ringold, Editor-in-
Chief
www.utulsa.edu/Nimrod
Biannual.

Noon
1369 Madison Avenue
PMB 298
New York, NY 10128
Diane Williams, Editor
noonannual@yahoo.com
New annual.

The North American Review
University of Northern Iowa
1222 West 27th Street
Cedar Falls, IA 50614
Robley Wilson, Editor
nar@uni.edu
www.webdelsol.com/
NorthAmReview/NAR
Bimonthly founded in 1815.

North Carolina Literary Review
English Department
East Carolina University
Greenville, NC 27858–4353
Margaret D. Bauer, Editor
BauerM@mail.ECU.edu
www.ecu.edu/english/journals/
nclr

Nicely produced and illustrated annual.

North Dakota Quarterly
The University of North Dakota
Grand Forks, ND 58202–7209
Robert W. Lewis, Editor
ndq@sage.und.nodak.edu
Quarterly.

Northeast Corridor
English Department
Beaver College
450 S. Easton Road
Glenside, PA 19038–3295
Susan Balée, Editor
Biannual.

Northwest Review
369 PLC
University of Oregon
Eugene, OR 97403
John Witte, Editor
Triannual.

Notre Dame Review
Creative Writing Program
English Department
University of Notre Dame
Notre Dame, IN 46556
John Matthias, William
O'Rourke, Editors
www.nd.edu/~ndr/
review.htm
Biannual.

Oasis
P.O. Box 626
Largo, FL 34649–0626
Neal Storrs, Editor
oasislit@aol.com

www.litline.org/OASIS/oasis.
html
Quirky independent quarterly.

The Ohio Review
344 Scott Quad
Ohio University
Athens, Ohio 45701–2979
Wayne Dodd, Editor
www.ohio.edu/TheOhioReview
Biannual.

Ontario Review
9 Honey Brook Drive
Princeton, NJ 08540
Raymond J. Smith, Editor
www.ontarioreviewpress.com
Biannual.

Open City*
225 Lafayette Street
Suite 1114
New York, NY 10012
Thomas Beller, Daniel
Pinchbeck, Editors
ocmagazine@aol.com
www.opencity.org
Downtown annual.

Other Voices*
English Department (MC 162)
University of Illinois at Chicago
601 South Morgan Street
Chicago, IL 60607–7120
Lois Hauselman, Executive Editor
Biannual with all-fiction format.

Owen Wister Review
University of Wyoming
Student Publications
Box 3625
Laramie, WY 82071

rotating editorship
Annual.

The Oxford American
P.O. Box 1156
Oxford, MS 38655
Marc Smirnoff, Editor
oxam@watervalley.net
www.oxfordamericanmag.com
*John Grisham–backed magazine
with Southern focus. Bimonthly.*

Oxford Magazine
English Department
356 Bachelor Hall
Miami University
Oxford, OH 45056
rotating editorship
Oxmag@geocities.com
www.muohio.edu/
creativewriting/oxmag.html

Oxygen
535 Geary Street #1010
San Francisco, CA 94102
Richard Hack, Editor and
Publisher
Oxygen@slip.net
Published irregularly.

Oyster Boy Review
P.O. Box 77842
San Francisco, CA 94107–0842
Damon Sauve, Publisher
obr@levee67.com
www.levee67.com/obr
*Quarterly with full text available
online.*

The Paris Review*
541 East 72nd Street
New York, NY 10021

George Plimpton, Editor
www.parisreview.com
Quarterly.

Parting Gifts
3413 Wilshire Drive
Greensboro, NC 27408
Robert Bixby, Editor
rbixby@aol.com
users.aol.com/marchst/msp.
html

Partisan Review
236 Bay State Road
Boston, MA 02215
William Phillips, Editor-in-
Chief
partisan@bu.edu
www.webdelsol.com/
Partisan_Review
Quarterly.

Passages North
English Department
Northern Michigan University
1401 Presque Isle Avenue
Marquette, MI 49007–5363
Anne Ohman Youngs, Editor-
in-Chief
vm.nmu.edu/passages/http/
home.html
Biannual.

Phoebe
George Mason University
4400 University Drive
Fairfax, VA 22030–4444
rotating editorship
phoebe@gmu.edu
www.gmu.edu/pubs/phoebe
Biannual, student-edited.

Playboy

Playboy Building
919 North Michigan Avenue
Chicago, IL 60611
Alice Turner, Fiction Editor
editor@playboy.com
www.playboy.com
Sometimes takes on a literary sheen.

Pleiades

English and Philosophy Depts.
Central Missouri State
University
Warrensburg, MO 64093
R. M. Kinder, Kevin Prufer,
Editors
rmkinder@sprintmail.com
www.cmsu.edu/englphil/
pleiades.html
Biannual.

PLOUGHSHARES*

100 Beacon Street
Boston, MA 02116
Don Lee, Editor
www.emerson.edu/
ploughshares/
Triannual. Well-known writ-
ers serve as guest editors.

POP Literary Gazette

P.O. Box 02071
Detroit, MI 48202
Karl Wenclas, Maz Sitting,
Editors
blah2@dhol.com
Billed as underground literature.

Potomac Review

P.O. Box 354
Port Tobacco, MD 20677
Eli Flam, Editor and Publisher

www.meral.com/potomac
Quarterly.

Potpourri

P.O. Box 8278
Prairie Village, KS 66208–0278
Polly W. Swafford, Senior
Editor
Potpourpub@aol.com
www.potpourri.org
Quarterly.

Pottersfield Portfolio

P.O. Box 40, Station A
Sydney, Nova Scotia
B1P 6G9 Canada
Douglas Arthur Brown,
Managing Editor
www.pportfolio.com
Triannual.

Prairie Fire

423–100 Arthur Street
Winnipeg, Manitoba
R3B 1H3 Canada
Andris Taskins, Editor
prfire@escape.ca
Quarterly.

Prairie Schooner*

201 Andrews Hall
University of Nebraska
Lincoln, NE 68588–0334
Hilda Raz, Editor-in-Chief
www.unl.edu/schooner/
psmain.htm
Quarterly.

The Prairie Star

P.O. Box 923
Fort Collins, CO 80522–0923
Mark Gluckstern, Editor
Est. 1999.

Press

125 West 72nd Street
Suite 3-M
New York, NY 10023
Daniel Roberts, Editor
pressltd@aol.com
www.pressmag.com
Quarterly. Publication suspended.
Web site may no longer be in
service.

Prism International

Creative Writing Program
University of British Columbia
Vancouver, British Columbia
V6T 1Z1 Canada
rotating editorship
prism@interchange.ubc.ca
www.arts.ubc.ca/prism
Quarterly.

Provincetown Arts

650 Commercial Street
Provincetown, MA 02657
Christopher Busa, Editor
Annual Cape Cod arts
magazine.

Puerto del Sol

P.O. Box 30001
New Mexico State University
Las Cruces, NM 88003–8001
Kevin McIlvoy, Editor-in-Chief
Biannual.

Quarry Magazine

P.O. Box 1061
Kingston, Ontario
K7K 4Y5 Canada
Rob Payne, Editor-in-Chief
Quarterly.

Quarterly West

317 Olpin Union Hall
University of Utah
Salt Lake City, UT 84112
Lawrence Coates and M. L.
Williams, Editors
webdelsol.com/Quarterly_West
Now biannual.

Raritan

Rutgers University
31 Mine Street
New Brunswick, NJ 08903
Richard Poirier, Editor-in-Chief
Quarterly. Edited by former
O. Henry Awards series editor
(1961–66). Only occasionally
publishes fiction.

Rattapallax

523 La Guardia Place
Suite 353
New York, NY 10012
George Dickerson, Editor-in-
Chief
rattapallax@hotmail.com
www.rattapallax.com
Biannual.

REAL

School of Liberal Arts
Stephen F. Austin State
University
P.O. Box 13007, SFA Station
Nacogdoches, TX 75962
Dale Hearell, Editor

Red Rock Review

English Department, J2A
Community College Southern
Nevada
3200 East Cheyenne Avenue

North Las Vegas, NV 89030
Richard Logsdon, Editor-in-Chief
Biannual.

Redbook
224 West 57th Street
New York, NY 10019
*Monthly women's magazine.
Sometimes publishes fiction.*

News from the Republic of Letters
120 Cushing Avenue
Boston, MA 02125–2033
Saul Bellow and Keith Botsford, Editors
rangoni@bu.edu
www.bu.edu/trl
Appears irregularly. Publishes some fiction.

Rio Grande Review
Hudspeth Hall
University of Texas at El Paso
El Paso, Texas 79968
M. Elena Carillo, Editor
Biannual.

River City
English Department
The University of Memphis
Memphis, TN 38152–6176
Thomas Russell, Editor
rivercity@memphis.edu
www.people.memphis.edu/~rivercity
Biannual. Formerly known as Memphis State Review.

River Styx
3207 Washington
St. Louis, MO 63103

Richard Newman, Editor
www.riverstyx.org
Triannual.

Rosebud
P.O. Box 459
Cambridge, WI 53523
Roderick Clark, Editor
www.rsbd.net
Quarterly.

St. Anthony Messenger
1615 Republic Street
Cincinnati, OH 45210–1298
Jack Wintz, O.F.M., Editor
StAnthony@AmericanCatholic.org
www.americancatholic.org
Monthly magazine published by Franciscan friars with about one story per issue.

Salamander
48 Ackers Avenue
Brookline, MA 02445–4160
Jennifer Barber, Editor
Biannual.

Salmagundi
Skidmore College
Saratoga Springs, NY 12866
Robert Boyers, Editor-in-Chief
pboyers@skidmore.edu
Quarterly.

Salt Hill
Syracuse University
English Department
Syracuse, NY 13244
rotating editorship
www-hl.syr.edu/cwp
Biannual.

Santa Monica Review
Santa Monica College
1900 Pico Boulevard
Santa Monica, CA 90405
rotating editorship
Biannual.

The Seattle Review
Padelford Hall
Box 354330
University of Washington
Seattle, WA 98195
Colleen J. McElroy, Editor
Biannual.

Seven Days
P.O. Box 1164
255 S. Champlain Street
Burlington, VT 05042–1164
Pamela Polston, Paula Routly,
Coeditors
sevenday@together.net
www.sevendaysvt.com
*Free weekly newspaper in the
Burlington, Vermont, area.
Occasional fiction.*

The Sewanee Review
University of the South
735 University Avenue
Sewanee, TN 37383–1000
George Core, Editor
www.sewanee.edu/sreview/
home.html
Quarterly.

Shenandoah*
Troubador Theater, 2nd Floor
Washington and Lee University
Lexington, VA 24450
R. T. Smith, Editor

www.wlu.edu/~shenando
Quarterly.

Snake Nation Review
110 #2 West Force Street
Valdosta, GA 31601
Robert George, Editor
Triannual.

Sonora Review
English Department
University of Arizona
Tucson, AZ 85721
rotating editorship
sonora@u.arizona.edu
www.coh.arizona.edu/sonora
Biannual.

South Dakota Review
Box 111
University Exchange
Vermillion, SD 57069
Brian Bedard, Editor
sunbird.usd.edu/engl/SDR/
index.html
Quarterly.

Southern Exposure
P.O. Box 531
Durham, NC 27702
Chris Kromm, Editor
southern_exposure@i4south.org
*A journal of Southern politics and
culture that publishes some fiction.*

Southern Humanities Review
9088 Haley Center
Auburn University
Auburn, AL 36849
Dan R. Latimer, Virginia M.
Kouidis, Editors
www.auburn.edu/english/shr/

home.htm
Quarterly.

THE SOUTHERN REVIEW*
43 Allen Hall
Louisiana State University
Baton Rouge, LA
70803–5005
James Olney, Dave Smith,
Editors
unix1.sncc.lsu.edu/guests/
wwwtsr
Quarterly.

Southwest Review*
Southern Methodist University
307 Fondren Library West
Dallas, TX 75275
Willard Spiegelman, Editor-in-
Chief
Quarterly.

STORY*
1507 Dana Avenue
Cincinnati, OH 45207
Lois Rosenthal, Editor
Quarterly. All fiction. Sadly,
this mainstay of the American
short story ceased publication
with the Winter 2000
issue.

StoryQuarterly*
P.O. Box 1416
Northbrook, IL 60065
Anne Brashler, M. M. M.
Hayes, Editors
Actually an annual.

The Sun
107 North Robertson Street
Chapel Hill, NC 27516
Sy Safransky, Editor

www.thesunmagazine.org
Spirited monthly.

Sycamore Review
English Department
1356 Heavilon Hall
Purdue University
West Lafayette, IN 47907
rotating editors
sycamore@expert.cc.purdue.edu
www.sla.purdue.edu/academic/
engl/sycamore/
Biannual.

Talking River Review
Division of Literature and
Languages
Lewis-Clark State College
500 8th Avenue
Lewiston, ID 83501
www.lcsc.edu/TalkingRiver
Review
Student-run biannual.

Tameme
199 First Street
Los Altos, CA 94022
C. M. Mayo, Editor
editor@tameme.org
www.tameme.org
Annual. "New writing from
North America." Publishes bilin-
gual fiction in English and
Spanish, the original language
and in translation.

Tea Cup
P.O. Box 825
Ithaca, NY 14851–0825
Rhian Ellis, J. Robert Lennon,
Editors
Published "whenever possible."

The Texas Review
English Department
Sam Houston State University
Huntsville, TX 77341
Paul Ruffin, Editor
www.shsu.edu/~eng_www/
trp.html
Biannual.

Thema
Box 74109
Metairie, LA 70053–4109
Virginia Howard, Editor
www.litline.org/THEMA/
themahome.html
For every issue, a theme.
Biannual.

Third Coast
English Department
Western Michigan University
Kalamazoo, MI 49008–5092
rotating editorship
www.wmich.edu/thirdcoast
Biannual.

The Threepenny Review
P.O. Box 9131
Berkeley, CA 94709
Wendy Lesser, Editor
wlesser@threepennyreview.com
www.threepennyreview.com
Quarterly.

Tikkun
60 West 87th Street
New York, NY 10024
Thane Rosenbaum, Literary
Editor
magazine@tikkun.org
www.tikkun.org
"A Bimonthly Jewish Critique
of Politics, Culture &
Society."

Tin House*
P.O. Box 10500
Portland, OR 97296–0500
Rob Spillman and Elissa
Schappell, Editors
Quarterly.

TriQuarterly
Northwestern University
2020 Ridge Avenue
Evanston, IL 60208
Susan Firestone Hahn, Editor
triquarterly.nwu.edu
Triannual.

The Urbanite
P.O. Box 4737
Davenport, IA 52808
Mark McLaughlin, Editor
"Surreal & Lively & Bizarre."
Published irregularly.

Urbanus
P.O. Box 192921
San Francisco, CA 94119–2921
Peter Driszhal, Editor
Published "approximately 3 times
a year."

The Virginia Quarterly Review*
One West Range
P.O. Box 400223
Charlottesville, VA
22903–4223
Staige D. Blackford, Editor
www.virginia.edu/vqr

Wascana Review
English Department
University of Regina
Regina, Saskatchewan

S4S 0A2 Canada
Kathleen Wall, Editor
Biannual.

Washington Review
P.O. Box 50132
Washington, DC 20091–0132
Clarissa K. Wittenberg, Editor
www.washingtonreview.com
D.C.-area bimonthly arts magazine.

Washington Square
Creative Writing Program
New York University
19 University Place, 2nd Floor
New York, NY 10003–4556
rotating editorship
Annual.

Weber Studies
Weber State University
1214 University Circle
Ogden, UT 84408–1214
Sherwin W. Howard, Editor
weberstudies.weber.edu
Triannual. "Voices and viewpoints of the contemporary west."

Wellspring
4080 83rd Avenue North
Suite A
Brooklyn Park, MN 55443
Meg Miller, Editor/Publisher

West Branch
Bucknell Hall
Bucknell University
Lewisburg, PA 17837
Karl Patten, Robert Love
Taylor, Editors
Biannual.

West Coast Line
2027 East Academic Annex
Simon Fraser University
Burnaby, British Columbia
V5A 1S6 Canada
Roy Miki, Editor
www.sfu.ca/west-coast-line
Triannual.

Western Humanities Review
University of Utah
English Department
255 South Central Campus
Drive
Room 3500
Salt Lake City, UT
84112–0494
Barry Weller, Editor
Formerly quarterly, now biannual, starting with 2000 volume.

Whetstone
Barrington Area Arts Council
P.O. Box 1266
Barrington, IL 60011–1266
Sandra Berris, Marsha Portnoy,
Jean Tolle, Editors
Annual.

Whiskey Island Magazine
University Center
Cleveland State University
1860 East 22nd Street
Cleveland, OH 44114
rotating editorship
whiskeyisland@popmail.
csuhio.edu
Biannual.

Willow Springs
526 5th Street, MS-1
Eastern Washington University

Cheney, WA 99004
Christopher Howell, Editor
Biannual.

Wind
P.O. Box 24548
Lexington, KY 40524
Charlie Hughes, Leatha
Kendrick, Editors
Biannual.

Windsor Review
English Department
University of Windsor
Windsor, Ontario
N9B 3P4 Canada
Katherine Quinsey, General
Editor
uwrevu@uwindsor.ca
Biannual.

Witness
Oakland Community College
Orchard Ridge Campus
27055 Orchard Lake Road
Farmington Hills, MI 48334
Peter Stine, Editor
Biannual.

The Worcester Review
6 Chatham Street
Worcester, MA 01609
Rodger Martin, Managing Editor
www.geocities.com/Paris/
LeftBank/6433
Annual.

Wordplay
P.O. Box 2248
South Portland, ME
04116–2248
Helen Peppe, Editor-in-Chief
Quarterly.

Words
School of the Visual Arts
209 East 23rd Street
New York, NY 10010–3994
Louis Phillips, Faculty
Advisor
www.schoolofvisualarts.edu
Biannual.

Writers' Forum
University of Colorado
P.O. Box 7150
Colorado Springs, CO
80933–7150
C. Kenneth Pellow, Editor-in-
Chief
Annual.

**WV: Magazine of the Emerging
Writer**
The Writer's Voice of the West
Side YMCA
5 West 63rd Street
New York, NY 10023
Kathleen Warnock, Editor-in-
Chief
WrtrsVoice1@aol.com
users.aol.com/wtrsvoice1/files/
WVmag.html
Launched in 1998.

Xavier Review
Xavier University
Box 110C
New Orleans, LA 70125
Thomas Bonner Jr., Editor
Biannual.

**Xconnect: Writers of the
Information Age**
P.O. Box 2317
Philadelphia, PA 19103

D. Edward Deifer, Editor-in-Chief
xconnect@ccat.sas.upenn.edu
ccat.sas.upenn.edu/xconnect
Pronounced "Cross connect."
Annual print version of trian-
nual Web 'zine.

The Yale Review
Yale University
P.O. Box 208243
New Haven, CT 06250–8243
J. D. McClatchy, Editor
Quarterly.

The Yalobusha Review
P.O. Box 186
University, MS 38677–0186
rotating editors
yalobush@suneset.backbone.
olemiss.edu
www.olemiss.edu/depts/english/
pubs/yalobusha_review.html
Annual.

Zoetrope: All-Story*
1350 Avenue of the Americas
24th Floor
New York, NY 10019
Adrienne Brodeur, Editor-in-Chief
www.zoetrope-stories.com
Quarterly. Published by movie
director Francis Ford Coppola.
Web site provides full text of sto-
ries and a related site allows for
online submissions and online
workshops, provided users first
read and rate five other stories.
Now quarterly.

ZYZZYVA*
41 Sutter Street
Suite 1400
San Francisco, CA 94104–4903
Howard Junker, Editor
editor@zyzzyva.org
www.zyzzyva.org
Triannual. West Coast writers
and artists.

Permissions Acknowledgments

Grateful acknowledgment is made to the following for permission to reprint previously published material.

Introduction to John Edgar Wideman's "Weight" Copyright © 2000 by Michael Cunningham.

"Weight" by John Edgar Wideman originally appeared in *Callaloo*. Copyright © 1999 by John Edgar Wideman. Reprinted by permission of the author.

Introduction to Beth Lordan's "The Man with the Lapdog" Copyright © 2000 by Pam Houston.

"The Man with the Lapdog" by Beth Lordan originally appeared in *The Atlantic Monthly*. Copyright © 1999 by Beth Lordan. Reprinted by permission of the author.

Introduction to Mary Gordon's "The Deacon" Copyright © 2000 by George Saunders.

"The Deacon" by Mary Gordon originally appeared in *The Atlantic Monthly*. Copyright © 1999 by Mary Gordon. Reprinted by permission of the author.

"Plains of Abraham" by Russell Banks originally appeared in *Esquire*, copyright © 1999 by Russell Banks. From *The Angel on the Roof* by Russell Banks. Copyright © 2000 by Russell Banks. Reprinted with the permission of HarperCollins Publishers.

"Flush" by Judy Budnitz originally appeared in *McSweeney's*. Copyright © 1999 by Judy Budnitz. Reprinted by permission of the author.

"These Hands" by Kevin Brockmeier originally appeared in *The Georgia Review*. Copyright © 1999 by Kevin Brockmeier. Reprinted by permission of the author.

"Salve Regina" by Melissa Pritchard originally appeared in *The Gettysburg Review*. Copyright © 1999 by Melissa Pritchard. Reprinted by permission of the author.

"The Smallest People Alive" by Keith Banner originally appeared in *The Kenyon Review*. Copyright © 1999 by Keith Banner. Reprinted by permission of the author.

"Bones of the Inner Ear" by Kiana Davenport originally appeared in *Story*. Copyright © 1999 by Kiana Davenport. Reprinted by permission of the author.

"The Fool's Proxy" by J. Robert Lennon originally appeared in *Harper's Magazine*. Copyright © 1999 by J. Robert Lennon. Reprinted by permission of the author.

"He's at the Office" by Allan Gurganus originally appeared in *The New Yorker*. Copyright © 1999 by Allan Gurganus. Reprinted by permission of the author.

"The Gilgul of Park Avenue" by Nathan Englander originally appeared in *The Atlantic Monthly*. From *For the Relief of Unbearable Urges* by Nathan Englander. Copyright © 1999 by Nathan Englander. Reprinted by permission of Alfred A. Knopf, Inc.

"Theories of Rain" by Andrea Barrett originally appeared in *The Southern Review*. Copyright © 1999 by Andrea Barrett. Reprinted by permission of the author.

"Whileaway" by Jeannette Bertles originally appeared in *The Gettysburg Review*. Copyright © 1999 by Jeannette Bertles. Reprinted by permission of the author.

"Rose" by John Biguenet originally appeared in *Esquire*. Copyright © 1999 by John Biguenet. Reprinted by permission of the author.

"The Gardens of Kyoto" by Kate Walbert originally appeared in *DoubleTake*. Copyright © 1999 by Kate Walbert. Reprinted by permission of the author.

"Easy Pickings" by Tim Gautreaux originally appeared in *GQ*. From *Wedding with Children* by Tim Gautreux. Copyright © 1999 by Tim Gautreaux. Reprinted by permission of St. Martin's Press, Inc.

"The Beautiful Days" by Michael Byers originally appeared in *Ploughshares*. Copyright © 1999 by Michael Byers. Reprinted by permission of the author.

"Watch the Animals" by Alice Elliott Dark originally appeared in *Harper's Magazine*. Reprinted with the permission of Simon & Schuster, Inc. from *In the Gloaming* by Alice Elliott Dark. Copyright © 2000 by Alice Elliott Dark.

"Kindling" by Raymond Carver originally appeared in *Esquire* (July 1, 1999) Copyright © 1999 by Tess Gallagher. Reprinted by permission of International Creative Management, Inc.